# SIDNEY SHELDON'S THE SILENT WIDOW

## ALSO AVAILABLE BY SIDNEY SHELDON

**Other Side of Midnight Novels**
*Memories of Midnight*
*The Other Side of Midnight*

**Tracy Whitney Novels**
*If Tomorrow Comes*

**Blackwell Family Novels**
*Master of the Game*

*The Other Side of Me*
*Are You Afraid of the Dark?*
*The Sky is Falling*

*Tell Me Your Dreams*
*The Best Laid Plans*
*Morning, Noon and Night*
*Nothing Lasts Forever*
*The Stars Shine Down*
*The Doomsday Conspiracy*
*The Sands of Time*
*Windmills of the Gods*
*Rage of Angels*
*Bloodline*
*A Stranger in the Mirror*
*The Naked Face*

## ALSO AVAILABLE BY TILLY BAGSHAWE

**Sidney Sheldon Novels**
*The Phoenix*
*Sidney Sheldon's Mistress of the Game*
*Sidney Sheldon's The Tides of Memory*
*Sidney Sheldon's Angel of the Dark*
*Sidney Sheldon's After the Darkness*

**Tracy Whitney Novels**
*Sidney Sheldon's Reckless*
*Sidney Sheldon's Chasing Tomorrow*

**Blackwell Family Novels**
*Sidney Sheldon's Mistress of the Game*

*The Bachelor*
*The Show*
*The Inheritance*
*Friends & Rivals*
*Fame*
*Scandalous*
*Flawless*
*Do Not Disturb*
*Showdown*
*Adored*

# SIDNEY SHELDON'S THE SILENT WIDOW

## A SIDNEY SHELDON NOVEL

## Tilly Bagshawe

CROOKED
LANE

NEW YORK

Published in the United States by Crooked Lane Books, an imprint of The Quick Brown Fox & Company LLC.

Crooked Lane Books and its logo are trademarks of The Quick Brown Fox & Company LLC.

Library of Congress Catalog-in-Publication data available upon request.

ISBN (paperback): 978-1-64385-961-3
ISBN (hardcover): 978-1-64385-093-1
ISBN (ePub): 978-1-64385-094-8
ISBN (ePDF): 978-1-64385-095-5

Cover design © HarperCollinsPublishers Ltd 2018
Cover photograph © Robert Jones/Arcangel Images (main image); Shutterstock.com (skyscrapers)

Book design by Jennifer Canzone

Printed in the United States.

www.crookedlanebooks.com

Crooked Lane Books
34 West 27th St., 10th Floor
New York, NY 10001

Trade Paperback Edition: May 2022
First Edition: May 2019

10 9 8 7 6 5 4 3 2 1

For Alice, with love.

# Prologue

'No! Please no! I can't . . .'

The old man's eyes widened in terror as he stared at the drill, straining against the ropes that bound him. He imagined the spiral metal bit grinding into his flesh, splintering his bones like shrapnel as they nailed him to the wooden beam.

As they crucified him.

Surely they knew he was good for the money? He would give them what they wanted – everything they wanted! He was no good to them dead.

How long had he been in the warehouse now? Days? Or only hours? Slipping in and out of consciousness between the beatings, he'd lost track, aware only of the pain in his body: the screaming burns on his skin, thin and creased with age like crepe paper. The fractured ribs and swollen eyes and lips. The tiny razor cuts to his genitals. They had tortured and humiliated him in every sadistic way imaginable, while the young woman stood in the corner impassively and filmed on her mobile phone. *Hateful bitch.* He despised her most of all, more even than his tormentors.

They appeared to be reaching a crescendo, some sort of grand finale with the drill. Or at least *he* did. Their boss. The ringmaster at this circus of terror.

The man with the brown eyes.

The devil incarnate.

'Please!'

The old man's sobs turned to screams as his torturers switched on the drill, passing it laughingly between them as they revved it louder and louder.

'I'll do anything! Oh God, no!' A warm river of liquid excrement exploded out of his bowels and streamed down his shaking legs.

The man with the brown eyes smiled.

'What's that you say?' he taunted, cupping a manicured hand to his ear. 'I'm sorry, my friend, with the sound of that drill I can't hear you.'

He looked on as his men did his bidding, aroused as always by the pleading and the shrieks and the blood, and finally by the silence, once the show was over. Aroused too by the young woman dutifully filming it all for his pleasure, as he'd commanded her to do. He preferred killing women. But ending a life, any life, was a high like no other. The ultimate expression of power.

Once, the battered old man hanging lifelessly from the beam in front of him had been rich and powerful. More powerful than him. Or so he'd thought.

But look at him now. Like a carcass in an abattoir.

'Should we cut him down, boss?' one of the goons asked his master.

'No.' The man with the brown eyes stepped forward. 'Leave him there.' Pulling a wad of hundred-dollar bills from his inside jacket pocket, he stuffed them violently into the corpse's mouth.

The stupid old man had never understood.

It was never about the money . . .

# Part One

# 1

**DR NIKKI ROBERTS**
**Brentwood, Los Angeles.**
**May 12, 11 p.m.**

It never rains in Los Angeles in May, so the light mist falling on my bare arms is a surprise. The last surprise I will have on this earth. But that's OK. I've come to hate surprises.

Our yard looks beautiful, lush and green. I am standing under the magnolia tree Doug planted in the spring, just a month before his accident. *Accident.* I have to stop using that word. I know now that my husband's death was no random act of fate. The night that Doug crashed on the 405, burned alive in his beloved Tesla: that was the beginning.

Not that I knew it at the time. I didn't know anything back then.

The gun in my hand, a 9mm Luger, feels small and harmless, like a toy. The man who sold it to me called it 'a lovely gun for a woman', as if I were buying earrings or a silk scarf. I tried to take my own life once before, right after Doug's . . . after he died. I took pills, more than enough, but I was unlucky. My housekeeper, Rita, found me and called 911. Not this time. This time my little toy gun will get the job done.

I'm not afraid of death. Never have been, although as a psychologist I've treated countless patients who are. It's a control thing, ultimately. Fear of the unknown. The way I see it, what I'm about to do is the ultimate act of control. Leaving the world on your own terms is a luxury.

Not everybody gets that chance.

Too many people have died because of me. Tonight another kind, decent man lost his life. A man I cared about. A man who cared about me.

This can't go on. I have to end it.

The rain is getting heavier. I wipe my hand on my jeans to dry it and make my grip less slippery. No mistakes this time. I raise the gun to my temple and turn around, looking back at the house that Doug and I built together. A white clapboard, East Coast 'estate', beautifully lit, with a romantic balcony off the master suite that has views all the way to the ocean. Our dream home. Back when we still had dreams. Before there were nothing but nightmares.

I close my eyes and see their faces, one by one, like patterns on a kaleidoscope.

The ones I loved: Doug. Anne.

The ones I could have loved. Lou. *We'll never know what might have been.*

The ones I let down: Lisa. Trey. Derek. *I'm so very sorry.*

My last thought is for the ones I hated.

*You know who you are. May you rot in hell.*

I start to cry. I know this is wrong. I wish there were another way. But wishing never fixed anything.

# 2

CHARLOTTE
**Ten years earlier . . .**

Charlotte Clancy felt the warm summer breeze caress her skin and with it a tingle of excitement. It was part sexual excitement, part happiness, and part the unfamiliar thrill of doing something illicit. Something naughty. Dangerous, even.

Charlotte wasn't usually the naughty type. At eighteen years old she'd always been a straight-A student at her San Diego high school, where the most trouble she'd ever gotten into was for allowing her girlfriend to crib her Social Studies paper on early Mexican civilizations. Charlotte just *loved* Mexico – the history, the language, the food. She'd literally had to beg and plead with her parents to allow her to work the summer in Mexico City as an au pair.

'I don't know, Charlie,' her dad said skeptically. Tucker Clancy was a firefighter and a deacon at the local Episcopal church, about as upstanding and conservative a family man as you could hope to find. 'You hear stories. People get kidnapped down there. And the drug gangs . . . you read about beheadings and God knows what other terrible things.'

"That's true, Dad,' Charlotte countered. 'But those things are only happening in certain *parts* of Mexico. Not where I wanna go. It's El Salvador and Colombia where you really have to be careful. And this agency, American Au Pairs International, AAPI – they have an amazing safety reputation. Like, zero incidents in twelve years working down there.'

Tucker Clancy listened with pride to his only daughter's negotiating skills. One thing you could say for Charlie: she never did anything half-assed. As usual she had all the facts and figures at her fingertips. And she was a very sensible girl.

In the end though, it was Charlotte's mother, Mary, who had tipped the scales in her favor.

'I'm nervous too, honey,' Mary told Tucker over dinner at the Steak 'n' Shake one Friday night. 'But I don't think we should let our fears hold Charlie back. She'll be at college in the fall, living on her own, making all these decisions for herself. She needs some independence.'

'College is in Ohio,' Charlotte's dad countered. 'They don't cut people's heads off in Ohio.'

Mary frowned. 'Well, according to Charlie, they don't in Mexico City either. And the lady at the au pair agency was super-reassuring. This family they've got lined up for her sound wonderful. The parents are lawyers, they live on this phenomenal estate . . . Come on, Tucker. Let the girl live a little.'

That conversation had been three months ago. Charlotte had been in Mexico for two months now, and boy, had she lived a *lot*. She'd smoked her first joint, got drunk for the first time, cheated on her boyfriend Todd for the first time and (she could hardly believe it, even when she said it to herself) fallen in love with a married man.

It wasn't the dad of the family she was working for, the Encerritos. That would be cheap and tacky, and besides, Charlotte really liked Señora Encerrito, her boss, and would never do that to her. Not that what she was doing was OK. She knew it was wrong to have an affair. In fact, it was worse than wrong. It was a sin, a mortal sin. Charlotte came from a solid 'church' family, and there wasn't much wiggle room when it came to morals, especially sexual morals. It wasn't that she didn't care, either. She cared plenty, and she felt guilty and all of that. But none of that mattered. Not when *he* was there. When he walked into a room, when he looked at Charlotte, when he said her name, even when she heard his voice on the telephone, everything else went out the window. Her caution, her values, her fear, her regrets. *Poof. Gone.* And when he took her to bed and made love to her? Good God. There were no words to describe the bliss, the absolute ecstasy. Charlotte had had sex with Todd hundreds of times, but never like this. Never, in Charlotte Clancy's wildest imaginings, had she believed sex could be this wonderful. So she wasn't going to heaven? Big deal. She had heaven right here and his name was . . . *Shhhh.* She giggled to herself. She mustn't say his name out loud. Not ever. Not to anyone.

'What we have is a secret, *cara*,' he told her, every time they made love. 'No one must ever know. You understand?'

Charlotte did understand. He was married, and much, much older, and an important man. Their affair had to be discreet. What she didn't understand was all his other secrets. The mysterious 'meetings' he would disappear off to in the middle of the night. The attaché cases stuffed full of US dollars that she'd seen him hand over to the local chief of police in one of the fancy hotels in town.

'You can tell me, you know,' she would whisper coquettishly in his ear in bed. 'I can keep a secret. I just . . . I want to know everything about you. I want to be part of your life as much as I can. I love you so much!'

He always smiled, and kissed her, and assured her he loved her too and that he found her little outbursts 'adorable – like you'. But he never told her anything. 'It's for your own safety,' he would say, throwing in a thrilling element of danger to the already exciting situation.

In short, Charlotte Clancy was having the time of her life.

And tonight was going to be even better, the best yet.

Following the map he'd given her – so romantic! – she got out of her car and weaved her way on foot through the maize fields and down towards the river.

She'd taken a big risk a few nights ago, following him in the little Nissan the Encerritos had provided for her use, headlamps off so as not to be seen, only a few hundred yards behind him. It was hard to see along the bumpy roads, no more than tracks really, that he turned on to once they'd left the city. She'd started to panic, wondering how she would ever get back if somehow she lost him, but at that moment the track gave way to a hidden clearing in the trees and he came to a halt. She could make out rows of semicircular sheds, like giant pipes cut in half; inside, men were working at tables, their stations illuminated by old-fashioned oil lamps that made each shed glow softly in the moonlight. Charlotte watched as her lover got out of his car and moved from shed to shed, overseeing the work. It was all quite fascinating, but Charlotte couldn't see what the men were actually doing from where she was parked. With a boldness she didn't know she possessed till that moment, she'd got out of her car and walked over towards the shed where *he* was. She'd got to within about ten yards of the door when two men armed with machine guns leapt out in front of her.

Charlotte screamed so loudly they could probably hear it back in the city. 'Don't shoot! Please!'

Her lover turned around, a look of shock and anger on his face. But it quickly softened to a smile, and then a laugh.

'*Cara!*' he chuckled indulgently. 'You *followed* me?'

'I . . . I wanted to know,' stammered Charlotte, her long legs still shaking involuntarily at the sight of the guns. 'You wouldn't tell me anything.'

He gestured for the men to let her pass, opening his arms wide and pulling her into a tight hug. 'I never would have thought you had it in you,' he grinned, ruffling Charlotte's hair as if she were a disobedient but adorable puppy. 'You're a brave little thing, aren't you, hm? I see I underestimated you.'

Charlotte swelled with pride and relief. He wasn't angry. He was pleased! She'd been right to take the risk, right to show him she was more than some silly little girl, some au pair he was having a summer fling with.

'Come.' He took her hand. 'As you're here, let me show you around.'

She'd seen it all then, all the workings of his empire.

*Cocaine.*

Even the word sounded dangerous to Charlotte, like something from an episode of *Miami Vice*. She'd never been offered coke in her life, never even seen it. And now, here she was, in the eye of the storm, actually watching the stuff being produced. It was fascinating, and he showed her around with pride, as if this were any other factory or business he'd built. It was also extraordinarily complicated.

In one of the sheds, sheaves of dry coca leaves were being finely ground and dusted with lime before going under a misting machine like a weak garden sprinkler to be moistened with water. From there, the mixture was taken to another shed where it sat in giant vats like cement mixers, into which kerosene was added. The third shed was the 'extraction plant', where cocaine was first separated from the leaves, and then subjected to a complicated process of heating, filtering, pressing, siphoning and mixing with sulfuric acid, before being transferred to yet another building where eventually a gummy, yellow solid emerged that he identified as 'coca paste'. The paste was then carried to a purifying shed, where it was mixed with diluted ammonia and filtered to produce cocaine hydrochloride.

All the while Charlotte listened, and nodded, holding his hand, acting as if this entire experience were perfectly normal, the sort of thing she did back in San Diego all the time.

'Are you shocked?' he asked her at the end of the tour. 'Do you still want me, now you know I'm a *criminal*?' He grinned as he said the word, tongue in cheek. But it was true, Charlotte thought. He was a criminal.

'I'll always want you,' she told him, gazing up adoringly into his mesmerizing eyes. He took her back to his car then and made love to her, more passionately than ever before. Then he drove slowly back to the city, with Charlotte following.

Afterwards, she didn't hear from him for almost a week. She was starting to panic that something had happened, that he'd decided to end things, when she'd finally got his text this morning: *I've missed you, cara. Meet me here at 7 p.m.*, he wrote, sending her a link to a map as well as written directions. *I have a surprise for you!*

Charlotte's heart soared. He'd never written anything like this to her before. *I've missed you.* That wasn't his style at all. Nor were little maps and romantic surprises. Something had shifted between them since she'd learned the truth. *He sees me as an equal now. As a partner.*

A feeling of deep happiness surged through her. This, then, was love.

*     *     *

She was almost at the meeting spot, a place so remote and isolated there couldn't possibly be anything there. *Maybe he's set up a picnic?* Charlotte thought, imagining a soft blanket laid with silver and crystal, and buckets of champagne on ice. It was the sort of thing she could see him doing. Private but luxurious. Different, special, like he was. She felt sure now that her future lay with this man, despite his wife and the age difference and the dangerous things he did for a living. She couldn't see yet exactly how this future would come to pass. How she would ever reconcile her parents to this new life she'd found. But she trusted, somehow. She was Charlotte Clancy, Charlotte the brave. *He'd* underestimated her, but only because she'd underestimated herself.

*I can be whatever I want to be.*

Frederique didn't understand. 'Don't go, Charlotte. Or at least don't go alone,' her friend had begged her, when Charlotte showed her the 'secret' map. Frederique Zidane was an au pair too, and Charlotte's only close girlfriend in Mexico City. She knew about Charlotte's older, married boyfriend, but not enough to piece together who he was or what he did. 'These places aren't safe in the daytime, never mind at night. Anyone who lives here knows that. *He* must know it.'

'Stop being such a scaredy-cat,' Charlotte giggled. 'I'll be fine.'

But Frederique wasn't laughing. 'There are bandits out there. I'm serious. People get robbed, kidnapped, murdered. People disappear.'

'Well, I'm not going to disappear,' Charlotte replied robustly.

'And you know this because . . . ?'

'Because I won't be alone,' Charlotte said. '*He'll* be there, won't he? He'll protect me.'

It was the last conversation Frederique Zidane and Charlotte Clancy ever had.

# 3

## LISA

'So, Lisa. How has your week been?'

Dr Nikki Roberts leaned back in her faded black leather armchair and smiled warmly at her patient.

*Lisa Flannagan. Twenty-eight years old. Former model and long-term mistress of Willie Baden, septuagenarian billionaire owner of the LA Rams. Recovering Vicodin addict. Narcissist.*

'Pretty good actually,' Lisa smiled back and, pressing her palms together, leaned forward in a little bow of gratitude. 'Namaste. I'm really feeling at peace about moving on from Willie. Like, I'm in a place of light, you know?'

'That's great.' Nikki nodded encouragingly. Raindrops were tap-tapping against the window. This was her last session of the day, thank God. All she wanted was to get home. Switch off. Let the rain lull her to sleep.

'I know, right?' Lisa beamed. 'Your advice in our last session helped me sooooo much.'

Lisa talked like this a lot: in clichés and exclamation points, like a teenage girl who'd swallowed her first self-help book whole, and now considered herself 'a spiritual person'. As a psychologist, and a highly successful one at that, Nikki didn't judge. She merely observed, and offered techniques to help her patient modify harmful behaviors and break destructive cycles.

As a person, however, it was a different story.

As a person, she judged plenty.

Lisa Flannagan was a user. A homewrecker. A baby-killer. A slut.

\* \* \*

Sinking back into Dr Roberts' soft, over-stuffed couch, Lisa Flannagan poured out her heart.

'I moved out of the apartment,' she announced proudly. 'I actually did it.'

God, it felt good! *Such* a release, to come to a place where she was truly seen and understood and just let it all out.

'Willie was, like, in shock. He was so mad, I thought he was going to hit me. Screaming and yelling and smashing things up.'

'Did he threaten you?' Nikki asked.

'Oh yeah. Sure he did. "You can't do this to me. I own you. I'll destroy you. You're nothing without me!" All of that. But I was super calm. I was like, "No, baby. You need to understand. This is something I need to do for *myself.* Like, I'm twenty-eight years old, you know? I'm not a child."'

Lisa looked forward to her Wednesday-night therapy sessions at Dr Roberts' plush Century City offices the way she used to look forward to scoring Vicodin, or getting laid by one of Willie's big, black NFL players in the Beverly Hills apartment he'd bought for her two years ago. Back then, she hadn't seen how totally controlling Willie was being. Like he was trying to buy her or something. Dr Roberts had totally opened her eyes on that score.

She'd also helped Lisa to realize how much inner strength she had. Like, kicking the pills was a big deal. Willie had picked up Lisa's tab at Promises, but it was *Lisa* who'd agreed to go to rehab, *Lisa* who'd changed her own life.

*I'm a good person.*

*If left the drugs behind, I can leave Willie Baden behind.*

She would keep the apartment, of course. Or rather, she would sell it and keep the money. Ditto the Cartier sapphire-and-diamond necklace Willie had bought her for her twenty-fifth. New starts were all well and good, but Lisa Flannagan wasn't about to walk away destitute from an eight-year relationship with a billionaire. That would be plain stupid. Besides, it wasn't as if Willie needed the money back. Plus she'd done the responsible thing and terminated his baby, not hung around and demanded baby-momma money for the rest of her life, like most girls would have. The way Lisa saw it, once Willie got over the initial blow to his pride, there was no reason why she and her married lover couldn't part as friends.

As she talked, sipping cucumber water from the jug on Dr Roberts' coffee table, Lisa Flannagan stole occasional glances at the woman sitting opposite her, the therapist she had grown to rely on and to think of almost as a friend.

*Dr Nikki Roberts.*

What was *her* life like, outside these offices?

Thanks to Google, Lisa already knew the basic facts: *Dr Nicola Roberts, née Hammond, thirty-eight years old. Graduated from Columbia before doing a postgrad in psychology at UCLA and an internship at Ronald Reagan Medical Center.*

Lisa wondered whether that was where Dr Roberts had met her husband, Dr Douglas Roberts, a neurosurgeon and specialist in addiction-related brain disorders. Unfortunately, she couldn't ask. Asking your therapist personal questions was against the rules.

What Lisa did know was that Dr Roberts' husband had been killed in a tragic car accident last year, right about the time she first started coming to therapy. The *LA Times* had reported on his death, because by all accounts Doug Roberts had been an amazing guy and a big deal in the LA charity world, campaigning tirelessly to help the city's addicts wherever he found them, from downtown's skid row to the mansions of Bel Air.

It was bizarre to think that the poised, attractive, professional woman sitting opposite Lisa, with her sleek brunette bob similar to Lisa's own hair, her slender figure and intelligent green eyes was actually a grieving widow, whose own inner life was presumably in total turmoil.

*Poor Dr Roberts,* Lisa thought. *I hope* she *has someone to talk to.*

*She deserves to be happy.*

'I'm afraid that's our time, Lisa.'

The therapist's mellow, soothing voice broke Lisa's reverie. She looked at the clock on the wall.

'Oh my God, you're right. Time passes so *fast* in here, it's crazy. Do you find that, Dr Roberts?'

Nikki smiled diplomatically. 'Sometimes.'

Lisa Flannagan stood up to leave.

'Don't you have a coat?' Nikki asked. 'It's pouring out there.'

'Is it?' Lisa hadn't noticed the pounding on the windows.

She was dressed in a tiny denim miniskirt that barely skimmed the top of her thighs, and a tank top with the words 'ALL YOU NEED IS LOVE' emblazoned on the front, a garment so tiny it would have struggled to adequately cover a child's chest, never mind Lisa's ample bosom.

'You'll be soaked to the bone out there,' said Nikki. Standing up, she reached for her own trench coat, hanging on the back of the door. 'Here. Take mine.'

Lisa hesitated. 'Don't you need it?'

Nikki shook her head. 'I'm parked downstairs. I can take the elevator right to my car. You can return it at our next session.'

'Well, if you're sure . . .' Lisa took the coat, smiling broadly. 'That is *so* kind of you, Dr Roberts. Really.'

She took the therapist's hand and squeezed it. It was little gestures like that, going the extra mile, that really set Dr Roberts apart from other therapists. She wasn't in this for the money. She actually cared about her patients. *She cares about me.*

\* \* \*

Outside in the alley behind the Century Plaza Medical Building it was cold, wet and dark. His legs ached from crouching for so long. His skin burned and so did his throat. Every breath felt like he was gargling razor blades, and every drop of rain felt like acid, a tiny burning dagger slicing into his frayed nerves. When it was over, he would get what he needed. Pain, unimaginable pain, would be replaced with exquisite ecstasy. It wouldn't last long, but that didn't matter. Nothing lasted long.

The streets of Century City were full of cars, but the slick sidewalks were deserted. No one walked in LA, especially not in the rain.

She did, though. Usually.

Sometimes.

Would she come out tonight?

*Come out, come out, wherever you are!*

There she was. Suddenly. Too suddenly. He wasn't ready.

His heart began to pound.

She belted her coat and put her head down against the rain. No umbrella. She was walking fast, crossing the opening to the alley.

'Help!' He tried to shout, but his voice was so raspy. Would she hear him? She had to hear him! 'Help me!'

Lisa Flannagan turned. There was a figure, a man, or maybe a boy – he was tiny – slumped beside some trash cans.

'Please!' he called again. 'Call 911. I've been stabbed.'

'Oh my God!' Pulling out her phone, Lisa moved towards him, already punching out the numbers. 'What happened? Are you OK?'

He was bent double, clutching his stomach. That must be where the knife had gone in. She squatted down beside him. He was wearing a hoodie that was soaking wet, covering his face and hair.

'Emergency, what service do you require?'

'Police,' Lisa blurted into her phone. 'And ambulance.' She touched the boy lightly on the top of his lolling head. 'Don't panic. Help's on the way. Where are you hurt?'

He looked up and grinned. Lisa felt the vomit rise up inside her. The face beneath the hood wasn't human. It was the face of a monster, green and rotted, strips of flesh literally curling off the bones and hanging down, like the skin of some rancid fruit. She opened her mouth to scream, but no sound came out.

'Ma'am, can you give me your location?'

He recognized the terror in her eyes as she crouched over him, open-mouthed. Still grinning, he plunged the blade deep into her abdomen and twisted. Oh, the scream came then all right! Loud and piercing and horrified. He pulled out the knife and plunged again, so hard that his fist followed the blade somewhere deep inside her, somewhere warm and wet and enticing.

'Ma'am, can you hear me? Ma'am? What's happening? Can you tell me where you are?'

\*    \*    \*

Dr Nikki Roberts leaned back against the soft leather of her Mercedes X-Class seats and waited for the garage doors to open.

Traffic permitting, she'd be back home in Brentwood in twenty minutes. Another long, empty evening stretched ahead, but she would fill it with mindless television and a bottle of Newton unfiltered Merlot and Ambien and sleep, and it would pass. Everything would pass.

Nikki felt guilty. She'd only been half-present during today's session with Lisa. Maybe even less than half. That wasn't fair, whether she liked the patient or not.

The garage doors inched open, agonizingly slowly.

Nikki edged the car forwards, towards the alley.

\*    \*    \*

Doors. Garage doors!

Lisa heard the grinding of mechanical gears and the close, familiar rev of an engine. Blood was pouring from her stomach and chest.

Not oozing but pouring, like milk from a jug. She couldn't move. Couldn't stand or run. She could only scream, and she did, again and again and again, each time the monster sliced into her arms and breasts and thighs. He wasn't even trying to kill her any more. At least, not quickly. He was playing with her, like a cat with a mouse, delighting in the agony he was causing, in shredding her perfect body, piece by tiny piece.

The engine grew louder. Hope soared in Lisa's heart.

*Someone's coming. Maybe it's Dr Roberts? Please God, let her see me!*

She drew in her breath and screamed, surely the loudest scream anyone had ever made in their lives. She could hear her own blood bubbling in the back of her throat and feel her eyes bulge as if they might burst from their sockets. Headlamps swept over her and the monster, lit them up like a stage spotlight.

The stabbing stopped.

So did the engine.

Lisa sobbed with relief. *She's seen me!* She heard the monster's knife clatter to the floor. She could feel her pulse slowing, and waited for her attacker to run, or for the car door to open.

Seconds passed. *Two. Five. Ten . . .*

Nothing happened.

*Wait . . . what's going on?*

The car's engine started up again.

*No!*

Headlights lit up the alley.

*NO! Please! I'm here! PLEASE!*

Nikki's silver Mercedes glided past them along the alley, then turned slowly into the street.

Rotted, scaly hands coiled themselves around Lisa's neck from behind. In front of her eyes, the shiny blade glinted, already slick with her blood.

'Where were we?'

The last noise Lisa Flannagan heard was the monster laughing.

# 4

Carter Berkeley III looked down at his expensively manicured nails and resisted the urge to bite them. What the hell was he doing here? He should be talking to the police, not a damn therapist.

Then he reminded himself that the police wouldn't help him. The police didn't believe him. No one did.

Carter thought about the two armed bodyguards he had waiting downstairs in the lobby, and tried to feel better. It didn't work. Then he tried imagining his therapist naked. That *did* work, at least a little. Dr Nikki Roberts was a deeply sensual woman. Carter pictured her gray, pencil skirt pushed up roughly around her hips, and her prissy white blouse ripped open. He imagined her . . .

'Carter? Are you with me?'

Her voice made him startle, then blush, then scowl. A highly successful investment banker, handsome, educated and rich, Carter was used to having people jump to his command and scuttle to gratify his every desire. Especially women. He did not appreciate being called out like a naughty schoolboy.

'Tell me again what you think you saw last night,' Dr Roberts said.

'I don't "think" I saw anything,' Carter snapped. 'I know what I saw, OK? I am not crazy.' He ran a harassed hand through his thick blond hair.

'I never suggested you were.' The therapist's voice was calm. 'But even sane people can be mistaken some of the time, can't they? I know I often am.'

'Yeah, well I'm not,' Carter growled.

*Jesus.* They'd all be sorry when he was dead. When these bastards finally got him and strung him up with electrical cord and beat him to death in some godforsaken dungeon. They'd all wish they'd listened then: the police, Dr Roberts, all of them.

\* \* \*

Nikki leaned forward earnestly while her patient rambled on, expounding the same conspiracy theory he'd been peddling since he first started seeing her, more than a year ago. Carter Berkeley believed he was being stalked by unnamed assassins. He never offered any reason for this, still less any evidence, other than the elaborate imaginings of his brilliant but tortured mind. And yet, no matter how many logical paths Nikki led him down, Carter's paranoid fears persisted. In fact, if anything, they were getting worse. Only last week he had informed Nikki solemnly that Trey Raymond, the sweet boy who ran her office and manned the front desk at Century Plaza, was a spy 'working for the Mexicans'.

'You can't trust him. What do you really know about Trey, Dr Roberts?'

'What do *you* know about him, Carter?' Nikki countered.

'Enough. I know enough,' Carter pronounced, cryptically. Although, again, he offered no evidence to back this up.

*I'm not making him better,* Nikki thought sadly. *I might actually be making him worse. Why am I even here?*

She knew the answer to that, deep down. She was here – at work, in her office, seeing patients – because she had nowhere else to be. Nowhere else except home, alone, with no Doug, and no answers. That prospect was quite unbearable.

*Unbearable . . .*

The word took Nikki back.

It was only a year ago, but it felt like a lifetime.

Doug was smiling at her across the table at Luigi's, wolfing down his spaghetti vongole as if he hadn't eaten in weeks, talking at a million miles an hour, the way he always did when the two of them were together.

'"It's unbearable." What do people even mean when they say that?' Doug asked Nikki. 'My patients say it to me all the time: "It's unbearable, Doc. I can't bear it." As if they have any alternative.'

Nikki and Doug Roberts had been married for seven years and together for almost three times that long. But the thrill of each other's company, of talking and sharing ideas and feelings and experiences, never faded. No lunch date with Doug was ever dull.

'I guess they're speaking metaphorically,' Nikki observed, toying with her own crab salad. Luigi's food was delicious, but even the salads were rich. Doug might be incapable of gaining weight, but since she turned thirty-eight Nikki found increasingly that she had to watch her figure. There was nothing worse than thinking you might be pregnant at long last, only to realize that your rounded belly was actually ugly, middle-aged fat.

'They mean that they don't want to bear it. It hurts. Don't forget, these are desperate addicts we're talking about.'

'You're right.' Doug nodded, slurping down the last of his pasta before reaching for the bread basket. 'I guess I just get frustrated sometimes. Because, at the end of the day, it really is that black and white. Do you want to get better or not? Do you want to die or not? That's it. That's the choice.'

To an outsider, Doug Roberts might sound compassionless toward his junkie patients, but Nikki knew that he was anything but. He'd raced to meet her for lunch today directly from the latest meth and opioid clinic he was busy setting up in Venice with his good friend from med school, Haddon Defoe. Helping LA's most hardened, most helpless addicts had become Doug Roberts' passion, his life's work.

'Anyway, enough about me.' He looked at Nikki lovingly. 'How's your morning been, sweetheart? Did you do another test?'

'Not yet.' Nikki looked down shyly at her half-eaten food. 'Maybe tonight.'

'Why not now?' asked Doug.

'Because. If it's negative and I feel shitty, it might distract me from my afternoon clients,' said Nikki.

Doug reached across the table and squeezed her hand. 'It could be positive, honey. No reason why it shouldn't be.'

'Yup,' Nikki forced a smile. 'No reason.'

*Except that the last six times we tried, it was negative. And with every month that passes my eggs are getting older and more worn out. And some cruel god out there, some malicious force beyond our control, seems to have decided that we'll never become parents.*

She and Doug had everything else, after all. A wonderful, loving marriage. Wealth. Status. Meaningful, rewarding careers. Great friends. Great family. In what alternate universe did they deserve children, as well as all that?

'I love you, Nik,' Doug said softly.

'I love you, too.'

'It'll happen. We still have time. So much time.'

*That's right,* thought Nikki. *We still have time.*

\* \* \*

'Dr Roberts?' Carter Berkeley sounded irritated. 'Were you even listening to me?'

'Of course.' Nikki dutifully repeated everything her client had just said. She'd long ago learned the knack of 'surface listening', using one's brain to multitask, in this case memorizing Carter's words whilst actively focusing on something else entirely. It was a trick Doug had taught her.

Why did everything seem to come back to Doug?

'Now, as we're almost out of time, I suggest we finish up with a mindfulness exercise,' Nikki told Carter, deftly regaining control of the session. 'If you don't mind putting your feet flat on the floor . . .'

Once Carter Berkeley had left, Nikki wandered out into the lobby.

Trey Raymond, her PA, office manager and general right-hand man, was busy updating patient files. Not that there was much to update any more. Since Doug's death, patients had been deserting Nikki's practice like flies. Perhaps they thought her grief was contagious. Or that her loss might make her less focused, less effective as a therapist. Perhaps they were right about that. Whatever the reason, Nikki now only had four regular clients, down from almost twenty a year ago.

Inevitably, her final four were the most desperate, the ones who simply couldn't let go.

Carter Berkeley, the paranoid banker, who came once a week.

Lisa Flannagan, the deluded mistress, who typically came twice a week.

Anne Bateman, the insecure violinist, who was Nikki's most frequent flier, coming to therapy almost daily. Therapeutically, this was overkill, but like many people Nikki found she had a tough time saying no to the young and beautiful Anne. In fact it worried Nikki quite how often she thought about Anne, and how important her patient was becoming to her.

And finally there was Lana Grey, the actress, who regularly failed to pay Nikki's bills on time, or even at all. Poor lost Lana. Once a mid-level TV star, she was washed up now and borderline bankrupt.

'Lana ain't your client,' Trey would tell Nikki, repeatedly. 'Clients pay. She's your charity case. Your lost cause.'

'Oh really? My lost cause.' Nikki would smile. 'And what does that make you, I wonder?'

'Me?' Trey would grin. 'Oh, I'm the patron saint of lost causes. But you can't get rid of me, Doc. I jus' keep on coming back, like a bad penny.'

To which Nikki would reply that she didn't want to get rid of him. That she didn't know how she would manage without him. Both of which were true, but not because she needed an office manager. The reality was that Trey Raymond was a last link to her husband. Doug had helped Trey, picked him up off the streets and turned his life around. He'd done the same for countless others over the years. But for some reason Trey was different. Doug had loved him like a son.

*The son I was never able to give him . . .*

Trey shot Nikki a sidelong glance now, as he finished his filing. 'You headin' home, Doc?'

'I was going to.' Nikki hesitated, casting around for reasons to stay. 'Do you need me for anything?'

'Nope.' The young man beamed, strong white teeth lighting up his ebony complexion. 'I got this covered.'

'Are you sure?'

'I'm positive,' said Trey. 'I'll call you if anything comes up.'

\*   \*   \*

Outside on the street, Nikki squinted. The sun was blinding, blasting out of the clear blue California sky with a vengeance after yesterday's unexpected rain.

Nikki used to love the rain but now she hated it. It reminded her of Doug, of the anguish and misery and rage – God, the rage! – that could never be washed away. She imagined the wheels of his Tesla, slick and slipping across the freeway. His panic as he hurtled towards the lights of the oncoming traffic. Nikki imagined Doug's foot stamping frantically on a useless brake pedal. Did he scream? *I hope he screamed.*

Up until that day, as far as Nikki knew, she and Doug had been happy in their marriage. Blissfully happy.

Clearly she was mistaken. That was the day it had all unraveled. All the smoke and mirrors had fallen away, and she was left staring at the raw truth. The ugly truth.

And now Doug was dead and she was alone, her life a never-ending nightmare of unanswered questions and 'what ifs'. Until the accident, Nikki wouldn't have believed it possible to love someone so much, miss them so much and hate them so much, all at the same time. But here she was, drowning in all three emotions, fighting simply to make it through the day.

She'd found solace in her work, to a degree. But sometimes, like Doug with his addicts, Nikki found herself so frustrated with her patients she wanted to pick them up by the scruff of the neck and shake them, like a terrier with a rat.

*Get over it, for God's sake.*

*STOP WHINING!*

She never used to be that way. Intolerant. Superior. Judgmental.

Grief had changed her.

Lisa Flannagan was a case in point. Nikki didn't approve of Lisa. Of her life, her choices. On the plus side, unlike Carter Berkeley, Lisa did at least sincerely want to change. Although, again unlike Carter, she was so stupid, so profoundly intellectually giftless, that getting her to see even the most simple correlation between her behaviors, thoughts and emotions was like trying to teach a swamp rat calculus. Was it frustration that had made Nikki so depressed after last night's session with Lisa? Or something else? Maybe it was envy. Envy at Lisa's positive outlook. Her happiness, her hope for the future. Hope was something that Nikki Roberts no longer possessed, in any area of her life. After last night's session she'd driven out into the rainy alley, so upset she'd had to stop the car to compose herself. Then she'd gone home, finished an entire bottle of wine alone (a nightly occurrence these days) and collapsed into bed, too drained even to cry. To her amazement, she slept deeply and well, not waking until almost nine this morning, feeling nauseous but more rested than she had in months.

The sleep had done wonders for her mood, carrying her through the morning on a mini wave of euphoria, right up until her trying session with Carter Berkeley. That had brought her down again. But now it was over, she made an effort to recapture her earlier good spirits.

Arriving home, she kicked off her shoes and turned on the TV news before running upstairs to change. Pathetic as it was, Nikki found that background noise from the television or radio made her feel less lonely, especially in the evenings. Up in the master bedroom it was off with the professional psychologist's clothes – skirt, pumps, silk jacket – and on with the shorts and sneakers. This evening, Nikki decided, she would run on the beach. She hadn't done that in forever, not since long before Doug's accident. Back then, in another life, running beside the ocean used to make her feel happy. Free. Blessed. She didn't expect any of those feelings today. That would be too much to ask. But getting out and moving had to be better than moping around the house. After all, if Lobotomized-Lisa Flannagan could take a step forward in her pampered, self-centered life, so could she.

The newscaster's voice droned on in the background as Nikki came back downstairs. She half tuned in.

'A young woman's body was found this afternoon, partially hidden in undergrowth close to the 10 freeway,' the anchor was saying. 'Initial reports suggest that the victim, a white woman in her late twenties, was stabbed multiple times, possibly even tortured.'

Was it Nikki's imagination, or did the newscaster seem to be lingering over the gruesome details?

'According to police, the injuries to the victim's face are so severe that no formal identification has yet been made.'

Nikki winced and grabbed a water bottle from the fridge. *Christ. There are some psychos out there.*

'Sports news now, and in a major setback for the LA Rams . . .'

Nikki tuned out. Opening the door, she ran out into the still bright evening light.

\*    \*    \*

She'd almost reached Sunset Boulevard when her phone rang. She stopped and answered, panting.

'Hello?'

It was Trey. He was crying, sobbing so violently it was hard to make out his words. Nikki slipped into doctor mode.

'Try to breathe, honey. Slow it down.'

Two long, rasping breaths shuddered down the line.

'Good,' said Nikki. 'Now can you tell me what's happened?'

'Lisa!' Trey blurted. 'Lisa Flannagan.'

Trey had always had a soft spot for Lisa. Nikki could tell. The way he stared at her when she walked down the hall to the restroom, the shy smile he gave every time she came to his desk to pay for a session.

'What about Lisa?' Nikki asked kindly. 'Whatever it is, I'm sure it can't be that bad, Trey.'

'She's dead!' Trey sobbed.

A low ringing had started in Nikki's ears. She watched the traffic crawl past her as if in a dream.

'What do you mean?'

'I mean she's dead. Murdered!' Trey started to weep uncontrollably. 'I heard it on the news.'

Nikki's knees buckled beneath her. She'd seen Lisa yesterday, alive and well and full of plans for her future. This couldn't be right. 'Are you sure?'

'I'm positive. Oh God, Doc, it's awful. Some sicko cut her to pieces! Dumped her by the side of the freeway.'

Nikki gasped. The news report she'd heard earlier! About the young woman dumped off the 10. That was *Lisa*?

'Dr Roberts? Dr Roberts, are you still there?'

Trey's voice whined out of her earpiece but Nikki didn't answer.

Guilt crept over her like a spider. While she'd been envying Lisa's hope and youth, while she'd been *judging* her, Lisa had been . . . *Oh God*.

She tried not to think about it, but the horrifying images crowding into Nikki's brain wouldn't stop.

'I'll talk to you tomorrow, Trey,' she rasped, and hung up.

A new nightmare had begun.

# 5

'**W**e're looking for Dr Roberts. Dr Nicola Roberts. Now it's a simple question, son. Is she here or isn't she?'

The two cops hovered menacingly in front of Trey Raymond's desk. At least, it felt menacing to Trey. Then again, they were cops, and Trey was black and a former meth-dealer from Westmont, South LA's 'Death Alley', so the three men weren't ever going to be friends.

'She's with a patient right now.'

One of the cops, the shorter, fatter, older one with big, wet, larva-like white lips, regarded Trey with unadulterated contempt.

'In there?' he asked, nodding towards Nikki's office door.

He wasn't wearing uniform and he hadn't showed Trey his badge. Neither of them had, for that matter. But he spoke with the innate, entitled authority of a police officer. It didn't occur to Trey to question him.

'Yes, in there,' Trey confirmed. 'But like I said, Dr Roberts is with a patient. She can't be disturbed while she's in session.'

'Is that a fact?' The fat cop smiled unpleasantly, moving towards the door.

'Leave it, Mick.' His taller, younger, more attractive partner put a restraining hand on his shoulder. 'We can wait.'

'Wait?' Larva Lips looked furious, but his partner ignored him, smiling at Trey and taking a seat on the Italian leather couch in the waiting room. Picking up a copy of *Psychology Today,* he asked casually: 'It's fifty minutes, right? A therapy session? I remember from when my wife left me.'

'Which one?' Larva Lips snarled, obviously not best pleased to have been 'reined in' in front of Trey.

'All of them,' his partner grinned. 'I was a wreck every time.'

Larva Lips didn't smile back but sat down, lowering his ample backside into an armchair where he simmered belligerently. Trey had encountered scores of LAPD like him growing up: knee-jerk racists, Blue Lives Matter assholes who shot first and thought later. Or not. Dude might as well have had a swastika tattooed on his forehead, so obvious were his prejudices. For all Trey knew, his partner might be every bit as rotten inside, but he was better educated and he hid it better. Maybe he thought he'd get more out of Dr Roberts if he played nice with her office staff?

Trey Raymond figured he'd learned a lot, working in a psychologist's office.

'How much longer?' Larva Lips demanded, glaring at the clock on the wall as if it were to blame for his impatience.

'The session ends in fifteen minutes,' said Trey. He assumed the police were here to ask about Lisa, which only made him feel worse. The thought of these bozos, picking through Lisa's private life like vultures pecking at a carcass, made him feel sick.

Trey had seen a lot of death growing up. A lot of murder too, but that was different. That was shootings, gang violence, and where Trey grew up that was a fact of life. Sad, for sure. But not shocking.

Not like this. Lisa wasn't part of that world. She was white and rich and beautiful, part of a white, rich, beautiful world where shit like this didn't happen. Dr Roberts came from the same world. Trey didn't, but he'd been invited in by Dr Roberts' husband, Doug, before he died. More than invited. Welcomed. Like a son.

These son-of-a-bitch cops had no business here, bringing their dark world into this bright one.

'Can I get you something to drink?' Trey offered the politer officer.

'I'm fine thanks.'

'You can get me a Coke,' the fat one replied, without looking up from his phone. An unspoken '*boy*' hung in the air.

Beneath the desk, Trey's fists clenched. He longed to refuse, to tell the man they were all out, sorry. But a deep-rooted survival instinct kicked in. *Don't mess with cops. Not to their face, anyway.*

*       *       *

Inside Nikki's office, Anne Bateman recrossed her slender legs beneath her long linen skirt. All her movements were so graceful, so thoughtful and composed. *Like a ballet dancer,* thought Nikki admiringly. Only last night Nikki had dreamed about Anne again, dreams that were not overtly erotic but that certainly had something obsessional about them, something voyeuristic. *Perhaps being a virtuoso violinist isn't so dissimilar to being a ballerina?* Nikki thought. Whatever the reason, Anne appeared to dance through life to the tune of some inner music, some rhapsody of her own creation.

'She was your patient, wasn't she? Like me,' Anne asked.

'You know I can't tell you that,' Nikki said gently.

Like everybody else, Anne had seen the grisly reports of Lisa Flannagan's murder on the TV news. She'd been distressed by them, and understandably wanted to talk.

'You don't have to tell me,' she said quietly, staring down at her lap. 'I know. I've passed her in the corridor a hundred times. Poor woman.'

'Yes,' said Nikki. She felt bad herself. Lisa had been so full of hope in their final session together, so focused on her future. A future that, as it turned out, didn't exist.

It was too late to help Lisa Flannagan now. But Nikki could still help Anne Bateman. Beautiful, intoxicating Anne. In fact, Anne was the one patient who Nikki felt she *was* helping, consistently. A violin prodigy with a coveted position at the LA Phil, at only twenty-six years old Anne was already wildly successful. Although childlike in some ways, in others she had already lived a life far beyond her years. As a teenager she'd traveled and performed all over the world, eventually marrying young to an extremely wealthy, charismatic, and much older man.

Anne was an attractive girl, in a tiny, fragile, doll-like way. Shy and meek in everyday conversation, with a violin in her hand Anne transformed into a frenzied, passionate woman, utterly lost in her own talent. Many men had been drawn to her on stage, to her alabaster skin and enormous, chocolate brown eyes, as well as to the intensity of her playing. But her husband had coveted her with an obsessive desire. After they married he had carried her off to his vast estate like a fairy-tale princess, showering her with gifts and clothes and attention and adoration, rarely letting her out of his sight.

It had taken immense courage for Anne to leave him and move back to her native Los Angeles. It wasn't that she didn't love him. But she'd married so young, and she'd changed, and her music was calling to her, its call becoming more and more insistent with each passing day. The collapse of her marriage was what had prompted Anne to start seeing a therapist, and she and Nikki had quickly formed a strong bond. Over the last three months, Anne had come to rely heavily on Nikki's support and advice in almost every aspect of her life.

'You mustn't feel frightened,' Nikki told her now. 'What happened to Lisa was terrible, but it had nothing to do with you. Don't internalize it. The fact that you happened to see her in this office doesn't mean anything. It doesn't tie the two of you together.'

'No.' Anne smiled shyly. 'You're right. I'm being silly.'

'Not silly,' said Nikki. 'Death is a traumatic event. Especially violent death. But you're still processing your own trauma, Anne. Try not to take on anyone else's, that's all I'm saying.'

Their time was up. Reluctantly, Nikki opened the door to the corridor to show Anne out. Most patients shook Nikki's hand at the end of a session, but Anne always hugged her, squeezing tightly like a child leaving its mother at the school gate. It was too intimate a gesture really, not appropriate between a patient and a therapist, but Nikki didn't have the heart to put a stop to it. The truth was that Anne's dependence on her felt good. Everything about Anne Bateman felt good.

This time, however, Nikki stiffened the moment Anne embraced her.

Two strange men were heading towards her from the waiting room, watching intently.

Extricating herself swiftly from Anne's arms, Nikki ushered her patient out before turning to the two men.

'Can I help you?' she asked curtly.

One of the men, the younger one, stood up and extended his hand politely.

'Detective Lou Goodman, LAPD. This is my partner, Detective Mick Johnson.'

Nikki shook Goodman's hand. 'I assume you're here about Lisa? Such a terrible thing.' She offered her hand to his partner as well, but the short, heavyset man jerked angrily away.

'Not here,' he barked rudely, with a sidelong, distrustful glance at Trey. 'In your office.'

Nikki bristled. *What's his problem?* She had the vague sense of having seen him somewhere before, but she couldn't place it. 'All right,' she said briskly, walking both men into her consulting room and offering them a seat, before closing the door behind them.

\* \* \*

Back in the waiting room, Trey waited until he could hear the three of them talking before he picked up the phone.

'There's two cops here!' he whispered down the line. He was close to tears. 'What do I do? I'm scared, man.'

The voice on the other end of the line began to talk.

Trey listened, and nodded, trying to calm himself down.

*They don't know.*

*Nobody knows.*

*Be cool.*

\* \* \*

Detective Mick Johnson watched and listened as Dr Nikki Roberts answered his partner's questions.

When did Nikki last see Lisa Flannagan?

*The day she died.*

Had Lisa mentioned anything in that session, or prior sessions, about being threatened, or having any fears for her safety?

*No.*

Did Nikki know of anyone who might have a reason to target Lisa, or hurt her?

*No.*

Goodman asked all his questions politely, and accepted all Nikki's one-word answers without question or comment, writing each one down in his little notebook like a schoolboy taking notes from a teacher.

Johnson watched in silent disapproval. He didn't trust Nikki and he didn't like her. The arrogant bitch didn't even remember him! But he remembered her. He would always remember her. Watching her now, poised and cautious, sweeping her shiny dark hair back out of her eyes as she talked with Goodman, he could feel the anger burn his chest like battery acid.

'Dr Roberts, you may have been the last person, other than her killer, to see Miss Flannagan alive,' Goodman was saying. Leaning forward in his chair, looking at Nikki intently, it was obvious he was smitten by her. 'It's vital that we understand as much as we can about exactly what happened, both in this office, and after she left here.'

'I understand that, Detective,' said Nikki. 'I'm not sure what I can add, that's all. The session was positive, as I told you. Lisa seemed happy. She'd made a break from her boyfriend—'

'Boyfriend? You mean her sugar daddy,' Johnson interjected. 'Willie Baden?'

These were the first words the angry little man had spoken since he sat down. There could be no mistaking the leer in his voice. The idea of a beautiful young girl like Lisa offering herself sexually to a dirty old man like Baden clearly turned him on, or at least amused him.

'Yes,' Nikki said evenly.

'But, to be clear, she didn't have a "boyfriend". She was sleeping with a rich old man, someone else's husband, for his money,' Johnson pressed the point, earning himself a dirty look from Goodman, as well as a horrified one from Nikki. 'She was a high-class whore, basically. Isn't that right?'

'I don't know why she was with him. It's not my place to judge my clients, Detective,' Nikki replied coolly, fighting down her distaste at this man's unabashed sexism. 'All I know is that in our session that evening, Lisa told me she'd taken steps to leave Willie, and she seemed to be feeling good about that. I'd say she left here in a happy, hopeful mood.'

'Did she plan to meet anyone after her appointment? A friend, maybe? Did somebody pick her up?' Goodman asked, glaring at Johnson as he resumed his questioning.

'No,' said Nikki. 'She left alone. Typically, she drove herself to our sessions but on Wednesday she didn't have her car with her.'

The two cops exchanged glances.

'Do you know why not?'

Nikki shook her head. 'No. Sorry. I only remember because it was raining, and she told me she was leaving on foot, so I lent her my raincoat.'

Forgetting his anger for a moment, Detective Johnson sat up eagerly. 'She was wearing the coat when she left?'

'Yes,' said Nikki.

'Can you describe the coat, Dr Roberts? In as much detail as possible.'

Nikki did so. It was a perfectly ordinary raincoat but both men seemed fascinated by it.

'Thank you, Dr Roberts,' Goodman said, smiling warmly. 'That's very helpful information.' He had an intense way of speaking, Nikki noticed, a sort of flattering, micro-focus that made you feel as if you were the only person in the room. It wasn't flirtatious exactly, but it wasn't far off.

By contrast, his partner was utterly charmless, firing off a few more questions without any sort of thanks, before both men took their leave. But even he, Johnson, had seemed excited by the raincoat revelation. *Could it really be that important?*

Once they'd gone, Trey knocked on Nikki's door.

'I'm sorry, Doc. I didn't know what to do,' he said anxiously to Nikki. 'I knew you wouldn't want them to interrupt your session, but I think the older guy didn't like that I made them wait.'

Nikki put a reassuring hand on his shoulder. 'That's OK, Trey. You did everything right. How are *you* feeling? I know you cared about Lisa.'

'I'm feeling OK, I guess,' he muttered awkwardly. 'I mean, I'm sad. Shocked.'

'Me too,' said Nikki.

'She was so beautiful.'

'Yes. She was.'

'Times like this, I wish Dr Douglas was here,' Trey blurted. 'You know?'

Nikki looked pained. Trey hung his head.

'Sorry, Doc. I shouldn't have said that. Not to you.'

'Of course you can say it, Trey,' Nikki said kindly. 'You miss him. I miss him too. I don't want you to feel Doug's name is taboo. He'd have hated that.'

Later, after Trey had gone home, Nikki sat in her office alone for a long time, thinking.

She thought about Doug, and what he'd have made of all this.

She thought about Lisa, about the horror of her death.

She thought about the angry detective, Johnson: *She was a whore, sleeping with someone else's husband.*

Nikki understood anger. Since Doug's death, it had been her constant companion.

Reaching into her pocket, she pulled out the card that the other detective had given her. The civil one. Detective Lou Goodman.

*Lou.*

How long would it be, she wondered, before she heard from him again?

# 6

The Medical Examiner, Jenny Foyle, replaced the plastic sheeting covering Lisa Flannagan's body and returned her attention to the two detectives. In her early fifties, with a short, unkempt bob of salt and pepper hair, a stocky frame and a make-up-free face, Jenny was no beauty. But she was smart, intuitive, waspishly funny and astonishingly skilled at her job.

'So you're saying only one of these stab wounds killed her?' Mick Johnson asked.

'The one to the heart. Yes,' Jenny confirmed. 'The others were all superficial. Designed to wound, to hurt, but never intended to kill.'

Lou Goodman raised a groomed eyebrow. 'All eighty-eight of them?'

Jenny sighed. 'I'm afraid so.'

Most people preferred Lou Goodman to his partner, probably because Lou was handsome and charming and, unlike Mick Johnson, rarely looked as if the thing he'd most like to do in the entire world was punch you in the face. But not Jenny Foyle. Detective Goodman's charms were lost on her. A New York Irish girl herself, Jenny had always had a soft spot for Detective Johnson. True, he lacked charm and was no oil painting. But Jenny liked the big man's permanently stained shirts, his gruff sense of humor and his take-no-prisoners directness. In a city that was all about style over substance, and a department in which political correctness had gone mad, the Medical Examiner had always found Mick to be a breath of fresh air.

'So she was tortured?' Mick asked her. 'That's basically what you're saying?'

'That's exactly what I'm saying,' said Jenny. 'She was tortured. Incapacitated, probably through terror as much as from her physical injuries. Then she was moved. And at a later time, killed. Then she was moved again to the dumping site.'

All three of them paused for a moment to take in the plastic-covered shape that had once been Lisa Flannagan. A gorgeous young girl with her whole life ahead of her, reduced to a mutilated carcass.

Goodman broke the silence first. 'And you're confident of this timeline?'

'I am.'

'Because . . . ?'

'Because the rate of healing clearly shows the fatal wound occurred some hours after the first injuries. And because the levels of blood loss at the scene, although substantial, are incompatible with the victim having been stabbed in the heart there,' Jenny answered matter-of-factly.

'No sexual assault?' asked Goodman.

Jenny shook her head. 'Nope.'

'And she didn't fight back?' Johnson asked quietly.

'Well,' Jenny peeled off her latex gloves, allowing herself a small smile. 'At first I thought she didn't fight at all. Terrified, as I said. But right at the end of my examination I found a tiny – and I mean *tiny* – sample of tissue under one of her fingernails.'

Johnson's brow furrowed. 'Why so tiny?' he asked. 'If she scratched him, fighting for her life, wouldn't there be more?'

'Indeed there would.' Jenny's smile broadened. 'Which is why I think her nails were cut and the fingers scrubbed. Post-mortem.'

'Jesus.' Goodman winced.

'But he missed a spot?' Johnson asked brightly. 'Lucky for us.'

'I hope it will be,' said Jenny. 'Like I say, the sample was tiny. It was also . . . strange.'

Both men waited for her to elaborate.

'The cells were unlike anything I've seen before. They appeared to be from rotten flesh.'

Goodman raised an eyebrow. 'Rotten?'

'Yes, rotten.' Jenny cleared her throat awkwardly. 'From some-thing . . . someone . . . dead.'

Detective Johnson's eyes narrowed. 'You think this chick was killed by a dead guy?'

'No,' Jenny replied, deadpan. 'That would be impossible.'

'So what are you saying?' asked Goodman.

'Simply that the cells I recovered were unusual. And that I can't guarantee whether the quality or quantity of what we found under that nail will yield a meaningful DNA match to a possible suspect.'

'Maybe our killer's a zombie.' Mick Johnson nudged the ME playfully in the ribs. 'The living dead are among us!'

Jenny laughed. 'I'd say you're proof of that, Mickey. I'll let you know when I have any more, but that's all she wrote for the moment, boys. You take care now.'

* * *

Standing outside the Boyle Heights Coroner's Office, the two detectives digested the ME's bizarre findings in silence. Johnson's zombie comment was obviously a joke. But exactly how had Lisa Flannagan wound up with a corpse's flesh under her fingernails?

Realizing someone had to say something, Goodman tried to focus on the facts.

'So, we're looking for three sites,' he observed. 'Torture. Murder. Disposal.'

'Uh huh,' Johnson nodded. 'Three sites.'

'I guess we focus on that first.'

'I guess we do,' Johnson agreed.

There were a whole bunch of things that irritated him about his slick, young, ambitious partner. But Mick Johnson had to give Lou Goodman credit for an ordered mind, even in the craziest of circumstances.

They were back in their car and about to drive away when Jenny Foyle came rushing out the building towards them, flapping her arms like a lunatic.

Johnson wound down his window. 'Did you forget something? What else you got for us, Jenny? Vampire teeth-marks on her neck?' he quipped.

'Ha ha.' Panting from exertion, the ME shoved a single sheet of paper into Johnson's hand. 'Looks like you got lucky, Mick. DNA results just came back. Turns out your zombie has a name.'

# 7

Lou Goodman drove alone to Pacific Palisades. He and Johnson had agreed long ago to divide and conquer on their homicide cases. Goodman always handled the rich, high-class, educated types, while Johnson bonded with the 'great unwashed', as Lou only half-jokingly called the blue-collar witnesses. The system didn't work perfectly. Johnson was great with low-income whites, and over his years in the drug squad had developed a decent working relationship in some of the rougher Latino communities. But he was old school LAPD when it came to black neighborhoods. He didn't like them and they didn't like him.

It was a problem.

But not today's problem.

Today's call was up in the wonder-bread-white community of Pacific Palisades. The wide streets and multimillion-dollar mansions were very much Lou Goodman's territory. He was in his element.

'Turn right on Capri Drive,' Google Maps commanded. Goodman obeyed, cruising past homes so opulent it beggared belief. 'Estate' was an overused word among LA real estate brokers, but these houses were the real deal: ten-, fifteen-, twenty-bedroom palaces with sweeping driveways and idyllically manicured grounds. Uniformed maids, all of them Latina, darted in and out of side gates, some walking dogs, others taking out trash or directing deliveries. Goodman saw a bouquet of flowers as big as he was being delivered to one house, and to another an entire van's worth of helium balloons emblazoned with the words 'Ryan is 9!'

*Lucky Ryan.* Goodman thought back to his own ninth birthday, a trip to the ice rink in White Plains with his buddy Marco. What a great day that had been. One of the last completely happy days of his childhood, before his father went bankrupt and the Goodman family's rapid descent into poverty, misery and loss began. By Lou Goodman's tenth birthday, his father was dead. But he never thought about that any more. He'd trained himself only to remember the good times, the happy times. He'd also learned young that while money couldn't always buy you happiness, a lack of money always brought anguish. Lou's father barely understood what real wealth was. Greg Goodman had felt rich when he owned a business and a house with a garage and a big backyard. Losing those modest successes had destroyed him.

His son was different. Lou Goodman knew very well what real wealth was, and the terrible things men would do to obtain it and maintain it.

'Your destination is ahead,' Google informed him cheerfully. 'You have arrived!'

*Someone's certainly arrived,* thought Goodman, staring up at the vast, Greek classical mansion that was 19772 Capri Drive, aka the Grolsch Residence.

He'd skim-read the family information in the car on the long drive over from Boyle Heights: Nathan Grolsch had made a fortune in waste disposal way back in the 1980s. Dumped his first wife and two daughters and married again in his fifties to a barely legal beauty queen named Frances Denton. Nathan and Frances had one son together, Brandon. According to the file, the kid had turned nineteen three days ago, the same day Lisa Flannagan was murdered.

If Jenny Foyle's DNA results were to be believed, Brandon Grolsch had spent his big day slashing Lisa Flannagan to death before tossing her corpse onto the side of the freeway like a bag of trash. Either that or someone else had managed to insert tiny traces of Brandon's flesh under Lisa's fingernails, an unlikely scenario, however Goodman looked at it.

Goodman hit the call button on the enormous front gates. Two stone lions gazed impassively down at him from marble pillars to his right and left.

'Yes?' a woman's voice crackled over the speaker.

'Good afternoon.' Goodman cleared his throat. 'I'm Detective Louis Goodman from the LA Police Department. I'm here concerning Brandon Grolsch.'

'Jus' a moment please.' The woman had a Mexican accent. *Probably the housekeeper.* Goodman heard a crackle of static, then a long silence. He was about to ring again when the gates suddenly whirred into life, swinging open to reveal the house and gardens in all their glory.

Making his way up the bluestone driveway, past a lavish marble fountain, Goodman climbed the formal steps up to the front door. Potted olive trees flanked the entrance, and an antique bronze lamp gleamed above the portico. The place looked more like a fancy hotel than a private residence, a small Ritz Carlton perhaps, or a Four Seasons.

'Come in, please.'

The housekeeper, indeed Mexican, led him through a light-filled foyer into a small sitting room. Goodman took in his surroundings. The furnishings were overtly feminine – white sofas, pale pink drapes, floral cushions and cream, fringed cashmere throws. A large vase of fresh peonies graced an otherwise bare coffee table, and a candle had been lit that smelled of something cloying and sweet. Maybe figs?

'Mrs Grolsch will be coming in a minute. Can I get you some tea?'

'No, gracias.' Goodman smiled. He was about to arrest this family's son on suspicion of murder. It didn't seem right to be drinking their tea at the same time. 'Is Brandon at home?'

The housekeeper looked down nervously. 'Mrs Grolsch is coming,' she mumbled, leaving the room before Goodman could ask her anything else. A few minutes later, the door opened again.

'Detective? Sorry to keep you waiting. I'm Fran Grolsch.'

The woman in front of him was not at all what Goodman had expected. Chubby and out of shape, with the bloated face and puffy eyes typical of pain-pill addicts, Frances Grolsch was unrecognizable as the attractive former beauty queen from her Google Image pictures. This afternoon she was wearing a stained pink Juicy Couture tracksuit that sagged around her backside, and wore her thinning, greasy hair tied up in a cheap elastic. If Goodman had to use one word to describe her, that word would be defeated. Even her voice sounded exhausted, each word elongated – '*I'm Fraaaaan*' – as if the effort of moving on to the next one was too much to bear.

'You're here about Braaaaandon?' She slumped down onto one of the couches.

'That's right. Is your son at home, Mrs Grolsch?' Goodman asked.

'Nooooo.' Frances Grolsch closed her eyes, offering no more information. *This woman needs help*, Goodman thought.

'Do you know when you expect him back?'

The eyes opened, but she didn't respond.

'Ma'am?'

To Goodman's embarrassment, Frances Grolsch opened her mouth and let out a long, low howl, an awful, animal moan of distress that went on and on, getting louder and louder. Goodman heard a door slam in the hallway, and heavy footsteps approaching. Seconds later the door swung open and a tall, elderly man in a dark suit stormed in.

'What the hell, Franny? Shut up! You sound like a goddamn air-raid siren. I'm trying to work.' Turning on Goodman, the old man barked, 'Why is she crying? And who the hell are you?'

Goodman produced his badge. The old man inspected it, unimpressed.

'Homicide?' he scowled. 'Who died? Franny, I said shut UP!' he roared at his wife, who ran whimpering from the room.

'Nathan Grolsch, I assume?' Goodman countered, doing his best to take control of the situation. Not easy with such a bullying, forceful man.

'Of course I'm Nathan Grolsch,' the old man grunted. 'The question is, who the hell are you?'

Goodman held up his badge again.

'So? Why are you here?' Grolsch asked, unimpressed. 'I'm a busy man, you know.'

'I need to speak to your son, Brandon.'

Grolsch rolled his eyes. 'Is that why she was bawling?' He nodded towards the door through which his wife had bolted. 'You asked her about Brandon?'

'Mr Grolsch, do you know where your son is?' Goodman asked pointedly. He was beginning to get irritated by the old man's attitude. 'A young woman has been brutally murdered and we need to eliminate your son from our inquiries.'

'Well, that shouldn't be hard,' Brandon's father said bluntly. 'Brandon's dead.'

Goodman did a double take. 'Excuse me?'

There was no record of Brandon Grolsch's death, or even of his being missing.

'He took an overdose,' Nathan Grolsch announced matter-of-factly. 'His mother got a letter around eight months ago, from a "friend" who saw it happen. Some friend, right? Fran's still in denial about it. Thinks Brandon's gonna walk back through that door some day like the prodigal son.' He snorted derisively.

'You received word eight months ago that your son died of an overdose, but you never thought to notify anyone?' Goodman asked, incredulous.

'What's to notify?' Nathan Grolsch shrugged. 'There was no body, no proof. Look, my son was an addict, OK? A useless, lying, no-good scumbag who threw his life away for drugs. That is the beginning and the end of the story. Brandon was dead to me long before that letter.'

*Wow,* Goodman thought. *What a prince of a guy. With a dad like that, no wonder the kid went off the rails.*

'Does Mrs Grolsch still have the letter?'

'Nope. I burned it.' The old man's pale, rheumy eyes glistened with spite. 'That meddlesome bitch Valentina Baden should never have shown it to Fran in the first place. She must have known it would screw her up. Better for everyone to get rid of the thing. Close the door on the whole sorry chapter.'

Goodman's mind raced. 'Valentina Baden? You mean Willie Baden's wife?'

'Right,' Grolsch grunted. 'She runs some charity for missing kids. I guess at one point Fran decided Brandon was "missing" and Valentina must've gotten involved. In any case, she passed on the letter. So you can go ahead and "eliminate" Brandon from your inquiries.'

'I'm afraid it's not quite that easy, Mr Grolsch,' Goodman said, pleased to have provoked a look of deep irritation on the old man's face. 'We have DNA evidence directly linking Brandon to the murder victim. And as you say, you have no proof your son is dead. No body. And, now that you've burned the letter, no hard evidence either. Other than your *word.*'

Goodman's tone made it plain how little store he set by Nathan Grolsch's word.

'What's the dead girl's name?' Nathan Grolsch sighed deeply.

'Lisa Flannagan.'

'Never heard of her.' Grolsch shrugged.

'She was Willie Baden's mistress,' Goodman shot back. 'Among other things. Small world, isn't it?'

A momentary flash of surprise registered on Nathan Grolsch's face, but he swiftly recovered. 'Not that small. From what I've heard, Baden's slept with half the pretty girls in LA. Probably why his wife needs charity work to distract her. Look I'm sorry, Detective, but I really can't help you. My son is dead, whether you choose to believe it or not.'

'Be that as it may, I'm going to need to know when, exactly, you last saw him,' Goodman insisted. 'Who his friends were. His dealers. Where he hung out.'

'I don't know any of that,' Nathan Grolsch snapped. 'I dare say his mother remembers some of the low-life scum he hung around with,' he offered grudgingly. 'You could ask her, although as you can see, Detective, Frances is not exactly at her best by this stage in the day. Now if you'll excuse me, I need to get changed. My racquetball coach should be here any minute.'

And with that, Nathan Grolsch left the room, without so much as a handshake.

Goodman wisely took a couple of moments to regain his composure before walking back into the hallway and accosting the housekeeper.

'Take me to Brandon's room.'

He could see the housekeeper's panic, her eyes darting around the foyer in search of Mr Grolsch, afraid to comply without his approval. Goodman flashed his badge and repeated the instruction, his tone making it plain this was not a request. Reluctantly she escorted him upstairs and nodded towards the relevant door, then scuttled away as fast as she could.

The room Goodman walked into was a large, brightly decorated boy's bedroom. He felt a pang of real sadness. There was so much warmth here, so much innocence and hope, traces of the happy child Brandon Grolsch must once have been, before drugs robbed him of his future. The desk chair shaped like a football. The Lamborghini posters on the walls. The trophies, for swimming and karate, wedged between books about NFL heroes and space exploration. The giant 'B' cushion, propped up against the Pottery Barn teen bed.

*Where did it all go wrong?*

A noise behind him made Goodman turn. Brandon's mother, her eyes still puffy from crying, hovered anxiously in the doorway.

'Did Brandon have a computer? Or a phone?' Goodman asked.

She nodded. 'Both. Once. But he sold 'em, long before he left. You know how it is, when kids have problems.'

Goodman nodded. He knew how it was.

Frances Grolsch gazed vacantly around her son's room.

'Maybe he got another phone . . . I guess he must have.'

'Mrs Grolsch, your husband believes that Brandon is dead. He said you received a letter—'

'We don't know!' Frances insisted, twisting her fingers round and round in her lap, like someone trying to wring the last drops of water from a dishcloth. 'That letter wasn't signed, or anything. Maybe it was a mistake.'

'But there *was* a letter?'

She nodded miserably.

'That Mrs Baden passed on to you?'

Another nod. Then, more lucid than before: 'He could be dead, Detective. I know that. I'm not stupid. He used to call me two, three, four times a week, no matter what state he was in. Then last summer the calls stopped, just like that.' Her eyes welled up with tears. 'Until it's beyond doubt, until I know for one hundred per cent *sure*, I can't give up hope entirely. You understand, don't you?'

'I do,' Goodman assured her. 'Which is why it's so important we find out what happened to Brandon, Mrs Grolsch. We need to know, for our investigation. And you need to know too, one way or the other. Right?'

She nodded vigorously.

'Were there any other adults he might have turned to, after he left home? When he stopped calling you. A teacher at school? A counselor? A doctor, even?'

Frances Grolsch sighed heavily. 'Brandon didn't like teachers. He had a lot of therapists, but I don't know if he'd've reached out to any of them.'

A thought suddenly occurred to Goodman.

'Did he ever see a therapist named Dr Nicola Roberts?'

Frances furrowed her brow and thought for a moment. Then, closing her eyes, as if the effort was too much for her, she shook her head. 'Uh-uh. Don't think so. I don't remember that name.' Looking up at Goodman, she suddenly asked, 'What is your investigation anyway? Is Brandon in trouble, Detective?'

Goodman stared back at this broken, lonely woman, with her bullying husband, rattling around this opulent prison of a house. *I suspect Brandon's been in trouble for a very, very long time,* he thought.

'We don't know anything for sure yet, ma'am,' he said aloud, pulling out his card and pressing it into her clammy hand. 'But if you remember anything – anything at all that you think might help – please call me.'

'Mmm hmmm,' said Frances Grolsch, looking dazed.

Goodman headed out to his car. It had been quite the elucidating visit. Clearly he and Johnson needed to speak to Mr *and* Mrs Willie Baden, and the sooner the better. But driving away, it was the toxic atmosphere in the Grolsch household that haunted him more than anything, sending shivers running down his spine.

Poor Brandon.

Families like that were how monsters were made.

No amount of money could compensate for a life that loveless and bleak.

Passing the neighboring home with the birthday balloons outside, he found himself saying a silent prayer for nine-year-old Ryan.

*Good luck, buddy. I think you might need it.*

# 8

'Treyvon? *Trey!*'

Marsha Raymond's voice echoed down the hall of the flimsy single-story house on Denker Avenue. Marsha had moved in here two years ago with her son, Trey, and her mother Coretta, after their last place got torched. The Hoovers, one of the worst gangs in Westmont, threw a petrol bomb through Marsha Raymond's bedroom window one night. No reason for it. No feud or bad blood. It just happened.

That was a bad time all around, back when Treyvon was still using, and dealing to fund his habit. A lot of good things had happened since then. Moving into this place. Trey getting clean. Getting a job. The Raymonds had Dr Douglas, *God rest him,* and his beautiful wife Nikki to thank for all that. Sometimes, Marsha thought, the Lord truly did work in mysterious ways.

'TREY!' she yelled now, struggling to make herself heard over her son's booming music. 'You got a visitor! Get out here.'

Haddon Defoe stood in the hallway and grinned as he watched Trey's formidable mother march into her son's bedroom and haul the boy out. What a long way Trey Raymond had come since Haddon first met him at the rehab clinic. With Doug. And not only Trey. The whole family. Back then the boy had been a desperate, wild-eyed addict, skeletally thin, his body covered in sores. He was having seizures, the whole nine yards. No one knew better than Haddon how often intervention attempts failed, especially with kids from hellholes like Westmont, kids as deep in their addiction as Treyvon Raymond was. But every now and then, things worked out perfectly. This was one of those rare cases.

'Hey, man!' Haddon high-fived Trey as his mom frog-marched him out into the hall. 'How you been?'

'Good, man,' Trey said proudly. 'I'm doing good. I wasn't expecting you.'

'I was in the neighborhood.'

Haddon winked and they both laughed. Westmont was not a neighborhood that a man like Haddon Defoe 'passed through'. Haddon and Trey might share the same skin color, but they came from very different worlds. Haddon had grown up in Brentwood, the son of a doctor and a UCLA history professor. The black kids at the Roberts-Defoe Venice Clinic had nicknamed him 'Obama', a reference to his educated, privileged upbringing and whiter-than-white tastes, including a passion for baroque classical music and an obsession with 1920s silent movies. There was nothing Haddon Defoe couldn't tell you about Charlie Chaplin, but Tupac lyrics drew a complete blank. Trey, on the other hand, was the product of a teenage relationship between his indomitable mother, Marsha Raymond, and a good-for-nothing troublemaker named Billy James who'd disappeared from their lives long ago and whom Trey assumed was either incarcerated or dead.

'Seriously, Dr Defoe, is everything OK?' Trey asked Haddon, leading him through to the tiny front room. 'Why are you here?'

Haddon rested a hand on the boy's shoulder. 'Everything's fine, Trey. I wanted to check in on you, that's all. I know Doug would have wanted me to.'

Trey nodded gratefully. Doug Roberts had been the closest thing to a father he'd ever had. He missed him terribly. Haddon Defoe had been the Doc's best friend, which made him honorary family in Trey's eyes.

'How are things going at work? How's Nikki?' Haddon asked.

'You mean since the murder?'

Haddon looked blank. 'What murder?'

'Seriously?' Trey frowned. 'You haven't heard? Don't you watch the news, man?' Trey told him about what had happened to Lisa Flannagan, and the LAPD visit to Nikki's office.

'Lisa was one of Dr Roberts' patients.'

'This isn't the girl they found by the freeway? Willie Baden's mistress?' Haddon asked, astonished.

'She was a lot more than that,' Trey said defensively. 'Lisa was a beautiful person, she really was. The cops think Dr Roberts might have been the last person to see her alive. Apart from her killer, obviously.'

'Obviously.' Haddon seemed lost in thought. 'What were they like?' he asked.

'Who?'

'The detectives who came to Nikki's office.'

'Oh,' said Trey. 'You know. They were cops. One of them seemed all right, I guess. But his partner was this short, fat, Irish guy. Real mean. Racist too. You could see it in his eyes.'

Haddon Defoe nodded, still thinking.

'How's Nikki taken it? Was she close to this girl?'

Trey shrugged. 'I don't know. Not especially, I guess. Dr Roberts seems OK. I mean, she's sad. Everyone's sad. It's a shock.'

'I'll bet,' said Haddon.

They chatted for a few more minutes before Haddon left, declining all Marsha's attempts to get him to stay for supper. 'We got plenty,' she assured him. 'C'mon, Dr Defoe. Where you gotta be?'

'Back at my office, I'm afraid.' Haddon smiled ruefully. 'You have no idea how much paperwork I still need to finish tonight.'

This was a lie. But then so was Marsha Raymond's claim that she could afford to feed an extra mouth. Even with Trey's salary coming in, the family were barely scraping by and Haddon knew it.

'That's a good man, right there,' Trey's grandma Coretta observed, tottering in from the backyard just in time to see Doc Defoe drive off in his fancy electric car. 'You don' know how lucky you are, Treyvon.'

'I do know, Gamma.' Trey kissed the old lady on the top of her balding head. 'Believe me. I know.'

It was kind of Haddon to stop by and see him. Thoughtful.

At the same time, a small part of Trey felt suspicious. Why had he chosen tonight to trek all the way out to Westmont? Doug Roberts had been dead a year and he'd never 'stopped by' before. And why all the questions about Nikki and the police? Was it really coincidence, Dr Defoe's visit coming so soon after Lisa Flannagan's sudden death? And did he *really* not know anything about Lisa's murder?

Trey helped himself to a large plate of El Pollo Loco wings, trying to push these irrational fears aside. *I'm being paranoid. What could Haddon Defoe possibly know?* A few minutes later, his cell phone buzzed. Reading the text, he stiffened.

'What's the matter, baby?' Martha Raymond asked. After all Trey's years of addiction, she'd learned to watch her son's reactions like a hawk.

'Nothing.' He smiled.

'You sure?'

He nodded, putting the phone away. 'Just work. Something I forgot to do.'

After dinner, Trey did the dishes and took out the trash. It was important to keep to his normal routine, not to look as if he were rushing. He knew his mom would worry if anything seemed out of the ordinary. Only once the kitchen was clean did he grab his jacket, as casually as he could.

'I'm going out,' he told Marsha.

Instinctively, her eyes narrowed. 'Out where?' Trey hadn't used in over two years, but 'I'm going out' still triggered a fear response. It probably always would.

'Jus' for a walk, Mama.' He kissed her on the cheek.

'A walk? In our beautiful neighborhood?' she raised an eyebrow.

Trey chuckled. 'I need some cigarettes. Today was a crazy day, you know? I won't be long.'

'OK, baby.' Marsha forced herself to relax. He was a grown man after all. She couldn't keep tabs on his every move. 'Watch yourself.'

'I will, Mama.'

\* \* \*

The cool evening breeze on his skin gave Trey Raymond no comfort as he walked down Denker Avenue. He was wired like an over-strung guitar, ready to snap at any moment.

He waited till he'd turned the corner, out of sight of his house, to pull out his cell phone and re-read the text:

*'Be at the corner of Vermont and 135th in 1 hr.'*

That was all it said. But it was all it needed to say. Trey knew who the text was from, and what it meant. He wanted to cry, but the tears wouldn't come. It was too late for that.

He could see the corner, less than fifty yards away. Apart from a couple of wasted hookers, slumped against the convenience store wall, it was deserted.

His phone buzzed again. MMS. A picture this time.

Trey clicked it open and felt the bile rise up in his throat. It was a woman's torso, what was left of it, covered in stab wounds. Her bare breasts had been sliced open grotesquely, like a split chicken ready for stuffing.

*Lisa? Or someone else, someone new? Another victim?*

Beneath the picture were two words. *'Hurry up.'*

Trey started to run. He reached the rendezvous, breathless, but there was no one there. No cars, no people, nothing. Only the hookers sitting on the curb. Crouching down over the girls, Trey shook one by the shoulder.

'Was anybody here? D'you see anybody waiting here earlier?'

The girl looked up at him blankly, her pupils dilating like the pulse of a dying star. Trey tried her semi-comatose friend. 'Please!' He could hear the desperation in his own voice and it scared him. 'I'm looking for someone. It's really important.'

The second girl sat up suddenly, like a robot whose batteries just got replaced. 'Looks like you found them, sugar!' she grinned. 'Behind you!'

Trey turned, just in time to feel the crackle of the Taser burning into his chest. The pain was excruciating. He fell backwards, slamming his head on the concrete.

Then everything went black.

# 9

'**T**wo pairs.'

Lou Goodman laid his tens and eights down on the Formica table. Mick Johnson, his partner, was addicted to heads-up poker. Goodman had learned the game to try to bond with the older man. It hadn't worked, so far, but Goodman kept trying.

'Straight.' Johnson cracked a smug smile, laying out his six-through-ten. 'Guess that means the breakfast's on you.'

*And the heart attack's on you, my friend,* Goodman thought, watching his partner begin to attack his second enormous stack of Denny's pancakes, drowning in syrup and whipped cream.

The two detectives had escaped the station together to compare their progress, or lack of it, in the Lisa Flannagan murder case. Flannagan's former lover, the billionaire Rams owner Willie Baden, still hadn't returned from his vacation home in Cabo San Lucas. Conveniently, he'd been in Mexico the night Lisa was killed, vacationing with his loyal, long-suffering wife Valentina, and the couple were no doubt planning to stay there until the salacious press coverage about his and Lisa's affair died down. Goodman had told Johnson about the connection between Valentina Baden and Brandon Grolsch's mother, Frances. But a cursory call to Valentina's charity offices had yielded nothing of use, which left the detectives with little option but to await the Badens' return.

Meanwhile Johnson had drawn a blank with the dead girl's family (no siblings, both parents dead, and an aunt in Reno who hadn't seen Lisa since she was six) and Goodman was no further ahead in establishing whether Brandon Grolsch was dead or alive, never mind how his DNA came to be under Lisa's fingernail. Like his parents, none of Brandon's old friends or girlfriends had heard from him in eight months, and Goodman's calls to all of the various rehabs and drop-in centers known to have treated Brandon in the past yielded nothing. Though it pained him to agree with Nathan Grolsch on anything, it did seem increasingly likely that Brandon was, indeed, dead. Unfortunately, 'likely' wasn't good enough.

The only other clue they'd managed to find turned out to be a damp squib. There had been a lot of excitement when one of the techs recovered pieces of Lisa's clothing from the stretch of freeway close to where the body was dumped. But when the lab reports came in they were inconclusive; the unusually heavy rain around the time of Lisa's death had washed away any useful DNA traces. That left them with only the baffling fingernail cells to go on. So far there'd been no sign of Dr Roberts' missing raincoat, the one she claimed to have lent Lisa the night she died, nor of the murder weapon.

All in all, it wasn't exactly a triumphant start.

'I don't trust that psychologist broad,' Johnson observed, as he did every time they discussed the case, pushing the cards aside and shoveling forkfuls of pancake into his open mouth. 'I think we should talk to her again.'

Goodman frowned. Johnson's growing obsession with and dislike of Dr Nikki Roberts, the victim's beautiful therapist, was almost as disheartening as their lack of evidence.

'Talk to her again and say what?' he asked, exasperated.

'We could ask for her notes,' Johnson mumbled, spooning more cream onto his stack. 'Session notes. With the victim.'

'Not without a warrant, we couldn't,' said Goodman. 'Doctor–patient information's privileged.'

Johnson snorted derisively. 'She's not a doctor! She's a frikkin quack. That lady has about as much medical training as the tarot card readers on Venice Beach.'

'That's simply not true, Mick,' Goodman replied. 'I don't understand why you hate her so much.'

'You wouldn't,' the fat man grumbled.

'What's that supposed to mean?' Goodman asked.

'She's attractive,' Johnson said simply. 'You like attractive women.'

'And you don't?'

Goodman pushed aside his cold coffee. He thought everything about Denny's was disgusting. He couldn't understand why so many of his colleagues seemed to love the place. 'Anyway,' he went on, 'it doesn't matter whether she's attractive or not. The point is, she has nothing to do with this. She's a distraction, a sideshow. We need to focus on speaking to the Badens and we need to find Brandon Grolsch.'

Johnson grunted noncommittally. His ringing phone interrupted the sullen silence. 'Yello?'

Goodman watched him slowly put down his fork and stop eating. He was listening intently to whatever was being said on the other end of the line. After what seemed like an age he said an abrupt, 'OK. We're on our way now,' and hung up.

'What was that about?' asked Goodman.

'Remember Treyvon Raymond?' said Johnson, pushing back his chair. 'The snotty little black kid from Doc Roberts' office.'

'The receptionist? Sure,' said Goodman. 'What about him?'

'Someone found him dumped less than half a mile from where the killer left Lisa Flannagan. Naked. Multiple stab wounds, including one to the heart.'

'Shit.' Goodman exhaled slowly. 'So we've got a serial.'

'Not yet we don't.' Johnson stood up and lumbered towards the door.

'What do you mean?' Goodman asked.

'Treyvon Raymond's still alive.'

# 10

In the heart of West Hollywood, Cedars-Sinai Hospital has always been synonymous with celebrity and glamour. Frank Sinatra and River Phoenix died there, Michael Jackson's kids were born there and Britney Spears was admitted to the psychiatric wing there after her head-shaving breakdown.

However Cedars was also a bustling, inner-city hospital and home to LA's busiest ER. Every day, ordinary Angelinos poured through its doors after car crashes or overdoses, ambulances offloading every type of human pain and misery from burns to gunshot wounds to victims of rape and domestic battery. Some of the city's top surgeons and specialists could be found here too. One of them, a slight, softly spoken Iranian by the name of Dr Robert Rhamatian had just finished surgery on Trey Raymond – what was left of him – when Goodman and Johnson arrived.

'When can we talk to him?' Goodman asked the surgeon anxiously. 'It's vital we hear what he knows.'

Dr Rhamatian sighed heavily. He was exhausted after six grueling hours in theater and not in the mood for two pushy cops and their demands.

'I don't think you understand, Detective,' he said, with a patience he didn't feel. 'Mr Raymond is very gravely ill. He's heavily sedated right now, which is why he looks so peaceful. The operation was successful, as far as it went, but the damage to his left ventricle is extensive.'

Goodman looked blank.

'He was stabbed in the heart,' the surgeon clarified. 'We've done the best we can for him, but I'm by no means certain he'll survive.'

'All the more reason we need to talk to him,' Johnson said gruffly. 'Can you wake him up?'

'No.' The surgeon looked at the sweating cop in the syrup-stained shirt with distaste. 'I can't.'

'Did he say anything before he went into surgery?' Goodman asked, hoping to get something useful out of the doctor before Johnson alienated him completely. 'Was he conscious at any time? I'm sorry to press you, Dr Rhamatian. But we think whoever did this to Treyvon Raymond may have murdered a young woman a few days ago. If Treyvon saw his attacker, or can remember anything at all, it's vital that you tell us.'

'I understand,' said the surgeon. 'But I'm afraid I don't know what happened before his surgery. You need to speak to the paramedics who brought him in. I'll get the names for you. Hey!' Turning around he glared at Johnson, who was trying to open the door to the recovery room. 'What the hell do you think you're doing? You can't go in there.'

'Oh, I think you'll find I can,' Johnson said rudely. 'I'm gonna ask that boy some questions while he's still alive to be asked 'em, whether you like it or not.'

'I told you, he's sedated. He won't be able to hear you.'

'Then I won't be bothering him, will I?' said Johnson. 'Look, Doc, you did your job already. Now it's time for us to do ours.'

Dr Rhamatian looked at Goodman as if to say, *Can't you do something?*

'I'm sorry,' Goodman muttered. But he did nothing to restrain his partner as Johnson pulled open the door and walked in.

'So am I,' said the surgeon angrily. 'For the boy's sake. This is an outrage.'

He stormed off, presumably in search of reinforcements. Goodman hurriedly followed Johnson into the recovery suite.

'Do you have to be such a dick?' he asked Johnson. 'The man was helping us.'

'No he wasn't.' Johnson didn't look up from the bed, where Trey Raymond was lying prone and still, his bandaged chest rising and falling in a slow, steady rhythm, with the help of a machine that looked like a cross between a prop from a 1960s sci-fi movie and a pool cleaner, complete with long, corrugated tubing. His arms, neck and cheeks were covered in shallow knife wounds, exactly as Lisa's had been, and his face was bruised beyond recognition. No wonder the killer had left him for dead.

'The kid's dying, Lou,' said Johnson. 'Even you can see that. It's now or never.'

'I know,' Goodman said somberly. 'But—'

He was interrupted by Johnson's loud clapping, his fat hands crashing together inches above Trey's unresponsive face.

'Wake up!' he shouted. 'Tell us who did this to you. TREY!'

'Mick, come on—'

'I said, WAKE UP, DIPSHIT!' Johnson bellowed. 'Open your GODDAMN EYES!'

'Jesus Christ.' Grabbing him by the shoulders, Goodman pulled Johnson back. 'Stop it. Leave him alone. What the hell is wrong with you?'

Johnson turned, and for a moment looked as if he were about to punch his partner in the face. But before he had a chance, Trey suddenly opened his eyes and let out a panicked scream.

'I don't know!' he yelled, his arms twitching manically. 'Please! Oh God! I DON'T KNOW!' His head was tossing from side to side. He screamed again and then an awful gurgling sound began from somewhere deep in his throat. Even Johnson looked alarmed. One of the machines started beeping and a stream of nurses and medics ran into the room, as Trey slumped back, unresponsive, onto the bed.

'Who let you in here?' one of the interns barked at Goodman and Johnson. 'This is medical personnel only. Get out!'

Johnson hesitated, but only for a moment. He followed Goodman out.

Out in the corridor, Goodman turned on him. 'What in God's name was that? We could get prosecuted! What if the kid's family make a complaint?'

Johnson laughed. 'What if they do?' There could be no mistaking the racist undertone in his words. The unspoken implication that nobody would listen to the likes of Marsha Raymond, a poor, black single mother from Westmont. Not for the first tame, Goodman felt a surge of real dislike for the man he was forced to work with.

'Where are you going?' he called after Johnson, who was already headed for the exit.

'Back to the precinct,' said Johnson. 'The boy's clearly not gonna make it, so that ship's sailed. Still, at least we now know one thing for sure.'

'We do?'

'Sure we do. It's the same killer. Assuming Trey dies, that's two victims inside of a week, both attacked and dumped the same exact way.'

'OK,' said Goodman, not sure why this obvious fact seemed to please his partner so much.

'So you tell me,' Johnson spelled it out. 'Who's the *one person* that connects both of the victims?'

The penny dropped.

It pained Goodman to admit it. But this time, Johnson was right.

As far as they knew, Lisa Flannagan and Trey Raymond had only one thing in common.

They were both close to Dr Nikki Roberts.

# 11

Earlier that morning, Nikki Roberts sat bolt upright in bed, gasping for breath. Her sweat-drenched T-shirt clung to her body and she was shaking, shivering, as if she'd just been pulled out of icy water. Her bedside clock said 4.52 a.m. Wearily she sank back against the pillows.

It was the same dream she'd been having for months, or a variant of it anyway: Doug was in danger, about to die, and was screaming out to Nikki, begging her for help. But she didn't help him, and he died, and it was all her fault. Sometimes he was drowning and she stood and watched from the beach, letting it happen. Sometimes he was in a car, careening out of control, and Nikki held some sort of remote control that could activate the brakes, but she refused to use it. In tonight's version, they'd been walking along the clifftop path at Big Sur and Doug had somehow lost his footing and slipped off the edge. He was reaching out to Nikki, pleading for her hand to pull him back to safety. But this time, instead of simply refusing or ignoring him, she'd actively peeled off his clinging fingers one by one and pushed him to his death, watching as he was dashed to pieces on the rocks below. She'd murdered him. And the worst part was, in the dream, the act had left her with a sense of elation, a tremendous feeling of power.

A few hours later, an emotional Nikki met her friend Gretchen Adler for brunch on Melrose.

'I had the dream again,' she said as the two women sat down at Glorious Greens café.

'The Doug dream?' said Gretchen.

Nikki nodded. 'Only this time it was worse.'

Nikki filled Gretchen in on her latest nightmare while a handsome waiter hovered over them. Nikki ordered her usual poached eggs, toast and triple-shot latte, while Gretchen went for a vile-looking kale-and-beetroot smoothie and a bowl of something involving sprouted grains. Gretchen was Nikki's oldest friend – they'd known each other since high school – and a sweetheart of the first order, but for most of her adult life she'd been fighting an on-off battle with her weight. As far as Nikki could tell, she rarely got any thinner, but was always raving about some new diet or other. At the moment it was raw-vegan.

'You look exhausted,' Gretchen told Nikki. 'You know, if you're having sleep problems you should really think about going vegan, or at least only eating raw last thing at night. What did you have for dinner last night?'

'A burger,' said Nikki.

'There you go.' Gretchen sat back, satisfied she'd proved her point. 'Red meat. That's the worst thing for nightmares.'

'Is it?'

'Yup. Apart from cheese. Oh my God, it wasn't a cheeseburger, was it?' Gretchen gasped melodramatically.

Nikki laughed and confessed that, unfortunately, it was, but that she really didn't feel her diet was to blame for her night terrors.

'Well, what do you think it is then?' Gretchen asked.

'I don't know,' said Nikki. 'Guilt, maybe?'

Gretchen didn't buy it. 'That's baloney. What have you got to be guilty about? Doug's death was an accident.'

'I know.'

'You were an amazing wife to him, Nikki.'

'An amazing, infertile wife,' Nikki added wistfully.

Gretchen frowned. 'Come on. You were the one who cared about that, far more than Doug ever did.'

Was that true? Nikki couldn't remember any more.

'Maybe it's anger, then,' she said. 'Maybe I'm still so damn angry at him, my subconscious is trying to ease the pressure by having me sadistically murder my already dead husband in fantasy?'

'You know what I think?' Gretchen said. 'I think all you psychologists are full of shit. It's a dream. It doesn't mean anything. I mean, Christ, Nik, you've been under a hell of a lot of stress. No wonder your subconscious is going a bit haywire. What you need is a distraction.'

'Such as?' Nikki asked wearily.

'Well,' Gretchen leaned forward conspiratorially. 'I assume you've been following all the stuff about your poor murdered patient and Willie Baden?'

Reaching down beneath the table for her pocketbook, Gretchen pulled out the latest copy of US Weekly. Paparazzi pictures of the

Rams' owner, looking paunchy and dreadfully old on the beach in Mexico, had been placed alongside glamour shots of Lisa Flannagan from her modeling days. Between these, and three pages of lurid prose about Willie and Lisa's affair, under the headline 'Baden's Betrayal', were a few pictures of Valentina Baden, Willie's wife.

Nikki studied them closely. Mrs Baden was an attractive woman for her age, which she guessed was probably early sixties. Slim and elegant with a neatly trimmed bob of gray-blond hair. But at the same time she looked haggard and hounded in all of the paparazzi photographs, using her sarong as a shield and cowering behind oversized sunglasses.

Leafing through the feature, Nikki shook her head angrily. 'Poor woman. Why don't they leave her alone?'

Gretchen shrugged. 'They never leave anyone alone. You know that. And whatever else Valentina Baden may be, she's not poor.'

'You know what I mean,' said Nikki.

'I do, but I suspect you're wrong about that too,' said Gretchen. 'My guess is she's completely used to his affairs by now. I mean, it's not as if this murdered girl was his first.'

'Bastard,' Nikki muttered under her breath.

'Maybe they have an "arrangement"?' said Gretchen jokingly. 'Valentina might be a cougar with a string of young lovers for all we know.'

'Don't be facile,' Nikki snapped. 'This is what *men* do. This is *his* shit, not hers.'

Gretchen recoiled at Nikki's anger, white-hot suddenly. Neither of them knew the Badens personally, after all. This was just gossip, something the old Nikki would have enjoyed. Before Doug's death knocked all the joy out of her.

'I don't understand you sometimes,' she observed quietly.

'What do you mean?' said Nikki.

'I thought you'd be outraged that the media are focusing on Willie Baden and the affair, rather than the actual murder. I mean, this poor patient of yours is dead. Shouldn't that be the story? But instead you seem more worried about Baden's wife, who isn't dead, and who knew what she was signing up for!'

'No one signs up for betrayal,' Nikki said bluntly. 'And besides, Lisa Flannagan is dead. She can't be hurt any more. Unlike Valentina Baden.' She jabbed a finger furiously at the magazine. 'I mean, *she's* the only innocent party here. Lisa wasn't innocent! Trust me, I knew the girl. She was a selfish, lying narcissist, sleeping with another woman's husband for money.'

Gretchen said nothing, but a feeling of deep unease settled over her, as it did so often with Nikki nowadays. Ever since the awful night of Doug's car crash, Gretchen had watched Nikki being whipsawed between grief and anger. The circumstances of Doug's death had changed her. Made her harder. Colder. Less forgiving. Gretchen hoped the change was temporary.

'Well, if it's any consolation, I think Valentina Baden's a tougher cookie than you give her credit for,' she said, trying to lighten the mood a little. 'Before she married Willie she was with some hotshot financier who she completely took to the cleaners in their divorce.'

'Really?' Nikki was intrigued, her anger apparently exhausted for the moment. Not for the first time, she marveled at Gretchen's vast knowledge of celebrity gossip. 'How do you *know* this stuff?'

'I read,' said Gretchen. 'Valentina's actually had an amazing life. She grew up in Mexico City and when she was a teenager her younger sister went missing and they never saw her again. Can you imagine? She's given interviews about it, how the family assumed the sister was dead but they never knew for sure. Or whether she'd been raped or kidnapped or what had happened to her.'

'How awful,' said Nikki, feelingly. 'That must have been torture.'

'Valentina never had children of her own,' Gretchen went on, 'but she used her husband's money to set up a charity to help families of missing kids. Do you remember the Clancy case?'

Nikki thought about it. *Clancy.* The name rang a vague bell.

'A young American au pair went missing while working in Mexico City,' said Gretchen. 'It was probably about ten years ago now.'

Nikki cast her mind back. 'I do remember! I think I saw the dad on TV. Wasn't he a firefighter or something?'

'Right,' said Gretchen. 'Well, it was Valentina Baden's money that put him on TV and brought public attention to the search for his daughter. I think Valentina felt a personal connection to the case, because of the Mexico City thing and her sister. Charlotte, the girl's name was. Charlotte Clancy.'

'Did they ever find her?'

Gretchen shook her head. 'Never. It was like Valentina's sister all over again. The endless not knowing. All I'm saying is, Willie Baden's wife has been through a hell of a lot worse in her life than this. It's your murdered patient I feel sorry for. So young!'

'She was young,' Nikki agreed, softening. 'And, you know, she was trying to improve her life. It's not that I don't feel terrible about Lisa—'

'Do you think Willie had her bumped off?' Gretchen interrupted breathlessly. 'You know, took out a hit on her?'

Closing the magazine, Nikki laughed. 'You've been overdosing on *The Sopranos* again, Gretch. A "hit"?'

'I'm serious!' protested Gretchen. 'I mean, he's rich enough, right? I'll bet he knows people who know people.'

Nikki shook her head. 'Willie didn't do it. It was already over between them. Although, he was angry about her leaving,' she mused, thinking back to her final session with Lisa, and Lisa's almost throwaway remarks about Baden smashing china and making threats when she called it quits.

'You see?' Gretchen warmed to her theme. 'He had motive.'

Nikki shook her head. 'I don't think it was Willie Baden. His pride was hurt in the moment. No one likes being dumped. But I never got the sense Lisa was afraid of him.'

'Maybe she should have been?' said Gretchen. 'Well, if it wasn't Willie, who do *you* think did it?'

Nikki looked at her old friend for a moment with a strangely intent expression. 'I have no idea,' she said eventually. 'Why does everyone seem to think I would know who killed Lisa Flannagan?'

Gretchen shrugged. 'You were her therapist.'

'Patients don't tell us everything, you know. I'm sure one of the detectives investigating the case thinks I'm hiding something from him.'

Gretchen frowned. 'Why would he think that?'

'Who knows?' said Nikki, thanking the waiter as he placed her poached eggs in front of her. 'He's an odd little man, full of testosterone and rage. He obviously hates me. He hasn't said it in so many words, but it wouldn't surprise me if he had me down as a suspect.'

'Don't be so ridiculous!' said Gretchen.

'Is it ridiculous, though?' asked Nikki absently. 'I *was* the last person to have seen her alive.'

'Well, yes, but—'

'And we all have our dark sides. Don't forget I spent last night pushing my beloved husband off a cliff to his death. And I *liked it*.' Nikki paused, then broke into a broad grin.

Gretchen exhaled.

*OK. That was a joke. She's joking.*

Black humor was a well-known coping mechanism for grief. Gretchen might not be a therapist, but even she knew that. Still, she found Nikki worryingly difficult to read these days. Joke or no joke, something was off about her, and that something seemed to be getting worse, not better.

This murder, coming on top of everything else, had clearly added to the stress she was under. One more blow and Gretchen worried Nikki might unravel completely.

The sooner they caught the maniac that did it, the better.

# 12

It was five o'clock by the time Haddon Defoe arrived at the hospital. Taking the elevator to the fifth floor, past the Addiction Recovery Clinic where he worked a couple of days a week, he hurried down the corridor, praying he wasn't too late. But when the nurses directed him to the Family Counseling Suite his heart sank. That could only mean one thing.

Marsha Raymond's tear-stained face instantly confirmed Haddon's worst suspicions.

'He's gone, Dr Defoe.' Trey's mother shook her head, her lower lip trembling. ''Bout fifteen minutes ago. I was sitting in there with him, holding his hand, and all of a sudden his heart jus' stops beating. He never said one mo' word after those police left this morning. They should never've been here, that's what the doctor said.'

Instinctively, Haddon pulled the grieving woman into his arms and held her. His own mind was racing wildly. It was all too much to take in. Only an hour and a half had gone by since Marsha had called him, giving him a garbled story about Trey being kidnapped and knifed and in the hospital, and begging him to come. He'd driven to Cedars as fast as he could, his mind jumping between thoughts of Trey and what the hell could have happened, and his old friend Doug Roberts, who had loved the boy like a son. What would Doug have made of all of this? And now Haddon was here but he was too late. Trey Raymond was dead. But not before the police had been here, quizzing him, defying his doctor's orders. The whole thing was a mess.

'He was cut, more than *fifty times*!' Marsha wailed, extricating herself at last from Haddon's embrace and sinking into an armchair. 'They stabbed him in the heart, stripped him, and dumped him by the road. They musta thought he was dead.'

*Yes,* thought Haddon. *They must have.*

'Who would do that, Doc Defoe? Who would do that to my baby?'
'I don't know, Marsha,' Haddon said quietly. 'I'm so sorry.'
'I don't want *sorry*.' The small woman's head shot up, her eyes alive
with anger. 'I want to know WHY. I want to know WHO. My Trey
never hurt nobody, Doc. He made his mistakes in the past, we all know
that. But he was *clean*. He was a good boy. He had a new life, everything
ahead of him! Dr Roberts . . .' Her voice broke, and the tears came again
in a great flood, leaving the thought unfinished.

'Have the police said anything to you?' Haddon asked gently.

Marsha shook her head, still distraught.

'Does Nik— Dr Roberts know?'

Another shake. 'Nobody knows. Only you. You the first. He's not
even cold, Doc!'

A family liaison nurse appeared at the door as the sobbing began
again, but Haddon waved her away. 'I'm a family friend, Nurse. I'll
handle this.'

He turned back to Marsha. 'Would you like me to talk to the
police? And to let Nikki know what's happened?'

Marsha Raymond dabbed at her eyes with a handkerchief and
nodded. 'Thank you,' she sniffed. 'I'd appreciate that. I need to get
back to my mother. She's waiting at home for news. And then, I
guess . . . arrangements . . . ?'

'Don't worry about any of that,' Haddon said smoothly. 'Let me
handle it. I'll speak to the police and we can take it from there. You just
focus on Coretta. I truly am so sorry, Marsha. He was a very special
young man.'

Trey Raymond's mother smiled gratefully through her tears.
'You're a good man, Dr Defoe. Thank you for coming.'

'No problem.' Haddon hugged her again. 'Call me if you need
anything.'

*   *   *

Nikki had no sooner stepped out of the shower than she heard the
doorbell. Wrapping her wet hair in a towel, turban style, and slipping
on Doug's over-sized toweling robe that she still wore in moments she
needed to feel close to him, she raced downstairs.

'Haddon! What a nice surprise.'

She was taken aback to see Doug's old friend and former partner
here. Although they kept in touch and met up for coffee every once in

a while, Haddon Defoe hadn't been up to the house since the day of Doug's funeral. Perhaps it was Nikki's imagination, but she always sensed a certain tension when she ran into Haddon, as though Doug's absence made him embarrassed to be around her. Today, though, it was clear from his strained expression that something more than the usual awkwardness was on his mind.

'Hello, Nikki.' He cleared his throat. 'Can I come in?'

'Of course.' She led him through to the kitchen, disturbed by the odd formality of his manner. 'Is everything all right, Haddon? You don't look well.'

'I'm afraid I have some pretty terrible news,' he said grimly. 'I wanted you to hear it from me before the police contact you, as I suspect they will. Nikki, I'm afraid Trey Raymond is dead.'

Nikki was silent. Reaching out a hand, she leaned on the kitchen island for support, then eased herself down gently onto a barstool. She felt faint.

This couldn't be happening. Not Trey too?

'What happened?' she asked at last, her voice raspy and dry.

'Well . . .' Haddon avoided her gaze, looking down at the floor, out of the windows, anywhere but at Nikki. 'I don't know all the details. I literally drove here straight from the hospital. But I'm afraid it appears he was murdered. Stabbed, multiple times, with a fatal wound to the heart.'

Nikki shook her head. *No. There must be some mistake.*

'He was found naked, by the side of the freeway. Very close to where—'

'Don't say it,' Nikki cut him off, shaking her head as if to dispel the awful truth. 'Please, I can't. It can't be. Not again.'

Haddon moved towards her. Secretly, he'd always found Doug's wife powerfully alluring; it was that rare combination of strength and vulnerability that drew him, her ambition combined with a sort of intense neediness. Naturally, it was Doug that Nikki had always needed, not Haddon. Doug, who'd never really realized what a jewel he had. But Doug was gone now and Haddon was here, and so was Nikki, her skin still wet from the shower, her dark eyes welling with tears like two great pools of loss . . .

He reached out to touch her arm, to comfort her, but she backed away with a jerk, as if he were a rattlesnake.

'What else do you know?' she demanded. 'Tell me everything.'

Haddon threw his arms wide. 'You know what I know. Like I say, I came straight from the hospital. He was alive when they found him, and I think they'd hoped . . .'

His words trailed off uselessly. Poor Nikki looked white with shock.

'Why?' she asked him. 'Why would anyone want to hurt a young boy like that? I don't understand.'

'None of us do. Yet,' said Haddon. 'Marsha Raymond's asked me to talk to the police for her. I'm going there after this. Hopefully, I'll know more then. I'm so sorry, Nikki.'

She turned on him, irrationally angry. 'Why are *you* sorry?'

The transformation was instant and total, like Jekyll and Hyde. Haddon was so stunned it took him a moment to respond. 'I only meant . . . you've been through so much already,' he said, blushing. 'And I know you and Doug both loved Trey like a son. I'm worried about you, that's all. Is there someone I can call? I hate leaving you alone like this.'

Nikki blinked, as if waking up from a dream and seeing Haddon for the first time. When she spoke again, she was calm.

'No need to call anyone. I'm fine. It's just shock. I'll be fine. It was sweet of you to come. Really.'

She hugged him and ushered him out, pulling herself together and making small talk as she walked him to his car, standing and waving as he drove away.

Once he'd gone, Nikki closed the door behind him and leaned against it, breathing heavily.

*So now there were two.*

Lisa Flannagan, who she'd never really liked.

And Trey Raymond, who she'd loved, if only for Doug's sake.

Two young lives, slashed to pieces, brutally cut down in their prime.

*Poor Trey.*

Nikki waited for the pain to hit her, for the appropriate torrent of emotion, but instead she felt strangely numb. Funny how grief did that to you. Turned you off like a light switch.

Wearily, she walked back upstairs alone.

Always alone.

# 13

Valentina Baden took another sip of her perfectly made espresso and leaned back in her chair contentedly. She adored Cabo San Lucas, adored their villa here, with its private whitewashed balcony off the master bedroom with views over the formal gardens and tennis courts and then out to the clear, azure-blue sea. Before Willie bought the LA Rams, they used to come down to Cabo a lot. But ever since his obsession with that godforsaken football team, getting Willie out of Los Angeles had been like trying to pry a barnacle off the keel of a rusty boat.

And it wasn't only the Rams that had been keeping him homebound. There was the girl too, Lisa, the ridiculous brunette tramp Willie had been running around with for the past eight years, mooning after her pathetically like a lost puppy.

*Not any more, though*, Valentina smiled smugly. *The girl was gone. Good riddance.*

Truth be told, Willie and his young mistress had been on the outs anyway. Even before Lisa Flannagan's untimely demise, Willie had started suggesting that he and Valentina spend more time together in Mexico. 'We should head down to the villa before the hoi polloi descend,' Willie had told Valentina over dinner last month, as if it were nothing out of the ordinary. 'Spend a few weeks in Cabo. Maybe more, depending on business.' Apparently, Willie had some property deal brewing down in Punta Mita and another in Mexico City, Valentina's hometown. His plan was to travel for work during the weeks and head back to Cabo at weekends.

'You'd like that, wouldn't you, darling?' he purred at his wife. 'The whole summer in Mexico?'

Valentina replied that she would like it, very much. And she had liked it, despite the unexpected irritation of the paparazzi following her around like a swarm of flies ever since Lisa Flannagan inconveniently went and got herself murdered and the news broke that the dead model had been Willie's latest lover.

Valentina had read the details of Lisa's grisly death and the meager 'facts' the press had been able to glean about her relationship with Willie, but the Badens hadn't discussed the matter between themselves at all. The time had long since passed when Valentina cared a fig about Willie's extra-marital activities. Indeed, if some girl was willing to sleep with him for a few paltry gifts of jewelry and a cheap condo on the wrong side of Beverly Hills, the way Valentina saw it they were doing her a favor, keeping the revolting old toad out of *her* bed and allowing her to enjoy her lavish lifestyle – not to mention her own freedom – in peace.

The one part of the whole episode that troubled her was that the Los Angeles police had asked to speak with her, as well as Willie, about the murder investigation 'as soon as possible', even going so far as to request her immediate return to the States, a request Valentina Baden had no intention of granting. She had no desire to speak to the police about Willie's murdered whore, or anything else for that matter. In her bitter experience, the police were no help at all when *you* needed *them*, but when *they* needed *you* they were prepared to harass you at the drop of a hat.

Draining her coffee cup, Valentina picked up the binoculars Willie kept on the balcony for birdwatching and trained them on her beloved spouse, down on the tennis court with his new young coach, Guillermo. The two of them made a ridiculous pair, Guillermo tall and young and athletic, exactly Valentina's type, his broad shoulders rippling beneath his tennis whites and his thick dark hair blowing in the breeze as he moved gazelle-like across the court. And on the other side of the net, Willie, short, fat and bald as a coot, mimicking the young coach's movements, his frail, liver-spotted limbs performing a grotesque parody of Guillermo's effortless forehand.

*He is old and disgusting,* Valentina thought, *sweating like a pig ready for the slaughterhouse.*

But, she had to admit, Willie had kept his side of the bargain. Valentina's credit cards were limitless. Willie made generous, annual donations to her pet charity, Missing, without ever delving deeper into their 'work'. Just like Valentina's poor, long-lost sister María, Willie could be gratifyingly trusting when it mattered most. Plus, he rarely made demands on her, either sexually or socially, the way that Richard, her last husband, used to do. On top of all that, until now anyway, he had kept his affairs low-key and discreet.

If only the stupid girl, Lisa, had kept her mouth shut, instead of bragging to all and sundry about her trysts with Willie, she might well be alive today. She'd even gone and poured her heart out to a therapist, the strikingly photogenic Dr Nicola Roberts. As it was, it was Lisa Flannagan who'd become the slaughtered pig, while Willie, her ancient lover, lived to sweat and wheeze his arthritic, self-centered way through another day.

*Ah well. We all make our sacrifices, I suppose*, Valentina Baden thought wryly. *Our deals with the devil.*

She only hoped that at some point Willie's mood would improve, ideally before they both had to face the music and head back to LA.

*  *  *

Down on the tennis court, Willie Baden mopped his brow and glared bad-temperedly at his coach.

'That last point was in,' he snarled, doubled over and panting with exertion.

'If you say so, sir,' the boy, Guillermo, replied indulgently.

*Patronizing asshole*, thought Willie. Guillermo was a talented coach but he practically shone with the arrogance of youth. Willie's players on the Rams were the same, most of them. Arrogant. Lisa had been arrogant too. *Narcissistic little slut, may she rot in hell.* She'd actually believed she could switch Willie off like a light when she grew tired of him, throw him out like a discarded toy. But it was Lisa who'd ended up discarded, tossed onto the side of the freeway like a rag doll. And now he, Willie, was paying the price for that too, being chased by photographers everywhere he went and having his good name dragged through the mud. It was a headache he could have done without.

'Willie!'

Glen Foman, Willie's attorney, was waving at him from the sideline.

'We need to talk!' Glen shouted. 'Can you take a break?'

Wordlessly, Willie handed Guillermo his racket and stalked off the court.

'What is it now?' he barked at Glen, unscrewing his water bottle and taking a long, shaky gulp.

'I've finished wording our statement,' said the attorney, unfazed by his client's rudeness. 'You need to take a look. Then I think we should fly back to LA tomorrow and go to the police voluntarily.'

Willie shook his head.

'You give them the prepared speech,' said Glen, ignoring him. 'Let the media take pictures, let me handle any questions—'

'We can't leave tomorrow,' Willie interrupted him. Glen Foman followed his client's gaze up to the balcony of the villa's master bedroom, where Willie's wife sat reading the newspaper, as cool and calm as Lady Macbeth. *He's scared of her*, Glen thought. *Even with a possible murder charge hanging over him, he's too afraid to cross Valentina.*

'Mrs Baden wouldn't need to come,' Glen reassured him. 'It would only be you and me. We could turn around and be back here within twenty-four hours.'

'No,' said Willie. 'The cops want to speak to her too.'

'Since when?' Glen frowned. 'Willie, you need to tell me these things. I'm your lawyer. What do they want to talk to your wife about?'

'How the hell should I know?' Willie barked. 'Anyway it's not just Valentina. I have business here, in Mexico City. Important business, with people who don't like to be let down.'

'Well, business can wait,' Glen said bluntly. 'You need to give the police something, Willie. Hiding out here makes you look guilty.'

Willie's eyes darted nervously from his lawyer, to the master bedroom balcony, to the ground at his feet. *He's like a trapped rat*, thought Glen. Was it only his wife he was afraid of? Or something else? If Willie Baden hadn't been such a thoroughly unpleasant man, Glen might have felt sorry for him.

Willie looked up at his attorney mournfully. 'I just want this to end.'

'Then end it.'

'It's not that simple.' Willie rubbed his temples. 'Like I said, my business associates here are people you don't want to cross.'

'Don't tell me,' said Glen, raising a hand. 'I don't need to know. One problem at a time, OK, Willie? Because your girlfriend's murder is a big problem for you right now, in case you hadn't noticed.'

'I've been reading in the press about this therapist woman, Roberts,' said Willie. 'Evidently, Lisa was talking to her. Do you think . . . ?'

'It's all handled,' Glen assured him. 'I'm on this shit, Willie, OK? You need to trust me. But you also need to follow my advice. Go back – with your wife, if the cops have asked to see her. Give the statement I've written, no more, no less. Be seen to be cooperating.'

Willie hesitated. His rheumy old eyes looked up again to the house, but Valentina had gone back inside.

'Do you want me to talk to Mrs Baden?' Glen offered.

'No,' said Willie. 'I'll do it. But whatever happens, we *need* to be back here by Friday. This business in Mexico City is more important than you realize, Glen.'

'By Friday,' the attorney nodded. 'You have my word. Now go pack.'

# 14

'Tell me please, Mrs Roberts. How long did you take off work after your husband passed away?'

Beneath the interview room table, Nikki dug her fingernails hard into her palms and counted to ten. *I must not let this man get under my skin. I must not let him provoke me. That's giving him what he wants.*

'Again, Detective Johnson, it's *Doctor* Roberts.' She used her softest, most patronizing tone to correct him. 'You seem to be having a tough time remembering that. Have you always had trouble with your memory? Or is it something age-related?'

Johnson's jowly face reddened to an ugly puce as his partner suppressed a giggle. Unlike Dr Roberts, Goodman noticed, Johnson showed no self-control when provoked, rising to Nikki's bait like a starving fish.

'Oh, I'm not having a tough time remembering anything, lady. I merely choose not to dignify your bullshit profession with a title that actually means something to some people. We both know you aren't a real doctor.'

*Mick looks like an overcooked hotdog about to burst out of its skin,* Goodman thought, wincing at his partner's crassness. Johnson had issues around women in general, but for some reason this particular woman seemed to bring out the absolute worst in him.

Goodman couldn't understand why. In his opinion, Dr Roberts was looking particularly beautiful this afternoon, in a taupe pencil skirt and matching silk shirt. The outfit was the same color as her tanned skin, giving an exciting, if fleeting, impression of nakedness. Her calm, collected manner was attractive as well, at least in Lou Goodman's eyes. He liked a woman who could handle herself.

'Answer the question. How long were you off work?' Johnson snapped.

'Around six weeks,' said Nikki.

'Seems a long time.'

'Does it?' Nikki deadpanned.

'Yeah, it does. Then again, most of us need to work to live. Unlike you. You just dabble as and when you please, don't you, Mrs Roberts? You had no money problems after your husband died. He left you a wealthy woman.'

Despite herself, Nikki stiffened. What was this bozo implying?

'I was perfectly well off when Doug was alive, Mr Johnson. His death didn't change anything.'

'Hmmm,' Johnson grunted dismissively. 'And when did Treyvon Raymond start working for you?'

Nikki sighed sadly. She hadn't had time yet to process the reality of Trey's death, and she certainly didn't relish talking about him with this slob of a policeman.

'I don't remember exactly.'

'Was it after you came back to work, or before your husband's accident?'

'It was not long after,' said Nikki. Turning to Goodman she added, 'I don't understand what any of these questions have to do with the murders. Shouldn't you be out there trying to find who killed Lisa and Trey, instead of grilling me about employment dates?'

'That's exactly what we *are* trying to do. Find the killer,' snapped Johnson. 'Working on the theory that it's the same perpetrator, first thing we need is a link between the two victims. And guess what? We have one.' Leaning back in his chair, he jabbed a pudgy finger at Nikki. 'You, *Doctor* Roberts.'

'You think *I* killed Lisa? And Trey?'

Nikki addressed the question to Johnson, who'd already opened his fat lips to respond when Goodman jumped in, cutting him off.

'Of course not,' he said evenly. 'But you are a link. A common factor, if you will. There's a good possibility, a likelihood even, that this killer has some connection to you personally or to this practice. A former patient, perhaps? Or even a current one? In your line of work, you obviously come across some deeply disturbed people. Might one of them have become obsessed with you and those around you? Perhaps violently so?'

Nikki conceded it was possible, theoretically. But nobody leapt to mind. Unlike many of her colleagues and peers, she'd never had a patient attack her, although one or two had probably formed unhealthy romantic attachments. Fantasies about one's therapist were incredibly common. Rarely, if ever, did they result in two mutilated corpses and a homicide investigation.

'We're going to need your patient records, past and present,' Goodman informed her gently.

'Right,' Nikki muttered, lost in thought for a moment.

'All of them,' Johnson added aggressively. 'No editing. And no "doctor–patient confidentiality" bullshit either.'

'Although it may not be a patient,' Goodman said quickly, before things descended into a slanging match between his partner and their most crucial witness. 'Do you have any enemies you can think of, Doctor? Anyone who might want to hurt you or people close to you?'

'No.' Nikki rubbed her eyes, like someone trying to wake up from a bad dream. 'No. I really can't. I mean, that's ridiculous. What sort of enemies?'

'Former lovers?' Goodman proposed tentatively.

Nikki shook her head, not offended but firm.

'No. There was only ever my husband.'

'Disgruntled business associates?'

'No!' she said, frowning. 'No offense, Detective, but someone's out there torturing people to death with a hunting knife. That's not a business deal gone wrong. That's a psychopath.'

'Who said it was a hunting knife?' Johnson, who'd sat quiet as a mouse since Goodman cut him off suddenly came back to life.

Nikki hesitated for a moment.

'I don't know,' she said eventually. 'You must have, I suppose. Or maybe I heard it on the news.'

Johnson looked knowingly at Goodman but said nothing.

Goodman continued with his good-cop routine, asking Nikki more questions about her relationship with Trey Raymond. She answered confidently and naturally, explaining how first Doug and Haddon, and then she, had taken the boy under their wing. And how proud they all were of the way Trey had turned his life around.

'Especially Doug,' Nikki added, tears stinging her eyes for the first time since Haddon had broken the awful news of Trey's death. 'We couldn't have children, you see, my husband and I.'

Goodman's kind blue eyes seemed to invite confidences. Nikki appeared to have forgotten Johnson was even in the room.

'I think Doug looked on Trey as a surrogate son. After Doug— When he died, I tried to keep the connection going. That's when I offered Trey the job here, in the office. He was good at it,' she added, with a sad smile.

'OK,' said Goodman. 'Thank you, Dr Roberts. I think that's all we need for now.'

'Don't leave town,' snarled Johnson, as Nikki slipped on her coat. She didn't dignify the comment with a look, let alone a response.

'One last thing,' Goodman said casually, walking Nikki to the interview room door. 'Did you ever treat a client by the name of Brandon Grolsch?'

'No.' Nikki looked blank. Not a hint of recognition. 'I don't know that name.'

'OK.' Goodman smiled, masking his disappointment. Both men were disappointed. A direct link between Nikki Roberts and Brandon Grolsch would have helped a lot right now, especially since Jenny Foyle, the Medical Examiner, had texted Johnson earlier to confirm that two hairs found embedded in one of Trey Raymond's many wounds was a DNA match for Grolsch. The way Johnson saw it, that meant either the kid was alive after all; or – more disturbingly, but a closer fit to the evidence – whoever murdered Lisa Flannagan and Trey Raymond had also handled Brandon Grolsch's corpse.

'Thank you for your help anyway, Doctor,' said Goodman. 'We'll be in touch.'

Nikki had left the building and was halfway across the parking lot when she heard Detective Johnson call breathlessly after her.

'Wait!' he panted.

Nikki stopped and turned, trying to quell the unpleasant pounding sensation in her chest. *What now?*

'Your coat.' Johnson gestured at the classic, sand-colored raincoat Nikki was wearing.

'What about it?' Nikki asked.

'Isn't that the coat you told us you loaned to Lisa Flannagan?' Johnson wheezed. 'The night she was killed?'

Nikki looked at him curiously.

'You described it exactly in your statement,' Johnson went on. 'Full-length raincoat, waterproof canvas, sand-colored, buckled belt. That's it.' He nodded at the coat again.

Nikki allowed her gaze to linger for a moment on this obnoxious, rude, sweating, accusatory pig of a man. Clearly he believed he was catching her out at something, that he'd outsmarted her in some way. As if that could ever happen. Smiling, she said simply, 'That's right, Mr. Johnson. I have two.'

*   *   *

'"That's right, Mr Johnson. I have two." Patronizing bitch.'

Johnson's impression of Dr Roberts, complete with exaggerated, hip-swaying walk and nonchalant flick of the hair, had not been improved by his third tequila shot.

He and Goodman were at Rico's, a dive off Sunset popular with the homicide division. Rico Hernandez, the eponymous owner, was ex LAPD himself and enjoyed hosting his former colleagues for their game nights and late-drinking sessions. Tonight Goodman and Johnson were at a table with two other teams, Hammond and Rae, aka Laurel and Hardy, the division jokers; and Sanchez and Baines, one of the few male–female pairings in the department. Although Johnson questioned whether you could call Anna Baines a woman.

'I'm telling you, Lou,' Johnson groused, 'the good doctor's in this shit up to her pretty little neck!'

Goodman rolled his eyes. 'No, she isn't.'

'You don't think the therapist lady could be involved, Lou?' Bobby Hammond asked, taking a contemplative sip of his Corona. 'I mean, Mick does have a point.'

'And what point is that?' Goodman demanded.

Bobby shrugged. 'A lot of people close to her do seem to be droppin' dead.'

'Starting with her husband,' Davey Rae chimed in. 'Let's not forget him.'

'That was an accident!' Goodman almost shouted. What was this, the conspiracy theorists' association annual drinks party?

The fact was that, ever since the ME found those bizarre 'dead cells' under Lisa Flannagan's fingernails, the entire homicide department had become hooked on the 'Zombie Killings'. Most of these detectives' regular cases involved either gang shootings or over-zealous domestic battery, or drug deals turned sour. Few if any had the glamour of this one: a beautiful shrink-to-the-stars, her young black protégé, and her patient – a billionaire's model mistress. Add to that the mysterious zombie DNA found on the first victim, and you had a full-on thriller on your hands. It wasn't right for Goodman and Johnson to keep the thing solely for themselves.

'I hate to be the boring grown-up here and rain on your parade with the cold hard facts,' Goodman drawled. 'But the facts are: a) Nikki Roberts had no motive for either murder. None *whatsoever*. And b) she's five foot three and can't weigh much more than a hundred pounds. Treyvon Raymond was six two and a hundred eighty-six pounds of solid muscle. You're telling me she overpowered, kidnapped, stabbed and dumped that boy? I don't think so.'

'Maybe she had help,' said Johnson. 'Maybe she hired someone.'

'Yeah, and maybe Angelina Jolie's about to walk in and ask you out on a date, Mick,' Anna Baines observed wryly as she drained her beer. 'Theoretically possible, but not exactly likely.'

There were snorts of laughter all round.

'Lou's right,' Anna added. 'You got nothing on this shrink woman.'

Johnson stood up, pushing his chair back with an angry clatter.

'Not yet I don't,' he snapped at Anna. 'But I will. She's got no alibi, and *I* think she's lying through her straight white teeth. So you can all go screw yourselves.' And with that he stormed out.

'Jeesh.' Anna turned to Goodman, open-mouthed. 'What's with him?'

'I was hoping you guys could tell me,' Goodman sighed. 'You've all known him longer than I have. Mick's obsessed with Dr Roberts. He hates the woman's guts, but he won't tell me why.'

'I might have an idea,' Pedro Sanchez said quietly.

Sanchez was a man of few words, unlike his partner Anna Baines. He rarely offered an opinion, but when he did it was usually worth listening to.

'The Roberts woman used to get called as an expert witness from time to time.'

'She gave psychiatric evaluations, you mean?' asked Goodman.

'Right. Usually on narcotics cases,' said Sanchez. 'She and her husband were involved with the junkies downtown – needle exchanges, counseling, all that shit. They were big-time bleeding-heart liberals.'

*Mick is ex drug squad*, Goodman thought. 'Did she testify in any of Johnson's old cases?' he asked Sanchez.

'I don't know. You'd have to ask him. But I do know the lady wasn't a big fan of the force in general, which wouldn't have endeared her to Mick. You know what he's like with holding grudges.'

Without another word, Goodman left a twenty on the table and ran outside after Johnson. What Sanchez had told him was interesting, but it was another thought entirely that had just occurred to him.

'Mick!' he called into the darkness.

Johnson turned around. Thankfully, he'd got no farther than the parking lot, where he was swaying drunkenly in the breeze, waiting for his Uber.

Goodman cut straight to the chase. 'Let's say Dr Roberts *is* involved.'

'She is,' Johnson slurred. 'I'm sure of it.'

'But what if it's not in the way you think. What if the Doc was the intended victim?'

Johnson rolled his eyes. 'Not this again. We've been over this.'

'Lisa Flannagan *was* wearing her coat when she left the office that night.'

'According to *her*,' muttered Johnson. 'Look, I was excited as you about that raincoat being a lead, but we've found nothing. All we have is Dr Roberts' word for it.'

'Yes, and why would she lie about something like that? Admit it, you can't think of a reason.'

Johnson grunted. It was true, he couldn't. Yet.

'It was dark. It was raining. Lisa was leaving Dr Roberts' office, wearing her coat. They're the same height. Same hairstyle. If the killer approached from behind . . .'

'OK, OK,' said Johnson wearily. 'I get it.'

'It's possible,' insisted Goodman.

'Fine. It's possible. But what about Treyvon Raymond? Your theory doesn't work so well with him, now does it? Six foot two, male and black as your hat?'

'Maybe Trey was killed because he was close to Nikki,' said Goodman. 'She used to testify on drug cases, didn't she? That must've made her a lot of enemies. Her, and her husband.'

Johnson's eyes narrowed. 'Who told you about that?'

'I'm a detective, dude,' Goodman dodged. He didn't want to land Sanchez in it. 'I find shit out. Maybe a disgruntled dealer, someone Dr Roberts testified against, killed Lisa accidentally, thinking she was the Doc. And maybe Trey figured out who that dealer was.'

Johnson raised a cynical eyebrow. 'He was a detective too?'

'Come on,' Goodman urged. 'It's possible, isn't it, Mick?'

Johnson brooded silently. The last thing he wanted was to re-frame Nikki Roberts as a victim. But he had to admit Goodman's theory was at least possible.

'Can we keep an open mind on this? That's all I'm asking,' Goodman pleaded.

'OK,' Johnson conceded grudgingly. 'But open minds gotta work both ways.'

'Meaning?'

'Meaning that we don't *know* Roberts wasn't behind this. She's still a possible suspect,' Johnson insisted. 'How about this scenario? Roberts secretly hated Lisa Flannagan.'

'Why?' Goodman asked, genuinely baffled.

'Lisa was a gold digger. A homewrecker. Maybe Roberts disapproved of her lifestyle.'

'Come on, man,' said Goodman. 'That's weak.'

'Is it? We know Lisa aborted Baden's baby. Roberts can't have kids, remember?' Johnson went on. 'That's a big deal for women.'

'In your vast experience of female emotion,' Goodman quipped.

'Maybe she's so jealous, so mad about the baby thing it drives her over the edge,' said Johnson, ignoring him. 'Makes her crazy. Homicidal.'

Resisting the urge to roll his eyes, Goodman decided to end the conversation before Mick's conspiracy theories got completely out of control. 'OK, OK, open minds on both sides. What do you say tomorrow we start talking to Dr Roberts' patients? I'll take half, you take half?'

'Fine.'

Johnson's car finally pulled up. Goodman waited as he heaved his unfit frame into the back of the Toyota.

Deciding to strike while the iron was hot in this rare moment of accord between them, Goodman stuck his head through the open window.

'One last thing, Mick. Is there any personal history between you and Nikki Roberts?'

Johnson grinned. The question seemed to amuse him.

'Anything I should know about?' Goodman pressed.

Leaning back in his seat, Johnson closed his eyes, an amused smile still playing on his alcohol-flushed face.

'Goodnight, Lou,' he said, closing the window. 'Sweet dreams.'

*   *   *

Nikki drove for a long time after she left the police station.

She didn't want to go home, but she didn't know where else to go, so she took the 10 freeway all the way down to the ocean and cruised blindly up the coast. Memories of Trey played through her head on a continuous loop.

The first time Doug brought him home, whippet-thin and as dirty as a stray dog, shivering from withdrawal. Nikki's heart had gone out to him right away, just as Doug had known it would.

'Hey, Nik. This is a friend of mine, Treyvon. D'you think the chicken can stretch to three?'

From the beginning, Trey had drawn Doug and Nikki even closer together, their common compassion for this poor, broken boy strengthening their love bond and cementing them as a team.

She thought back to Trey's graduation ceremony out in Palos Verdes, after he'd completed his full sixteen-week detox program, dancing with Nikki to Nina Simone's 'Feeling Good'.

Nikki had caught Doug's eye over Trey's shoulder and smiled. Doug smiled back, and she'd felt so happy, so full of love for him and the miracle he'd helped happen for this sweet boy he'd come to love as his own.

It was a beautiful memory. But it had been ruined by what had happened since, slashed and mutilated and destroyed, just like Trey. And Lisa.

A million tiny cuts. Then one, final, fatal stab to the heart.

Doug's death, and the shock of everything she'd learned afterwards, had been the final stabs to Nikki's heart. So deep, so wounding, she'd believed for a while that she wouldn't survive them. But she had. She'd survived, and picked herself up and carried on. And she was still carrying on, even in the midst of this new nightmare.

Torture and terror.

Murder and lies.

I ought to call Trey's mother, Nikki thought, but she couldn't bring herself to do it. Her own grief was still so raw, so real, she couldn't cope with anyone else's. Perhaps that was selfish, but it was the truth. She knew her own limits.

She drove on for a long time. By the time she got home it was late, very late, and she couldn't remember where she'd been. That was happening a lot lately. The driveway lights were on, triggered by a timer, twinkling merrily as if all were right with the world. Locking her car, Nikki walked up to the key panel by the front door and was about to tap in her code when she noticed that the door was ajar.

She froze. Today was Monday. Her housekeeper, Rita, came on Mondays. Had she forgotten to close the door properly when she left? It had never happened before. Not once in six years. Rita was extremely reliable.

*Someone must have broken in.*

Nikki's heart pounded.

*What if they were still inside?*

She contemplated getting in her car and driving away. Calling the police. Asking for help. But then an unexpected emotion took over: anger.

*This is my home. My sanctuary. I'm not going to be afraid here. I refuse.*

Pushing the door open wide, she turned on the hall lights. 'Hello?' she called loudly. 'Is anybody here?'

She walked from room to room, making as much noise as she could, like a hiker hoping to scare away mountain lions. 'Hello?'

After a few minutes, she exhaled. No one was here. And as far as she could tell, nothing had been taken or touched. In fact, the house looked spotless. *It must have been Rita after all.*

Pouring herself a large nightcap from the whiskey bottle in the pantry, Nikki went up to bed, proud of herself for not having given in to her fears. Only once she was undressed and slipping between the sheets did she notice.

Her wedding photograph.

The silver framed picture of her and Doug she kept propped on her nightstand, despite the pain it caused.

It was gone.

# 15

## LANA

Lana Grey tossed back her Titian hair and gave Anton Wilders her signature smolder as she delivered the last line.

'Because I said so, Rocco.'

Lana leaned forward, her ample bosom threatening to spill over the top of her Victoria Beckham dress at any moment and into Anton's lap. 'Because. I. Said. So.'

'*Scene*,' a bored voice called from behind her as the stage lights went back up. Lana didn't care about the bored voice, or the ennui on the faces of the USC interns hanging around the set, hoping against hope that the great director would remember them.

*He won't,* Lana thought triumphantly. *He'll remember* me. *I nailed that audition. Anton Wilders is going to relaunch my career with a bang.*

What a struggle it had been, to get Wilders to see her! Lana's agent, Jane, had had a terrible time getting past his people, the Rottweilers that surrounded him, as they surrounded all the big-name directors.

'Lana Grey's too old to play Celeste,' Wilders' right-hand man, Charlie Myers, told Jane bluntly. 'The casting note clearly says twenty-two to thirty-two. Lana's, what, forty-five?'

'She looks twenty-five,' Jane had insisted. She was a good agent, Jane. Just the right amount of push. 'She was born to play this role. Let me speak to Anton.'

'No.'

'I won't stop calling.'

'Please do, Janey. She's too old!'

*Screw you, Charlie,* Lana thought now, smiling at Wilders as he walked onstage and enveloped her in a lingering, distinctly lecherous hug. *He wants me. I'm going to get this part.*

'Lana. Darling. Bravo!'

She could feel Anton's warm breath on her neck, and his left hand snake down onto her pert ass. All the twenty-something USC girls hated her right now. *Bad luck, ladies.*

'You were incredible.'

'Thank you, Anton.'

*I was incredible. I knew I was. I've still got it.*

Easing herself out of his embrace, Lana fluttered her eyes coquettishly. 'I knew I was right for this part. As soon as I read the script, I said to Jane, "This is me. It's *me*."'

'It is you,' Anton agreed. 'And I wish I could cast you, darling, I really do,' he went on, still smiling and staring longingly at Lana's tits. 'I know you'd rock it. But I'm in a bind. The studio want Harry Reeves as Luke. I only heard this morning.'

*Harry Reeves.* The nineteen-year-old Disney star, without a decent film credit to his name? *Harry Reeves?*

'I didn't know that.' Lana felt her jaw locking as hope and happiness left her body. 'Is that definite?'

'Looks like it.' Wilders' hand was back on her backside. 'You're so gorgeous, baby, but with the best will in the world, I can't cast you as Harry Reeves' girlfriend.'

Out of the corner of her eye, Lana saw two of the USC girls sniggering.

Leaning in closer, Wilders whispered in Lana's ear, 'I'll cast you to suck my dick, if you're interested. I'm staying at the Standard.'

Lana kissed him politely on the cheek and reached for her coat. 'You're sweet, Anton,' she smiled. She wasn't going to give those bitches the satisfaction of seeing her humiliated. 'Some other time.'

'You can name your price!' the director called after her cruelly as her borrowed Louboutins *clack-clacked* across the floor. Lana heard open laughter now, and a bored 'Next!' from the stagehand.

A familiar feeling of rage flooded through her veins.

*Screw you. Screw all of you. I hope you all die in a fire.*

\*    \*    \*

Outside on Cahuenga Boulevard, Detective Lou Goodman sat in an unmarked car a few yards from the theater. He watched Lana Grey emerge onto the street, take a few steps and then double over, gripping her knees and panting as if she'd run a marathon, or been punched in

the stomach. It was a crowded sidewalk but, Hollywood being Hollywood, nobody stopped to help, or even to look.

Goodman glanced at Lana's file, open on the seat beside him.
Nikki Roberts handwrote her patient notes, in the sort of beautiful
cursive you never saw these days. Each new client's file began with a
summary, followed by dated and detailed session notes. Like so much
else about Dr Roberts, Goodman was impressed.

'*Grey, Lana: forty-five years old, divorced*,' Lana's opening para-
graph read. '*Actress. Initially presented with acute anxiety and panic
attacks. Fear of aging, loss of career – self-worth issues.*' In the margin,
Nikki had written '*Financial worries??*' which she'd later underscored
in red. '*Divorced 2005. Subsequent abusive relationship, ended 2011.
Lost both parents, 2012/13. Run for the Hills ended 2009, no steady
work since.*' And then the final three words of the summary, stark and
unexplained: '*Sexually compulsive. Angry.*'

Lana straightened up and appeared to take two deep breaths. She
was still a strikingly attractive woman, with her trademark mane of red
hair, long, coltish legs and a face that Goodman had always thought of
as having a rather old-fashioned beauty. Like most teenage boys of his
generation, Goodman had followed *Run for the Hills* slavishly growing
up, and had always admired Lana Grey's brand of retro-glamour. Red
lips, lacquered hair, big boobs and a sassy comeback for everything.
She'd been so sexy back then. Every man in America wanted her.

*Must be tough to get older when you've had a youth like that.*

Pulling out her phone, Lana gazed down at the screen. Her fingers
began moving deftly across it in what Goodman recognized instantly
as a Tinder swipe. *Really? Lana Grey used a hook-up app?* Talk about
the mighty fallen. After a few minutes, she put the phone down, apparently settled on a mate, got into her car and drove away.

Lou Goodman followed.

*   *   *

Three hours later, Nikki Roberts listened intently as Lana Grey sat in
her office, leaned back on the couch, and poured her heart out.

And what was pouring out of Lana's heart was rage. Lava-hot,
toxic rage, of a kind that was painful to listen to. But that was Nikki's
job. Reactionless, she let it flow.

'He put his hands on me. His stinking, disgusting hands.' The
words flew out of Lana's mouth like bullets. 'Asked me to suck his dick,

like I was a prostitute. Offered to *pay me,* with all these pathetic, twenty-something little bitches standing there laughing. Like it was the funniest thing for him to humiliate me like that. I wanted to stick my hand down their throats and pull their non-existent hearts out. Have you ever felt like that?'

Lana's eyes flashed up at Nikki like two flares.

'Like you could kill someone with your bare hands and enjoy it?'

'We're not here to talk about my feelings,' Nikki responded evenly.

Lana laughed bitterly. 'So you *have.* Thought so.' She paused and stared out of the office window. 'I guess everybody has at some point. Wanted somebody else to suffer. I mean, *really* suffer.'

*Poor Trey really suffered,* Nikki thought. Since Haddon broke the news, she hadn't been able to go more than a few minutes without an image of Trey's torn and mangled body leaping, unbidden, into her head. Lisa Flannagan had suffered too, of course. But Lisa didn't haunt Nikki the way Trey did. Despite her feelings of guilt and sadness over her death, despite everything, Nikki still couldn't bring herself to *like* Lisa. Even now, the young model's entitlement and her casual cruelty towards other women left a sour taste in Nikki's mouth.

She still hadn't reported the break-in at her house – if you could call it a break-in. Somehow she suspected that Detective Johnson, for one, wouldn't dignify it with such a title. 'An unlocked door and a single missing photograph?' She could hear his sardonic, mocking voice now. 'That's not a crime, Ms Roberts. That's middle-aged memory loss catching up with you.'

With an effort, Nikki wrenched her attention back to Lana. 'I'm curious,' she observed. 'Why would you choose to focus your anger on these young women around Wilders, and not on the director himself? It seems to me *he's* by far the worst offender here. Him and the man who abused you afterwards, at his apartment.'

Lana uncrossed and recrossed her legs in an oddly provocative manner.

'It's not abuse if you ask for it, Dr Roberts,' she said bluntly.

'Isn't it?' asked Nikki.

Lana's eyes narrowed. *Who was this woman to judge her? This beautiful doctor who men still lusted after, and who was only now reaching the peak of her career? What the hell could someone like Dr Roberts possibly know about how it felt to be left on the shelf, discarded by the world, dumped in a box marked 'Too old. Too ugly. Finished. Worthless.'? She didn't know shit.*

'I don't see how,' she responded coolly. 'I told him what I wanted him to do to me and he did it. That's the joy of Tinder. No questions. No strings.'

'So you *wanted* him to hurt you? To humiliate you?' Nikki frowned. Minutes ago, Lana had sat there shaking while she described a sexual encounter of such bestial brutality even Nikki had gasped listening to it. After almost two decades as a therapist, it took a lot to shock her. But the things that Lana Grey had been subjected to – willingly, she now claimed – had done it.

'Don't you get it? I wanted to *own* the humiliation!' Lana shrieked. 'I wanted to take it back. To control it. Anton Wilders wants to treat me like a whore? "I'll see you and I'll raise you, dude!" It's called feminism,' she added defiantly, sitting back with an 'I rest my case' flourish.

*Letting a guy urinate in your mouth is feminism?* thought Nikki. Most of her patients twisted external reality to some degree to fit with their own neuroses, their own skewed self-perception. But Lana took the proverbial cake.

'Have you heard from Johnny lately?' Nikki threw out the question casually, as if it weren't charged with a hundred pounds of Semtex. Johnny was Lana's abusive ex-partner. He still called her from time to time or 'dropped by' her place; this despite the fact he was married now to a much younger, much more successful actress and the father of two small boys.

Lana looked out of the window.

'No.'

Nikki could see at once she was lying.

'I told you. I blocked his number,' Lana explained, unnecessarily. 'He's dead to me.'

'So when *did* you last see him?' Nikki pressed.

Failed auditions always brought Lana down, but they were also a part of her life routine, a commonplace disappointment. More often than not, when she went off the rails like she had today, acting out sexually and putting herself in danger, 'Johnny' was involved somewhere.

'No idea. Months ago,' Lana lied.

'I want you to try and think again about transference, Lana. That's your "homework" for this week. Try to notice the way that you take emotions that are about one thing or person – like your *anger* with

Anton Wilders; or your *shame* about your *own* behavior – and misdirect those feelings towards others. The young women in that auditorium. Me.'

'I don't know what you're talking about,' said Lana, her voice and body both brittle with repressed pain.

Nikki gave her an *Oh, I think you do* look.

'Try it,' she said. 'See what you notice as you move through your week.'

Lana left, stalking out of the room almost as angry as she'd been an hour ago, and only slightly more enlightened.

'Take care of yourself,' Nikki called after her as she left, an ugly sense of foreboding suddenly seizing her out of nowhere.

Too many people were dying around her. She hoped Lana wasn't about to take any more stupid risks.

*   *   *

Goodman watched as Lana Grey pulled out of Nikki's building in her leased Prius. He'd already learned that the actress was six months in arrears on the car and owed thousands in unpaid interest on the subprime loan she'd used to pay for it. The Victoria Beckham dress and pumps she wore to the audition had already been returned to Neiman Marcus, right after she finished with hook-up guy but before she swung by therapy. Goodman wondered how Lana was affording Nikki Roberts' fees. He made a note to check the accounts later.

He assumed she was heading home now to her lonely, rent-controlled apartment in Ocean Park, and an evening of what? Another meaningless encounter with a stranger, perhaps? Or pills, booze and bed? *What a tragic life.* But he knew everything he needed to for now. He was done following Lana for the day.

Five minutes into his drive home, his phone rang.

'Anything to report?' Johnson's voice sounded crackly. Bad line.

'I'll fill you in tomorrow. But no, not really. How about you?' Goodman asked. 'Any leads on Brandon Grolsch?'

'Nothing,' Johnson admitted. 'I'm calling it a day. See you bright and early tomorrow.'

'Mañana.'

Goodman hung up. Then, on a whim he pulled over. Waiting for a break in the traffic, he did a U-turn and headed back towards Century City.

About twenty minutes later, his patience was rewarded. Nikki Roberts' Mercedes pulled slowly out of the garage beneath her office building, turned into the alleyway and then out onto Avenue of the Stars.

Re-starting his engine, Detective Lou Goodman slipped into the stream of cars behind her.

# 16

Anne Bateman tightened her bow fractionally and brought it down to rest on the bridge of her violin. Anne's violin was something between a dear friend and a love object. An early eighteenth-century Pietro Guarneri, it was one of the first really valuable gifts her husband had given her, the week after their wedding.

'But this must be worth seven figures!' Anne had gasped, opening the beautifully inlaid case it came in, a work of art in itself, before lovingly lifting the Guarneri into her arms. 'It's exquisite.'

'Like you,' Anne's husband had purred, delighted to have been the source of such joy.

They'd been on honeymoon in Tahiti at the time. So it must have been eight years ago. *Eight years,* thought Anne, gripping her precious violin more tightly. Some days it felt like eighty.

She was sitting in the orchestra pit at Disney Concert Hall, about to start the first rehearsal for the LA Phil's sold-out performance of *The Best of Stravinsky* on Friday night. Anne knew the great composer's violin concertos inside out and backwards, but it didn't stop her experiencing the same mixture of excitement and fear she always felt before a big performance. She'd tried to talk about her stage fright in her session with Dr Roberts earlier. But Nikki (*'You really must call me Nikki, Anne.'*) had insisted on bringing the conversation back to Anne's husband, and what she would keep referring to as Anne's 'backsliding'.

'Think of how far you've come,' Nikki had pleaded with her. 'Think how hard-won your freedom was. Are you really prepared to give all that up, to let him back in?'

'I don't know,' Anne answered truthfully.

'You need to ask yourself why you would do that,' Nikki pressed. 'Why you would even *consider it,* after everything that's happened.'

She was right, as usual. When Anne was sitting in Nikki's office, it seemed so obvious, so clear what she should do. Or not do. But the moment she walked out, that certainty deserted her, and with it her resolve. It was as if the further away Anne Bateman got from her therapist – the more miles she put between her Prius and Nikki's Century City office – the weaker Nikki's influence over her became. And in the vacuum left behind, her husband's power grew.

'First violin! Anne, my dear. Are you with us?'

Henrik Leinneman, the conductor, kept his tone polite – he lusted after Anne Bateman too much to lose his temper with her – but he was clearly irritated. All this daydreaming was unprofessional, not to mention unfair to her fellow musicians. Anne was a brilliant violinist, but still terribly young. At times like these, her inexperience showed.

'Sorry, Maestro. Everybody.' Anne bit her lower lip, a nervous gesture that made her look even younger. 'I'm ready.'

Leinneman led them back into the second movement, and Anne swiftly lost herself in the music, allowing Stravinski to transport her to a world without her ex, a world without pain or conflict or denial or despair. How she wished she could stay there forever!

*　*　*

Anne Bateman had been only sixteen years old when she first met her future husband, a wealthy and powerful real estate developer some twenty-five-years her senior, at a concert in Mexico City. Already a well-travelled musician by then, this was the first professional trip Anne had taken without her mother as a chaperone. (Linda Bateman had come down with the flu the weekend before, and the tour managers had assured her that Anne would be well taken care of in Mexico. Besides, Anne was a sensible girl, who took her music deadly seriously. She'd have no time to get into any mischief between her grueling schedule of rehearsals and performances. What harm could possibly come to her?)

Anne's soon-to-be husband was forty-one when they met, newly married to his second wife, and a notorious womanizer. The moment he laid eyes on Anne, he knew he had to have her. And not just have her. Keep her. Hold her. Protect her. She was by no means the most beautiful girl he'd ever bedded. But never in his life had he felt such love, such instant and powerful yearning. Or at least, not for a long, long time.

Anne never stood a chance. It was like an iron filing meeting a giant magnet. The overwhelming force of his personality sucked her in like the death-star. Despite her inexperience, the teenage Anne was profoundly attracted to him from the start. Handsome, exciting, radiating sexual energy like a sun god, as soon as he came backstage and took her hand she felt a charge of desire jolt through her, unlike anything she'd known before. Except perhaps the charge she felt when she was playing, lost in her music on stage. But this was stronger. Deeper.

They became lovers immediately. As soon as Anne left Mexico, he began flying all over the world to snatch a few hours with his young mistress; although it wasn't until two years later, the day after Anne's eighteenth birthday, that he finally ditched his heartbroken wife and swept Anne away to Costa Rica, where they secretly married. Anne's parents, Linda and Gerry, were appalled. 'You're his third wife? And this fella is *how* old?' But they soon got over their new son-in-law's past – including no less than five children from two former wives, the oldest only a year younger than Anne – after he bought them a new, five-bedroom house in San Diego as a 'wedding present' and then invited them out to stay at the palatial beach-house in Cabo he now shared with Anne, flying them there by private jet.

Not only did their daughter seem deliriously happy, but she was also a newly minted member of the Latino superrich. True, Anne's new husband was the same age as Gerry Bateman and had what might politely be referred to as a 'checkered past' with women. (His first wife had left him after numerous affairs, the last of which had culminated in a love child, Rico.) But really, didn't everyone deserve a second chance? And since when should a little thing like age stand in the way of true love? The main thing was that he supported Anne's music.

'Naturally she must keep playing! It was her playing that made me fall in love with her in the first place,' he told Linda, over Cristal and oysters on the beachside terrace that first trip to Cabo. 'All I want on this earth, Mrs Bateman, is to make your daughter happy.'

'He meant it,' Anne told Nikki, remembering the happy times during therapy. 'He really did at the time. He tried.'

But Anne's husband was controlling by nature. He simply couldn't help himself. The love he felt for his new young wife, the *need* she aroused in him, terrified him. It wasn't long before he began erecting walls around her. At first it was a few, specific concerts that he objected to.

'Let's not do Paris this year, angel.'

'Not do Paris?' Anne looked perplexed. 'But I have to. I'm committed.'

'I'll un-commit you.' He waved a hand regally. 'It's so far, Anne. And I can't travel with you this time. Tell them you'll do New York in September instead. They'll understand.'

'But my love, that's not how it works.'

'You know I hate it when we're apart. I need you, angel.'

He reached between her legs, and Anne felt her own desire overwhelm her, as it always did with him, and the fight – if it ever was a fight – was over before it began. But it wasn't long before one concert became many. Soon all foreign tours were vetoed. Even when Anne performed locally, in Mexico City, she was tailed constantly by heavily armed guards. Before long the same guards were taking her shopping or to the gym. Lunches with girlfriends were spied on. Anne began to feel lonely and oppressed.

'You don't understand, angel,' her husband would tell her lovingly. 'You're not in Kansas any more. This is Mexico City. Wealthy women get kidnapped every *day* here. Some of them are released for ransom money, but many others are raped or killed. The drug gangs show no mercy.'

He told her the story of Valentina Baden, whose sister had been kidnapped, never to be seen again, and who had founded a charity to help support families of the missing. And about the young American au pair girl, Charlotte Clancy, who had also disappeared without trace, right here in the city. Those who were found were often returned to their family cut up into little pieces and stuffed in plastic bags.

'You don't see it, because I try to protect you from the news, from the reality of what's out there. But the danger is real, Anne.'

'Then let's move,' Anne pleaded. 'We have money. We don't *have* to live here, darling. We could go back to the States, or even Europe. We could travel—'

'I have to be here. For my business,' he said, more curtly than usual.

'But surely you could develop real estate somewhere else?' Anne pressed. 'It's not as if there aren't other markets.'

He grabbed her wrists, not painfully but forcefully, and pulled her to him, stopping her mouth with a kiss that was similarly forceful. 'We cannot leave, Anne. I'm sorry, but that's the way it is.'

Something in his eyes warned her not to argue.

That conversation marked a change in their relationship. The love was still there, on both sides. But from that point on, it went hand in hand with fear. Anne had more and more questions but she was too afraid to ask any of them. For the first time it dawned on her that she was now officially stepmother to five children. Why was it that their father barely saw them? Leaving a wife, or even two wives, was one thing, but surely it wasn't normal to walk away from one's own children? Anne knew her new husband paid maintenance and school fees and the like. But she'd only met the children from his first marriage once, and the two younger ones from his second marriage a handful of times. None of them had seemed to have any real relationship with their father.

Lonely, unable to play her violin other than privately, for him, and cut off from family and friends, Anne started to panic. Life in the gilded prison of her marriage was rapidly becoming unbearable. But life without her love was equally unthinkable. He had been her world, her rock, her idol since she was sixteen years old. And he still needed her, and adored her, every bit as passionately as he had back then. Anne was physically afraid of him, yet he had never hurt her. Was she becoming paranoid? Was it all in her head?

It was only after he started pressuring her to have a baby – a sixth child he would barely know – that Anne knew she had to get out. By now estranged from her parents, who would have taken her husband's side anyway, she managed to contact an old friend from the San Diego Youth Orchestra, who helped her book a flight and return in secret to the US while her husband was away at a business meeting. Despite arriving in California with only her precious violin, her passport and a few hundred dollars in her wallet, Anne swiftly reconnected with her old contacts in the music world and began to work again. It felt like a rebirth, and for a while the joy of performing and having her freedom back eclipsed all the feelings of loss and guilt over her abandoned marriage. By the time her husband tracked her down, about a month later, and began his campaign to win her back, she was already much stronger, almost a different person.

*Almost.*

The problem was, she still loved him. Still missed him, even though she knew she couldn't go back. Even after she landed her dream job with the LA Philharmonic, the feelings of pain and regret over abandoning her marriage continued to creep up on her, to the point where she worried she might be on the brink of some sort of breakdown. She had already started forgetting things, sometimes blacking out entire evenings or stretches of the day, overwhelmed by stress.

That was when a friend introduced her to Dr Roberts – to Nikki. For the first time since the early days with her husband, Anne felt that she had someone in her corner, someone looking out for *her* and protecting *her*, only this time in a good way. A healthy way. Therapy was the answer, she felt sure of that now. Nikki was the answer. She just had to keep going, to stay strong.

Lifting her bow, she dived back into the music with renewed devotion, each note elevating her to a higher plane, to a future full of hope and promise and wonder.

* * *

Nikki checked her reflection in the rear-view mirror as she pulled into Tigertail Road.

*I look old,* she thought. *Old and exhausted.*

It was hardly surprising. She'd had a tough day. A tough month. A tough year, in fact, since Doug died. But at some point, these were all excuses. That's what Doug would have said, anyway. 'Snap out of it, Nik! You're better than this. Where there's life, there's hope, right? We're blessed.'

That was a catchphrase of his. 'We're blessed.' And they had been. At least, Nikki thought they had been.

*No. To hell with that. We* were *blessed. Just because Doug kept secrets from me, it doesn't take all that away. We* were *blessed. I still* am *blessed.*

That was the key point, surely? Doug might be dead. *His* blessings were over. But Nikki was still very much alive. Still here, still helping people, still doing important work. *Where there's life, there's hope.* That was another of Doug's catchphrases, one he used to trot out to the recovering addicts at his clinic all the time. He was always so upbeat, the bastard. Those junkies must have hated him for that, in all the moments when they weren't throwing themselves at his feet as their lord and savior.

The truth was, although Nikki struggled to admit it, it wasn't only grief over losing her husband that had etched the lines around her eyes or punched the two dark, plum shadows underneath them. It was also Anne Bateman.

*Anne.* Beautiful, talented, weak, volatile, intoxicating Anne – was threatening to go back to her husband. A man who, by Anne's own account, she was afraid might kill her. A man whose jealous, controlling nature had so crushed her spirit that Anne had arrived at Nikki's office three months ago, starvingly thin and shaking, like a dog that had been dumped on the freeway, terrified to make even the smallest decision about her own life, such as what to eat for dinner or which skirt to wear to a performance. Nikki had taken her in, comforted her, helped her. Nikki had *rebuilt* her, piecing back together Anne's shattered ego, her wasted sense of self, and returning it to her intact. And all for what? For her to hand it back to her bastard husband, to be stamped on and broken all over again?

Nikki knew she shouldn't take it personally. But *God* it was frustrating when patients did this. When all their hard work – all *Nikki's* hard work – was for nothing. Doug used to deal with it all the time, working with addicts at his clinic. The recidivism, people sliding back into the depths of hell after months, years, sometimes even decades clean, for no apparent reason at all. Love, especially toxic love like Anne Bateman's for her controlling ex, was an addiction like any other. With her professional hat on, Nikki knew that.

The problem was that, with Anne, her professional hat kept slipping. Nikki's feelings for Anne Bateman went well beyond professional boundaries. They exhausted her, and kept her up at night, and aged her horribly, as her reflection grimly attested. To be honest, they embarrassed her. They weren't sexual, at least not overtly. But they were certainly obsessional and unhealthy and . . . *Eeeugh.*

Pulling up to one side of her driveway gates, Nikki got out of her car to punch in the code. Nothing happened. She was rocking on her heels, waiting for the stupid panel to reset, when her cell phone rang.

'It's happened again.'

Anne's voice was ragged, fearful.

'What's happened?'

Nikki felt a wave of protective feelings rise up inside her.

'The man. He's back. He's following me again!'

*Poor thing,* thought Nikki. Years of living under her husband's Stasi-like surveillance had left Anne deeply paranoid, jumping at her own shadow. She was constantly complaining of being 'followed' but never seemed able to describe the cars or surveillance operatives in question, or any way in which she was being threatened.

For the next few minutes Nikki spoke to her soothingly, talking her down from the ledge, as she always did when her fears took hold. 'This isn't real, Anne,' she said. 'None of it's real. It's only your ex, getting into your head. This is why you need to escape him. For good.'

'Maybe . . .' Anne wavered. 'But what if it *is* real, and nothing to do with him? I mean, there have been two murders.'

'Anne. No one is following you.'

'You say that. But how do you *know*? The police said we should all be on our guard, all your patients. That if we see anything suspicious we should report it.'

'But, Anne, you *haven't* seen anything, have you? This is only a feeling you get. A sort of sixth sense that someone's tailing your car, that something sinister is over your shoulder?'

'Well, yes. I suppose so. But . . .'

Nikki took a few more minutes to reassure her before she hung up. As always after speaking with Anne, she felt conflicting emotions. Happiness, that Anne had chosen to turn to her for advice; and frustration that she still allowed her husband so much power over her life. There was something indefinable about Anne – her youth and vulnerability, combined with her huge talent and an overpowering, almost tangible neediness – that spoke to Nikki in a way that other patients didn't. Perhaps, at its core, her attraction to Anne was about need. Anne Bateman needed her. At this chaotic juncture in her own life, Nikki needed to be needed. Perhaps that was *her* drug of choice.

*Whoosh!*

A gust of air was the first thing Nikki felt: hot and fast and very close.

Then the noise. The scream of an engine.

*A car.*

She turned – half turned, for it all happened so quickly, in a fraction of a second. An SUV, big, and black with tinted windows, coming towards her at breakneck speed. There was no time for anything, not even fear. Instinctively Nikki flattened herself back against the wooden gates, closing her eyes.

Another screech of brakes and it swerved, missing her by millimeters.

Nikki opened her eyes. *What just happened?* The driver must have come in at an angle, swinging violently to the left as he hurtled down the narrow road. *Had he lost control?* Rooted to the spot, her heart pounding, Nikki watched in mute horror as the car skidded to a halt, turned, and came at her a second time, this time backing up very deliberately, straightening up so that it would hit her head on, the engine revving like a maddened bull about to charge.

This was no accident.

She looked desperately to left and right for a means of escape, but about three feet of jutting garden wall hemmed her in on both sides of the gate. By the time she maneuvered around it, the car would have hit her. Above her was a small wooden ledge she could conceivably grab onto and try to pull herself up, but it was too high for her to reach.

*I'm trapped!* Nikki thought helplessly. *I'm going to die.*

Everything slowed down – her senses, her perceptions, her heartbeat. Even the car's roaring engine seemed to go quiet, drowned out by the low, deep thud of her pulse.

Right as this peaceful sense of acceptance was settling over her, a red sports car suddenly appeared around the corner. Nikki watched as if it were a dream, or an out-of-body experience as both drivers slid across the road, their brakes squealing as they frantically tried to avoid a side-on collision. Being so much lighter, it was the sports car that spun out of control, shooting past Nikki like a bright red child's spinning top before miraculously coming to rest, tail end first, in Nikki's neighbor's hedge.

A momentary silence fell. Then the SUV backed up, turned and disappeared down the hill.

The owner of the red car staggered out into the road, shaken but unhurt. 'Holy shit!' A young Iranian man in his early twenties, he was well dressed and handsome in the way that LA's privileged youth so often were. Good dentistry. Good skin. Good body, courtesy of some expensive private gym membership. 'Did you see that maniac? He was coming straight at you!'

Nikki tried to speak but no words came out.

'Are you OK?' the young man asked.

Nikki shook her head. 'Not really,' she gasped. 'I think somebody's trying to kill me.'

# 17

The Badens' return to Los Angeles was a low-key affair, unreported by the media and distinctly fleeting. Willie's private jet touched down in Burbank on a Tuesday night, and his pilot had instructions to fly his boss back to Cabo first thing Friday morning. Mrs Baden would stay in town a little longer, through the weekend, to take care of some loose ends at her charity offices downtown. But their lawyer made it plain to the LA police department that if detectives wished to interview the couple, then Wednesday would be 'the only convenient day.'

'Doesn't it bug you?' Goodman asked Johnson, as his partner headed off to Willie's apartment to interview the billionaire Rams' owner about his affair with the victim. 'All this special treatment for the rich?'

They'd agreed to quiz the Badens separately, with Goodman meeting Valentina at the Polo Lounge in Beverly Hills while Johnson grilled her husband.

'Depends.' Johnson shrugged. 'Old man Baden's been good to the department. Plus he flew back of his own free will to talk to us. So in this case, no.'

It was an open secret that Willie Baden was one of the LAPD Benevolent Fund's largest 'anonymous' donors, a fact that carried a lot more weight with Johnson than it did with Goodman. It was also strongly rumored that Willie had effectively shut down an investigation into his wife's charity's finances a year or two ago – some 'oversight' on taxes and unreported income. Nothing had ever been proved but the nascent case against Missing was dismantled before it began. The whole thing left an unpleasant taste in Goodman's mouth.

'You be nice to Mrs B now,' Johnson taunted his partner. 'Don't let your liberal outrage about "special treatment" get the better of you or you'll have the chief to answer to.'

'I'm always nice,' growled Goodman.

It turned out to be easier to be nice to Valentina Baden than Goodman had expected. Rising from her poolside seat in the Beverly Hills Hotel's iconic Polo Lounge to greet him, in a simple white shirtwaister dress, Willie Baden's wife was a lot less flashy and high maintenance than he'd expected. She wore minimal make-up, and her gray-streaked hair was tied up in a casual topknot. She was also disarmingly apologetic about the time it had taken her to return to the US.

'Unfortunately, it's not always easy with Willie's business. We can't move as freely as we'd like,' she explained. 'And it has been a difficult time for me personally, having to process my husband's infidelity in the full glare of the media.'

'Of course,' Goodman said understandingly, accepting a proffered glass of Pellegrino. 'We appreciate you taking the time to talk to us.'

'I must admit, I was a little surprised that you wanted to interview *me*,' Valentina observed coolly. 'I mean, obviously Willie had a relationship with the girl who was killed, so I knew you'd want to talk to him. But I knew nothing about her. *Lisa Flannagan*.'

She turned the name over on her tongue, like an unusual and potentially unpleasant-tasting fruit.

'The affair was a total surprise, then?' Goodman asked guilelessly.

'Well,' Valentina admitted, leaning forward and enveloping Goodman in a cloud of Gucci perfume, 'I knew my husband had affairs, naturally. I'm not a fool, Detective. But this specific girl I had never heard of. So I'm not sure what I can add to your investigation.'

'You accepted your husband's affairs?' Goodman raised an eyebrow.

Valentina smiled sadly. 'I never said that. Marriages are complicated things, Detective. Elements of my marriage have brought me pain. But other elements have been . . . more positive. I have a lot of freedom to pursue my own interests and passions. My charity work, for example,' she clarified, although Goodman could have sworn he detected a certain tongue-in-cheek element to this response.

'Have you heard of a young man named Brandon Grolsch?' he asked, deciding to steer clear of the tax-evasion rumors surrounding her charity and focus on the matter at hand.

Valentina sat back, startled. 'Brandon? Yes, sure I have. What has Brandon got to do with this?'

'Would you mind telling me how you know him?' said Goodman, ducking the question.

'Well, I never *knew* him, as such. I know his mother, Fran. Poor woman,' Valentina shook her head sadly.

'Poor in what way?' Goodman played along.

'Well, Brandon went missing. That's how I got to know Fran, through my charity. I assume you're aware of our work?'

Goodman nodded. 'I know the basics. You raise awareness of missing person cases?'

'Oh, we do a lot more than that, Detective,' Valentina said knowingly.

*Is she daring me to ask her about the tax investigation?* Goodman wondered. There certainly seemed to be an air of challenge in Mrs Baden's tone that was borderline flirtatious. But again, he let it go.

'Tell me more about the Grolsches.'

'I'm afraid theirs was a familiar story,' Valentina sighed. 'Brandon had substance abuse problems. No one takes it seriously when an addict falls off the grid. It happens all the time, right? But we at Missing took his disappearance seriously.'

There was a fierceness in Valentina Baden's voice and expression that impressed Goodman. This was not your run-of-the-mill rich wife, throwing herself into charity work to stave off boredom between shopping trips. This was a lioness, passionate about her cause. Whether or not she'd fiddled her taxes, this woman cared about Missing like a mother with a child.

'We helped Fran to search for her son when nobody else would – including your colleagues at the police department, I might add. Even though the outcome was tragic in that case, and not what any mother would hope for, I think Fran appreciated our efforts. Between you and me, Nathan, her husband, is a difficult man. Very cold. I don't think he loved Brandon, and he couldn't begin to understand what his wife was going through.'

'You said the outcome was tragic?' Goodman coaxed.

Valentina Baden sighed. 'Yes. We received a letter from a young woman known to my staff: Rachel, someone we'd contacted who'd been close to Brandon. Rachel was a heroin addict herself. She was with Brandon when he died from an overdose. Somebody with him gave him Narcan, but it was too late.'

'Mmm hmm.' Goodman sipped his water. 'Do you know Rachel's last name?'

'I'm afraid not,' said Valentina, with a smile that clearly implied that she wasn't about to divulge it to Goodman, whether she knew it or not.

'Other than this letter, did you find any physical evidence to suggest that Brandon Grolsch had, in fact, died?' he asked.

'No,' Valentina admitted. 'But then again, we didn't look for any. Fran did ask us to keep searching for Brandon, but our resources are limited, Detective, and the truth is we had no reason to doubt the story Rachel told us. We already knew from hospital records that Brandon had overdosed before, at least twice. At some point, the heart simply gives out.'

'Did the letter say where this happened? Or when?'

Valentina shook her head. 'There were no specifics.'

'So you don't know what happened to Brandon's body?'

The question seemed to surprise her. 'I assume it was taken away by the police. I'm not sure what the procedure is after that. You'd know better than I would, Detective. If I might ask you – what is all this about? Is there some sort of connection between Brandon Grolsch and my husband's . . . and Lisa Flannagan?'

'There might be,' Goodman answered cautiously. 'We're not certain about anything at this stage, Mrs Baden. But the information you've given me today was very helpful. Just to be clear: do you, personally, believe that Brandon Grolsch *is* dead?'

'I'm certain of it,' Valentina said firmly. 'I only wish I'd been able to convince his mother. You know, Detective, I watched my own parents waste decades of their lives on false hope for my sister. Since then I've seen countless other families do the same. Part of what we do at Missing is searching for lost loved ones. But a bigger part is helping the families to let go, once we know someone isn't coming back.' Leaning back in her chair, she looked Goodman square in the eye. 'You can take my word for it, Detective. Brandon Grolsch is not coming back.'

\* \* \*

A few hours later, Goodman and Johnson compared notes over a beer at Murphy's on Santa Monica Boulevard. Evidently, Willie Baden had been a lot less transparent than his wife, reading from a prepared statement with his attorney by his side and refusing to be drawn a millimeter from his script.

'I got a timeline of his affair with Lisa, some bank statements showing cash he'd given her and the deeds for her condo, and he volunteered fingerprints and a cheek swab. But that was it. According to him, the only thing they did together was have sex. He claimed not to know any of her friends or family, or how she spent her time when she wasn't with him. He confirmed Lisa had ended the relationship in the weeks before she died, but he said he was fine with that, it had "run its course", whatever that means.'

'Was he believable?' Goodman asked.

'Not really,' admitted Johnson. 'But his alibi's rock solid. I don't know. My gut is he wasn't involved. I don't think he cared enough about her to pay someone to cut her up like that.'

'You call that "caring"?' Goodman spluttered on his beer.

'Well, it ain't exactly detached,' Johnson replied, deadpan. 'She wasn't shot in the head. She was tortured, terrorized, made to suffer. Maybe I'm wrong, but I don't see any of that as Willie's style. What was the wife like?'

'Interesting,' said Goodman. 'Smarter than I thought. I can't quite put my finger on it, but I got the feeling she was almost playing with me at times. As if there were a double meaning to everything she said.'

He filled Johnson in on his interview with Valentina Baden, how she'd confirmed almost to the letter the story he'd been given by the odious Nathan Grolsch.

'She's convinced Brandon's dead. No doubt in her mind.'

'I think so too,' said Johnson.

Goodman thought for a moment. Did he agree? He remembered the forcefulness of Valentina Baden's parting words to him. *'Take my word for it, Detective. Brandon Grolsch is not coming back.'* He'd had overdoses before. All told it did seem the most likely scenario.

'OK. So let's assume he's dead. Where does that leave us?'

The two men sat and sipped their drinks in quiet contemplation. Johnson broke the silence:

'How about this. Our perp kills Brandon first. Figures he's a junkie, he's a nobody, nobody's going to miss him. He, or she, holds on to the corpse. Then, when they kill Lisa, and later when they *think* they've killed Trey and leave him for dead, they plant Brandon's DNA on the victims, to cover their tracks.'

'You don't buy the overdose story, then?' Goodman asked.

'Maybe,' said Johnson. 'Maybe Brandon's already dead, and our perp gets hold of his corpse somehow. That would explain us having no record of it at the morgue.'

'Like how?' Goodman frowned. 'How would someone get hold of Brandon Grolsch's corpse?'

'Maybe this "Rachel" sold it,' said Johnson, matter-of-factly.

'That's sick,' said Goodman.

'It's a sick world we live in,' observed Johnson. 'We need to find her, you know.'

Goodman nodded.

Both men relapsed into silence as they finished their beers.

\* \* \*

Later that night, Willie Baden stared out of the window as his private plane took off. He'd managed to secure a slot to fly out of LA early, the one really good thing that had happened all week. Not that he enjoyed leaving Los Angeles, or his beloved team behind him. But needs must. He had to return to Mexico. His associates there had made that point brutally clear, and for now they held the upper hand in Willie's latest business arrangement. Not for long, though. Once the focus of operations shifted back to Los Angeles, he would have the home field advantage. If he played his cards right, that stood to make him an obscene amount of money.

If . . .

Below him the lights of the city spread out like a blanket of fireflies, glinting in the darkness. At least it had been a successful trip. The chubby detective had got nothing useful out of him. With Glen by his side, Willie had stuck doggedly to the script, and they'd let him go.

'Something to drink, sir?' the flight attendant asked. She was new, this one, and not at all attractive. Valentina had replaced the old model, the luscious Conchita, in a fit of pique after his affair with Lisa hit the headlines.

'Vodka tonic,' Willie grunted. Perhaps it would help him relax.

He'd wanted Valentina to fly back with him, but to his surprise and irritation, she'd insisted on staying on a few more days.

'I want to get my hair done,' she told him. 'And I have people to see.'

'What people?' Willie demanded.

She turned on him angrily. 'I don't have to account for my movements to *you*, Willie,' she spat. 'You forced me to come all the way here and talk to the police. I may as well make use of the time. God knows when we'll next be back, after all.'

The thought of his angry, vengeful wife staying on in LA alone was not a reassuring one. But he was hardly in a position to prevent it, and on the grand scale of Willie Baden's worries right now, it was nowhere close to the top. Still, it baffled him. Twenty-four hours ago, Valentina had ranted and raved about not wanting to leave Cabo, yet now she refused to return.

Whatever. Willie had long ago given up trying to fathom the workings of the female mind. Hopefully, his wife's beloved charity would continue to distract her while he focused on how to make his 'arrangement' with his new Latino business partner work to his advantage. Ironically it was Valentina who'd introduced them, although Willie suspected his wife knew little of what a dangerous man he really was. *It's like being in bed with a cobra,* thought Willie. The rewards could be huge. But the risks were appalling and constant.

*I'm too old for this,* he reflected, as his drink arrived and he downed it in one long, tremulous gulp. Closing his eyes, he tried to sleep.

\* \* \*

From the balcony of her suite at the Beverly Hills Hotel, Valentina Baden watched the tail lights of a plane move through the night sky.

Willie would be in the air by now. Soon, she would have to follow him. But not yet. Not tonight. The thought of a few days alone, a few precious hours of total freedom, was exhilarating beyond anything Valentina had felt in years. It was almost like being young again. Young and beautiful and desired . . .

The detective she'd spoken to earlier had been handsome and charming and as biddable as a puppy. So easy! The LAPD didn't make them like they used to. Talking to him, and outsmarting him, had felt exciting. Even more so when he'd brought up the subject of Brandon Grolsch.

*Ah. Brandon.*

If she closed her eyes, Valentina could practically feel his strong, young body pressing down on hers. The firmness of his skin, the confidence of his touch. Such a beautiful boy he'd been back then. *What a waste!*

Walking back into her suite, Valentina Baden stripped off and stepped into the shower, allowing her own hands to play the part of Brandon's, losing herself in the fantasy.

She had a lot to do, tonight and in the days to come. But it could wait.

It could all wait.

# 18

'**S**o where is he, then? This kid in the red car, who supposedly witnessed everything?'

A small muscle was jumping beneath the sagging skin on Detective Mick Johnson's neck. Leaning across the desk in the interview room, the same room Nikki had been in the last time she spoke to the police, he thrust his face belligerently towards her, like an angry toad about to spew venom.

'I don't know where he is,' Nikki explained again wearily. 'I gave you the number he gave me.'

'Which doesn't work.'

'Look, he didn't "supposedly" witness anything, OK?' Nikki was angry. 'He was *there*. He saw this guy try to mow me down like a damn bowling pin. He saved my life.'

*Anger suits her,* Lou Goodman thought admiringly, watching Nikki Roberts cross her slender legs and narrow her intelligent almond eyes to slits as she glared back at his partner. *Like a beautiful, exotic cobra, ready to strike.* And God knew Johnson deserved to get bitten. Despite his promise to keep an open mind, he'd behaved like a total asshole ever since Nikki walked into the room. She'd come to give a more detailed statement about the attack she'd reported the previous day, an attempt on her life, right outside her home. But Mick had been nothing but hostile. This despite the fact that forensics had been up to the Roberts residence yesterday, so he knew full well that skid marks on the road, as well as a large hole in the neighbors' hedge, bore out Nikki's version of events. There *had* definitely been two cars, both definitely traveling at speed, and neither of them had been Nikki's Mercedes X-Class. Flecks of red paintwork had been retrieved from the shrubbery, bearing out her claims about the color of the witness's car. Mick's 'disbelief' was nothing but pure pig-headedness and a determination to cast Nikki as a perpetrator, not a victim.

He yawned rudely at her now. 'So you took down the wrong number. But you never thought to get this guy's name? Or his license plate?'

'I was in shock,' Nikki said, through gritted teeth. 'Someone had just tried to crush me to death, Detective, and they damn nearly succeeded.' She rubbed her eyes like a tired child. 'My patient is dead. My assistant is dead. I have other patients in fear for their safety, for their lives. You're the one who insisted that I'm the link between these murders. And it looks like you were right, because now it appears some maniac is trying to kill me too. So you'll have to forgive me if I wasn't at my most clear-headed.'

Johnson gave her a withering look. 'I'll tell you what I think, *Doctor.* I think you made this whole thing up. The SUV, the witness, the race-car driver. It's all an invention.'

'What?' Nikki looked at him, incredulous.

'Your husband's gone,' Johnson went on. 'You're all alone. No one's paying you any attention. So you dream up someone else, some knight in shining armor to come and rescue you. You invent some spurious attack, and then you sit here and tell us all about this handsome stranger, who can validate your story except . . . *oh no!* . . . you happened to take down his number wrong.'

Nikki turned to Goodman. 'Your partner appears to have lost his mind.'

Goodman, who wholeheartedly agreed, glared at Johnson.

'I'm sorry, Dr Roberts,' he began, but Johnson cut him off.

'Don't apologize to her!' he shouted, banging his fist on the table. 'If anybody's crazy here, it sure as hell ain't me. I mean, come on. A mysterious truck. Blacked-out windows. No plates. No injuries. No *witnesses.* It's like something out of a bad late-night movie, Dr Roberts. One that casts you very firmly as the victim. Surprise, surprise.'

Nikki stood up. Smoothing down her pencil skirt in a dignified manner, she turned away from Mick Johnson and addressed herself only to Goodman.

'Please let me know if you make any progress, Detective. In the meantime, I'm going home. I'm afraid I don't have time for your friend's bullshit armchair psychology, or for his puerile insults. Good day.'

*She really is magnificent when she's pissed,* Goodman thought, watching Nikki strut out of the room, her stiletto heels clacking briskly on the linoleum floor as she walked.

'"*Puerile*"!' He smirked patronizingly at Johnson. 'You'll have to look that one up, Mick, eh?'

'She's a bitch,' Johnson grunted, unamused. 'A bitch and a liar, wasting our time.'

Goodman stood up, exasperated. 'What is going on with you and this woman? What happened to "open minds"?'

'*She* happened,' Johnson snapped. 'I'm only calling it like I see it. I don't believe anyone tried to kill her. I think she's a fantasist.'

'For Christ's sake, Mick. We have evidence, actual, forensic evidence.'

'A couple of tire skids? Give me a break. They don't prove shit and you know it.'

'Why would she make up something like this?' Goodman threw his arms wide in frustration. 'Why?'

Johnson shrugged. 'For attention.'

'Whose attention? Yours? No offense, Mick, but I don't think she's that interested.'

'I don't know, Lou. Maybe yours,' Johnson shot back, irritated. 'Maybe she sees your tongue hanging out and your pants bulging every time she walks into a room and she wants a closer look.'

Goodman shook his head. What was this, third grade?

'I don't know what her motives are and I don't really care,' Johnson went on. 'All I know is that I don't trust her. I think she's messed up in the head.'

Exhausted, Goodman let it go. There was no reasoning with Johnson in this sort of mood.

Interpreting his partner's silence as a sign the conversation was over, Johnson changed the subject. 'Any more leads on Brandon Grolsch?'

'None we can use.' A troubled look came over Goodman's face. 'I traced the girl who wrote to Valentina Baden about his overdose. Rachel Kelsey, her name was.'

'"Was"?'

'Uh huh,' Goodman confirmed with a sigh. 'OD'd eight weeks ago. Her family buried her down near San Diego. Twenty-two years old.'

Johnson scowled. 'What the hell is happening with these kids?'

'I know,' Goodman muttered. 'It's tragic.'

'I'm sure Nikki Roberts is involved in these murders somehow,' said Johnson, animated again suddenly. 'I don't know how. But I'm sure of it. I feel like we're *this* close to seeing the connection. But then poof, it's gone.'

Goodman didn't feel 'this close' to anything. He just wished that Johnson would quit harassing Dr Roberts and shutting the door on potential new leads she gave them, like the witness in the red car. Because the depressing truth was, if Brandon Grolsch was dead, the driver of the SUV with blacked-out windows might be the only suspect they had.

*    *    *

'So I've got a question for you.' Haddon Defoe smiled warmly across the lunch table at Nikki. He hadn't seen her since the night he'd broken the news about Trey Raymond's death. Thankfully all the awkwardness and pain of that encounter was absent from today's meeting. It almost felt like old times.

'Fire away,' said Nikki.

Haddon fixed her with a gimlet stare and asked seriously: 'What exactly *is* a Meyer lemon?'

Nikki laughed. They were in Venice, at one of the newest and most self-consciously trendy bistros on Abbot Kinney, where the menu definitely scored an 'A' for pretention.

'And while we're at it, what's an *heirloom* tomato, a *Dungeness* crab, and a *Jidori* chicken?' asked Haddon. 'It's like invasion of the killer adjectives on these menus. Whatever happened to good ol' fried chicken?'

'Oh, they still have that,' said Nikki, slicing into the last, juicy stem of her steamed asparagus. 'About six blocks away at El Pollo Loco, for a tenth of the price. But we both know that's not your style, Haddon.'

Haddon was glad to see her looking happier, even teasing him as she used to before Doug's accident. Ever since Doug's death, Nikki had changed, a dark cloud descending over her that was part grief, part anger and, Haddon suspected, part utter bewilderment at the things she'd learned about her husband after his death, sides to him she'd never known before.

'Did you want dessert?' Haddon asked, finishing up his crayfish (with Meyer lemon crème fraiche). 'Or shall we get going?'

'Let's go,' said Nikki. 'I don't think I'm in the mood for deconstructed, gluten-free chocolate ganache.'

They were headed to the new Venice clinic, an off-shoot of the downtown facility that he and Doug had run together for the last eight years. Doug had been heavily involved in the planning for Venice, an LA neighborhood that, despite its rising real estate values, remained home to a growing number of homeless and mentally ill, many of them long-term addicts. Doug had helped pick the site for the new clinic, negotiating bargain-basement rates on everything and getting a variety of local artisans and contractors to revamp the building, most of them giving up their time for free. Now, of course, it would be Haddon who would run the place, alone. They'd only opened a couple of months ago but already the clinic was full to capacity every single day, with lines of would-be patients forming around the block from before 7 a.m.

Haddon had made the offer of lunch and a tour before Trey's murder, and was both pleased and surprised that Nikki had kept the date. For Nikki, it wasn't even a question. Haddon Defoe was a kind man, and a precious link to Doug and happier days, days that seemed so long ago now. She'd come to today's lunch straight from the police station and her bruising interview with Detective Johnson. She decided not to share that with Haddon, or to tell him about Tuesday night's attack at the house. Once she told him, he would likely insist on getting involved and trying to help, keeping an eye on her. Nikki knew better than anyone that Haddon didn't have time for that, not with running the downtown drop-in center *and* Venice, *and* having his own medical practice to manage at Cedars. Besides, what could he do really, other than worry? He could hardly guard her around the clock, and Nikki wouldn't have wanted that, even if he could.

As they walked from the restaurant to the clinic, it struck Nikki what a difference six blocks could make. Within minutes, overpriced clothes and antiques stores had given way to run-down 1920s cottages and shabby corner drugstores. A few minutes more and it was all vacant lots, chain-link fences and weeds. Up-ended shopping carts lay littered around amid the familiar detritus of despair that Nikki recognized from the downtown neighborhoods Doug use to work in: old shoes, cans, bicycle parts and trash of all kinds, including discarded needles, foil and other drug paraphernalia. Here and there amid this sea of filth, a few buildings popped up, many old but some new and clean and hopeful, stores and apartment blocks and offices, even an art gallery, trying its luck. Like the palm trees swaying tall and proud, these seemed to offer the promise of something better. After a few more minutes, Haddon strode up the steps of one of them proudly, a whitewashed wooden building on a corner lot that had once been a large home with a wraparound porch and gardens that would have stretched for blocks on all directions. A simple sign out front read *Roberts-Defoe Venice Clinic – All Welcome.*

'Here she is.' Haddon turned expectantly to Nikki. 'What do you think? He'd have liked it, wouldn't he?'

It took Nikki a second to compose her emotions. 'He'd have loved it, Haddon. Show me inside.'

As soon as they walked through the doors, the clean, hopeful, white-picket-fence vibe of the exterior was gone, vanished like a popped bubble. Men and women – but mostly men – lay sprawled out on floors in the corridors, or bent double in misery on hard plastic chairs that had been nailed to the floor. In the two waiting rooms, wretches in various stages of addiction stared or rocked or moaned or yelled out angrily, demanding help, lashing out either at the real nursing staff who patiently attempted to keep order, or at the imagined adversaries created by their addled, psychotic minds.

Two boys in particular caught Nikki's attention as she followed Haddon through the bedlam to his office. Both were young, late teens, and white, although that word no longer accurately described their skin color. Leaning helplessly against the wall, side by side, these kids literally looked green. Flakes of skin were peeling off their forearms, necks and faces, like old paint coming off a wall.

'Is that heroin?' Nikki whispered in Haddon's ear. 'Poor things. They look like they have blood poisoning.'

Haddon led her into his office and closed the door before answering.

'It's not heroin,' he told Nikki. 'But it's similar. It's a desomorphine derivative called Crocodile – or *Krokodil* in Russian. The Russians are the ones bringing it over here.'

'Because of what it does to the skin?' Nikki asked.

Haddon nodded. 'It's pretty horrific. Did Doug ever talk to you about this?'

Nikki shook her head. 'I don't think so.'

'It's sort of the "new new thing" in LA right now,' Haddon explained. 'The Russians are basically making a big push to maneuver the Mexicans out of the drug business here, or at least to set up some viable competition. It's a trade war, and those kids you saw out there are the victims. Krok's the dealers' latest weapon of choice.

'It's a problem, because it can be easily home-made, which means the supply gets contaminated with all kinds of shit: paint thinner, hydrochloric acid – you name it. It's been huge in Russia for a long time, but it's still relatively new here. Gaining ground though.'

'Are you seeing more kids like that?' Nikki couldn't get the image of the two green-skinned boys out of her head.

'Oh yeah. Every week,' Haddon confirmed grimly. 'Like I say, it's a trade war. So the Russians came in and wowed everyone with this stuff, which has a bigger high than meth, by the way. But now the Mexican cartels are pushing back with their own brand of Krok, supposedly cleaner than the Russian product – which wouldn't be hard. The Mexican stuff is more expensive, but still cheap enough to be accessible. So yeah, long story short, it's cheap, it's unbelievably potent and it's everywhere.'

'Can I do anything to help?' Nikki asked.

Haddon was touched.

'Not really, sweetheart.' He squeezed her hand. 'Although I appreciate the offer. Right now I'd say you have more than enough to deal with without throwing this chaos into the mix.'

He waved around vaguely, a gesture meant to encompass the drop-in center, drug addiction generally and all that went along with it.

'Doug always tried to protect you from the worst of it, you know. I know he'd want me to do the same, especially now, with what happened to Trey and the Flannagan girl and everything. Have the police made any progress, by the way?'

'No.'

All of a sudden her tone was harsh and abrupt. In an instant, something had changed in Nikki, like a light switch going off. Haddon had seen this reaction before. The mere mention of Doug's name at the 'wrong' time could do it. Nikki's face would harden and her muscles tense.

'I'm sorry,' Haddon said gently. 'I didn't mean to upset you.'

'You didn't,' Nikki lied, fighting back tears. 'I'm fine.'

They made it through the rest of the tour without incident. Nikki met the staff and volunteers, shaking hands and enduring the many reminiscences and condolences about Doug. Half an hour later she left. To Haddon's surprise, she hugged him tightly in farewell.

'I'm sorry again, about before,' she said. 'It was when you said something about Doug "protecting me". It made me think about all the things he kept from me. All the secrets. You know? It's hard sometimes.'

'I know it is,' said Haddon, hugging her back. 'You don't have to apologize, certainly not to me. Just try to focus on yourself, Nikki, and on the future. Look forward, never back.'

Nikki smiled. 'OK, Dr Defoe. I'll try.'

\* \* \*

Haddon watched her walk back towards her car, until she turned the corner out of sight. He said a silent prayer that she would find the strength to take his advice and let go of the past. The alternative didn't bear thinking about, for any of them.

Dr Haddon Defoe knew better than most that some doors should never be opened.

His friend Doug Roberts had protected his wife from more than she knew.

# 19

The sun had already started to set by the time Lou Goodman arrived at Avenue of the Stars. The towers of Century City looked dreamlike, bathed in the pinkish-orange light of a perfect LA evening, and the palm trees along the avenue swayed drunkenly in the warm breeze.

Badge in hand, he approached the front desk.

'Detective Louis Goodman, homicide. I need access to suit 706,' he told the Latina receptionist, in the firm-but-friendly tone he always employed when winging it without a search warrant. 'I assume you have a key?'

The girl smiled back helpfully. This cop was handsome, not like the usual Columbo lookalikes. 'I do have a key, but you won't need it,' she told him. 'Dr Roberts came in about an hour ago. I'm pretty sure she's still up there. Second bank of elevators, on your left.'

'Thank you,' said Goodman, hiding his momentary sting of disappointment. He'd hoped to snoop around Nikki's office alone. *What's she doing here, this time of day?* But he quickly regrouped. Perhaps, after all, Nikki being here was an opportunity? Johnson had been so rude to her at the station this morning, he'd shut her down before she'd been able to tell them anything really useful. Now might be the time to rectify that.

Taking the elevator up to the seventh floor, he padded along the hallway to Nikki's suite. The door to her waiting room was ajar. Goodman slipped in, unheard, his footsteps muffled by the sound of a shredder.

Nikki stood with her back to him, utterly engrossed in what she was doing. A large, almost empty cardboard box sat at her feet. Reaching into it, Nikki began feeding the remaining documents into the greedy mouth of the machine. Goodman watched as it spat out confetti at the other end, into a tray already full to overflowing.

'Hey there.'

Nikki spun around with a gasp, her face flooding with color.

'Oh my God! You scared the life out of me!'

'Sorry.' Goodman raised a curious eyebrow at the sheaf of papers still in her hand. 'What have you got there?'

'Oh, nothing exciting,' said Nikki. 'I'm just tidying up.' Regaining her composure, she slipped the remaining papers into the machine. 'Long overdue housekeeping. Don't worry,' she added. 'It's not vital patient records or anything like that. Before your partner comes up with yet another reason to distrust me.'

'Glad to hear it,' Goodman smiled. It was easy to play good cop with a woman as attractive as Dr Nikki Roberts.

'So what brings *you* here on a Saturday night, Detective?' Nikki asked, switching off the machine.

'Actually, I came to apologize. About this morning.' The lie tripped off Goodman's tongue. 'Detective Johnson had no right to talk to you the way that he did.'

'I agree,' said Nikki. 'Although I think that's his apology to make, not yours. Don't you?'

Goodman shrugged. 'We're partners. And honestly, apologies are not Mick's strong point.'

Nikki laughed. 'Now why am I not surprised?' She liked Detective Goodman and found him remarkably easy to talk to. 'I'm not lying, you know,' she added, more seriously. 'Someone really did try to run me down the other night. Someone who knows where I live.'

'I believe you,' said Goodman, truthfully. 'For what it's worth, I think Johnson believes you too. Our techs found plenty of evidence to back up your story.'

'Really?' Nikki frowned, perplexed. 'Then why was he accusing me of being a fantasist? What has he got against me?'

'I don't know,' said Goodman, seizing the moment. 'But I'm hoping maybe together we can figure it out. Can I buy you a drink, Dr Roberts?'

*    *    *

He took her to the bar at Dan Tana's, possibly the least private place in the whole of Los Angeles. Nikki ordered a Jack Daniels, straight up, which she downed in one gulp. Encouraged, Goodman gestured to the barman to leave them the bottle.

'Do you think whoever tried to kill me the other night was the same person who killed Lisa and Trey?' Nikki got straight to the point.

'Either the same person or someone connected to them. Yes, I do.' Goodman sipped his drink. 'I actually believe you may have been the target all along.'

He explained his theory about the raincoat Nikki had loaned Lisa Flannagan the night she died potentially leading to a case of mistaken identity. Combined with Tuesday night's overt attempt on her own life, as well as the fact that Nikki was the only known link between Trey and Lisa, the evidence was mounting.

'Let's say you're right,' Nikki responded calmly. 'Let's say this person has been after me all along. What do you think their motive could be for wanting me killed?'

'Right now, I don't know,' Goodman admitted. 'But the fact that whoever killed Lisa and Trey tortured both of them first suggests maybe it has something to do with information. People torture victims to get them to talk, right?'

Nikki thought about it. 'I suppose so. Either that or because they're sadists. Because they enjoy it.'

Goodman gazed into his drink. This was also a possibility.

'Is it true they found dead human skin cells on Lisa's body?' Nikki asked bluntly.

Goodman looked shocked. 'Who told you that?'

'I read it online,' said Nikki. 'There's a whole bunch of nonsense on the net about "killer zombies" roaming the streets of LA.'

Goodman groaned. That was all they needed. Once an investigation started getting leaks, especially a case as 'juicy' as this one, it was only a matter of time before it became a tabloid free-for-all.

'Is it true?' Nikki pressed him.

'That Lisa and Trey's killer is a zombie?' Goodman quipped. 'No. That's not true.'

'That they found dead skin cells?' said Nikki.

'I can't talk about specifics,' Goodman deflected her. 'But I will say all those conspiracy theories are a waste of time. The question you asked me before was a better one. About motive. And while you're right about sadists being out there, my guess is that whoever is behind this believes you *know* something. Something that Trey or Lisa might also have known. Now I don't know whether that "something" is about a patient of yours? A secret somebody wanted to stay hidden? Or maybe someone your husband treated, in one of his clinics? But my guess is . . .' Goodman took another long sip of bourbon, '. . . you *do* know.'

Nikki looked at him despairingly. 'You're wrong! I have no idea. My God, if I knew what this was about, if I knew anything, don't you think I'd tell you? I cared about Trey. And I cared about Lisa too, although in a different way.'

'Did you?' Goodman raised an eyebrow archly.

'Yes!' Nikki insisted. 'Professionally, as her therapist. Yes, I cared. But more to the point, I care about myself. Do you think I want to be murdered? That I want to be run down outside my own house? Believe me, no one's more motivated to catch this maniac than I am, Detective Goodman.'

'It's Lou.' Goodman poured them both another drink. 'And no, of course I don't think you want to get hurt. I'm not suggesting you know consciously what it is the killer is after. Only that I suspect that, deep down, *you* hold the key to this riddle. And that in the end, only you can unlock it.'

He sipped his liquor, and Nikki did the same. She was starting to feel a definite buzz now, which, mingled with the recent chain of bizarre and traumatic events, was having a distinctly disinhibiting effect. She wasn't sure whether he reached for her hand, or if it was the other way around. Either way, she felt a rush of blood to her groin as their fingers entwined. After months of wrestling with her complex feelings for Anne Bateman, it was almost a relief to experience straight-forward sexual desire. Whatever it was Nikki felt for Anne, it wasn't *this*. When her eyes met and locked with Goodman's, it took a real effort of will not to lean in and kiss him, to give herself up to a sensa-tion she hadn't felt in so long.

Goodman obviously felt it too. When he spoke, his voice was hoarse with desire.

'Why did you become a psychologist?'

It was the last question Nikki had expected. She wasn't sure she had an answer. 'I don't know, exactly. Lots of reasons, I guess. I knew I didn't want to do anything boring, like being a lawyer or an accoun-tant. Medicine kind of appealed. But I've never been good with blood, so surgery was out.'

'Really?' Goodman was amused. 'You're squeamish?'

'Kind of.' Nikki blushed. 'Why did you become a cop?'

'Ah.' Goodman sat back, his mood and expression visibly changing. 'That was . . . I liked the idea of stopping bad guys I guess. Sounds stupid, right?'

'Not at all,' said Nikki.

'When I was a kid, some guys ripped off my dad,' Goodman went on. 'Common fraudsters really, nothing sophisticated. But they suckered him into some deal and he lost everything. Our house. His marriage to my mom. I hated those guys.'

'I can imagine,' Nikki nodded, listening closely. The liquor had loosened his tongue, but this wasn't the drink talking; the emotions pouring out of him were real. 'Did your dad ever re-marry, or get his life back on track?'

Goodman laughed awkwardly. 'Unfortunately not. He killed himself a week before my tenth birthday. Gassed himself in our garage. The house *and* the car were repossessed the next day.'

Nikki gasped. 'Oh my God. How terrible! I am so sorry, Lou.'

He waved an embarrassed hand, as if to brush the conversation aside. 'It's OK. I mean, it was terrible, but it motivated me, in lots of ways. Not only becoming a cop. It taught me the importance of money, of financial security. And never letting anyone else scam you, or control you. I'm master of my own destiny, you know?'

Nikki nodded, although she wasn't sure she did know. The sad truth was she'd never felt fully in control of her own life. Less so now than ever, in fact.

'Can you think of anything unusual or surprising or strange that happened in the months leading up to Lisa's murder?' Goodman asked, bringing the conversation back into safer, less personal waters.

Nikki closed her eyes and squeezed his hand again, more tightly this time. She felt closer to him now, since he'd trusted her with one of his own, painful secrets.

'Happened to Lisa, or to me?'

'Either.'

'Well . . .' Nikki swallowed. Her whole throat suddenly felt dry. 'Lisa left Willie Baden. I guess you could call that surprising.'

Goodman nodded. 'How about you?'

Nikki opened her eyes and gazed directly into Goodman's.

'The most surprising thing that happened to me,' she said matter-of-factly, 'was losing my husband.'

Raising her hand to his lips, Goodman kissed it.

'Tell me what happened,' he urged Nikki softly. 'Tell me everything.'

\* \* \*

At the very back of the bar, alone in a corner booth, a man looked on unnoticed while Dr Nikki Roberts and Detective Lou Goodman leaned into one another like limpets.

*She's got him where she wants him,* the man thought, watching Nikki's lips part as Goodman's hand toyed with her hair, his blue eyes fixed on her green ones. Whatever sob story she was telling him, it was working. She was reeling him in like a credulous fish. *Fool.*

The man nursed his beer discreetly as Goodman paid the check, then he and Dr Roberts walked out onto Santa Monica Boulevard, hand in hand like a pair of teenagers. It was frustrating, being an observer, unable to act. He liked to think of himself as a man of action. But the past few weeks had taught him that patience was also a virtue. He wouldn't have to stay passive for long.

Soon the time for watching would be past.

Very soon . . .

# 20

Detective Mick Johnson watched as Carter Berkeley fiddled with his shirt, picking anxiously at the platinum Tiffany cufflinks with a perfectly manicured fingernail. It struck Johnson that everything about Nikki Roberts' rich banker patient was 'manicured', from the neatly trimmed lawns of his Holmby Hills estate, to the gleaming collection of vintage Jaguar sports cars in his garage, to the immaculately furnished interior of his home office, where the two men now sat. Even the words Carter chose to explain what had happened seemed carefully chosen.

Last night while he was out at dinner, according to Carter, a rat – a dead, poisoned, rat – had been left at the foot of his bed as a mafia-style 'warning'.

'There was no note or anything like that,' he told Johnson, twirling the cufflink between finger and thumb. 'But obviously it was intended to intimidate. And it hit the mark, Detective. I don't mind telling you, I was terrified. I *am* terrified. Especially after the other two murders. It was rather a stroke of luck that you were already in my schedule today, or I'd have been calling you out here.'

Johnson nodded, looking again around the room with all its polished wood and neatly arranged books, shelf after shelf of self-help and business manuals. Everything around this man was controlled and ordered, the result of careful thought and planning. Everything was perfect, on the outside. Inside Carter Berkeley's head, however, it was a different matter.

Johnson had read Nikki's notes earlier: '*Neurotic. Delusional. Convinced he is being pursued by Mexican criminals but presents no evidence to support this belief. Long history of anxiety. Childhood trauma?? (Spent time in Mexico as teen/young adult. Did something happen?) Regressive/immature in intimate relationships. Excessively controlling.*'

It pained Johnson to agree with Dr Roberts on anything, but her assessment of Carter Berkeley chimed with his own. Although he would probably have added 'attention-seeking' to the list. Perhaps Dr Roberts couldn't see that because she suffered from it herself? Carter's rat story was obviously an invention, a deliberate attempt to place himself at the center of the drama surrounding the two murders.

*He needs to feel important,* Johnson thought. *Either that or he's trying to distract me from something else. Some evidence he doesn't want us to find.*

'I assume you have security here, sir?' Johnson asked, although he already knew the answer. He'd passed the bored, poorly trained guards on his way in, and observed the CCTV cameras throughout the property.

'Naturally,' said Carter. 'It's a valuable property.'

'Including cameras?'

'Yes. But not in the master bedroom.'

The cufflink twirling took on a more frenzied pace.

'Not in the master bedroom,' Johnson repeated. 'Why's that?'

The banker gave a smirk worthy of a thirteen-year-old. *Puerile,* as Dr Roberts would say. 'I'm sure you can take an educated guess, Detective. My security guards receive a live feed from those cameras. Let's just say I value my privacy. Besides, I don't need cameras in the master suite. All the entrances to the house are filmed, as is the upstairs hallway. Anyone coming in or out would be visible.'

'Right,' said Johnson. 'And I imagine you reviewed the footage from those cameras yourself. After you found the rat.'

'Naturally.'

'But no one was there?'

'No one other than my regular household staff, no. That's the uncanny thing.' Carter twisted the cufflink again, so violently he was in danger of ripping it off.

'So.' Johnson asked the obvious question. 'How do you suppose this "warning" was placed in your room?'

Carter looked irked. 'I have no idea. You're the detective. You tell me.'

'Well, if no one else showed up on the footage, then it had to be put there by a staff member, didn't it, sir?' Johnson said, with a patience he didn't feel.

'That's not possible,' Carter insisted with a shake of the head. 'I trust my household employees. They've all been subject to exhaustive background checks – and I mean exhaustive. There's no way—'

'Perhaps you can show me the rat, sir?' Johnson interrupted, standing up. 'I'll have it removed and we can run some tests.'

'Show you? Oh no, I can't show it to you.'

*I knew it,* Johnson thought. *Delusional is right.*

'And why's that, sir?' he asked wearily. He had no idea how therapists like Nikki Roberts dealt with this shit on a daily basis. Didn't they ever want to punch these people's lights out?

'Well, I found it late last night, as I explained,' Carter began defensively. 'My housekeeper doesn't arrive until eight in the morning and naturally I couldn't leave the thing lying there till then. God knows what diseases it might carry. So I took it out to the trash myself.'

'You disposed of the evidence,' said Johnson.

'I had to.'

'And did anyone else see this rat, before you threw it out?'

'Well, no. Like I say, it was late—'

Johnson got to his feet.

'Where are your trash cans, sir? Might it still be out there?'

At least Carter Berkeley had the decency to blush.

'I'm afraid they'll be empty by now. The garbage men came early this morning. I guess I should have considered that . . .'

*   *   *

It took Johnson over an hour to drive back to headquarters, in heavy rush-hour traffic. He arrived in a foul mood. His visit to Carter Berkeley had confirmed the banker's mental instability, but not much else. There'd been no new leads relating to either murder – Carter didn't know Lisa, had barely interacted with Trey and had never heard of Brandon Grolsch. Not that he was a suspect, but he also happened to have cast-iron alibis for both crimes. In other words, the trip had been a complete waste of Johnson's time.

His spirits weren't improved when Goodman cornered him the moment he walked into the building and announced they'd been summoned to the chief's office for a progress report.

'Now?' Johnson groaned.

'Right now. In fact,' Goodman looked at his watch, 'he's pissed you're late.'

'Late? How am I late?' Johnson protested. 'He only just called the meeting! I was in here at seven thirty this morning, for Christ's sake. Which reminds me, *w*here the hell were you?'

'Sorry,' Goodman mumbled. 'I had a late night. Something came up.'

Something *had* come up, last night at the bar with Nikki Roberts, and again this morning as Goodman lay in bed alone, thinking about her warm, slender, needy body and what might have been yesterday evening, if only he'd allowed himself to give in to it. He wanted to. God knew he wanted to, wanted *her*, Nikki, more than was good for him, or for this investigation. Despite her opening up to him about her husband's death and her struggles with grief, Goodman had resisted the temptation to take things further – for now. But in terms of new leads the fact was he had nothing concrete to show for last night's investigative efforts beyond his still-raging hangover.

'Goodman! Johnson! Anytime today!' Chief Brody's booming voice echoed down the hall, slicing into Goodman's aching head like a meat-cleaver.

'Sir.'

Both men shuffled obediently into their boss's office, taking the seats he indicated.

'So,' Brody began grimly. 'Your case.'

A heavyset man in his early sixties with a quick temper, not unlike a darker version of Mick Johnson, Chief Brody was evidently not in a good mood either.

'We've got two bodies, both cut up like rag dolls. No arrests. No suspects. We've got a leading psychiatrist getting death threats. And as one of the victims, her patient, was a hot piece of ass with a married, billionaire boyfriend, we've got the press all over it like mold on a stinking cheese.'

'Yes, sir,' said Goodman, looking at the floor.

'But it gets even better,' Brody went on, glaring at both detectives. 'We've also got a leak! The internet's going crazy with trash talk about some zombie killer on the loose. This morning they were covering this zombie nonsense on the NBC 4 news! I mean, what the hell, boys?'

'The leak could be from the ME's office,' Johnson said defensively.

'Do I look like I care where it's from?' Brody countered.

Johnson pressed on: 'Jenny Foyle found skin cells under the first victim's fingernails that were a DNA match for hairs found on the second victim. Both belonged to a junkie called Brandon Grolsch, whom we believe to be deceased. That tallies with what Jenny found, sir. The dead cells under the nails.'

Chief Brody sighed deeply. 'So you're telling me your chief suspect – your only suspect – is dead?'

'Brandon Grolsch isn't a suspect,' said Goodman. 'He died of an overdose eight months ago. Our working theory is that the perp had access to Brandon's corpse. That he deliberately planted Brandon's DNA on the bodies, knowing that Grolsch was officially still "missing", in hopes we'd pin the murders on a dead man and stop looking.'

'That's one of the working theories,' muttered Johnson.

Chief Brody grimaced. 'What's the other one?'

Goodman's face echoed the question. Last he heard, he and Johnson were on the same page about this.

'It doesn't involve zombies, does it?' asked Brody.

'No, sir. It doesn't.' Johnson cleared his throat. 'It involves Dr Nicola Roberts, the psychologist at the center of all this.'

Goodman rolled his eyes. Johnson ignored him.

'Detective Goodman and I have spent the four days sifting through Dr Roberts' patient records and session notes, among other things. We both agreed that she was the obvious link between the two victims. Goodman felt – feels – that Dr Roberts herself may have been the killer's target.'

Brody's eyes narrowed. 'But you don't agree?'

'No, sir, I don't,' said Johnson. 'Dr Roberts' notes on the first victim, her patient Lisa Flannagan, reveal as much about Roberts herself as they do about Flannagan. We know she was deeply disapproving of Lisa's affair with Willie Baden, and of her abortion, and that she was less than sympathetic about Lisa's struggles with Vicodin. The tone of Roberts' comments struck me as odd for a therapist, someone whose job is to listen without judging. But these notes are full of judgment, sir. And they're full of rage, too.'

Chief Brody turned to Goodman. 'You've read them, Detective. Do you agree?'

Goodman shifted uncomfortably from foot to foot. It was true that Nikki's notes on some of her patients, including Lisa, could seem unduly hostile at times. Then again, they were never intended to be read by outsiders, but were merely personal musings, aide-memoires to help with future sessions. More importantly, the picture Johnson was painting of Nikki pointedly failed to mention his *own* rage towards *her*, his relentless twisting of the evidence to try and make Nikki look guilty and paint her in the blackest possible light.

'The notes do make judgments, sir,' he admitted grudgingly.

Johnson let out a mocking laugh. 'Judgments? Roberts makes it abundantly clear that she's morally repulsed by this young woman. She talks about Lisa Flannagan needing to be "made accountable" for her actions, about the suffering she's caused Baden's wife and others. It's a theme that runs through a lot of the notes.'

'What's a theme?' the chief asked, confused.

'Nikki Roberts has a grudge against mistresses,' Johnson said matter-of-factly.

'That's a stretch, Mick,' Goodman jumped in.

'Is it? I don't think so,' said Johnson, warming to his theme. 'So anyways, her notes got me thinking about *why* she might bear that particular grudge,' he continued, 'and I realized, it must have had something to do with her husband.'

'Isn't the husband dead?' Chief Brody sighed, rubbing his temples wearily. He could feel a headache coming on.

'Yes, he is.' Johnson sounded excited, as if he was moving towards some sort of punchline. 'Dr Douglas Roberts was killed in an unexplained auto accident on the 405 last year. But guess who he was with when he died?'

Chief Brody and Goodman both stared at Johnson. Neither of them were in the mood for guessing games.

'His mistress!' Johnson announced triumphantly. 'Some Russian chick. She was in the passenger seat. Died too, killed instantly. The first Dr Roberts knew about her husband's affair was the day he died, when the emergency crew cut two bodies out of the wreckage! Can you imagine what that must feel like? The pain? The humiliation? When the whole world believed you had some perfect, fairytale marriage? Including you?'

Johnson was looking directly at Goodman now, with an infuriating *I told you so* expression on his face.

Goodman struggled to process this new information. Nikki had opened up to him about her husband's death only last night. She'd alluded to feelings of anger, mixed in with the loss, and to finding things out about Doug that she hadn't known before. But she'd never said anything about a mistress. Apart from anything else, Goodman found it hard to believe that anybody lucky enough to be married to Nikki Roberts would *want* a mistress. Willie Baden cheating on over-the-hill Valentina was one thing, but this? It almost made him wonder whether Johnson was making the whole thing up.

'How'd you know this?' he asked, more aggressively than he'd intended.

'It was reported online,' Johnson answered. 'Not at the time but a few weeks later. A brief, one-line mention of a female passenger. But I did some digging with Doug and Nikki's friends, and they all confirmed it. The dirty secret she's been trying to hide, how the anger's been eating away at her—'

'OK, so the shrink's husband was playing away,' Chief Brody said gruffly, cutting him off. 'What does this have to do with our murders?'

'Well, sir, I'm curious about this whole mistress thing, especially as Roberts never so much as hinted about it to us,' said Johnson. 'So two days ago I go looking for the accident report, to see what I can find about Doug Roberts and this Russian woman he was seeing.'

Goodman could contain himself no longer. 'You never told me any of this!' he exploded.

'Hey, you were "busy", remember?' Johnson shot back. 'You haven't exactly been Captain Transparency yourself, my friend. In any case, there was nothing to tell because, guess what? Turns out, there *is* no accident report.'

'What do you mean?' Chief Brody asked. He was growing tired of riddles.

'Exactly what I say,' said Johnson. 'There is no report in the system. Either one was never filed, or it was filed but someone deleted it later.'

This was interesting. But it still wasn't a theory on who killed Lisa Flannagan and Trey Raymond, as Chief Brody pointed out.

'I'm getting there, sir, I swear,' insisted Johnson. 'So now I'm really curious, because this accident *did* happen. It was in all the papers at the time, along with a big, whitewashed obituary in the *LA Times* about what a great and saintly guy Doug Roberts was, his beautiful, grieving widow, they're both so young, yadda yadda yadda. But no mention of the Russian broad. That little nugget only came out later, online. So anyways, I tracked down the shop where they took what was left of Doug Roberts' Tesla after the accident. Spoke to an engineer there who told me they'd checked out the car's computer systems and it looked as though they might have been messed with before the crash.'

'"Messed with"?'

'Hacked into remotely,' Johnson explained. 'He couldn't be sure, but it looked to him like faulty code might have affected both the steering and the brakes, once the car reached a certain speed. He says he told his boss, who said he would report it to the police.'

'And did he?' Chief Brody asked.

'There's no way of knowing. Because like I said, there is no report. And because Damon's boss dropped dead of a heart attack on Easter morning.'

Chief Brody took this in silently. As did Goodman.

'So,' the chief asked Johnson eventually. 'Your theory?'

'My theory, sir, is that Nikki Roberts is a psychopath. She finds out her husband's doing someone else, while she's in the middle of fertility treatment; totally loses it, pays someone to tamper with his car. She stages an accident, killing him and the mistress.'

'For Christ's sake!' Goodman muttered, but Johnson was on a roll.

'The plan works like a dream. Her husband and his Russian fancy woman are both dead, and no one suspects a thing. She's emboldened, but she's still mad as hell about the affair, and that anger needs somewhere to go. So she develops a grudge against all mistresses, all marriage wreckers – like her patient Lisa Flannagan. It becomes an obsession with her. And remember, at this point she's already killed once and gotten away with it. I think Nikki Roberts had Lisa Flannagan murdered. I think she paid a hitman to do it, possibly using Brandon Grolsch's remains as some sort of forensic cover story, like Goodman suggested.'

'Don't drag me into this!' Goodman's frustration was mounting. 'This is total bullshit, Mick. You have no evidence against Nikki Roberts. None!'

'I don't agree.' For once Johnson kept his cool. 'It's circumstantial, sure, but there's a pattern here, a pattern of deceit. She said she was "fond" of Lisa Flannagan, but her notes plainly show otherwise. She said she loved her husband, but multiple friends have attested to her flashes of rage over his affair. I think Nikki Roberts is a very smart woman. But I also think she's a pathological liar and a murderer. She's behind this, Chief. I know it in my bones.'

'Your *bones*,' Goodman scoffed. 'What does that even mean? You've had it in for her from the start.'

'And you wanted to sleep with her from the start!' Johnson retorted furiously. 'It's clouded your judgment.'

'All right, all right,' Chief Brody stepped in. 'Knock it off, both of you. What about Trey Raymond?' he asked Johnson. 'Weren't he and Nikki Roberts close?'

'On the surface, maybe. But underneath, who knows?' said Johnson. 'Maybe Trey knew about Doug's affair all along and helped hide it from Nikki? Or maybe he found out she was behind Doug's "accident"? Or that she killed Lisa Flannagan, who we know Trey had the hots for. I don't have the details yet, sir,' Johnson admitted. 'Like I said, it's a theory.'

'OK.' Chief Brody laid his palms down on the desk in a gesture meant to indicate the conversation was over, at least for the moment. 'It's a theory, and I'm open to it.'

'Chief!' Goodman protested, but Brody cut him off.

'Just like I'm open to the frankly *insane* idea that someone stole a corpse in order to pin these murders on some "missing" junkie. OK, Detective Goodman? I'm an equal opportunities employer. But what I need now isn't theories. It's facts. I need hard evidence. I need an arrest, boys.'

'Sir,' Johnson mumbled submissively.

'Mick, until you get me that evidence, Goodman's right. You gotta stop harassing Nikki Roberts and her patients.'

'Harassing?' Johnson bridled. 'Who's harassing?'

'I've had three complaints, Detective. *Four* official complaints. One from Dr Roberts, one from the mother of Treyvon Raymond, one from Carter E. Berkeley III, and one from Willie Baden. All of them described you as rude, belligerent . . .'

Goodman watched in amusement as his partner's complexion turned from white to red to something close to purple. To Goodman's surprise, however, Johnson managed to regulate his tone when he replied.

'With respect, Chief, Nikki Roberts is a psychopath, Carter Berkeley is a fantasist with well-documented psychological problems, and Willie Baden's an old-fashioned asshole—'

'He's also a rich and powerful asshole, Detective,' said Brody, leaning back in his chair. 'As is Carter Berkeley. You may not be aware, but Willie Baden donates six-figure sums to the LAPD benevolent fund every year, and Carter Berkeley's bank has given us over a million dollars.'

Johnson frowned. 'I wasn't aware of that.'

'Me neither,' chimed in Goodman.

'And is that supposed to buy them something, sir?' Johnson asked archly.

'You can lose the insolent tone, Detective,' Chief Brody snapped back. 'Yes, it's supposed to buy them something. It's supposed to buy them this department's time, and understanding and respect. These men aren't criminals. They aren't suspects in a crime. Nor is Dr Roberts, for that matter. Not yet.'

Johnson looked fit to explode. 'They could be. They all could be. Roberts lied to us about her husband's affair. Carter Berkeley deliberately wasted police time today, and lied during a murder investigation. And as for Baden, the guy didn't so much as fart in his interview without checking with his lawyer first! If he's not guilty of something, Chief, then I'm Shirley Temple.'

'I don't wanna hear it.' Chief Brody held up a hand. 'Stop pissing off donors, Johnson. And stop alienating witnesses. And you needn't look so smug either, Goodman,' he added caustically. 'You better find this Grolsch kid's body, or that missing accident report, or something that looks like evidence, or I'm taking you off this case. That goes for the both of youse.'

The two partners shuffled out. As soon as the door to the chief's office closed behind them, Goodman quickened his pace, striding away from Johnson as if the older man were an unexploded bomb.

'I meant what I said in there!' Johnson shouted after him. 'She's got you totally blind to what's happening. Ask her about her old man's affair.'

Goodman kept walking, pushing open the double doors that led out to the parking lot.

'Ask her!' Johnson followed him. 'You were with her last night, weren't you?'

It was a guess, a try-your-luck shot across the bows. Goodman wasn't stupid enough to answer it. Instead he climbed into his car.

'She never said a word about the husband's affair, did she? Not a word. She's using you, man! She's playing you. Open your eyes.'

Goodman sped away, with Johnson's words ringing in his ears.

A few blocks from the station he pulled over and took three deep breaths.

Johnson's revelations in Chief Brody's office had unnerved him. For one thing, his own attraction to Nikki Roberts was clearly a lot more obvious than he'd thought.

Mick was right about one thing, though. He was getting too close to her, too close for his own good. But was that closeness clouding his judgment?

He tried to think dispassionately about Mick's specific accusations. Namely, that Nikki knew her husband had been having an affair, and had somehow rigged his accident while he was with his mistress, then covered it up. And that she'd then gone on to mastermind the murders of Lisa Flannagan and Trey Raymond.

On the last point, Goodman had no doubts: Nikki didn't kill Lisa or Trey. That much he *knew*. But as for murdering her husband and his lover . . . was it possible? He wanted to believe not. That Johnson was way off the mark on this, as on so much else. But right now there were too many missing pieces for Goodman to form a clear picture.

Who was Doug Roberts' mistress?

Why had her name, and existence, been withheld from press reports on the accident?

What had happened to the official accident report?

And why had Nikki never brought this up, even when they'd discussed her marriage and her husband's death? Even when she was opening up to him.

Johnson's words haunted him now. '*She's playing you. Open your eyes.*'

*Was* Nikki Roberts playing him?

Against his better judgment, Goodman dialed Nikki's number.

*      *      *

In the dimmed lights of Disney Concert Hall, Nikki saw Detective Goodman's personal cell number pop up on her phone screen. Tapping 'decline' she turned her phone off and slipped it back into her purse, a black satin clutch she'd bought especially for tonight. She'd also splashed out on the elegant, backless Balenciaga dress in floor-length black crepe that clung sensuously to her petite frame, earning her approving glances from many of the male concert-goers, and less approving ones from their wives.

Anne Bateman was coming to the end of the fourth movement of Stravinsky's Violin Concerto in D, the finale of a two-hour-long medley of the composer's works, and obviously the highlight. Nikki was no music buff, but even she had been blown away by the power of Anne's playing, the sublime swell of emotion with which she interpreted each note and phrase, pulling the audience along with her.

The thought of a talent like that being wasted – of Anne return-ing to her jailer of a husband, locked in a gilded cage, never to per-form again – was tragic. Scandalous. Nikki's eyes welled with tears, although whether they were for Anne, or for the beauty of the music, or for her own life's tragedies, she couldn't say.

Last night had been a close call. With hindsight, she knew she'd been incredibly foolish. Reckless, even. She'd allowed herself to get drunk with one of the detectives in charge of the murder investiga-tions. Worse, she'd come within a whisker of sleeping with Detective Goodman, battling a physical attraction stronger than anything she'd felt in a long time.

*What's wrong with me?* she thought miserably. *This isn't me. I don't do this. Get drunk. Almost sleep with a stranger. Put myself in danger.*

Then again, in recent months Nikki had done all sorts of things she would never have done in her past life. Such as spending well over a thousand dollars on an outfit to impress a patient. A married, female patient. A patient she needed to detach from, badly, but whose pres-ence in her life had helped her more than anything else to overcome her terrifying anger towards Doug.

*Poor, dead Douglas. Gone, but not forgotten.*

Nikki would never forget.

Anne lowered her bow, and with a flourish the conductor brought the concert to a close. After a split second's silence, the crowd erupted in applause, rising to their feet and stamping and whistling their approval as the lights went up. Despite her hangover and the acute stabbing pain in her cranium brought on by the sudden noise and light, Nikki felt a warm rush of pride watching Anne stand to take her bow. She looked even tinier and more fragile than usual up on the stage, her pale skin like porcelain against the muted gray of her simple shift dress, a vision of grace and understatement. Like a child.

*She needs my protection,* Nikki thought. *My professional support. I can't let her down. I have to get a grip.*

Flashing the pass Anne had sent her, Nikki slipped backstage while the encores continued. By the time Anne reached her dressing room, Nikki was already waiting.

'Oh! Hello.' Anne hugged her shyly, as if her presence were unex-pected. Which was odd, and slightly irritating to Nikki after Anne had made such a big deal of asking her to come tonight and inviting her backstage. 'You made it.'

'Of course I made it.' Nikki hugged her back. 'I said I would, didn't I?'

'What did you think?' Anne asked anxiously.

'I thought it was incredible. You were incredible,' Nikki replied truthfully. 'I was blown away. The entire audience were.'

'Really?' Anne asked. 'Was it truly OK?'

'It was light years beyond OK,' said Nikki.

Sometimes Nikki wondered whether Anne manipulated her, psychologically. Toyed with her, 'playing' the needy patient in order to feed Nikki's ego. But in this case, Anne's insecurity was obviously sincere. The standing ovation she'd just received wasn't enough. She needed Nikki's reassurance. It was flattering.

'It's such a rare thing, Anne, to have a talent like yours,' Nikki told her. 'If I had a fraction of your gifts I would die happy.'

Anne smiled. 'Don't be silly. I've never met anybody more accomplished than you. You look beautiful tonight, by the way.'

The compliment was unexpected. Ridiculously, Nikki felt her cheeks flush with pleasure. 'Thank you. So do you.'

A knock on the door interrupted them. Being closer, Nikki opened it, her eyes widening as a young man staggered in, completely engulfed by the largest bouquet of white roses Nikki had ever seen. The thing must have weighed as much as him, with literally hundreds of stems bound together at the base in a satin bow as wide as two outstretched arms.

'For you, Ms Bateman,' the boy panted, resting the floral monster on the ground beside Anne's dressing table as there was nowhere else to put it. He handed Anne the card. 'Congratulations.'

'Oh my goodness!' Anne gasped. The bouquet was bigger than she was. 'What on earth am I going to do with all these? Do you want any flowers?' She turned back to Nikki. 'Please, take some home with you. Or to the office, I can't possibly . . .'

Her words tailed off as she opened the card and read the note inside. Nikki watched her reactions with a therapist's trained eye. The fluttering hands, pressed against her chest. The nervous bite of her lower lip, followed by a smile that seemed to be full of both sadness and love.

Nikki felt her own chest tighten. 'They're from him, aren't they?'

Anne nodded with a sigh. 'They're from my husband. He says he wishes he could be here. That he hears my music every day in his dreams, and carries it in his heart.'

Nikki rolled her eyes. 'It's a shame he didn't "carry it in his heart" while he was keeping you prisoner in his house against your will and refusing to let you perform at all. For six years.'

'I know,' Anne admitted, still staring wistfully at the flowers. 'But look. There's a bloom for every day I've been gone. Ninety-six, he says here. You have to admit, it's romantic.'

Nikki felt a rush of fury overwhelm her. How could women be so stupid? How could they allow men to manipulate and control them like this? To get away with it?

'Romantic?' she snapped. 'For God's sake, Anne, grow up! This isn't some Harlequin romance. This is your future. Your life.'

Anne flushed, but this time it was with anger. She'd never lost her temper with Nikki before but her feelings came tumbling out now like water through a shattered dam.

'You're right, it is my life. Mine, not yours. So back off.'

'I care about you, Anne,' said Nikki, stung. 'As your therapist—'

'Oh, STOP IT!' Anne shouted, the first time Nikki had ever heard her raise her voice. 'This isn't about you being my therapist and we both know it.'

Nikki stared back at her, stunned. An awkward silence fell, with neither woman knowing what to say or do next. In the end it was Anne who attempted to normalize the situation.

'Look. I appreciate your advice. I do. And your support. You changed my life,' she said. 'But you don't need to be so hateful about my husband all the time. Even when he does something nice, something kind.'

'But it's *not* kind. That's the whole point. It's controlling!' Nikki couldn't help herself. 'It's manipulative. And by the way, he's your ex-husband. I'm sorry, Anne, but you have to ask yourself, just how blind are you willing to be?'

'How blind am *I* willing to be? What about *you*?' Anne snapped, fighting back tears. 'How blind were you in your own marriage? Hm? Did you *really* not know about *your* husband's affair?'

Nikki blanched. The world seemed muffled suddenly, as if she were having this conversation in a dream, or underwater. 'How did you know about that?' she asked Anne, her voice cracking. 'Who told you?'

'I think you should leave now.' Anne's voice was quiet but her resolve was clear. She wasn't going to answer Nikki's questions. A line had been crossed, and there was no coming back.

'Fine.' Nikki felt as if someone were pouring acid down her throat, right into her chest and then down to the pit of her stomach. 'I'll go.'

Turning at the door, she looked back at Anne.

'He'll kill you, you know. One day. If you go back to him. Men like that always do. It's kill or be killed.'

Anne stifled a sob as the door slammed shut.

*   *   *

Driving through downtown, crawling towards the 10 freeway in gridlock traffic, Nikki felt sick to her stomach. It was that awful sour sickness, as if her veins were running with turned milk. Part self-pity, part shame, part anger, part regret.

She was right about Anne's husband. He might be generous and charming, but he was also a bully, and bullies never changed. They both knew, deep down, that his 'romantic gestures' were really controlling gestures in a wafer-thin disguise. But Anne would no longer hear that from Nikki, because Nikki had stopped behaving like her doctor and started behaving like . . . what? Her friend? Her lover? Her stalker?

She was wrong to have spoken to Anne the way she did.

And now, finally, Anne had called her on it. Not just on her own inappropriate feelings – *'This isn't about you being my therapist and we both know it!'* – but on Doug's affair. How on earth had Anne found out about that? Nikki had certainly never discussed it with her or alluded to it in any way. In fact, other than Gretchen, and Haddon Defoe, nobody close to her knew – or if they did, they were diplomatic enough never to speak of it.

The sick feeling intensified. Through her car window, Nikki saw four homeless men huddled together in a theater doorway. One looked up and right at her, with the wide, empty gaze of the hopelessly addicted. Nikki waited to feel something, the familiar stab of compassion she used to have when Doug was alive, before that Russian bitch destroyed everything Nikki held dear. But there was nothing. Something in Nikki's heart, her soul if such a thing existed, had died. Or perhaps it hadn't died so much as run out of gas. One day, maybe, her tanks of love and care and human feeling would be replenished and she'd be able to feel again?

Maybe.

Or maybe not.

At the freeway on-ramp, she noticed another desperate case, a middle-aged woman this time, like her, only this woman had the same revolting, scaly skin Nikki remembered from the boys at Haddon's Venice clinic. Krokodil, he'd called it. The 'new new thing' that the cartels in LA were battling to control.

She'd felt sympathy back in Venice, for the two boys. But not now. Not tonight. Perhaps her shameful encounter with Anne Bateman had been the final straw, the last blow Nikki was capable of sustaining before total emotional shut-down.

She drove home, blind and unthinking. Two plainclothes policemen sat parked outside her gates, courtesy of Detective Goodman, who apparently wouldn't take no for an answer.

'You need protection,' he'd told her last night in the car, his hand somewhere between her knee and upper thigh while she was pouring her heart out about grief. God, it felt good.

'I don't want protection.'

'It's not about what you want, Nikki. It's my job to protect you.'

That felt even better.

'And what if I refuse your protection, Detective?' Nikki couldn't remember where her own hand was at the time, but she suspected nowhere good.

'Then I'll ignore you, *Doctor.*'

Detective Johnson had used her title as an insult. With Goodman, it was a come on.

The cops' presence proved he hadn't simply been flirting. He'd meant it. Nikki smiled to see the officers in place now, as Goodman had promised they would be. Stubbornness was a trait she had always admired in men. Doug had had it in spades. *Darling Doug.* If only things hadn't ended the way they had.

Tears stung the back of Nikki's eyes but she blinked them away angrily and pulled into the driveway. Inside the house she switched off the alarm, kicked off her shoes and walked into the kitchen, dumping her new clutch bag on the counter. Still too hungover from last night to contemplate a real drink, she poured herself a large Virgin Mary instead from the ready-mixed bottle in the fridge and sat at the counter, flipping open her laptop for a last check of her emails.

That's what she told herself anyway. In fact she just wanted to see if Anne had messaged.

She hadn't.

But another email caught Nikki's attention. Under the title 'I saw you last night' the anonymous sender had attached an image. Clicking it open, Nikki saw a shot of Dan Tana's restaurant with a second image pasted over the top. It was a crudely photoshopped photograph of Nikki's face above a naked woman's body. The woman was swinging from a cartoon noose. Beneath it was a two-word missive: 'Die, bitch.'

Nikki sat back. She felt a moment's shock. Then a brief fluttering of fear. Then nothing. Nothing at all.

Despite her emotional numbness, the intellectual part of her brain insisted she do something. This wasn't a prank. This was a death threat. A specific death threat, from someone who knew her movements, who knew she'd been to Dan Tana's last night, and presumably who she'd been with. She must tell the police immediately. She must tell Goodman.

And yet, she hesitated. Did she really want to give the handsome detective a reason to intrude even further into her life? To creep closer and closer, on the grounds of 'protection'?

Part of her definitely did. But another, wiser, part knew that wasn't the answer.

Goodman was a good man and he seemed to be trying his best to solve the case. But his partner, the odious detective Johnson, was the devil incarnate, and whether Nikki liked it or not, the two cops were a team. A team who seemed to be making grindingly slow progress catching Lisa and Trey's killer, not to mention the maniac who'd tried to mow her down, and almost succeeded.

Meanwhile, her own life was in danger.

Nikki did need protection. But more than that she needed answers, not only about the murders, but about the one question that had haunted and poisoned and destroyed her since the moment she first learned of Doug's betrayal.

Clicking open Google she typed in the search bar:

*Private Detective, West Los Angeles.*

It was time for Plan B.

# Part Two

# 21

'So, Andrea. What's the definition of a bachelor?'

Derek Williams leaned forward over the Formica table at I-Hop and looked up at the waitress expectantly.

'It's seven in the morning, Derek,' the exhausted young mother replied, refilling his coffee cup. 'If this is another one of your dirty jokes, I ain't in the mood.'

'It's not dirty!' Derek Williams protested. 'You know, it wouldn't kill you to cheer up every once in a while, Andrea.'

The waitress raised a sardonic eyebrow. 'Look around, Derek. You show me where it says "service with a smile".'

Williams laughed loudly, an open-mouthed guffaw that shook his out-of-shape body like a giant jello. Andrea was his kind of girl. The kind who made single parenthood on eight bucks an hour funny.

'A bachelor is a man who never makes the same mistake once!' He blurted out the punch line. 'Come on, admit it, sweetheart. That's funny. I got another one for you too.'

Andrea rolled her eyes affectionately, tossing two menus down on the table.

'What's the definition of alimony?'

She started to walk away.

'The high cost of leaving!' Derek called after her retreating back.

That last joke was true enough, as Derek Williams knew to his cost. His ex-wife (witch, she-devil), Lorraine, was wringing him out like a wet dishcloth in the courts right now. Derek felt like a desiccated lemon who was somehow still being squeezed, long after the last drop of juice was gone.

'I'm a private detective, Your Honor,' Derek had pleaded at their last hearing, representing himself. (A mistake, but needs must.) 'I'm not a lawyer or an investment banker or a silicon . . . computer . . . one of those San Francisco guys. I can't even spell Palo Alto.'

'Well, I'm sorry to hear that,' the female judge had replied, looking anything but sorry. *Damned feminists.* 'But I trust you can spell J-A-I-L, which is where you'll be going if you miss one more maintenance or child support payment to Ms Sloane.'

*Ms Sloane.* That irritated the crap out of him. Lorraine had gone back to her maiden name after the divorce, and had even had it added to their son's birth certificate by court order. *Hunter Sloane-Williams.* What kind of a pretentious, dumbass name was that for an eight-year-old boy? Or any boy, for that matter? Lorraine was clearly dead-set on raising him gay. Not that Derek had anything against gays, if you *were* gay. But Hunter . . . aw, who was he kidding? He didn't know shit about Hunter. Lorraine was right on that score at least. *'You never spend any time with him, Derek. You wouldn't know what to do with joint custody, and you know it.'*

'Mr Williams?'

Startled, Derek sat upright and promptly spilled scalding coffee all down his crisp white shirt. 'Motherf—' he cursed under his breath, pulling the burning, wet material away from his skin. Out of the corner of his eye, he could see Andrea sniggering from behind the counter.

'Oh my goodness, I'm so sorry!' The pretty, professionally dressed brunette looked aghast. 'Was that my fault?'

'No, no,' Williams winced, dabbing at himself ineffectually with a handful of paper towels. 'Not at all. I was miles away. Daydreaming. Actually, it was more of a nightmare. Day-mare. You must be Dr Roberts?'

'Nikki, please. And thank you for agreeing to meet me so early.'

The woman extending her hand in Derek's general, coffee-soaked direction was even better looking in person than she was on TV, where he'd seen her several times since the 'zombie killer' story made it into the mainstream media. Dr Roberts had called him at midnight last night, no doubt expecting to leave a message, but Williams had picked up and the two of them had had the beginnings of a conversation about her 'predicament'. Half-cut on home brew and not at his sharpest, Williams had nevertheless agreed to meet her at the crack of ass this morning, partly because he desperately needed the money a new client might bring in, and partly because of the genuine desperation in Nikki Roberts' voice.

In Williams' experience, genuine desperation could usually be translated into up-front fees. Already familiar with the murder case, thanks to the breathless news coverage of Lisa Flannagan's relationship with Willie Baden, twenty minutes of internet research into Dr Roberts' own background told him the rest of what he needed to know. Lisa Flannagan's shrink was a renowned West Side psychologist and the widow of a prominent doctor. In other words, this particular damsel in distress was seriously loaded. Nikki's call was the *ker-ching* moment Derek Williams had been waiting for, the fee that might just keep him out of J-A-I-L. He hoped he hadn't ruined his chances by spilling coffee all over himself like a freakin' toddler.

As it turned out, Nikki Roberts' own nerves were such that she seemed barely to notice his. Sliding into the booth opposite him, she pulled out a crisp manila envelope and handed it to him.

'I wasn't sure where to start, so I put a few notes together,' she explained. 'I need your help, Mr Williams. The police . . . well, as I explained last night, they're really not making any headway with these murders.'

'If I had a dollar for every time I heard that, Dr Roberts. Nikki.' Williams leaned back, feeling more confident. Setting the envelope to one side he said, 'I'll take a look at this later. For now, why don't you tell me in your own words what's been going on?'

Nikki took a deep breath, surreptitiously using the pause to take stock of Williams' appearance. *Overweight. Sallow skin. Slow physical reactions. Yellow in the eyes.* She swiftly put him down as a drinker, probably a divorcee, and struggling financially. Then again it didn't take Einstein to figure that out. Not many wealthy professionals at the top of their game chose to conduct their breakfast meetings at I-Hop.

But, she reminded herself, Williams had outstanding reviews from past clients, as well as a reputation for being willing to push limits, legally, to get the evidence he needed. More than once he'd been in trouble with the courts. It was exactly the sort of risk-taking, get-it-done attitude Nikki was looking for.

'Like I said, I'm not sure where to begin.'

'Try the beginning,' Williams said, beckoning Andrea back over to the table. 'I'll have the bacon platter please, sweetheart, with a stack of pancakes on the side. And for my friend?' He looked at Nikki.

'Oh, nothing, thank you. Just coffee.'

'She'll take the toast and eggs,' said Williams. Then, turning to a bemused Nikki, 'You need to eat, honey. Whatever's going on in people's lives, if they're calling me, there's stress involved. You need to eat and you need to sleep, period.'

It was presumptuous and bombastic, but at the same time endearing, perhaps because it was so kindly meant. Nikki found herself instantly warming to Derek Williams.

'Well,' she said. 'If I'm starting at the beginning – the real beginning of all of this, for me – I guess that would be: *My husband had an affair.*'

\* \* \*

Valentina Baden said a silent prayer of thanks as her G6 touched down at Cabo San Lucas International Airport.

Valentina wasn't afraid of much. Ever since her sister's disappearance almost five decades ago, Valentina had learned that there were few things in life she couldn't survive if she put her mind to it. But her irrational fear of flying remained a constant. Friends insisted it must be the lack of control that bothered her. Perhaps they were right? It was certainly true that in the rest of her life, Valentina kept a tight grip on the reins, from her marriage, to her family to her business decisions and personal relationships.

She'd achieved everything she'd set out to during her time in LA. Showing up unannounced at the Missing offices downtown, she'd demanded to be shown the status of all the charity's outstanding cases, as well as a detailed breakdown of the last six months' accounts. Ever since the IRS had started sniffing around their foreign income sources, Valentina had become obsessive about checking the reporting personally. Very few people in the organization understood the full, true nature of their 'work', and the profound need for secrecy. Thankfully, Willie was too lazy and self-absorbed to pay his wife's pet project much mind. But the IRS were a different matter. Willie had shut them down this time and paid off the LA police. But no one knew better than Valentina that they couldn't afford a next time. Not ever.

It pleased her to watch her staff scurrying around like frightened ants whose nest had been kicked over, scrambling to appease their queen. Charities, she reminded them, should be run to the same, exacting standards as for-profit businesses, and that meant results. She prided herself that, in Missing's fifteen-year history, only a handful of the cases they'd taken on remained unsolved. There was Ritchie Lamb, the toddler who went missing in Turkey on a family vacation, almost certainly snatched by child traffickers, who sadly they'd never been able to trace. And Charlotte Clancy, the au pair girl whose disappearance had so deeply, and publicly, tugged at Valentina's heart-strings because it happened in Mexico City, where she'd lost her sister María all those years ago. She could almost feel a photogenic tear rolling down her cheek at the memory. But in the vast majority of Missing's cases, they were able to provide families with closure. Even if, as in Brandon Grolsch's case, the news they had to break was not good. Those sorts of results only came from constant vigilance and consistent best efforts, qualities Valentina encouraged in her employees through a deft use of both carrot and stick.

This week in LA had mostly called for the stick. Within an hour of her arrival, Valentina had summarily sacked her accountant and both his assistants.

'If you want something done properly, do it yourself,' she'd complained to Terry Engels, the LA office manager, as the hapless accounts team cleared their desks – the second team to do so in less than two years. 'The last six months' files are a total shambles. I'll sort them out myself while I'm here and then appoint someone new to take over.'

With the finances back under her own beady eye and a fire lit under the rest of Missing's LA employees, Valentina had had ample time to attend to her other business. Namely, making sure that *certain people* knew that she was watching them – no one made a fool out of Valentina Baden – and that outstanding issues of a business nature with some troublesome Russians were resolved to her satisfaction. On the last day she'd even squeezed in a hair appointment and a trip to Neiman Marcus, in case Willie should get suspicious. Besides which, Cabo might be heaven in most respects, but from a retail perspective one's options were limited.

So as far as Valentina was concerned it had been a very successful trip, and the break from Willie's constant, cloying presence and growing paranoia about his new partner had restored her sanity. All they needed now was for the furor over Lisa Flannagan's murder to die down and the irritating Dr Nikki Roberts to crawl back into her hole so that the media could move on to the next story, and life would stand a chance of returning to something close to normal.

'Thank God you're back.' To Valentina's astonishment, Willie had come to meet her on the tarmac. He looked terrible; pale and disheveled in a repellent velour jogging suit like some dying Floridian retiree.

And his breath smelled. 'He hasn't returned my calls in two days!' he blurted nervously to his wife. 'Two days! He's clearly angry.'

'Who's angry?' Valentina asked, as one of Willie's minions stepped forward to take her suitcase.

'Who do you think?' Willie snapped at her.

'You mean Rodriguez?' Valentina sighed.

'Of course Rodriguez!' Willie snapped. 'We should never have gotten involved with him. This stupid deal—'

'Is going to make us a fortune,' Valentina reminded him calmly, laying a red-taloned hand firmly on his thick arm. 'You have to calm down, Willie. This isn't a good time to lose your nerve. Men like Rodriguez can smell weakness like a shark can smell blood. Believe me, I know. I grew up with men like him, remember? Things are different here.'

'I know all that,' said Willie.

'Then act like it,' said Valentina. 'You've done your part, and you've offered him fair terms. If he's angry about it, too bad.'

'Too bad?' Willie gulped down air, opening and closing his mouth like a stranded fish. '*Too bad?* Valentina, don't you know what he's capable of? What all these damned Mexicans are capable of? He'll kill me. He'll kill us both. Slit our throats in our beds.'

Calmly, Valentina climbed into the back seat of the Bentley. She waited for the chauffeur to drive away before replying.

'Speaking as one of those "damned Mexicans",' she regarded her husband archly, 'I can assure you you're wrong. Naturally I know what Rodriguez is capable of. I've had dealings with him over Missing, remember?'

'That's a goddamn charity!' shouted Willie. 'It's not the same! He doesn't have skin in the game.'

*That's what you think,* thought Valentina, but she kept her reflection to herself.

'The point is, you're right, he *would* kill us both in a heartbeat if it served his purposes to do so. But it doesn't. He needs you, Willie. He needs your presence in LA, he needs your network, he needs the legitimacy you give this. You're holding a lot of cards here, my love. All you need to do is play them.'

Willie opened his mouth to say something else, but Valentina held up a hand imperiously.

'I'm tired now, my darling. It's been a busy few days. If you want to talk more, we'll do it at dinner.'

She closed her eyes.

'Should I call Rodriguez again?' Willie asked, unable to contain himself.

Her eyes still closed, Valentina responded coolly. 'Absolutely not. For God's sake, Willie. Please try to grow at least a tiny pair of balls.'

With an effort, the chauffeur stifled a giggle.

They drove on.

\* \* \*

It was past ten o'clock when Derek Williams finally pulled out of the I-Hop parking lot and headed for his office, a mere eight blocks away on Centinela. If you could call the poky, windowless, twelve-by-eight cell he rented by the month an 'office'. Above a busy auto shop, where the guys downstairs had been known to make more in an hour than Derek did in a week, Williams' room was one of six rented out to independent businesses. One was leased by loan sharks, another by a down-at-heel lawyer named Alan Clarkson with whom Derek had struck up a wary friendship, and a third to a very affable pimp named Fabrizio. The fourth office was currently empty, and Williams' nearest 'neighbor' at the end of the row was a woman from Phoenix who made bead purses and necklaces that, as far as Williams could tell, she never even attempted to sell. It was Sad Sack City, no question. But it was dirt cheap, safe enough, and the internet connection was reliable, which was pretty much all Derek Williams asked of an office these days. That and a bunch of friendly guys downstairs with tire irons, in case any of his clients ever got nasty.

Not that he anticipated that in this case. Not from the client herself, anyway. After three full hours in Dr Nikki Roberts' company, Derek had emerged in possession of three important new pieces of information.

The first was that he stood to make a LOT of money here, if he played his cards right.

The second was that fate had handed him a rare chance to put one over on his old enemy, the Los Angeles Police Department.

And the third was, taking this case would mean putting himself in real and immediate physical danger.

Ironically, it was the third fact that gave him the biggest thrill of all. It had been a long, long time since Derek had put himself out there. Since he'd been on the edge, taking real risks, living on adrenaline like he used to in the old days, B.L. (Before Lorraine). He hadn't realized until this morning's conversation with Nikki quite how much he'd missed it.

Dropping two Alka-Seltzers into a large glass of tap water – last night's heavy drinking combined with this morning's bacon-and-syrup fest had not helped his digestion – he eased his ample backside into the creaky faux leather of his desk chair, stretched out his short legs, and downed the unpleasant mixture in one gulp. Then he pulled an old-fashioned notepad out of his desk drawer and began writing. He started with the familiar, shorthand bullet points he always used after the first client meeting, at the beginning of every case. But soon his prose was flowing, his observations filling page after page.

Nikki Roberts was a fascinating woman, and the mystery she'd presented him with was even more unusual than she was. In fact, the way Williams saw it, it was two mysteries, as he explained carefully when he charged Nikki double his usual fees.

'There's your husband's affair. You want to know who the lady was, how they met, all of that stuff?'

'Right,' said Nikki.

'So that's case one. And then there's these murders, and the threats against you. You want me to find out who's behind them. Basically to do the LAPD's job for them?'

'Precisely.'

'And that's case two.'

Nikki hadn't batted an eyelid, writing Derek out a check on the spot for a month's full-time work at double his usual rate, plus a generous expenses allowance. Williams was starting to like this lady more and more.

He quickly ascertained that it was the husband's affair that would prove to be the biggest cash cow here. Not least because that case was all his – presumably the LAPD didn't give a shit who Dr Doug Roberts had or hadn't been banging – and why should they? Which meant that, theoretically at least, Derek could drag that investigation out longer. Like all PIs, adultery was the bread-and-butter of Williams' business, and he thanked the Lord daily for all the sinners out there in West Los Angeles.

The homicide cases were more complicated. On the downside, there was always a chance that the useless LAPD would catch this so-called Zombie Killer or at least make an arrest soon, before Derek's first month's money was spent. On the other hand, according to Nikki, they'd achieved diddly squat so far and weren't taking the threats against her seriously. No one seemed to be following up on the SUV driver who'd tried to run her down, or on the witness who'd saved her life. Nikki's faith in the police was so low at this point she hadn't even bothered to show them the email threats against her, but instead brought those directly to Williams.

Another excellent sign. The more evidence he had, the better his chances of getting to the finish line before LA's finest.

Yup, all in all, this had the makings of quite an assignment.

The murders themselves fascinated him. Like everyone else, Derek had followed the story in the papers and on TV. Willie Baden's very young, very beautiful mistress – who also happened to be one of Nikki Roberts' patients – had been horribly tortured by a knife-wielding maniac, before being stabbed in the heart and her corpse dumped, naked, in scrubland beside the freeway. Three days later, a young African American boy named Treyvon Raymond – Nikki Roberts' assistant and close family friend – had met the exact same fate, surviving long enough to make it to the hospital, but passing away before he could identify his assailant. So far so horrible. But it got worse. Baden's mistress had evidently fought for her life, and some of the killer's DNA had been preserved under her fingernails. After multiple leaks about those samples containing dead human cells, the whole 'zombie' soap opera took off in earnest, first on the internet and later in the mainstream media. It was truly ridiculous what people were prepared to believe these days. Back in the real world, however, no one had been arrested for either killing, never mind charged. No clear motive had been established. The whole thing was a genuine mystery.

'So LAPD still have no suspects?' Williams asked Nikki.

'Not officially. Although I think one of the detectives on the case, Johnson, suspects me. He certainly treats me like a criminal every time I speak to him.'

'I wouldn't read too much into that,' said Williams. 'All cops are rude.'

*Not all,* thought Nikki, thinking of the charming Goodman. But she kept the thought to herself. Instead, to Williams' astonishment, she blew things wide open right off the bat by admitting to him that she'd lied to detectives in her interview.

'They asked me if I knew a boy named Brandon Grolsch. I said no. But I do know him. At least, I did. He used to be a patient of mine. My husband referred him to me, through one of his clinics.'

'Why were they asking about this boy? And why'd you lie?' Williams asked.

Nikki shrugged. 'I'm not sure why they were asking. I presume because they thought he might have been involved in the murders. But I know he wasn't. Brandon wasn't capable of anything like that. He was very gentle, very sweet.' She smiled wistfully. 'I suppose I lied to protect him. I didn't really think about it at the time.'

'You do realize that's obstruction of justice?' Williams pointed out. 'If the cops found out and wanted to get nasty about it, they could.'

'I know, but I don't care,' Nikki said boldly. 'The fact is, I don't trust them, Mr Williams.'

Williams could have high-fived her then and there. *Well, that makes two of us, honey.* 'But you trust me?'

'I'm paying you,' Nikki grinned. 'That creates a very different dynamic.'

'Yes, ma'am, it sure does.' Williams grinned back. 'So this Brandon kid. When did you last hear from him?' he asked.

'Quite a long time ago. More than a year,' said Nikki. 'He called me from Boston. He was using again, feeling very low. He wasn't in a good place at all, I'm afraid.'

'Do you think he's dead?' Williams asked bluntly.

Nikki shrugged. 'It's certainly possible. But I don't know.'

'OK.' Williams changed tack, filing Brandon Grolsch under pending. 'Tell me about the detectives running the case.'

With a heavy sigh, Nikki launched into a description of Detective Mick Johnson: his raging hostility and paranoia towards her, his determination to view her as a perpetrator rather than a victim. 'He told me to my face that he thought I'd made up the story about the guy in the SUV trying to kill me. It's absurd. His partner's much more reasonable. Detective Lou Goodman.' Williams noticed the way Nikki's face instantly brightened when she said his name. 'He's different.'

'Different in what way?'

'In every way. He's polite, he's hard-working, he's educated. Open-minded.'

'But still not getting anywhere with the case,' Williams reminded her.

'I suppose not,' Nikki admitted reluctantly. 'Not fast enough anyway. He believes that I may have been the killer's target all along. That
Lisa Flannagan could have been killed by mistake, because she was
wearing my raincoat and outside my office when she was attacked.'

Williams looked skeptical. 'That seems a bit of a stretch.'

'I don't know,' said Nikki. 'It was dark and raining. And we did
look somewhat similar, Lisa and I. Superficially, at least. I mean, obviously Lisa was much younger and more beautiful.'

Williams didn't correct her. Nikki Roberts was a good-looking
lady for her age, no question, but he'd seen pictures of Lisa Flannagan.
The girl had been a knockout. What a waste.

Later, Nikki told Derek about the photograph stolen from her
bedroom, and filled in the gaps about the mysterious black SUV that
had tried to run her down and the young man who'd come to her aid.
She also gave him a copy of the death-threat email she'd received the
night before. He couldn't understand why this detective Johnson
wouldn't take those incidents seriously, especially in the context of
these gruesome murders and Nikki's close connection to both. It
made no sense. Did Johnson know something that his partner didn't?

He made notes of all his questions, then sat back and listened
patiently while Nikki brought the conversation back around to the *real*
reason she'd hired him: her husband's affair.

The story Nikki told him was gut-wrenching. But Williams' gut
told him it was also incomplete. There seemed to be several vital pieces
of the puzzle missing, facts that Nikki either didn't know or wasn't
ready to tell him – yet.

According to Nikki, the first she knew about her husband's mistress was the night of his death. Doug Roberts had lost control of his
car on the 405 one night and been killed instantly. When Nikki got the
call from police, she learned that he hadn't been alone. A woman passenger had been in the car with him.

'They asked me if I knew who she was, but I had no idea. At that
time I assumed maybe she was one of Doug's patients, or a colleague
he was giving a ride home. It was a few days later when I learned the
truth. I overheard two of the cops talking. They'd interviewed staff at
the hospital where Doug worked and multiple people had told them
the woman was Doug's girlfriend. I didn't believe it at first. It made no
sense to me at all – it still doesn't. But when I confronted Doug's best
friend Haddon, he admitted Doug had been seeing someone. As you

can imagine I was devastated. I begged Haddon for details, but he claimed not to have any.'

'You didn't believe him?'

'Would you?' Nikki asked. 'He and Doug were best friends. Maybe he thought he was protecting me, or protecting Doug's memory. I don't know. But I need answers, Mr Williams. All I've been able to find out so far is she was Russian and that her first name was Lenka. The rest is a total blank.'

'What would you like to know?' asked Derek.

'Everything.' Nikki's eyes flashed with anger. 'I want to know everything. Who she was, how long it had been going on, how they met, where they met. I want to know how often they slept together, and where, and I want to know why. Why did he do this? *Why?* We were happy. He didn't need anyone else! We were incredibly, incredibly happy.'

Williams said nothing to this, but he watched Nikki's reactions closely. Watched as all the poise and control, all the calm with which she'd discussed the murders and the attempts on her life, flew out of the window, replaced by an unstable mix of grief, denial and a powerful, almost tangible anger.

*There are two sides to this woman,* he thought.

*One that's in control of her emotions. And one that's not.*

*One that lives in the real world. And one who takes refuge in fantasy.*

*One that tells the truth. And one that lies. Even to herself.*

It also struck him that even when her own life was in danger, the thing that mattered to Nikki Roberts most was solving the riddle of her husband's mistress. Was there something she wasn't telling him? Something about 'Lenka' she was holding back? Perhaps that obsession was also where her courage came from? The poor woman had already died inside a thousand times over. She'd already been tortured by the circumstances of her husband's death, and the betrayal it had revealed to her.

Perhaps, after that, nothing scared her any more?

In Williams' experience, there were few people more dangerous, or more powerful, than those with nothing left to lose.

By the time he'd finished making his own initial notes, another hour had passed. It was now eleven thirty, almost lunch time, but for once Derek Williams' stomach wasn't his number one priority.

Running a hand almost lovingly over the manila folder Nikki had handed him earlier, he opened it now for the first time.

He was curious to see which details she had chosen to include in her dossier of 'facts' and which she had omitted or edited out. Her honesty about Brandon Grolsch and lying to the police had been disarming. So, on one level, she trusted him. But Derek Williams wasn't naive enough to believe that any client ever gave him the unadulterated truth. If such a thing even existed.

'What have you got for me sweetheart?' he muttered under his breath.

Pulling out the first page from Nikki's folder, it took him a moment to recognize the unfamiliar feeling in his chest. It wasn't stress, or indigestion, or heartburn. It was happiness. He was happy.

Overnight, it seemed, his luck had changed. He had a new case, a new client, a new challenge.

Derek Williams was *back*.

Thorough to a fault, he read the files in silence for a long time. Then he read them again. And again. Minutes turned into hours. There was a lot here, a lot of different places where he could choose to start.

In the end though, one name leapt out at him, from the scores Nikki had chosen to mention. In terms of the two murders, it was the name of a bit player, a minor figure, tangential at best to the case. And yet it was a name that Derek Williams knew well – too well – from another case, another time.

His mind wandered back.

Almost a decade back . . .

# 22

**Nine years earlier . . .**

Derek Williams peeked through the glass door of his office at the couple sitting in the waiting room.

It was a great office, new and expensive, and the waiting room was impressive – high-ceilinged and furnished with designer couches and high-end 'lifestyle' magazines, as advised by Williams' new wife, Lorraine.

'You gotta spend money to make money, baby,' was one of Lorraine's favorite catchphrases, along with 'You never get a second chance to make a good first impression.' Derek tolerated Lorraine's greeting-card philosophizing because he loved her, and because she had a terrific ass and great tits and he was lucky as all hell that she'd chosen him, out of all the guys who wanted to bone her. Also, so far at least, she seemed to be right about the 'spend money to make money' thing. Since taking the lease on the fancy offices he'd raised his rates sixty percent *and* seen his volume of business triple. 'People feel reassured when they pay a lot of money for something. No one wants a cheap service,' said Lorraine. She was right about that too.

Today's couple had paid Derek a small fortune in fees, plus hefty expenses, for the job he'd recently completed on their behalf. He couldn't help but feel bad for them, and nervous about their imminent meeting. They sat together, hands clasped, but staring straight ahead, as stiff and rigid as statues.

The man, Tucker Clancy, was stocky and well built, the type who looked as if his shirt collar was permanently choking him. He dressed in the classic preppy uniform of khakis and a white shirt, and probably had the Republican Party elephant tattooed somewhere on his super-fit body. There was nothing disheveled about him, nothing undone. And yet his face was a craggy ruin, bearing all the hallmarks of devastation and grief. He was only in his mid-forties but looked twenty years older at least. To have a child die was terrible enough. But to have your only daughter disappear into thin air, to be left with an agonizing sliver of hope that perhaps she might one day return to you, against all the odds, that the nightmare might end? Derek Williams could not imagine anything worse.

The wife, Mary, seemed to have held up better. She looked exhausted too, but resigned, somehow, to her fate in a way that her husband wasn't. If she still held out hope for her daughter, it didn't show on her kindly middle-aged features.

*That's good,* Williams thought. *At least one of them has accepted reality.*

He'd spent the last three weeks down in Mexico City, hunting for any traces of the Clancys' daughter, Charlotte, trying to piece together her last-known movements and come up with some sort of credible theory as to what might have happened to her. A slim, attractive blonde, unusually tall for her age, Charlotte would have cut a striking figure anywhere, but especially in a place like Mexico where she towered over the local girls, as All-American as apple pie. And yet no one, it seemed, had laid eyes on her since the evening she disappeared.

The Clancys hadn't given him much to go on in their initial meeting, largely because the Mexican police had given *them* nothing. In the beginning, Tucker Clancy had put this down to his ingrained, knee-jerk belief that all foreign police, and especially the Mexican police, were useless and that as soon as 'superior' American officials got involved, things would improve. It had caused Tucker great pain to discover that neither the FBI nor the staff at the US consulate were any improvement on the Mexicans. In fact in some ways, they were worse, seeming at times to be actively dismissive of the Clancys' concerns, rather than simply incompetent.

'They don't give a damn about Charlie!' an outraged and astonished Tucker Clancy had ranted to Williams the day that they decided to hire him. 'She's an American citizen, for God's sake. Why aren't they out there looking for her? Beating the damn bushes?'

Williams shared Tucker Clancy's outrage, but not his surprise. 'The sad truth is, Mr and Mrs Clancy, unless you're wealthy or politically connected in some way, the FBI are simply not going to devote resources to a case like this. Your daughter was eighteen when you last heard from her. Plenty of young people take off on their own without telling their parents.'

'Not Charlie,' Tucker Clancy growled.

'And not for a *year*,' his wife added, more calmly. 'We know something's happened to her, Mr Williams,' she said bravely, fighting back tears. 'We just don't know what. People, tourists, do get kidnapped down there. I mean, it's dangerous. Mrs Baden gave us some statistics . . .'

'Who?' Williams asked.

'Valentina Baden,' Tucker Clancy responded gruffly. 'She's Willie Baden's wife and she runs a charity that helps search for Missing Persons. They've helped us more than anyone. Tried to get the word out there.'

Suddenly things clicked in Williams' mind. He'd seen the Tuckers before, on television. One of those tear-jerker ads that charities put out. He'd only half tuned in, but the thing had aired on a game night in one of the commercial breaks, which must have cost a fortune. Ignobly, he wondered whether any of the Baden coffers had been opened with regards to his own fees, but he let the thought go as Tucker Clancy plowed on.

'I should never have let her go,' Tucker muttered furiously.

'The thing is, according to Mrs Baden, with kidnapped foreigners there's usually a ransom request,' Mary Clancy told Williams. 'We've heard nothing. Now, I don't know whether that's good or bad.'

*It's bad*, Williams wanted to tell her. He wondered if Willie Baden's do-gooder wife had told these people that at this point the odds had to be a hundred to one against finding Charlotte Clancy alive. Life was cheaper south of the border than most ordinary, middle-class Americans could imagine. Plus Charlotte was young and naive and attractive. It didn't look good.

In any event the Clancys had hired Derek Williams to do a job and he intended to do it, to the best of his abilities.

He'd landed in Mexico City four days later armed only with the name and address of Charlotte's employers, the first name of a local girlfriend she'd mentioned in a rare phone call home, and some photos and personal details, including her Mexican cell phone number. That was it. He had low hopes, but as Lorraine reminded him, 'Ten thousand dollars is ten thousand dollars, Derek. And at least you'll get a tan.'

He did get a tan. He also got an education. None of his research had prepared him for the utter lawlessness of Mexico City. It was like living in the Wild West. The Clancys must have been out of their minds to allow their naive teenage daughter to take a job out here alone. Drug gangs operated with virtual impunity, and both kidnappings and murders were jaw-droppingly common, genuinely everyday occurrences. Some of the local police were phenomenally brave, facing the menace on their streets head on despite the risks of torture or beheadings or reprisals against their own families. But plenty of others were venal, in the pay of either the gangs or wealthy local families, whom they served exclusively and at the expense of ordinary citizens. As for the elected officials, corruption ran from top to bottom in the city, affecting every aspect of life, like a blue vein of bacteria spidering its way through Roquefort cheese. Charlotte's employers, the Encerrito family, had lived in the city for generations and seemed wearily accepting of both the corruption and the constant threat of violence.

'Sadly, I am certain that Charlotte is dead,' Juan Encerrito told Williams, in a deep, resonant baritone that betrayed no trace of shock. 'These things happen here, I'm afraid.'

'Do you have any idea why anyone would want to kill her?' Williams asked. 'Anti-American feeling, perhaps? Or an assumption her family would be rich and willing to pay a ransom? Although as you know, no demands were ever made to the Clancys.'

Angelina Encerrito, a pretty woman with elaborately braided dark hair, offered her opinion. 'In our city, Mr Williams, the gangs don't need a reason. We did warn Charlie about always staying in the safer neighborhoods, and never driving alone after dark. But I think she was maybe a little impulsive.'

'And you didn't think to stop her? To step in and say "no" when she took off at night alone, in your car?' Williams asked, more accusingly than he'd meant to. It got to him that these people sounded so calm, so nonchalant about a young woman's possible murder.

'We employed Charlotte to take care of our children,' Juan answered defensively. 'It was not our job to take care of *her*, to follow her around in her own time.'

'Also, you know, she was young and blonde and attractive,' said Angelina, not in the least offended by Williams' last question but still brooding on the one before. 'So perhaps, in her case, the motive was a sexual one?'

'Did she have any boyfriends that you knew of?'

Both Encerritos shook their heads. 'No.'

'No one who came to the house?'

'Not that I saw,' said Angelina. 'She was with the kids, mostly. There was a girl she liked in the Colonia Juarez – another au pair, I think. But no boys. She didn't seem the type, to be honest.'

Williams looked at his notes.

'The girl – her name wasn't Frederique, by any chance?'

'That's right!' Angelina smiled. 'Frederique. That was it.'

'I don't suppose you remember her last name.'

Angelina Encerrito shook her head.

'*I* do.'

A boy of around ten had wandered on to the terrace to join them. With his olive skin, jet-black hair and long, dark lashes and dressed head to toe in Ralph Lauren tennis whites, he looked like he'd stepped straight off the pages of *Town & Country Magazine*. 'It was Zidane,' he said confidently. 'Like the soccer player. That's why I remember.'

'Thank you.' Williams smiled at him. 'What's your name, kid?'

'Antonio,' said the boy. He seemed delighted to be part of the grown-ups' conversation, but Williams noticed that both his parents looked uneasy, as if they were waiting for an opportunity to shoo him away.

'So did you ever meet Frederique, Antonio?' Williams asked. 'While Charlotte was taking care of you?'

'Sure. Lots of times.'

'Do you remember where you met?'

The boy nodded. 'At the park. And at the house where she was staying. There were only girls there, but they had a water slide and a trampoline and—'

'All right, Antonio, thank you, darling,' his mother interrupted, exchanging pained glances with her husband. 'Off you go to tennis now.'

'Where was the house?' Williams grabbed the little boy by the arm.

'He's late for his lesson,' Juan Encerrito said sternly. 'Please, Mr Williams, do not abuse our goodwill. Your business does not concern my son.'

'Sure it does.' Williams matched the older man's irritated tone. 'I need that address, Señor Encerrito. Frederique Zidane may be the one person who actually knows what might have happened to Charlotte. Imagine how Charlotte's poor family feel right now, sir, not knowing anything. How would *you* feel if it was your child?' He nodded towards Antonio, who hovered anxiously, not sure whether to stay or go.

The boy's father relented. 'Do you remember where this house was, Antonio?' he asked, gently.

'Oh yes.' The boy smiled. 'I have an excellent memory.' Turning to Williams he added helpfully, 'I could take you there right now if you like?'

* * *

Frederique Zidane was a plain young woman in her early twenties, short with mousy brown hair and the sort of pale, doughy figure more usually associated with middle age. Her dress sense, however, made no concession to these shortcomings. She answered the door to Williams in a denim skirt so short it barely merited the name, and a tight white T-shirt beneath which a straining red lace bra was plainly visible. She was also obviously a kind person. When Williams explained the nature of his business, she bent over backwards to help.

'Do you know, you're the first person who's bothered to come and talk to me about Charlie?' she informed him, clearing a space on the messy sofa for him to sit down and pressing a glass of iced water into his hand. 'Apart from that charity lady.'

'Charity lady?'

'From Missing,' Frederique clarified. 'They've been trying to help, getting Charlie's name and picture out there. Which is great, 'cause the police here couldn't care less.'

*That's interesting,* Williams thought. He'd understood from Tucker and Mary Clancy that Valentina Baden and her charity had only contacted them recently, in the States, to offer them some free publicity. But now it seemed Valentina had taken an interest in Charlotte's disappearance from the start. *Strange she'd never mentioned that, or her meeting with Frederique, to the Clancys.*

'I was told the American police would be getting involved,' Frederique went on, 'but I never heard from them either.'

Born and raised in Rouen, she spoke English with only the slightest of French accents. Williams was impressed.

'I traveled all over as a kid,' Frederique told him. 'I learned English as a baby but I also speak Spanish and Italian. I think that made it easier for me here. Poor Charlie was kind of isolated, because her Spanish wasn't that great. She relied on me a lot to translate for her. And because I was older, you know? This job was her first time away from home. God, it's so *sad*.'

'I'm trying to build a picture of her life here, in the months she worked for the Encerritos,' said Williams.

'OK.' Frederique leaned forward eagerly, a thick roll of belly fat escaping over the elastic of her skirt as she moved. 'What do you want to know?'

'The family she worked for said they never saw a boyfriend. Is that true?'

'It's probably true they never saw one,' said Frederique. 'But Charlie was seeing somebody, for sure. I already told the police this, and Missing, but they didn't seem interested.'

'I'm interested,' Williams assured her. 'Did you meet him? Do you know his name?'

Frederique shook her head. 'No. That's the whole thing. He was a secret. Charlie was really into him, she talked about him all the time. But he was married, and a lot older than her, and really rich and powerful – that's what she said anyway. None of us were allowed to meet him or know who he was.'

Williams listened eagerly. This was a break, of sorts.

'Was he Mexican? American?'

'I don't know his nationality, she never said. I assumed he was local, but maybe that was wrong . . . I do know he traveled a lot. He wasn't always in town and Charlie would pine for him like a lost kitten whenever he was away.'

Williams made a note. 'Do you know how they met?'

Frederique thought for a moment. 'I think she met him at her employers' house. Maybe he was a business associate of the dad?'

'Anything else?' Williams pressed her. 'Did she tell you what job this man did, or any details about his family, his background? Anything that might help me track him down?'

'Not really.' Frederique bit her lower lip. 'I'm not being much help, am I? I think he might have been in finance. It was some big-money job, anyway. And like I say, he was married but beyond that I don't know. All she really talked about was how great he was in bed. That, and the presents he bought her.'

'Presents?'

'Oh, yeah.' Frederique's big brown eyes lit up. 'He bought her diamonds and thousand-dollar shoes. Really fancy, expensive stuff. She adored him, but it looked as if the feeling was mutual.'

'And were they still together when she went missing?' Williams asked. 'Had they had a fight, or broken up?'

Frederique shook her head. 'No. Definitely not. If anything, I'd say they were closer than ever. She was supposed to meet him that night, and she was so excited. I remember her sitting right where you are now, telling me how she was going to spend her life with this guy.'

'Is it possible she ran off with him?' Williams asked. Up till now he'd been totally sure that Charlotte was dead. But the picture her friend painted of her romance did open the door to other, less gruesome possibilities. 'Maybe the two of them are living on a beach somewhere right now.'

'I wondered about that,' said Frederique. 'I mean, I'd love to believe it. But it doesn't add up, does it? Rich, powerful businessmen with families don't simply disappear. And Charlie may not have seen eye to eye with her parents, but I don't believe she would run off into the sunset without saying a word to them. She was a nice girl. She wouldn't do something that cruel.'

Williams left, thanking Frederique for her help and handing her his business card in case she remembered anything else. 'I'll be at the Hilton for the next ten days. But you can reach me on my cell after that if something comes back to you, any time.'

\* \* \*

Things moved fast after that. The Encerritos were less than welcoming when Williams returned to try to talk to them a second time about male visitors to their home, specifically married business associates of Juan's. Luckily, in exchange for a few pesos and some American whiskey, most of their household employees were considerably more forthcoming. More than one of them told Williams about a handsome American who had visited the compound a few times over the course of that summer, and who had often been seen chatting with the young au pair.

'She liked him. They like each other,' the Encerritos groundsman informed Williams with a toothless grin. 'You could tell.'

The general consensus was that 'the American' was either a banker or a lawyer and that he'd been introduced to Juan Encerrito by a man named Luis Rodriguez, another wealthy local businessman and philanthropist.

'Rodriguez is a wonderful man,' the groundsman told Williams, a sentiment echoed by the housekeeper, the maid and just about everybody else Williams spoke to. 'He came from nothing, and he still cares about the poor. Not like them.' A nod towards the house was intended to indicate the groundsman's employers, Juan and Angelina. 'But the people around him, like the American banker? I don' know about those guys.'

A few days after his meeting with Frederique, Williams called home in high excitement.

'I'm gonna ask the Clancys to pay for another week out here,' he told Lorraine breathlessly from the balcony of his pool-view suite at the Hilton. Below him, a cluster of lithe, bronze-skinned young women lay sprawled out on sun loungers in tiny bikinis, but Williams barely noticed them. 'I know this American dude had something to do with Charlie's disappearance. The family she worked for claim not to know who he is, but they're obviously lying. You know who else is lying, weirdly? Or at least holding back the truth?'

'Who?' Lorraine asked dutifully.

'Valentina Baden – Willie Baden's wife. Her charity has been helping the Clancys, but it turns out they'd already been looking for Charlotte for months, asking questions. I mean, why wouldn't you mention that to the parents?'

'I don't know, Derek,' Lorraine said wearily.

'Anyway, this American guy Charlotte was seeing worked for some local big shot named Rodriguez, kind of like a Robin Hood figure around here. So I have another lead into him, which is great. Assuming Mrs Baden doesn't return my call, which so far she hasn't. All I need is a name, babe. I'm *this* close, I can feel it.'

'OK, Derek.' For some reason, Williams' young wife didn't seem to share his enthusiasm. 'One more week's OK. But after that you gotta come home. We're getting calls every day and I'm having to turn business away.'

'But this *is* business. The Clancys are paying, honey,' Williams reminded her.

'Yeah, they're paying, but you're down in Mexico spending literally all your time on one case,' Lorraine protested. 'You can't afford that, Derek. Not with a baby on the way. You got a family to think about now.'

Williams hung up. He was surprised and disappointed that Lorraine couldn't see what a big deal this was. All he needed to do was speak to this Luis Rodriguez, and he should be able to unearth his precious name, maybe as soon as tomorrow! Finding Charlotte's married boyfriend would be a huge leap forward in the case. If he could solve the mystery of what happened to her after she left Frederique Zidane that night, not only would he be putting an innocent family out of their misery, but he would have succeeded where the FBI, not to mention the Mexicans, had failed. Thanks to Missing, Tucker and Mary Clancy had been all over the talk-show circuit back home. Millions of Americans knew about the Charlotte Clancy case. Cracking it would make Williams' name, and seal his reputation as a top-class private investigator. If that wasn't good business, he didn't know what was.

But most of all, solving this case would mean justice for Charlotte. Sometimes Williams wondered whether he was the only person on earth, other than her parents and Frederique, who genuinely cared about that.

Just as he had the thought, the phone rang.

*Please be Valentina Baden. Please be Valentina Baden . . .*

In fact, it was Frederique, sounding almost as excited as Williams felt.

'I remembered something!' she panted breathlessly.

'Great.' Williams smiled broadly, reaching for his pen and pad.

'I remember his car. I saw Charlie once getting into a car and I'm sure it was his. I mean, I didn't actually see the driver. But she was dressed for a date, and her expression was like—'

'What sort of car was it?' Williams couldn't contain himself. Please let it be something unusual, something he could trace.

'It was a Jaguar. One of the old ones,' said Frederique. 'And it was dark green. I think they call it racing green?'

Williams could have kissed her.

'That has to be a rare car, right?' said Frederique. 'I mean, how many of those can there be driving around Mexico city?'

*Not too many,* Williams thought triumphantly. *Not too many at all.*

\* \* \*

The next seven days were some of the most frustrating in Derek Williams' life. Having raised the Clancys' hopes, not to mention relieved them of another three thousand dollars they could ill afford, he'd hoped to get back to them with an imminent breakthrough. Instead he quickly learned that getting anything done in Mexico City was like trying to run a marathon with your sneakers dipped in treacle. It was a mystery to Williams how anybody did business here, never mind amassed the sort of fortunes that men like Luis Rodriguez seemed to have conjured out of thin air.

Rodriguez was frustration number one. Robin Hood he may be, but he was also literally impossible to get to. Not difficult – Williams was used to difficult. Impossible. A wall of receptionists, secretaries, and secretaries' secretaries were in place to deny access to the great man, both in person and on the phone. Emails were returned by faceless minions, and phone calls transferred and transferred and transferred again until the would-be caller lost the will to live.

Williams had tried showing up at Rodriguez's offices, hoping to 'doorstep' him there as he came in or out, but a small army of machine-gun-toting goons soon dissuaded him from that approach. As for Rodriguez's home, that had no doorstep, only a long, winding drive behind reinforced steel gates, another set of goons and the less than reassuring sound of Dobermans barking hungrily somewhere inside the grounds.

Meanwhile, researching car ownership records here was not a simple matter of calling the DMV as it was back home. Williams was sure there must be some old Mexican saying that people were taught at birth, that translated to something like 'Why keep a record when you can *not* keep a record?'

Infuriatingly, he assumed that Valentina Baden's charity must already have at least *some* of this information. But as they'd chosen not to share it with the Clancys, for reasons best known to themselves, and had steadfastly refused to return a single of Williams' calls, he was left trying to reinvent the wheel.

He used the wasted hours of waiting for someone to get back to him to do some research into Luis Rodriguez, everybody's favorite billionaire and a local legend for his generosity, down-to-earth manner, and support for any and all causes that helped the city's poor.

'*I came from these streets. I know these streets,*' Rodriguez had told an interviewer from *La Jornada* last year in a piece Williams had now read at least a dozen times: '*Some people don't like that I give money to* the police. *But we need the police. They are the front line in the war on drugs, and no one should doubt that this is a war.'*

Yeah, thought Williams. *It's a war all right. Problem is that half of the local police are really spies for the other side.*

'*That's why I also give to rehabilitation centers,*' Rodriguez went on. '*I lost my own sister to drugs. So I make a point of employing recovering addicts in my businesses. I am not a political man. I am a compassionate man.*'

The interview was a bit too 'Pharisees in the temple' for Williams' taste. A bit too 'look at me, I'm such a great guy'. A puff piece, basically. But the numbers bore Rodriguez's boasting out. The man really had given away a boat-load of money to good causes, especially ones related to fighting drugs. He could be something of a player when it came to women, but that only seemed to add luster to his legend. The poor of Mexico City worshipped him and it wasn't too hard to see why.

It was a Wednesday when Williams finally got his opening, accosting Luis Rodriguez as he emerged from his regular weekly session with a chiropractor.

'I'm investigating the disappearance of a young American girl,' Williams gabbled breathlessly as the lone bodyguard Rodriguez had brought with him leapt out of his car and started barreling towards him. 'I only need a minute of your time, sir. I believe one of your business associates may have known her. Her name was Charlotte Clancy.'

Just as the bodyguard was about to body-slam him to the floor, Williams saw Luis Rodriguez raise his hand, stopping the man dead, like a remote-controlled toy. For the first time, Rodriguez looked at Williams directly.

'Charlotte? *Carlotta,*' he mused. 'That was my sister's name. You're looking for an associate of mine, you say?'

'Yes, sir, that's right. An American. He may be a financier or a lawyer. And I believe he drives a racing green Jaguar sports car.'

Rodriguez frowned. 'No one's leaping to mind. But I work with a lot of American lawyers, Mr . . . ?'

'Williams. Derek Williams.'

They shook hands.

'I'll tell you what. Why don't you come to my offices on Colonia del Valle tonight around six. I'll have my secretary look into it for you in the meantime. Maybe between us we can come up with a name for you.'

'Thank you, Mr Rodriguez,' Williams said sincerely. After all the fruitless phone calls, the days and days of waiting, he had a result at last. 'I'll be there.'

\* \* \*

At six o'clock on the nose, Williams presented himself at the reception desk on the ground floor of Luis Rodriguez's offices on Colonia del Valle. He'd shaved, showered and changed into a pale linen suit for the meeting, and was looking his spruced best as he sauntered across the marble-floored lobby.

It was hard not to feel excited to be here.

This was it, at long last. This was the turning point in the case.

Of course, he had yet to prove that Charlotte Clancy's lover had had a hand in her disappearance, and what Williams now felt quite certain was her death. But once he knew who the man was, he could start building a case against him. At a minimum he'd have something concrete to report to Charlotte's poor parents, even if it wasn't good news.

'I'm here to see Luis Rodriguez.' He handed the receptionist his card. 'He's expecting me.'

The girl smiled and picked up the telephone. After a brief conversation in Spanish she replaced the receiver and looked up at Williams.

'Are you certain the meeting was today, Mr Williams?' she asked politely. 'It doesn't seem to be in Mr Rodriguez's calendar.'

Williams stiffened. *Here we go again.*

'I'm quite certain. I spoke with him this morning and he asked me to come by at six. I—'

Before he could get any further, two armed policemen appeared at his side.

'Derek Williams?'

'Yes?' Williams looked up, baffled. Not only because they seemed to have sprung up out of nowhere, but because they knew his name.

'Mr Williams, you're under arrest.'

Before Williams could say anything, the men unceremoniously grabbed an elbow each and physically lifted him off his feet, dragging him backwards towards the street door he'd come in by.

'Under arrest? For what?' Williams demanded, aware of the curious looks from everybody else in the lobby and strangely embarrassed by them. 'This is a mistake!'

'For visa violations,' one of the cops answered, while his partner dug an elbow painfully and deliberately into Williams' ribs. 'We have orders to deport you immediately.'

'Deport me? *What?*' Williams erupted. 'This is bullshit. I don't need a visa. I'm a tourist on—'

A hard blow under the jaw stopped him mid-sentence. A second aimed directly at his nose broke the bone with an audible crunch. Blood poured from Williams' face like an open faucet. The pain was excruciating, but it was the shock, the total surprise of what was happening, that slowed his reactions. Before he knew it, he was being bundled into the back of an unmarked car. And then the beating began in earnest.

He assumed he must have been conscious boarding the plane, but he had no memory of it, or of passing through Mexico City International. He did remember waking mid-flight with indescribable pain in his face and ribs, and a man in a white lab coat sitting next to him pulling out a syringe and plunging it into his leg. When he landed at LAX, however, the seat beside him was empty, so perhaps he'd imagined that part?

Lorraine's anxious face, waiting to meet him, was the first 'real' thing he remembered.

'I got a phone call from some rude asshole at the embassy in Mexico City telling me you'd be on this flight,' she told him. 'I almost didn't come. I thought it was a prank call at first. Jesus Christ, Derek, what happened? What did they do to you?'

'I'm not sure,' Williams mumbled, a fat lip muffling his words. 'One minute I'm waiting for a meeting with this businessman I told you about, and the next thing I know two lunatics are beating the crap out of me and I'm being deported.'

'Well, you need to see a doctor,' Lorraine insisted. 'I'll take you to the urgent care on Pico on our way home. And then we should go to the police. I mean, seriously, Derek, you're an American citizen. You have rights.'

'No.' Williams interrupted her. 'No police. And I don't need a doctor either.'

'Of course you need a doctor, are you nuts?'

'NO!' he said, more loudly than he meant to. 'Sorry, honey. All I want is to go home and sleep and then I need to call the Clancys. See if you can get them in for a meeting first thing tomorrow.'

\* \* \*

Williams' head was exploding with pain even before Todd Clancy started yelling.

'How dare you!' Charlie's father shook his fist threateningly in Williams' general direction, like an angry cartoon character. 'We sent you out to Mexico to find out what happened to our daughter. Not to have you come back here and slander her, drag her name through the mud. You repeat these allegations and I swear to God I'll sue you for every miserable cent you own!'

'They're not "allegations", Mr Clancy,' Williams said, keeping his cool in the face of this unexpected onslaught. 'Think about it. I have no reason to make any of this up, do I? I'm talking to you both privately, as my clients.'

'Ex clients,' growled Tucker Clancy.

'Sir, all I'm interested in is getting justice for your daughter,' Williams protested. 'And I believe we just got a whole lot closer. What happened to me proves it. We're rattling some pretty powerful cages over there.'

'We're not "closer" to anything,' Tucker Clancy snarled, his white button-down shirt looking tighter and more uncomfortable than ever.

'Were you aware that Missing had been investigating Charlotte's disappearance long before they contacted you?' Williams asked, abruptly changing tack.

'What do you mean?' Tucker's eyes narrowed.

'Frederique Zidane, Charlotte's friend, had already been visited, by Mrs Baden personally, months before I showed up. Do you have any idea why Mrs Baden might have kept that from you?'

Mary Clancy and her husband exchanged troubled glances.

'No,' said Tucker, still visibly angry. 'All I know is, whatever this French girl told you, or Valentina Baden, or anybody else, it's a lie. My daughter would never have an affair with a married man. Never! Charlie wasn't even . . . she was eighteen, for God's sake. She was still a virgin.'

'Oh, Tucker!' His wife rubbed her eyes wearily. 'Come on, honey.'

'Come on what?' If possible, Tucker Clancy sounded more outraged.

'She wasn't a virgin,' Mary Clancy insisted calmly. 'She'd been dating that Todd for at least a year.'

'Dating, yes. But that doesn't mean . . .'

Tucker Clancy's wife gave him a pitying look. 'It doesn't do any good yelling about it, honey,' Mary persisted. 'If Mr Williams has found a suspect, or even a motive for someone to want to hurt Charlie, that's progress. Especially if Missing have been keeping things from us – although I can't imagine why they would have.'

'Like hell it's progress!' Tucker Clancy roared, banging his fist on the table and getting to his feet. 'It's bullshit is what it is. You're fired,' he told Williams. 'And I expect a full rebate for the additional week we paid you for, seeing as you managed to get yourself booted out of the goddamn country. Come on, Mary.'

With an apologetic look, his wife followed him out of Williams' office.

A few minutes later, Williams' own wife came in.

*Thank God I got married,* Williams thought, admiring Lorraine's curvaceous bosom under her tight lemon yellow sweater, the baby-bulge beginning to show in the pencil skirt that clung to her ass like saran wrap over a pair of peaches. It made it easier to bear the slings and arrows of outrageous fortune – in this case getting fired for doing exactly what you'd been hired to do – when you knew somebody had your back. Life was better as a team. Maybe later he'd take that trip to the doctor after all. And afterwards Lorraine could tend to his bruises and tell him how much she loved him and comfort him the way that only a woman could . . .

'What the hell, Derek?' Her waspish tone put an end to his fantasy like a pin in a balloon. 'They *fired* you! We needed that money. Do you know how many paying clients I turned away so you could run off to Mexico for those bozos? And now you're out?'

She made it sound like it was his fault.

'I did a damn good job in Mexico,' he shot back angrily. 'A little support might be nice, Lorraine, especially after this.' He pointed to his swollen face, the black eye and distended cheek making him look like a boxer who'd lost a title fight.

But Lorraine was unrelenting.

'It was bad business. I told you that from the moment they walked in the door.'

'Oh yeah? Well, that's too bad. Because it ain't over,' said Williams, finally losing his temper. 'I'm gonna find out what happened to Charlotte Clancy if it's the last thing I do. Whoever's protecting this lover of hers, this American, thinks they've won. But they've got another think coming. And so has Mrs Baden, if she thinks she can keep hiding from me.'

'Is that a fact? Well, so have *you*, Derek Williams, if you think I'm going to stay married to a man who refuses to provide for his family and insists on throwing good money after bad. You think about that while you're off on your wild goose chase.'

And with that she stormed off, slamming the door behind her.

*   *   *

Six beers later, the barmaid at Luca's was a lot more understanding.

'I think it's great that you care about finding this girl, sweetie. I totally get it.'

'I mean someone should care, right?' Williams slurred, his eyes mesmerized by the steady rise and fall of the barmaid's breasts. 'Her ol' man's living in cloud cuckoo land. Doesssn't wanna hear the truth.'

'I hear ya,' the girl said, refilling his glass.

'And my wife . . . my so-called *wife* . . . ish all about money. All about the Benjamins.'

'That's too bad.'

Williams gazed morosely into his glass. He was at the stage of drunkenness where time lost all meaning, and the minutes and hours flew by, indistinguishable from one another. He wasn't sure when, exactly, the red-headed man had sat down beside him or when he'd started talking. But at some point the guy was grabbing him painfully by the shoulders and squaring up to him like he was gonna hit him or something.

'Now you listen to me, you fat moron,' the man told Williams. 'Back off the Clancy case or you'll regret it.'

Belatedly, Williams shrugged him off, raising his own fists in a rather disoriented show of defiance.

'I'll regret it, will I? Says who?' He jabbed the man in the chest with an angry finger.

'Says the professionals.' The redhead pulled out his badge and flashed his gun.

'You call the FBI professional?' Williams scoffed. 'Don't make me laugh.'

'I mean it, Williams, you're an amateur and you're way out of your depth. You don't know what you're doing.'

'I know what *you're* doing, though,' Williams retorted, his beer-addled brain trying to work out how this douchebag knew his name, or where to find him. 'Nothing! You guys never even *tried* to find Charlotte.'

'That's because Charlotte was a cheap whore who more than likely got popped by some small-time drug dealer out there.'

'You don't know what you're talking about,' mumbled Williams.

'Actually, I do,' the man said. 'You need to drop this. And while you're at it, you need to stop harassing the Badens. And Luis Rodriguez.'

'Harassing? I didn't harass anyone!'

'Rodriguez is a good man, a great man actually, and a friend to this country.'

'I never said he wasn't.'

'You're not fit to shine the man's shoes.'

'Ah, go screw yourself.' Williams waved an arm dismissively. He was done arguing with this idiot, and too hammered to try to figure out his cryptic insults.

The man stood up and left a twenty on the bar.

'Consider this a friendly warning,' he told Williams. 'The next one won't be so polite.'

# 23

**Present day . . .**

'**A**aaaagh! Luis. Ay, yes! Yes!'
Luis Rodriguez closed his eyes and tried to tune out the girl's exaggerated moans of pleasure. Why did women do this? Did they think he was too stupid to realize they were faking it? Or that he cared, in any way, about their pleasure?

With his wife – his ex-wife – it had been different. With her it had been making love. Something real. But these twenty-something model/actress/whores that flocked to his bed since his wife left him, hoping for crumbs from his vast fortune? They were there solely for Rodriguez's own pleasure. He couldn't care less whether they lived or died.

'Grrrrrr-aaaagh!' he grunted, climaxing at last inside the writhing beauty beneath him. Annabella. Or was it Isabella? Something like that. They were in his office on Colonia del Valle after a lunch date that had spilled into the early afternoon. The girl had gotten a Tiffany gold bracelet out of it, and Rodriguez had enjoyed an excellent meal, accompanied by the envious stares of his fellow diners, followed by twenty minutes of decently satisfying sex with the girl showing off her yoga moves as he bent her backwards, then forwards, over his couch.

'Oh my God! That was incredible, baby.' She was still gushing as she stepped back into her panties and dress. But he was already back in work mode, sitting at his desk and flipping open his laptop. He had a big deal to close this afternoon with Willie Baden, owner of the LA Rams, and an important new contact to meet before he boarded his private plane to Los Angeles tonight.

The Baden deal had ended up being more complicated than he'd anticipated. Luis had been introduced to Willie through his wife, Valentina, who grew up in Mexico City and who often attended the same charity functions that he did. As two committed philanthropists with a common tragedy in their pasts – Valentina's younger sister had 'disappeared' in her teens, never to be seen again, at the exact same age that Luis's beloved sister, Carlotta, had lost her life to drugs – Luis and Valentina had instantly understood one another. As a result, he'd expected business with Willie to be plain sailing. Unfortunately, the man's greed had made negotiations difficult. Willie was attempting to play hardball. But when push came to shove, no one's balls were harder than Luis Rodriguez's. He could be generous and compassionate, qualities that had won him an adoring fan base amongst the city's poor. But he remained a street-fighter at heart.

Nonetheless, he was anxious about the trip. The streets of LA were Willie Baden's streets, not his, and the rules of warfare were different there.

His nerves were one of the reasons, probably the main one, that Luis had needed sex this afternoon. Isabella's attentions had been a distraction and a release.

He tried to analyze his fears, as he tried to analyze everything. The Baden deal was a part of it, for sure. A bigger part was the fact that this would be the first time in some years that he had set foot on US soil, an event that always raised his stress levels, but that felt even more unpleasant than usual now, amid the new political climate in Washington. This wasn't a good time to be an extremely rich Mexican national, known to the FBI, however decent and honorable your intentions might be. It didn't matter to the American Government that you'd donated millions of dollars to drug rehabilitation charities and other worthy civic causes. It didn't matter that you were part of the solution in Mexico. Once you were a marked man, that was it. They hated you.

*Bastards!* What was it about Americans that made them so envious of success in others, no matter how hard those others might have worked to earn it? Luis Rodriguez was a businessman, pure and simple. The way he saw it, his only 'crime' had been to succeed. Half of Mexico City already belonged to him and the other half would one day, yet he had come up from nothing, from less than nothing. Dirt poverty of a kind that most ordinary Americans couldn't even imagine.

'You look stressed, baby. Let me help.' The girl had crept up behind him and was attempting to massage his bull-like shoulders with her long, bony fingers. She smelled of some heavy, musky perfume and sex. Like a fish dipped in patchouli. Luis felt revulsion, his earlier desire utterly spent and his excellent lobster linguini churning violently in his gut.

'You have to go now. I need to work.'

'Really?' she pouted. But the look on his face answered her question succinctly and she took the hint. 'OK, baby. Well, you've got my number. See you soon.'

Luis didn't even look up as she sashayed out in ridiculously high wedge heels, her narrow hips swinging along with her waist-length hair. *Stupid whore.* He longed for his wife like a child longing for its mother. Everything was worse since she left him.

As soon as the girl had gone, Marisol, his secretary, stuck her loyal, unattractive head around the door. 'The Colombian delegation has arrived, Mr Rodriguez. Should I show them up or do you need a few minutes?'

Luis smiled. He loved Marisol for her tact and discretion. He paid her well, but at the same time he knew that her loyalty ran deeper than money.

'Have them wait in the blue room. Offer them some coffee and tell them I'll join them shortly.'

Luis looked at his watch. In four hours he'd be at the airport. In seven, he'd be in Los Angeles. In the belly of the beast. Now that the day was actually here, it was hard to believe somehow.

Los Angeles, for Luis Rodriguez, meant danger. It meant risk. But it also meant rewards, or at least the opportunity for rewards, of both a business and a personal nature. *It's worth it,* he told himself. *It's time to go. To stake your claim and take what's yours.*

Closing his eyes, he shut his computer and pulled his mother's rosary out of his inside jacket pocket where he always kept it. Three Hail Marys, for Mama, three more for his wife, and he'd be ready for the Colombians.

And after that, for Willie Baden.

*God's on your side, Luis.* He reminded himself of his mother's mantra. *God is always on your side.*

* * *

'How much longer?'

Andrés Malvino felt his chest constrict. He longed to loosen his tie, but knew that it would be a mistake to show the slightest sign of weakness, or even mild discomfort, in front of his boss.

'Hopefully only a few minutes. Control say we're next up for runway two.'

Working as Luis Rodriguez's private pilot for the last eight years had made Andrés a modestly wealthy man. But his frayed nerves had paid the price. Señor Rodriguez did not like being disappointed, and had no qualms about shooting the messenger.

'We'd better be,' Rodriguez grunted and withdrew, displeased, from the cockpit.

Paola, the G650's outrageously sexy stewardess, rested a manicured hand on the pilot's shoulder. 'Don't worry,' she said. 'He's stressed about the whole trip. It isn't you.'

*It doesn't have to be me*, Andrés thought. *He'll turn on the nearest available punching bag.*

'I think he's missing his wife,' Paola whispered.

More bad news. Nothing, but nothing, could put Luis Rodriguez in a worse mood than thinking about his broken marriage. Andrés had flown his boss's wife once or twice when they were together and had always liked her, although she and Rodriguez seemed a strange match to the pilot. Luis was larger than life, a superstar in Mexico City for his generosity and for his championing of the underdog, the common man. His wife was the opposite: shy, quiet. Kind, certainly, but never in a flashy way. She also lacked Luis's legendary, explosive temper, and spent a lot of time apologizing to staff or others in their inner circle for his outbursts, some of which could be genuinely terrifying. It made you wonder what *she'd* been through, living with him . . .

Andrés' headphones crackled. 'Piper 175JP, you are cleared for take-off. Repeat, Piper 175JP, you are cleared.'

'You'd better get back there,' he told Paola with a deep sigh of relief. 'We're off.'

*       *       *

Back in the cabin, Luis Rodriguez leaned back in his custommade, calf-leather chair and sighed with relief himself as his plane roared along the tarmac and shuddered noisily up into the cloudless night sky. His meeting with the Colombians had gone well, and all was set – hopefully – for some productive business in LA. It was Valentina Baden he needed to focus on, he realized now. Willie might wear the crown, but it was plain that his wife was the power behind the throne.

*I must try to focus on the business,* Luis reminded himself, *and not on her.*

He'd been a strong, powerful businessman, full of confidence, when his wife met and fell in love with him. If he were ever going to win her back, he needed to project that same strength now, more than ever.

*Never be needy. Never be weak.*

Putting his computer to one side, he turned his attention instead to the stack of American magazines the flight attendant had handed him. Opening one at random – the latest edition of *Time* – he stumbled upon a feature that instantly grabbed his attention.

Michael Marks, the new, hardline Republican US President, had launched a slew of new initiatives in his first hundred days in office. Luis wasn't a fan of Marks, a tiresome bore of a man who'd taken his predecessor's anti-immigrant rhetoric a step further and already done much to worsen American relations with Latin America – something that, before the election, few Mexicans would have believed possible. One of President Marks' splashiest efforts had been his renewed war on drugs, and in particular the opiate epidemic, which he described as his nation's 'public enemy number one'. On that point, at least, Luis reflected, he was probably right, although his strategy for solving the problem was doomed to failure.

The *Time* journalist had begun his piece as an interview with Marks' new opiates tsar, a man named Richard Grier, but then allowed the article to morph into a broader feature on the latest drug flooding the US market and its devastating impact on users and their families: the Russian desomorphine derivative, Krokodil.

Horrifying pictures of dead-eyed people with gangrenous limbs made Luis's stomach churn. But the images were not as shocking as the statistics. Already on a par with crystal meth in terms of the number of users, only two years after it was first introduced into the US, within the next twenty-four months Krokodil usage was predicted to outstrip meth, heroin and crack cocaine *combined*. As the *Time* writer pointed out, this was bad news not only for the American population, but for the Mexican cartels, who'd seen their business decimated by the Russians. In the long term, however, Krokodil might end up being bad news for all traditional illegal drug suppliers, including the Russians. '*Because, like the meth from which it's derived, this stuff is pretty easy to cook up at home.*'

The journalist went on to compare the predicted collapse of the drug cartels to the downfall of other traditional businesses like record labels, TV networks and book publishers. *'Once a consumer knows they can access a product either for free or much more cheaply themselves – whether that's a Beyoncé song or a hit of narcotics – market forces dictate that the middleman gets pushed out.'*

*Interesting*, Rodriguez thought. Pulling out his phone, he dictated a note to himself. 'Have Marisol look into drug rehab charities in the US. Who's focused on Krokodil?'

He had yet to finalize his philanthropic plans for the year, but a splashy donation to the fight against Krok had just made its way to the top of the list. The pictures of those poor wretches were haunting, the sort of thing that would catch the attention of even the most jaded public. Plus, if Luis channeled the money correctly, it might even impress the right people in Washington and President Marks' administration. As an added bonus, acts of generosity in any form were bound to impress his wife.

It was uncanny how everything came back to her in the end.

# 24

Detective Mick Johnson scratched at the skin on his forearm till it was red and raw. The itching had started as soon as he got out of the car on Denker Avenue, outside Treyvon Raymond's family home. It was as if he had hives. As if he were violently allergic to this shitty neighborhood. *Westmont.* The name sounded so innocuous, even gentrified. In fact, the streets where Trey Raymond had lived his short, brutal life were a human cesspit of violence, drugs, corruption and filth.

A lot of people considered Mick Johnson to be a racist. He used to defend himself against the accusation, but at this point he figured it might be true. And he didn't give a rat's ass. Two of Mick's closest friends, including his last partner, Dave Malone, had been killed on these very streets, both shot to death by young black dealers. The murders had happened in broad daylight, and yet, surprise surprise, not a single witness had come forward to identify the shooters. If it hadn't been for Dave's own hated dash-cam, his killers would never have been caught. As it was they were both now on San Quentin's death row, where they belonged.

It was tough to stay neutral about a community that killed your friends and lied about it. What happened on the streets of South Central LA every day was a war – a war, pure and simple – and black junkies like Treyvon Raymond and his buddies were the enemy. Bleeding-heart liberals like Doug and Nikki Roberts could bleat on all they wanted about reform and rehabilitation and the effects of poverty and gang culture and how 'the system' was failing young African American males. But they weren't in the trenches like the LAPD. It wasn't 'the system' that had executed Dave Malone and stood there laughing about it while he bled to death on the sidewalk.

Johnson hammered on the door of the Raymond house as if it were a raid.

'Open up!' he yelled, his corpulent form bristling with hostility. 'Open the damn door! Police!'

A thin, frail woman's voice answered. 'I'm comin', I'm comin'!'

'Come faster!' Johnson commanded.

\* \* \*

Parked across the street about a hundred yards away, sprawled out in the driver's seat of his battered Nissan Altima, Derek Williams watched Detective Johnson at work, a deep feeling of loathing lodged in his chest. The utterly unprovoked aggression in Johnson's body language and manner as a diminutive, elderly black woman – presumably Treyvon's grandmother – opened the door, made Williams' stomach turn. Here was a grieving family, *victims* of crime, guilty of precisely nothing, being treated like criminals in their own home. Williams could only presume because of the color of their skin, and Detective Johnson's racism. This was what the LAPD called 'community policing'. It was why people hated them.

Derek Williams hated them too, although not for the same reasons. Derek had applied himself to join the police force, three times in total. But each time he'd been rejected, deemed 'not worthy' by the faceless powers-that-be that decided these things. He'd passed the physical. He'd passed all the written exams. And yet three times the letter had arrived: '*Dear Mr Williams, We regret to inform you . . .*'

That was twenty years ago now, but it still stung. Especially when ignorant, prejudiced fools like Mick Johnson, or vain pricks like his partner, Goodman, evidently made the grade.

Johnson spent forty minutes in the Raymond household, eventually emerging red-faced and apparently even angrier than when he went in. Williams waited until the detective had driven off before heaving himself out of his car and approaching the house and knocking respectfully on the door.

'What now?' the voice of a middle-aged woman, weary and resentful, came towards him. 'We already told you all we know. Why don't y'all leave us al— oh!'

A small, attractive black woman in her mid-forties opened the door and did a double take at Williams. Clearly, she'd assumed it was Detective Johnson coming back for more. But her surprise soon gave way to hostility. With narrowed eyes, she asked Williams, 'You another one? You know your friend just left here. Y'all should be out there catching my son's killer instead of wasting yo' morning harassing two innocent women.'

'I'm not a cop,' Williams assured her, extracting a slightly grubby business card from his pocket and handing it over. 'I'm a private investigator. And I *am* trying to catch Trey's killer, Mrs Raymond. That's exactly what I've been hired to do. May I come in?'

Ten minutes later, Williams was sitting on the couch in an immaculately clean living room, sipping coffee from a rose-patterned china cup. Opposite him, in matching armchairs, were Treyvon Raymond's mother and grandmother, both as polite and welcoming as could be.

'So you're working for Dr Roberts?' Trey's mother asked. 'I think she's a good woman. She ain't as warm or easy to talk to as her husband was. The other Dr Roberts. I mean, that man was a saint on earth.'

'A saint,' the older woman echoed, nodding.

'But, you know, she gave our Trey a job, and she was real kind to him, even after Dr Douglas passed away. So we'll always be grateful to her. And she hired you?'

Williams nodded. 'She felt the police weren't doing enough to catch Trey's killer. And she herself has been threatened.'

The two women looked at one another, concerned. 'I did not know that,' Trey's mother said. 'That's too bad.'

'And then there was the other young woman who was killed, Lisa Flannagan . . .'

Trey's mother pulled out a handkerchief and dabbed her eyes. 'Trey was very fond of her, I think. She was one of Doc Roberts' patients, wasn't she? Poor girl. The trash they've been writing about her in the papers, about her boyfriend and all that. I mean, the poor girl lost her life! It's not right.'

'No, ma'am, it's not,' Williams agreed. 'I wonder, would you mind telling me what Detective Johnson was asking you about before? I'm curious as to what lines of inquiry they're pursuing.'

Trey's grandmother rolled her eyes. '"Lines of inquiry?" He wasn't inquiring 'bout nothin'. He jus' came in here to accuse Trey of dealin' drugs.'

'Which is a flat-out lie,' Trey's mother added, indignation blazing in her eyes. 'My son had been clean nearly two years when he died. Thanks to Doc Roberts.'

'I know that, ma'am,' Williams said reassuringly. 'So Johnson was asking about drugs?'

She nodded. 'Who Trey's dealers were, who his friends were, what "gang connections" did he have. I mean, my *God!* My son was a good boy, Mr Williams. So we told the detective that, and he got madder and madder, and then he started asking about Dr Roberts, and what exactly Trey's job was with her.'

'He felt Trey's job might be important to the case?'

'I don't know what he felt. I think mostly he wanted to yell and cuss. He said some terrible things about Dr Roberts and poor Dr Douglas. Said it was the likes of them that kept this neighborhood full of drugs and crime, that made it impossible for the police to help us. Like they want to help us! He basically implied that Dr Roberts never really cared about Trey, that she might even have had something to do with the people who took him . . .' She welled up with tears again, too choked with emotion to go on.

'Take your time, Mrs Raymond,' Williams said gently.

Trey's grandmother leaned over and rested a comforting hand on her daughter's shoulder. 'We told the detective we didn't believe that,' the old woman informed Williams. 'But the truth is, that man didn't care what we had to say. He's got his own ideas about Dr Roberts, and about Trey. He doesn't want to know no truth.'

Collecting herself, Trey's mother added, 'He accused us of being obstructive and he said if he found we'd deliberately withheld information he'd throw both our "black asses" in jail. Then he left. He said he could find Trey's dealer buddies himself. Which is gonna be hard, Mr Williams, as my son did not hang around with *any* of those guys. I mean, none.'

Williams offered his condolences and left, thanking them both for their time and the coffee. 'If you think of anything that might be helpful or important for me to know, you can call that number on my card, anytime. Day or night,' he told Trey's mother.

'Thank you.' She shook his hand gratefully. 'I surely will. And you say hello to Dr Roberts from us.'

Outside on the street, Williams stopped, considering his next move. He was only a few blocks from the corner where all the Westmont dealers hung out. It was one of the few spots where whites were allowed to pass by the local gang enforcers, because it wasn't in anybody's interest to shoot potential customers.

Johnson had probably headed straight there himself from the Raymonds' place, angry and reckless. The man was an out-and-out asshole, but he also had a reputation for being brave, and less likely than most of his colleagues to be intimidated by Westmont's notoriously violent dealers. Williams looked at his cheap watch. It was over an hour since Johnson had left Denker Avenue. The coast must be clear by now.

Jumping back in his car, Williams did a slow drive-by first, to get the lie of the land. All seemed peaceful enough, although he knew from experience that in places like this violence could erupt out of nowhere in an instant. Pulling over about fifty yards from the corner, he warily made his way over to a trio of young Latino men.

In perfect Spanish – after his abortive to trip to Mexico City looking for Charlotte Clancy all those years ago, he'd decided to learn the language – he asked them if a cop had been here in the last hour, asking questions about Trey. He was met with three blank stares. Handing each man a twenty-dollar bill and a packet of cigarettes he tried again.

'The cop was very fat, very white and very rude,' he elaborated, eliciting a smile from one of the trio. 'Kind of an asshole.'

'He was here,' the smiler confirmed. 'No one spoke to him though. He was talking to those junkies before he left.' The man nodded towards a small group of homeless men sprawled out on a sliver of green at the end of the street, opposite the official city park.

'Thanks,' said Williams, handing over another twenty. 'And I'm assuming none of you guys knew Trey?'

The smiler shook his head. 'We know who he is, though. The kid who got knifed, right? By the zombie?'

'There's no such thing as zombies,' Williams said quietly.

'Whatever,' said the smiler. 'That kid never hung around here.'

'Was he a user?' Williams chanced his hand.

'Like I say, I never saw him.'

'Dealer?'

'Not around here. Maybe on the West Side? I heard he had some pretty fancy friends.'

Williams nodded and headed over to the addicts clustered on the verge. Two of them were asleep or passed out, curled up in sleeping bags that were more dirt than fabric. One poor man, a white guy with a big ZZ Top beard, was rocking back and forth on his haunches, muttering something unintelligible to himself and intermittently bursting into possessed laughter. Which only left one young girl, also white and skeletally thin, in a fit state for conversation. Guiltily, Williams slipped her a twenty, knowing exactly what it would be spent on.

Her face lit up. 'Thanks! Oh my God . . . thank you!'

From the depths of his pocket, Williams pulled out a slightly battered Snickers bar. 'Take this too. You need to eat something.'

He asked the girl the same question he'd asked the dealers. She confirmed that Johnson had grilled her and her friends, threatened to arrest them on the spot for possession. 'But we could kinda tell he was bullshitting. He wasn't interested in us. Wanted to know about this boy.'

'Trey Raymond. What did you tell him?'

'Nothing.' She opened the Snickers and began to chew the top half-heartedly. 'Never heard of him. Then again, this ain't my neighborhood. I came here with my boyfriend.' She gestured to the bearded rocker. 'He's not usually like that,' she added, with a blush that was so sweet it broke Williams' heart. *She was somebody's perfect little baby once.*

'No?'

'Uh-uh,' she shook her head sadly. 'It's this new shit he's been on. Krok. Do you know it? It's the worst.'

'I don't,' Williams admitted. 'He scores it around here?'

Suddenly, belatedly, the girl's face clouded over with suspicion and fear. 'Who are you, anyways?' she asked Williams. 'Why are you asking all these questions?'

'I'm a friend of the boy that cop was asking you about,' he replied, pulling a second twenty slowly out of his wallet and turning it over thoughtfully between his fingers. The poor girl stared at it, unable to disguise the longing in her eyes.

'He was abducted, close to where we are now. Whoever took him tortured and killed him. They'd done the same thing to a young girl a few days before.'

The girl shivered. 'That's terrible.'

'Yup,' said Williams, still fingering the bill. 'I don't know if there's a drug connection to what happened to him, but there might be. What can you tell me about the dealers that work here?'

She shook her head. Williams could see the struggle inside her between her desperate need for the money and her fear. Fear was winning. 'Nothing.'

He pulled out a second bill, a fifty this time, and watched the girl's eyes widen as if he were Jesus and he'd just fed the five thousand. Nikki

Roberts' expense account was already proving mightily useful. 'That's a shame,' he said.

'OK, look,' she whispered urgently, beckoning Williams closer. 'Westmont's a war zone right now, but it's also the place you can guarantee the Krok will be clean. You know what I'm saying?' She reached out for the money but Williams held it back.

'Go on,' he said.

'It's a Russian drug, OK? Everywhere else, all over LA, it's Russian business. Those bastards sell cheap, but they cut their stuff with other shit. Like, really, really bad shit. A lot of people have died. A *lot*. Terry and I came here because we heard the Mexicans are running Krok in Westmont now. Don't get me wrong, I hate those guys too. It's not like they're good guys. But their stuff is clean.'

She reached again for the fifty. This time Williams let her touch it, but he kept his grip on the other end. 'What Mexicans?' He looked into her terrified eyes.

'I don't know, man. I don't! They're Terry's dealers, not mine. I don't touch Krok.'

'I need a name, sweetheart,' he said. 'No one will ever know you told me, OK? I'm not a cop. I'm trying to help a friend.'

The poor girl looked as if she might be about to explode with indecision. Eventually, she could stand it no more. Cupping both hands around Williams' ear, she whispered into it.

A name.

Williams' blood ran cold. He let go of the bill and she grabbed it triumphantly, stuffing it into the same pocket into which she'd dispatched the earlier twenty.

'Thank you!' she said again, as Williams turned to leave. 'And good luck, you know. With your friend.'

'Good luck to you too,' said Williams.

After what she'd just told him, they were both going to need it.

# 25

Wiping the sweat from her forehead and underarms, Anne Bateman staggered out of her Soul Cycle class into the bright, Brentwood sunshine in a joyous mood.

Her performance in the Stravinsky concerts had won rave reviews everywhere, and offers were flooding in to her agent on a daily basis. All of which meant she could enjoy her three-week hiatus from the LA Phil without needing to worry about money, or where her next gig was coming from.

Everything was calm on the personal front too. Her husband had stopped bombarding her with texts and calls and flowers, a development that had caused her a brief, sharp pang of sadness followed by a profound flood of relief. Anne still loved him. Part of her would always love him. But Nikki had been quite right: in their case, love simply wasn't enough.

That was the other reason for Anne's good mood this morning. She and Nikki were on good terms again. After their awful, painful fight in her dressing room the night of the concert, when her ex's truckload of roses arrived, Anne had begun to fear it was the last she would ever see of her therapist and dear friend. Too embarrassed to attend her next therapy session, she'd skipped without calling to cancel, and then been so embarrassed about *that* she ended up skipping the next one too. She'd been expecting a call or an email from Nikki's office warning her she'd be charged for the missed appointments, but there'd been nothing. She'd been on the brink of swallowing her pride and apologizing, despite the fact that, even now, in the calm light of day, she didn't feel she'd been in the wrong to call Nikki on her behavior that night. But her life was too lonely and painful to lose the few close friends she had, so she had been steeling herself to make the call when Nikki unexpectedly stepped up. This morning a handwritten letter had arrived at Anne's apartment, containing a brief but heartfelt apology.

'*I'll understand if you feel you prefer a new therapist. Absolutely no hard feelings,*' Nikki wrote. '*But I hope you don't. Because I do genuinely feel that our work together has been helping you. And I think, deep down, you feel the same.*'

Anne wasn't sure what she felt. Other than a happiness bordering on elation that Nikki had come back to her. And yes, she knew that wasn't normal, but she didn't care. It felt great! She'd accused Nikki of crossing the doctor–patient line, and that was the truth. But it was also true that she'd done the same thing herself. If Anne hadn't seen that before, she saw it now.

Crossing the street to the Coral Tree Café, she picked up an overpriced kale juice and jumped in her car, heading over to Nikki's office. Her session wasn't till noon, but she had nowhere else to be, and the desire to see her therapist's face again was so strong she didn't bother trying to resist it. Maybe, if she didn't have a patient prior, the two of them could grab a coffee or have a quick chat before the session?

Cranking up the radio and opening the roof, Anne let the rushing air cool the sweat from her limbs as she sped through the Wilshire Corridor, making a right at Beverly Glen. Palm trees swayed on either side of her to the strains of Justin Bieber and Wiz Khalifa, and above her a lapis blue sky seemed to glow with joy, reflecting Anne's own happiness. Pulling up outside Nikki's building, she was about to hand her keys to the new valet when a familiar voice behind her made her freeze.

'*Hola*, angel.'

And suddenly there he was. Her husband.

Anne's heart leapt into her mouth. She'd imagined this moment countless times since the day she left him. Him, coming to get her, showing up on her doorstep. In the beginning, those thoughts had been nightmares, loaded with dread that she would be dragged back to the cloying life she'd escaped. But as time passed and the distance between them grew, her physical fear faded. As her husband amped up the romantic gestures and loving, conciliatory rhetoric, she'd allowed the scenario to morph into something closer to a romantic daydream. A fantasy.

But now it was real. He was here. He had come for her.

All at once the terror was back.

'Leave me alone! Get away!' Instinctively, she edged closer to the valet stand with its small group of waiting drivers. *Safety in numbers.*

'Anne.'

Luis Rodriguez gazed at his beloved wife with wounded, reproachful eyes.

'It's me, my darling. It's Luis. Why are you afraid?'

There was no anger in his tone. Only sorrow. Anne felt her racing heartbeat start to slow marginally.

He was immaculately dressed as usual in a Savile Row suit and silk tie, was newly shaven, and smelled of the Gucci aftershave he always wore, a scent that even now produced an involuntary response between Anne's legs. In his left hand he carried a bouquet, much more simple than the lavish affair he'd sent to the concert hall. This was a modest, hand-tied posy of spring blooms, but it was full of Anne's favorites: sweet Williams and irises and softly windblown peonies. *He remembered.*

'What are you doing here, Luis?' she asked, softening but still suspicious.

'I had some business in LA,' he replied casually. 'I'll be here for a few days at least.'

Anne's eyes narrowed. 'You told me you could never return to the US. That you can't leave Mexico City.'

'I try hard not to. But this . . . was very important.'

She wondered whether 'this' meant the business or her. Despite herself, a part of her hoped it was the latter.

She studied his face in silence as if trying to work out a puzzle, while a torrent of conflicting emotions raced through her. Was he telling the truth about having business here? Or had he really come for her? And if he had, what did that mean? Should she be flattered, or afraid?

'You know I miss you, Anne.' His voice broke, leaden with love.

'I miss you too,' she said truthfully. 'But you can't . . . you should have called.'

'I don't have your number.'

'You could have left a message with the orchestra. I'm not hard to find. You could have warned me, instead of ambushing me on the street like this.'

'If I'd warned you, you might not have agreed to meet,' Luis said simply.

'Well, wouldn't that have been *my* decision?' Anne asked.

'It would have been. If I'd warned you,' he agreed, smiling. 'This way, it's *my* decision. I like that better.'

Anne couldn't help but smile back. This was classic Luis logic. He really was incorrigible, but somehow he always managed to combine his outrageous arrogance with enough charm to make it endearing. She had never met a man like him, and for all Nikki's warnings, she knew she never would.

'Have lunch with me.' He proffered the flowers, trying to press his advantage.

Anne took them and for a split second their fingertips touched. It was the first physical contact between them since the night before she bolted, and it was electric, charged with both desire and fear.

'I can't.' Anne looked away. 'You know I can't.'

'Why not?' Luis's voice hardened. 'Because *she* says so?' He nodded up at Nikki's building. 'Your so-called therapist?'

The cold fear crept back into Anne's veins, as if someone had changed the drip.

*How did Luis know about Nikki? Come to think of it, how did he know I'd be here at all?*

Suddenly she thought back to the mysterious cars she'd been convinced were following her. The ones Nikki said were all in her head.

'You've had people tailing me!' She backed away again, farther this time. 'Just like you did in Mexico. Spying on me!'

Luis was unapologetic 'The fact we aren't together any more doesn't mean that I've stopped being concerned for your safety, Anne.'

'What do you mean, my "safety"? I'm perfectly safe. Why wouldn't I be safe?'

'Well,' he responded, still smiling, 'in case you haven't noticed, my dear, people close to your therapist friend seem to have developed a nasty habit of showing up dead. I know the police warned you to be cautious, but what are they actually doing to protect you? And what are you doing to protect yourself? Nothing, as far as I could see.'

'I don't need your protection, Luis,' Anne whispered, frightened by how quickly her own resolve was crumbling. 'I didn't ask for it. I don't want it.'

Lunging forward, he grabbed her suddenly by the wrists. Anne struggled half-heartedly, waiting for a bystander to step in, but nobody seemed to notice or care.

'You *do* need it,' Luis whispered in her ear, pulling her close. 'Trust me when I tell you, your Dr Roberts is not who she claims to be. Do you understand me, Anne? She's no innocent in any of this.'

'Don't be ridiculous.' Anne looked at him defiantly. 'Nikki's completely innocent.'

'No.' Luis shook his head urgently. 'There are things you don't know, my darling. Many, many things. She's poisoning you against me, but it's not me you should be afraid of. It's her.'

With one hard yank, Anne wrenched herself free from his grip.

'Leave me alone, Luis!' she shouted at him, loud enough that no one in the valet line could pretend not to hear. 'I mean it. If I see you again, I swear I'll call the police.'

'Anne! Please!'

But it was too late. Anne had already turned and fled, bolting inside Nikki's building like a hunted rabbit.

'Are you all right, miss?' The elevator attendant came over, seeing Anne shaking and repeatedly pounding on the call button.

'I'm fine, thank you,' she lied.

She didn't believe what Luis had said about Nikki. Even so, his words seemed to have embedded themselves in her brain:

'*Dr Roberts is not who she claims to be. She's no innocent.*'

What did he mean by that? And why would he say such a thing?

*Oh God!* Why did he have to come here at all?

Anne waited until she was alone in the elevator with the doors safely closed. Only then did she give way to tears.

# 26

Kim Choy held her breath and pretended to be typing something into her computer as Lana Grey emerged from Dr Nikki Roberts' consulting room.

A graduate intern at the UCLA Semel Institute for Neuroscience, Kim was Nikki's newly hired assistant, a hasty replacement for poor Trey. Although both brilliant and beautiful, with perfectly smooth Asian skin, wide eyes and a long mane of silken black hair, Kim had been raised by strict Chinese parents and had led a very sheltered existence thus far in her twenty-four years on earth. As a result, she was utterly star-struck to see Lana, *a famous TV star*, walk right past her *in the flesh!*

'May I schedule another appointment for you, Miss Grey?' Poor Kim's heart was pounding so fast it was hard to get the words out. She'd never interacted with a 'celebrity' before. Evidently her new part-time job was going to bring her into contact with a whole new world, a side to Los Angeles that she'd heard about but never seen, beavering away at the library on UCLA's Westwood campus or spending late nights cramming in the neuroscience department. It was all too exciting for words!

Lana looked at the slim, attractive Asian girl behind the desk in Dr Roberts' lobby and felt envy choke her like a golfball lodged in her throat. As if the therapist's smugness weren't bad enough on its own, with Nikki rubbing her perfect life and beautiful figure and barely lined skin in Lana's face at every session, now the bitch had gone and hired some teenage beauty queen to run the office.

There was no way she wasn't doing it on purpose. *She wants my self-esteem on the floor, so she can keep me coming back for more therapy at three hundred dollars an hour.* You couldn't trust anyone these days.

Leaning over Kim's desk threateningly, Lana snarled: 'If I wanted to schedule another appointment, I'd say so, wouldn't I?'

'Oh.' Kim blushed to the roots of her hair. She'd put her foot in it somehow, made a mistake. Was she not supposed to speak to clients, or ask about appointments? 'I'm sorry, Miss Grey. I just thought . . .'

'Yes, well don't. I won't be coming back,' Lana announced, sweeping out of the office and slamming the door behind her.

Hearing the commotion, Nikki emerged to find her poor receptionist close to tears.

'I'm terribly sorry, Dr Roberts,' Kim blurted. 'I think, somehow, I must have offended Miss Grey. I asked about scheduling another appointment and she . . . she . . . well, she became very angry with me.'

'Don't worry, Kim, it wasn't your fault,' Nikki said reassuringly. 'I'm afraid Lana's been very angry for a long time. I'm sure it had nothing to do with you.'

'She said she wouldn't be coming back,' Kim admitted nervously.

'Yes,' Nikki smiled. 'She says that a lot too. You'll get used to it. You can send Carter Berkeley in as soon as he arrives.'

Back inside her consulting room, Nikki closed her eyes and began her own breathing exercises, the ones Doug had taught her years ago as a way to calm her emotions and that she still relied upon to this day.

*First, breathe.* Nikki could hear Doug's voice in her head, as if he were standing next to her. *Then separate your thoughts out one by one, slowly and calmly, as if you were laying out individual leaves on a table, or seeds in a tray.*

Thought number one: Lana was getting worse, not better, and edging into psychosis. Every prettier, younger woman was a threat, an enemy. The time had come to gently guide her towards another therapist. In all honesty, she probably ought to see a psychiatrist too. But would Nikki be able to get her there?

*Breathe.*

Thought number two: No one else had been killed, or hurt, since Trey and the threats to Nikki had also stopped, for now. Was the person trying to kill her done? Or merely biding their time, toying with her like a cat with a cornered mouse? If so, would Derek Williams be able to catch them before they struck again? Everything had gone ominously quiet on the police front, which she took to mean that Johnson and Goodman were no further forward. It was Williams or bust.

*Breathe. One step at a time, Nikki. Focus on your patients. Focus on the now.*

Thought number three wasn't a thought, so much as a series of faces. Doug's. Anne's. Goodman's. And a fourth, hidden face, still obscured by shadows: Lenka, Doug's mistress. Would Williams succeed where Nikki had failed, and find out something, anything, about the woman whose death had ripped apart Nikki's life?

The 'patient waiting' light on Nikki's wall suddenly turned red. Carter Berkeley must be here. Nikki found sessions with Carter difficult at the moment. His paranoia, always a problem, seemed to be escalating out of control. Ever since Lisa Flannagan's murder, he'd become so jumpy, so wildly suspicious of everybody, it was tough to get any effective work done in treatment. *I'm failing him too, just like I'm failing Lana,* Nikki thought miserably. *I wasn't a good enough wife, I couldn't even get pregnant, and now I'm failing as a therapist too.*

Stamping down her depression, like someone throwing a damp blanket over a fire – she could hear her friend Gretchen Adler's voice, telling her to 'get a grip' – she pulled herself together and opened the door, smiling serenely.

'Carter. Do come in.'

Carter stood up, revealing heavy bandages on his left leg from the knee down. Looking around him furtively, he grabbed a pair of crutches from the other side of his chair and limped through into Nikki's office.

'What happened?' Nikki asked, as soon as they were alone.

Setting his crutches to one side Carter eased himself down onto Nikki's couch. His face was white, with beads of sweat glistening on his forehead like tiny pearls, and his legs were shaking uncontrollably. Looking up at Nikki, he said through gritted teeth, 'I was shot. They shot me.'

'Oh my God!' Nikki was suitably horrified. 'Carter, I'm so sorry. Who shot you? And when did this happen?'

'I didn't get a good look at their faces. But it was the same guys, the Mexican gang I've been telling you about. I've had threats . . . they broke into my home. I told the police, but they didn't do anything. They acted like I was making it up.'

A shiver ran down Nikki's spine at the similarity to her own experience. Mysterious break-ins. Disbelieving police . . .

'Whatever,' Carter said angrily. 'Screw them. I know the truth. It was the same guys. Last Saturday. I came out of a club downtown around one thirty a.m. They must have followed me there. I was outside, waiting for my car, and this car pulls up, two guys get out, one of them shoots me in the shin and they drive off.'

He finished this monologue in an oddly flat tone. When he was done, Nikki noticed his teeth were chattering. It was as if he were still in shock – as well he might be, if his story was true.

'Did anyone else see it happen?'

Carter shook his head. 'No. I was the only customer outside and the valet had already left to pick up my car. By the time he got back I was on the ground, bleeding and barely conscious.'

'Right,' said Nikki, her mind whirring. On a human level, she wanted to believe him. He did, after all, appear to have been shot. So if his story wasn't true, that would imply that he'd deliberately shot himself, in some sort of Munchausenesque bid for what? Attention? She couldn't believe Carter was that far gone. He was still functioning in his job at the bank, still lucid.

On the other hand, yet again these mysterious 'Mexicans' seemed to have struck at a time when there were no witnesses, and left no evidence to corroborate his story.

'Did you call the police? Or did the valet? He must have been shocked to find you like that?'

Carter's eyes swiveled wildly around in his sockets. For a moment he looked truly insane. 'Maybe.' He dropped his voice to a whisper. 'Or maybe he was in on it. Maybe he tipped these guys off? Did you think of that? They have people everywhere, all over LA, all over the US. They're like a *plague*.'

'Who are "they", Carter?' Nikki asked softly. 'You've told me that you believe they're from Mexico but beyond that—'

'I don't believe it. I *know* it,' Carter insisted. 'And I know who they are but I can't tell you because it would be dangerous for you to know. And dangerous for *me* if anyone were to find out I'd told you.' He was speaking at a hundred miles an hour, the words tumbling out in a bizarre, paranoid stream-of-consciousness. 'They shot me in the leg, but they could have killed me. Right? But they didn't. So that means they're sending a warning. They don't want me dead, they want me *quiet*.'

'OK,' said Nikki.

'But it's not OK, because I need to talk about it, Doc! I need to tell someone what happened! I was there. I saw it. I saw them kill her. They made me watch, like it was some kind of show. *Oh God!*' Slumping forwards onto his knees, Carter broke down in terrible, wracking sobs.

Nikki moved to sit next to him, wrapping an arm around his shaking shoulders. This was important. Very important. It could be the breakthrough she'd been waiting for.

'What did they make you watch, Carter?'

He shook his head violently. 'I can't!'

'Yes, you can,' said Nikki. 'Close your eyes.'

He did as she asked.

'Now breathe deeply. And now imagine yourself there. What do you see?'

'I see trees.' His voice took on a trance-like quality. 'I see a clearing in the trees. It's nighttime. It's dark but there's moonlight. It's hot.'

'Good, Carter. Very good. What else?'

'I see the girl. She's in the clearing.'

'OK. What does she look like?' asked Nikki. Guiding clients through these sorts of retrieved memories was notoriously tricky, like walking a tightrope. Not enough prompting and the images could slip away, back into the deep unconscious mind. Too much and the client could become frightened and oppositional. Once the flow was broken it was damn near impossible to get it back.

'She's naked,' said Carter. He frowned. 'No, not naked. She has panties on. She's standing there, sort of swaying. And then . . .'

He stopped, and winced, like a dog running into an invisible electric fence.

'And then?' Nikki repeated softly.

Carter's breath quickened and his hands began worrying at his pant legs. He let out a sharp, frightened cry, like a yelp.

Nikki waited.

'I hear the guns,' he said. 'Like a drum beat. *Pop pop pop pop pop!* Machine guns. I don't see them. But I see her, the girl. Jerking. Jumping. It's awful! The blood, it's . . .' He gasped for breath, clawing wildly at his own legs. 'Bits of her are coming off! Oh God! I think she's dead, but she's still moving . . .'

He started to sob again. Nikki realized she probably only had seconds left.

'Do you know the girl, Carter?'

He nodded.

'What's her name?'

Opening his eyes with a jerk, he looked directly at Nikki. 'He made me watch. He made me! He was laughing. There was blood everywhere. *Everywhere*. The most disgusting thing I've ever seen. He's an animal.'

'What was the girl's name, Carter?' Nikki asked. But she already knew she'd lost him.

'If I told you that, Doc, he'd kill you too.'

'And who's "he"?'

Carter smiled then, a weary smile, but sincere. He got to his feet.

'I appreciate everything you've done for me, Dr Roberts. Especially today. I needed to get that out. To say it out loud.'

'I'm glad you did, Carter,' said Nikki. 'Maybe next time we can—'

'No,' said Carter. 'There won't be a next time. There can't be, I'm afraid. I can't escape him.' He looked at her with tears in his eyes. 'I thought I could. Start again, you know. But I see now that was never an option. You, though? You can escape. You can still get away. Reinvent yourself. Start again.'

'I'm not going anywhere, Carter,' said Nikki firmly.

'I hope you change your mind,' he said, shaking her hand with real feeling. 'Good luck, Dr Roberts. And goodbye.'

Nikki watched him limp out of her office, a strange feeling lodged in her chest. She'd helped him today, more than in all their past sessions combined. That much was clear. Like a doctor lancing an infected boil, it had been painful, but emptying his subconscious mind had brought Carter Berkeley instant and visible relief.

Now whether the story he'd told her was *true* or not was another matter. The girl might be a real girl. Or an imagined one, representing some aspect of Carter's own personality, or some figure from his past.

It wasn't the story itself, but Carter's last words to Nikki that pressed down heavily on her heart. '*You can still get away. Reinvent yourself. Start again.*'

Could she?

It was certainly an intoxicating thought.

Anne Bateman had called not long ago to cancel their midday session. At the time Nikki had felt disappointed, but now she was relieved to be alone and done for the day. Leaning back in her chair she felt dizzy all of a sudden and realized she hadn't eaten or drunk anything since breakfast.

As she was scrabbling about in her desk drawer for a protein bar, her cell phone rang. Nikki was about to ignore it, but then saw Derek Williams' name pop up on her screen.

'Any news?' she asked anxiously.

'I do have news,' he responded, sounding surprisingly downbeat. 'Where are you right now? Can you come to my office?'

'I can,' Nikki answered cautiously. 'I'm in Century City. But can't you tell me over the phone?'

Williams hesitated. 'I'd rather we met. How about in an hour?'

'OK,' said Nikki, her pulse already starting to quicken.

He had news. News too important to tell her over the phone. To her own shame, Nikki found herself praying that it wasn't about the murders at all, but about the mysterious Lenka.

*Please let him have found something,* she entreated the God she didn't believe in.

*Please, after all this time, let me find some peace.*

Before she could even think about taking Carter Berkeley's advice and starting again, she needed to know the truth.

# 27

'**P**lease, please, sit down.'

The fat PI made a sweeping, welcome gesture with one arm, while with the other he literally swept piles of old papers off of his fake leather 'client' seat.

'How's your day been so far, Dr Roberts?' he asked Nikki cheerfully. After his reticence on the phone earlier, he seemed in a surprisingly ebullient mood.

'My day? It's been exhausting, actually,' Nikki answered truthfully, running a hand through her hair. 'Two of my clients seem to have totally lost the plot.' She didn't know why, but something about Derek Williams made her feel safe, willing to let her guard down in a way she wouldn't with other people. Certainly not other men. It struck her now that perhaps it was because he didn't flirt with her. At all. In Nikki's experience, that was pretty unusual.

'Only two? I'd call that lucky,' he quipped, rearranging things so that his own seat and desk were relatively clear before they got started. 'Pretty much all of my clients have lost the plot. Most of them a very long time ago. Present company excepted, naturally.'

He smiled again and Nikki couldn't help but smile back.

'So what's this news?' she asked him eagerly. 'Please tell me it's about my husband's mistress.'

Williams spread his fingers wide over his chubby thighs and turned his empty palms over.

'It is not,' he informed her. 'Sorry.'

Nikki's face fell.

'It's early days,' Williams reminded her. 'We'll get to the girl eventually, believe me. And what I *do* have for you,' he looked at her proudly, 'is a pretty awesome start, if I say so myself.'

'OK,' Nikki sighed. She could use a shot of awesome right now. 'Impress me.'

Derek Williams cleared his throat. 'So I read everything you gave me, all the information. And I decided to start with Trey Raymond.'

He told Nikki about his trip out to Westmont, which began as a simple tail on Detective Johnson. 'Luckily for me, our favorite racist cop made things real easy for me, throwing his weight around and antagonizing everyone from the Raymond family to the neighborhood dealers he was trying to pump for information. It won't come as any surprise that no one told him anything. After that, all I had to do was walk in and be civil and the floodgates opened.'

Nikki waited for him to go on.

'Trey stopped using two years ago, shortly after he met your husband.'

'That's right,' Nikki confirmed. 'Doug brought him back from the brink.'

'He did,' Williams agreed. 'But things weren't that simple. Before he got clean, Trey had been dealing to feed his habit. Heroin, mostly. But later, at the end, he was pushing a new kind of desomorphine. It's codeine-based and it's incredibly nasty stuff. The street name for it is Krokodil.'

'I know what it is,' said Nikki. 'Doug's partner, Haddon Defoe, says they're running into it all the time at the clinic. It's horrific. He said the Russians introduced it.'

'That's right,' said Williams, impressed. 'Well, Trey had been working for a Mexican cartel, in competition with the Russians, before he met your husband. The guys he was working for back then, they don't believe in "fresh starts". I don't think they ever had any intention of letting him walk away.'

'But he did walk away,' Nikki insisted. 'Doug took him under his wing and Trey totally changed his life. I gave him a job. Trey came to work in my office every day, always on time, always professional.'

'That was his day job,' Williams said bluntly. 'I don't doubt your husband was a good man, Nikki, but for someone who worked closely with addicts, I'm afraid he was incredibly naive about the business side of the narcotics world. Trey's "other" boss was a Mexican drug lord by the name of Carlos de la Rosa.'

He looked up at Nikki, but the name obviously meant nothing to her. She was still in shock at the idea that Trey had been dealing drugs behind everyone's back.

'Do you think this man was the one who killed Trey? Or had him killed?'

'I don't know for sure. But I'd say it was a fairly safe bet, especially if Trey *was* trying to walk away, like you said, or had defied him in some way. De la Rosa is a big fish in Westmont,' Williams explained. 'But he's small fry in the world of the cartels. His boss is a far, far more dangerous man. And that's where this gets really interesting.'

'Who's his boss?' Nikki asked.

'Believe it or not, Dr Roberts, it's someone you know. Or at least know of. Luis Domingo Rodriguez.'

Nikki frowned, trying to place the name.

'Your patient Anne Bateman is his estranged wife,' said Williams. Turning around his laptop, he showed Nikki a picture on Google Images of a suave, attractive, Latin man with black hair graying at the temples and intense, watchful eyes.

Nikki looked confused. 'I think you must be mistaken, Mr Williams. Or gotten your wires crossed somehow. Anne's husband is a real-estate developer.'

'Please, call me Derek,' Williams reminded her. 'And I'm not mistaken. Luis Rodriguez married Anne Bateman in a private ceremony in Costa Rica eight years ago. I can show you a copy of the marriage certificate if you're interested. *I* was interested because I've run across Luis Rodriguez before on an old case. It was a missing persons case officially, although unofficially everybody knows the girl was murdered. Have you ever heard of Charlotte Clancy?'

Nikki closed her eyes and rubbed her temples. Her conversation with Gretchen a few weeks ago suddenly came back to her. *Charlotte Clancy, the au pair? The one Valentina Baden had been looking for?* Nikki felt as if she'd somehow slipped into the twilight zone, some bizarre alternate universe where everybody's lives were joined together by mysterious dark forces in a spider's web of misery. A world where Trey was a drug dealer, and Anne's husband was a drug lord. None of it made any sense at all.

'But . . . Anne told me her husband worked in real estate,' she repeated numbly, trying desperately to cling to reality. 'That's how he made his fortune.'

'No,' said Williams. 'It's how he *invests* his fortune. He *made* it twenty years ago, flooding Western US cities with cocaine.'

For the next fifteen minutes, Derek filled Nikki in on the case that had turned his life upside down – Charlotte Clancy's disappearance. He told her how he'd hoped Luis Rodriguez might lead him to Charlotte's secret, married lover, the Jaguar-driving American who Williams felt sure had had a hand in her disappearance. But how, instead, he'd been abducted by Mexican cops, beaten severely and deported back to the States. He told her how Valentina Baden and her charity had purported to 'help' the Clancys, paying for TV adverts about their daughter's disappearance, but had in fact been investigating all along in Mexico City and hiding information from the family. And how once he got back home he'd been visited by the FBI and 'warned off' from looking into the Badens or Rodriguez, again and again and again.

'Rodriguez wasn't even my main focus at that time,' he explained to Nikki. 'I don't think Luis was directly responsible for Charlie Clancy's disappearance, only that he might have known the man who was. And Valentina Baden might have known him too. But when everybody's telling you *not* to look at someone, *not* to ask questions . . . you get curious. At least, I do. So over the years I learned a lot about Luis Rodriguez.'

'Such as?' Nikki asked. She'd long been fascinated by the strange, Svengali-like hold Anne's husband seemed to have over her. Perhaps Williams could fill in the blanks?

'Well, for one thing, the man is basically two people. A real Jekyll-and-Hyde character. He came up from nothing, which makes him a hero to a lot of the poor over there. They see him as some sort of Robin Hood figure, and in a way he is. He gives away a ton of money, especially to drug-related causes. The whole of Mexico knows the story of his sister's death from heroin addiction, how it changed his life.'

Nikki cast her mind back to her sessions with Anne, where she'd mentioned something about her husband's philanthropy and his tragic past.

'That's all real,' said Williams. 'And his real estate empire is real too. It just happens to be the best cover story *ever* for a major cocaine producer. Which is what he is.'

Williams explained how Rodriguez had evaded justice both at home and in the US by a skillful directing of his resources towards both the police and the impoverished communities, ravaged by drugs, they purported to serve. 'He's everybody's friend. It's kind of incredible. Ordinary people don't know about his cartel, and they wouldn't believe it if they were told. Meanwhile, those in authority who *do* know have had it made worth their while to turn a blind eye. We're talking more than lining the pockets of corrupt officials. That's Rodriguez's genius: he's generous and he's charming, and he's embedded himself in every possible aspect of these communities' infrastructures. So in Mexico he pays for schools and roads and hospitals. Here in the US he funds senatorial races, gives a ton of money to our friends the LAPD. He's a master manipulator.'

That last part rang true to Nikki from her many long and torturous conversations with Anne. As for the rest of it, she wasn't sure what to believe. She was perfectly happy to imagine that Anne's husband was a 'bad hombre' with illicit businesses behind his legitimate ones. But Williams' characterization of Luis Rodriguez as some sort of untouchable drug kingpin smacked of a conspiracy theory worthy of Carter Berkeley.

'Can you prove any of this?' she asked Williams outright.

'Not much of it,' Williams admitted. 'Not yet anyway. But I'm working on it. I've been working on it for almost a decade, ever since Charlotte's father, Tucker Clancy, fired me.'

'Why'd he fire you?' Nikki asked.

Williams shrugged. 'He didn't want to hear the truth about his daughter. That she'd been seeing a married man and all that. I mean, I get it. He was her dad.'

Nikki thought for a moment. 'What about Valentina's charity? You said you thought they were involved.'

Williams inhaled deeply. 'I did. I mean, I still do, potentially. But that's been a lot harder to unravel, a real hornets' nest. And to be frank with you, after a while I let it go, because Rodriguez was clearly the bigger fish in all of this. But' – he cleared his throat – 'I'm pretty sure Missing isn't all it seems to be. I heard rumors when I was down in Mexico City that they had a hand in orchestrating some of these kidnappings that they then helped to "solve".'

Nikki frowned. 'Why would they do that?'

Williams rubbed his fingers together to indicate money. 'There's a whole bunch of ways to make a profit from abduction. I heard that Valentina "helped" families to pay ransoms and then took a cut from the kidnappers. That's the most obvious business model. Other times Missing were paid by the gangs to smuggle members or associates out of the country – supposedly some of them into witness protection programs here in the States. Which would mean Mrs Baden must have had inside help.'

'From the police, you mean?' asked Nikki.

Williams chuckled. 'Don't sound so shocked. The LAPD are as bent as an old coat hanger. I also got good information that Missing were involved in people-trafficking. Young girls were being picked up off the street and sold to Russian sex-gangs. Nothing I could prove. But there were a lot of rumors.'

Nikki's eyes widened. 'You don't think . . . Charlotte Clancy?'

Williams shook his head. 'Unlikely. Sex-trafficking is usually low income, Favela kids, young girls – and boys – with no status, no family to look out for them. An eighteen-year-old American girl would have been more trouble than she was worth. But one way or another I got the strong impression that the charitable side of Missing's work was a front. Huge sums of money were flowing through that organization – way more than you'd see for a legitimate NGO.'

Nikki lapsed into silence. It was difficult squaring Williams' 'rumors' with what Gretchen had told her about Valentina Baden. About her sister going missing when they were teenagers, and how that tragedy had changed and inspired her life. Nikki wasn't sure why, but she desperately wanted to believe the inspirational version over the corrupt one. Too much around her was rotten at the moment. Was it too much to ask that Williams be wrong about this one?

'In any case,' Williams broke the silence, 'Mrs Baden is kind of a sideshow here. The real linchpin has always been Luis Rodriguez. In the last two years his entire focus has shifted from cocaine to Krok. He's been trying to wrest control of the supply chain from the Russians, right here in LA. He has guys all over the city right now. They're like a plague.'

Nikki's pulse quickened. *Plague.* Wasn't that the exact word Carter had used in her office earlier about these mysterious Mexican assassins he claimed were trying to kill him? Or at least to scare him into silence, perhaps about a murder, if Carter's stream-of-consciousness ramblings were to be believed?

*Another link. Another dark thread in the spider's web.*

She forced herself to think rationally, to sift out the facts from this sea of speculation.

'Let's assume you're right about Luis's drug business. Do you think Anne knows?' she asked Williams.

'I am right,' he replied. 'As to whether his latest wife knew where his cash came from, I have no idea. I've never met Anne. But from what you've told me about her, I doubt it. Like I said, Rodriguez has a split personality. He may well have kept his business and personal life totally separate.'

*I have to tell her,* thought Nikki. *She has a right to know who her husband really is. Every wife has that right. The right not to live a lie, because of her husband's secrets.* She wondered how many of Anne's friends had known about Luis and kept the truth from her. The same way that Haddon Defoe and countless of Doug's colleagues had kept the truth from Nikki.

'But you say the police *do* know?' Nikki looked at Williams. 'The FBI and the police here in LA?'

'Oh yeah. They know.' Williams nodded grimly. 'You can bet the LAPD drug squad has got files as big as the telephone book on Rodriguez and De la Rosa. They know where and how this so-called "clean" Mexican Krok is coming into the city. But they seem to be letting Rodriguez's guys act with impunity.'

'Because . . . ?' Nikki raised a questioning eyebrow.

Williams shrugged. 'Either they prefer the Mexicans to the Russians, so it's a lesser of two evils thing. Or, someone senior in the department is getting a cut.'

Nikki digested this for a moment.

'So you're saying the police are in on the deal? That they're sharing the cartel's profits, in the same way they did with Missing?'

'I believe so, yes,' said Williams. 'The police are in on it and maybe others in the community too. Rodriguez is doing exactly what he did back in Mexico. Making friends, oiling the right palms, but also speaking up for the underclass – his customer base.'

Registering Nikki's skeptical face Williams doubled down on his theory.

'I'm certain the Mexican cartels are a part of this. That they're involved in Trey's death, and Lisa's. You should prepare yourself for the possibility that they had something to do with your husband's "accident" as well.'

Nikki's eyes glazed over. She let the PI's words wash over her, retreating into self-protection mode. She didn't want Doug's death to be a part of this spider web. His accident, his mistress, had nothing to do with Anne Bateman's ex-husband. How could they possibly?

'So. That's the summary so far.' Williams sat back in his chair, satisfied. 'What would you like me to focus on next?'

Nikki looked at him blankly.

'This week I focused on Trey,' Williams recapped. 'Starting tomorrow, I could dig deeper into Lisa Flannagan. Her past drug use – maybe find a connection to one of the cartel's dealers? Or her affair with Willie Baden. Maybe Willie and Valentina are a bigger part of this than I realized. Or I could try to find out why the police are so interested in your old patient, Brandon Grolsch. Or, I could keep following our friend Detective Johnson, see if his corrupt, racist fingers are jammed anywhere in this shit-pie? You're the boss,' Williams reminded Nikki. 'She who pays the piper calls the tune.'

The old-fashioned expression made Nikki smile.

'Is something funny?'

'No, not really,' said Nikki, still smiling. 'It's just . . . you're a nice man, Derek. You're working really hard on this, and you seem to have so much energy. My head is spinning, but I'm grateful, that's all. I trust you.'

Williams looked down awkwardly. It had been a long time since anybody had paid him a compliment, never mind a beautiful woman.

'Well. Thank you.' He cleared his throat, visibly embarrassed. 'I appreciate that. Could you maybe put that in writing to my ex-wife? The "nice man" part? I'll waive next month's fees.'

'Really?' asked Nikki.

'Nah, not really. I need the money,' Williams grinned. 'Speaking of which, I could use a tiny top-up on expenses . . .'

Nikki pulled out her checkbook. She was well aware she was paying over the odds, but she didn't care. In four days, Williams had achieved more than Johnson and Goodman had in almost two weeks. Although exactly what she was supposed to do with all his half-baked rumors, theories and connections she wasn't sure. Yet.

'This week I'd like you to focus on my husband's accident,' she told him, tearing off the check and pressing it into his clammy palm. 'I want to know more about Lenka.'

Williams considered this. 'Are you sure? That's your priority?'

'That's my priority,' said Nikki.

'You do realize that your own life is probably still in danger?' Williams pointed out, reasonably. 'These cartels are multimillion-dollar businesses. And they're run by psychopaths. I'm not only talking about

Luis Rodriguez here. The Russians, Mexicans, Chinese, they're all the same when it comes to disposing of their enemies.'

'How am I their enemy?' asked Nikki.

'I don't know yet,' replied Williams. 'But I'd like to spend this week trying to find that out – before you wind up cut to ribbons and dumped by the side of the freeway, or knocked down like a bowling pin on the road. No offense.'

'None taken,' said Nikki. 'And I appreciate your concern, Derek, I really do. But if there's a risk I might die tomorrow, what I actually *need* more than anything is to know the truth about my husband. This other woman, this Lenka – who *was* she? Surely that shouldn't be so hard a question to answer?'

'You're the boss,' said Williams again.

He watched from the window while Nikki drove off. She was a strange one, Dr Nikki Roberts. Then again, everyone was strange in their own way. He liked her. He especially liked the fact that she'd called him a 'nice man'. Not the most earth-shattering of compliments, perhaps. But it was sincere and it had touched him, more than he liked to admit.

As he drove home, Williams tried the words on for size, repeating them out loud to himself:

'You're a nice man. You're a nice man, Derek.'

*I'm a nice man.*

He would find out the story behind Doug Roberts' mistress. Because Nikki was right, really – how hard could that be? And he would find this killer too, and the people behind him, the dark forces threatening Nikki. The Badens were caught up in it somehow. And Rodriguez of course. Although, as with Charlotte Clancy, Williams suspected Luis was probably only one player in a larger, more sinister play. He, Derek Williams, would solve the mystery of the Zombie Killings and save the day and make everything OK for his beautiful client.

Not because she paid him.

But because he was a nice man.

\*   \*   \*

Nikki was a few blocks from Williams' office when she saw headlights flashing her from behind. At first she thought it must be some ticked-off driver she'd accidentally cut in front of. LA rush hour was full of angry, impatient assholes. But the lights kept flashing until at last they were followed by a single '*whoop*' of a police siren. She realized she was being pulled over.

Irritated, she pulled to the side of the road and wound down her window.

'Was I doing something wrong offic— Oh! It's you.'

Detective Goodman's handsome face smiled down at her. 'I've been trying to get your attention for the last mile. Ever since you left Derek Williams' office, in fact.'

Nikki flushed. 'How do you know about Williams? Were you following me?'

'Don't sound so outraged,' Goodman replied. 'That's my job. Part of it, anyway. I'm a detective and this is a murder inquiry. One in which *you*'re a potential target, in case you'd forgotten.'

His blue eyes locked with hers and once again Nikki was surprised by the strength of her attraction. 'Sorry,' she mumbled. 'I didn't mean to accuse you. I know you're only doing your job. You surprised me, that's all.'

'Where are you headed right now?' Goodman asked her.

'Home,' said Nikki.

'Have you eaten yet?'

The question caught her off guard. 'Not yet.'

'Good. Follow me,' Goodman said decisively. 'I know a Greek place a few blocks away – you'll love it. We should talk,' he added, seeing Nikki hesitate. 'About your new friend Mr Williams. There are some things you should know about him.'

*   *   *

Ten minutes later, Nikki found herself seated at a booth in the back of Stavros' Taverna on Westwood Boulevard, opposite a noticeably relaxed Lou Goodman. The top two buttons of his shirt were open and his sleeves were rolled up, revealing muscular forearms. His skin was smooth and tanned, and his teeth almost offputtingly white when he smiled. *Like the Big Bad Wolf,* thought Nikki, although in truth there was nothing predatory about his manner. The reality was, she simply wasn't used to spending time with single, attractive men. The awkwardness wasn't helped by the fact that the last time they'd had dinner together, at Dan Tana's, she'd gotten hammered and very nearly ended up in bed with him. And all the while, someone – perhaps the killer – had been watching them.

'Maybe we'd better steer clear of the Retsina,' Goodman said, reading her mind and ordering water and appetizers for the table. 'I wouldn't want to be accused of taking advantage of a lady.'

Sexual tension crackled in the air between them, but Nikki determinedly ignored it. Her life was complicated enough without romantic entanglements. Her feelings for Anne Bateman already took up three quarters of her available emotional energy, besides which she was still grieving Doug. She wasn't ready.

'So what is it that I need to know about Derek Williams?' she asked.

'Aside from the fact he's a slob and a conspiracy theorist and a card-carrying cop-hater, you mean?' Goodman observed caustically. 'Quite a lot, actually.'

'I like him,' countered Nikki boldly.

'Is that so?' Goodman rose to the challenge with good humor. 'Why?'

'He's authentic,' said Nikki.

'*Authentic . . .*' Goodman repeated the word, apparently amused. 'Well, that's one way of putting it, I suppose. His loathing of our department is definitely authentic.'

'And why is *that*, do you think?' Nikki asked, genuinely curious. It was true that she had heard Derek badmouth the LAPD more than once.

Goodman took a sip of his drink. 'He'd tell you it's because we're all corrupt and lazy and stupid,' he told Nikki. 'But the truth is it's his own bitterness that drives him. He applied to join the force himself when he was younger, a bunch of times, and they turned him down.'

'On what grounds?' Nikki asked. 'If you ask me, he's a gifted detective.'

'No idea,' said Goodman. 'Bad character? Impulsiveness? Derek Williams is not exactly what you'd call a team player. Whatever the reason, I guess he took it personally, because he's been a thorn in the department's side ever since. Sabotaging and obstructing cases. Compromising evidence, influencing witnesses. The drug squad literally have his picture on the wall of their rec room. They stick pins in it. Williams screwed those guys over so many times, they've lost count.'

Nikki felt confused. Goodman was obviously being sincere – and yet his description of a bitter, vengeful man didn't square with the Derek Williams she knew.

'This case is not about justice for him, whatever he might have told you,' Goodman went on bitterly. 'It's about settling scores, a personal vendetta with us. That and money. He'll bleed you dry if you let him. Out of interest, how much has he charged you already?'

Nikki halved the number she'd actually given Williams, but even that was embarrassingly high when she said it out loud.

'Look, sweetheart, it's your call,' Goodman said, not unkindly. 'But you heard it here first: the man's a charlatan. Be careful what you share with him.'

Having successfully sowed at least a small seed of doubt in Nikki's mind, he deftly switched the subject.

'I actually wanted to ask you about something else,' he said.

'Oh?' Nikki sipped her own drink, still glowing inside from his earlier endearment.

'Brandon Grolsch,' Goodman said bluntly, extinguishing the glow. 'I know you said you never treated him. But might your husband have run across him, at one of his clinics? He was a hardcore heroin addict, among other things.'

'It's possible,' Nikki said cautiously. 'Doug and Haddon helped so many people.'

'But they must have kept records, right? Of their patients?'

'Yeeeees. Some.' Nikki was hesitant. 'But it wasn't like my practice, or a normal medical office. This was a drop-in center. People passed through. Many were homeless, with no ID, no insurance, no social security number. To try to track down one individual would be like looking for a needle in a haystack.'

'You know, Johnson's like a dog with a bone on this,' Goodman warned her. 'If it turns out there *was* a link between Grolsch and your husband, or with you – that won't look good for you, Nikki.'

'I don't see why.' Nikki sat up taller, rising to Goodman's challenge, if that's what it was. 'I can't be expected to remember every addict my husband ever treated.'

'True.' Goodman smiled, his eyes twinkling again.

Nikki wasn't sure what to make of it. The entire conversation felt like a strange game of tennis that was part flirtation and part deadly serious. Should she trust him?

'Why are you so interested in this Brandon Grolsch anyway?'

Goodman looked at her for a few moments, as if weighing up how much he should divulge. 'We found his DNA on both bodies,' he said eventually. 'OK? So now it's your turn.'

'My turn to what?'

'Oh, come on, Nikki!' Goodman rolled his eyes. 'If you know anything about Brandon, you should tell us. We think he's dead, by the way.'

If he was waiting for a reaction from Nikki, he was disappointed.

'That's where all these stupid "zombie" stories came from,' he went on. 'The DNA we found didn't come from a living human but from a corpse. Brandon's corpse. So if you figure you're protecting him, you're not. The only person you're protecting is the murderer.'

'Firstly, I'm not protecting any murderer,' Nikki insisted, defiantly. 'So your partner Johnson can go digging for that needle as hard as he likes. And secondly, you should let him know that I'm well aware of how to handle myself in a courtroom. I've been called as an expert witness many times in the past, and I don't bully easily.'

'I'm sure you don't,' Goodman said, a clear note of admiration in his voice.

'No offense to you,' Nikki went on, glad that the conversation had moved on from the subject of Brandon. She'd made her decision on that score and having begun in the lie it was too late to turn back now. 'But more than once I've had to testify against police officers. Your friends in the drug squad, the guys sticking pins in Derek Williams' picture? Well, guess what? Williams is *right* when he calls those guys corrupt.'

'Some of them, maybe,' Goodman admitted.

'Many of them,' said Nikki. 'Too many.'

Somewhere in the back of Goodman's mind, a penny was slowly dropping.

*'I've been an expert witness . . .'*

*'I've had to testify against police . . .'*

'I've seen your colleagues stand up in court and lie through their teeth to protect each other,' Nikki warmed to her theme, conveniently forgetting that she, too, had just lied about Brandon Grolsch. 'Doug told me countless horror stories about police planting evidence, framing addicts and small-time dealers to get convictions, and all the while the big suppliers went free. Derek Williams is not the only one with mixed feelings about you guys.'

'OK, OK.' Goodman held up his hands in a gesture of innocence. 'I get it. But try to remember, *I'm* not the enemy, OK?'

'I know that.' Nikki softened. 'I never thought you were. I only hired Derek because I needed some answers. And because I was getting tired of being treated like a suspect.'

Goodman got the check and again refused to let Nikki split it. Afterwards he walked her to her car.

'Be careful,' he repeated. 'Until we catch this guy. Please be careful.'

'I will,' said Nikki, adding, tongue in cheek, 'Derek Williams gave me the same advice earlier.'

Goodman scowled. 'Williams wants your money, Nikki. I don't. Remember that, when you're thinking about who to trust.'

As he drove off, his parting words rang in Nikki's ears.

# 28

The town of Chowchilla, in Madera County California, had only two features deemed interesting enough to warrant a mention on Wikipedia. The first was that the town's name itself meant 'Murderers', a reference to the notoriously warlike Chaushila tribe of Native Americans who first settled there. And the second was the presence of Valley State Prison, formerly a women-only institution, but now home to almost a thousand male inmates.

Classified as 'medium security', from the outside the low, squat quadrangle of concrete buildings ringed with barbed wire and electric fences appeared forbidding enough to make any visitor wonder what a 'high-security' prison might look like.

Jerry Kovak hadn't seen the outside of Valley State in six years, not since the day he first arrived here, transferred from an overcrowded hellhole of a prison in LA County. Jerry had his pal Mick Johnson to thank for his move, and for many other things too. Jerry's waste-of-space attorneys had told him not to squander his time on another 'hopeless' appeal – as if he had anything better to do, stuck in here! But Mick Johnson hadn't given up and had helped Jerry lodge the paperwork. Without it, or some other kind of miracle, Jerry would never see the outside of Valley State's walls or anything beyond them until he was carried out in a coffin.

Shuffling into the visitors' room, an attempt at a cheerful space with brightly colored walls and a play area for children in one corner, Jerry took a seat and waited. He'd hoped his daughter might have made it today. It was almost six months since he'd last seen Julie. But she had three kids of her own now, and a husband who disapproved of Jerry, plus Chowchilla was a four-hour drive from LA. *You can't expect too much,* he told himself, doing his best to mask his disappointment when Mick Johnson waddled in alone. *She has her own life to live now.*

Taking the seat opposite Jerry's, Mick handed over the few meager gifts he'd been allowed to bring: a fishing magazine, a book of Sudoku and some herbal tablets supposed to help with joint pain. 'How are you, man? You look good.'

'Thanks,' said Jerry. 'I'm doin' OK, considering.'

This was an obvious lie. When Mick Johnson and Jerry Kovak first met as junior detectives, Jerry had been a seriously handsome guy. A football player, super-athletic, with the kind of chiseled jock's features that made him every woman's type. But despite his great looks and endless opportunity, Jerry had been a one-woman guy, utterly devoted to his wife Marianne and their kid, Julie.

That was fifteen years ago now. They'd all aged since then. But whereas Mick and the rest of the guys had simply grown fatter and balder, Jerry had withered like a tree in the desert. Stooped and frail, his skin as cracked and dry as parchment, his eyes rheumy and red, he had become an old man. Arthritic. Broken. Pathetic, in the true sense of the word.

It was the year he turned forty-five that it all came crashing down, the blows raining on poor Jerry Kovak like hailstones from a vengeful heaven. First Marianne got sick. Then, really quickly, faster than anyone expected, she died. Mick would never forget Jerry during those days, howling like a wounded dog, wracked with a tormenting grief beyond anything that Mick had ever witnessed.

He should have taken time off then. Some sort of compassionate leave, time to process things, to grieve in private with his daughter. But things were different in those days. Jerry had not long transferred into the drug squad, the first Pole in an almost entirely Irish division, and that was a big deal. Those guys didn't go home and cry. They were fighting a war, and the war didn't stop because somebody's wife had dropped dead of cancer at forty-two. Besides, Jerry didn't want to stop work. He needed the distraction, he told Mick at the time, not to mention the money. 'It's only me and Julie now. I have to provide for her.'

So Detective Kovak had gone back on the streets, and at first he seemed OK. But as his grief shifted through despair, to denial and into anger, things began to change. Jerry would start losing his temper at colleagues, flying off the handle over the smallest thing. In an argument over a parking spot, he threw a punch at a junior officer, breaking the poor kid's nose. That was all handled on the down low, and Jerry apologized. But out on the streets, in his daily interactions with the junkies and dealers and hookers and informants that were the bread and butter of drug squad life, he became a different person. Hardened. Battle weary, yet at the same time, looking for a fight.

Eventually, he found one. Kelsey James, a lowlife, piece of shit pimp and part-time crack dealer from Watts, gave Jerry some false information that led to the collapse of his first big case. Jerry drove straight from the courthouse to find James, pulled him out of his car in broad daylight and beat him to a bloody pulp on the street. For three weeks the boy was in intensive care, and for a while there it looked like he might not make it. In the end, he lived – more was the pity as far as Mick Johnson was concerned – but the doctors said he would spend the rest of his life in a wheelchair and need constant nursing care to be able to perform even the most basic functions.

Jerry was charged with aggravated assault and attempted murder. The boys all rallied round in court – it was in the line of duty. Kelsey looked like he was reaching for a weapon. Jerry could have used his firearm but he didn't. He showed restraint. But then Kelsey James's mama showed up, sobbing and wailing, and his sisters yelling blue murder about police brutality and what a 'good boy' their dealing, scumbag brother was, how Jerry had robbed him of his bright future.

Mick Johnson attended the trial every day. He could see the judge – a liberal, bleeding heart woman – buying every word of the James family's baloney. It made Johnson's stomach turn, listening to them lie through their teeth and blacken a good man's name. But there was nothing he could do about it. Clearly, Jerry needed some other line of defense, some sob story of his own to soften the judge's heart.

Luckily, he had one. Diminished responsibility, due to his mental state after Marianne's death. His attorney was doing a pretty good job with it too, bringing little Julie up on to the stand to tell everyone how much she loved her dad and how hard losing her mom had been on the family. Character witnesses from Julie's school and soccer team spoke up for Jerry. Even the local pastor came and sang his praises.

But then that bitch Nikki Roberts took the stand. And just like that, Jerry Kovak's case unraveled, and with it his future. Dr Roberts was called as an expert witness, to talk about the psychological effects of grief. Could grief explain what Jerry had done? Could it excuse or mitigate a sudden, compulsive display of violence? Was it at least possible that Jerry Kovak was not in his right mind when he attacked Kelsey James?

*No.*

*No.*

*No.*

'Doctor' Roberts never wavered in her damning judgment of poor Jerry. In her expert opinion, he showed zero signs of mental incapacity. His attack was premeditated, not compulsive or spontaneous. His motives, according to Nikki, were racist and selfish, his actions rooted in rage rather than grief. Mick Johnson could do nothing but sit and watch helplessly as this young slip of a girl who knew nothing about Jerry, and even less about the dangers cops like him faced on the streets every day at the hands of the Kelsey Jameses of this world, annihilated any hope his friend had of clemency.

Jerry Kovak was found guilty and sentenced to twenty-five years in jail.

Twice he'd appealed his sentence. Twice, Nikki Roberts had come forward *voluntarily* to re-state her case: that there should be no mercy for Jerry, no compassion, no 'special circumstances'. 'Justice for Kelsey' was all that mattered, apparently. Nikki Roberts had gone out of her way to ensure that Jerry Kovak would spend the rest of his days behind bars.

Mick Johnson would never forgive her for that.

Smiling at his old friend, doing his best to project an optimism that he didn't feel, Mick told Jerry he'd filed his appeal.

'You think we have a shot?' Jerry asked querulously.

'Sure we do,' said Mick. 'But these things take time. We won't hear anything back for at least six weeks. And that's only the initial processing.'

'I got time,' Jerry said wryly. 'That's the one thing I've still got. So tell me, how's your case going? You said it was knife murders, right?'

'Yeah,' Johnson muttered. 'It's going OK, I guess. Slower than I'd like, but I think we're closing in.'

He'd made a conscious decision not to tell Jerry about Dr Nikki Roberts' connection to the Zombie Killings, or to share any of the lurid details about the case. At this point, he was certain that Nikki was involved in both murders, and the death of her husband. But he needed to prove it. Only once he had her safely behind bars and suffering would he share the good news with Jerry. Maybe then, at last, the courts would throw out her earlier, damning testimony? Either way, Mick wasn't about to raise poor Jerry's hopes again only to dash them.

So far he had no concrete evidence. Shit, he hadn't even been able to convince his own *partner* that Dr Nikki Roberts wasn't the saintly, butter-wouldn't-melt do-gooder she pretended to be, but was in fact a vengeful woman, certainly capable of premeditated spite, and very possibly of serial murder.

For the rest of Johnson's visit, the two men talked about nothing much. Baseball, old friends from the drug squad days. Mick promised to come back next month, and to try to talk Julie into coming with him. He had no children of his own, but it shocked and saddened him to see a man's only daughter turn her back on her dad the way Julie Kovak had with Jerry. That was another thing Nikki Roberts had stolen from his friend – his relationship with his daughter. Julie had been thirteen when her father was put away. Too much time had passed, too much distance.

It was all such a waste.

＊　＊　＊

Halfway back to LA, the air con broke in Johnson's car. He opened all the windows, but still found himself driving drenched in sweat, his shirt stuck to his flabby back and his clammy palms sliding on the wheel as he weaved through the lanes of traffic. By the time Goodman called he was panting like an overheated dog. It was like taking a call in a sauna.

'What?' Johnson snapped.

'Where are you?' Annoyed, Goodman mirrored his curt tone.

'Driving.'

'Driving where?'

'Jesus, what is this?' said Johnson. 'If you must know, I'm driving back from Valley State Prison.'

'Visiting your friend Detective Kovak, I assume?' Goodman said slyly. 'Well, what a coincidence. It so happens I'm sitting here looking at the transcripts from Kovak's trial. And you'll never guess who popped up as the prosecution's *key expert witness*.' Goodman sounded triumphant. 'I had dinner with Nikki Roberts last night.'

'Course you did,' muttered Johnson bitterly.

'And she mentioned something about her court experience,' Goodman continued, ignoring him. 'For some reason it resonated, so I did a little digging and whaddaya know? Turns out you two *do* have history.'

'OK, OK,' said Johnson gruffly. 'You can lose the sarcasm.'

'Why didn't you tell me?' Goodman asked accusingly.

'Nothing to tell,' said Johnson.

'"*Nothing to tell*"? Oh, come on! This is why you hate her, isn't it? Because she testified against your best friend.'

'No,' said Johnson slowly. 'I hate her because she's a spiteful bitch. And because I happen to believe she orchestrated the murders of three innocent people.'

'You should have recused yourself from the investigation, Mick,' Goodman said angrily.

'Bullshit. Why?'

'Because you're predisposed against her!'

'Oh, I am, am I? Well, what about you?' Johnson shot back defensively. 'You've been trying to get the woman into bed since day one! You had dinner with her last night, for Christ's sake! Doesn't that make you equally biased the other way?'

'No,' Goodman snapped. 'And for your information, I have not been trying to get her into bed. I've been trying to get close to her, to win her trust. There's a difference.'

Johnson snorted derisively, but deep down he was shaken. He hadn't expected his partner to make the Kovak connection. Now that he had, Johnson would have to tread even more carefully around Nikki Roberts.

'I don't suppose you got "close" enough last night to get her to stop lying about Grolsch and come clean?' he asked Goodman, knowing this was the one weak spot in his partner's otherwise unwavering faith in Dr Roberts.

'I'm still pushing,' Goodman admitted. 'But brace yourself for this my friend: I did learn we have a third wheel on this case. It seems your lack of trust in Nikki Roberts is reciprocated.'

'*Reciprocated?*' Johnson mocked him. 'That the sort of big word they teach you at Harvard, is it?'

'She's hired Derek Williams, Mick,' Goodman said bluntly.

Johnson swerved, narrowly missing a semi in the left-hand lane. From the other end of the line Goodman heard a wild screeching of brakes, followed by a stream of the sort of language no one's grandmother ought to hear.

When Johnson finally came back on the line he sounded winded, like he was gasping for breath. 'You arc kidding me, right?'

'I wish I were,' Goodman sighed. 'I followed her to his office yesterday.'

'That fat bastard . . .' Johnson muttered. It was the pot calling the kettle black, but Goodman decided this was no time to quibble over insults.

'According to Nikki, she hired him to come up with some answers. Because we haven't given her any. And because she's tired of being treated like a suspect.'

*We've given her plenty of answers,* thought Johnson. *But she doesn't like them because they all point back to her.*

His mind scrambled to process this new information. Why had Dr Roberts hired Derek Williams? If Johnson was right, and Nikki was behind these killings herself, then it made no sense for her to hire a PI. *Unless she's using him to dig up dirt on us? So she can discredit our investigation and get away with murder. Literally.*

His head started to swim. Part of him wanted to share these doubts with Goodman. But his partner already thought he was biased against Nikki. This latest theory would be the icing on the cake. On the other hand, he couldn't sit by and do nothing while she instructed the appalling Williams to trample all over their investigation like a god-damn elephant.

'We have to stop him,' he told Goodman.

'At last, something we agree on,' Lou replied. 'The question is how?'

Both men were silent for a moment. Then Johnson said, 'One of us needs to pay him a visit.'

'Not one of us,' said Goodman. 'Both of us. We'll talk about it when you get back here.'

\* \* \*

Goodman hung up and began placing the transcripts of the Kovak trial back in the file.

So. It looked as though he and Johnson were partners again, albeit uneasy ones. It was a small step in the right direction. He remembered his father's old advice about keeping your friends close but your enemies closer. Lou Goodman had always tried to live by those words.

They were one of the reasons he was still alive.

# 29

**D**erek Williams flipped awkwardly through the latest copy of *Angelino Magazine*, sneaking regular glances at the clock. He was in the waiting room at Haddon Defoe's private medical practice in Beverly Hills, his ample backside ensconced in an expensive Italian leather armchair. The room, in Williams' view, was self-consciously 'fancy', as if the prints of silent movie stars lining the walls, or the exquisite Venetian glass vase full of peonies on the coffee table could make up for the outrageous fees Defoe charged his private patients.

He was aware that for-profit work was only a small part of what Haddon Defoe did for a living – Williams had done his homework and was familiar with the doctor's tireless work helping the city's addicts and providing basic healthcare services for the homeless. Not to mention his private but extensive donations to African American causes in some of LA's roughest neighborhoods. On paper at least, the man was a borderline saint. Williams had no reason to begrudge him his fancy Beverly Hills office, or his luxurious house in the Palisades Riviera, or his priceless collection of silent movie memorabilia. But a part of him couldn't help but chafe at the pretentious opulence of this waiting room, all Diptyque scented candles and silk cushions and piped classical music drifting out from state-of-the-art Bose speakers.

'Mr Williams?'

Haddon's beautiful secretary, a coffee-colored goddess with coltish legs and a dazzling smile, gestured to the door behind her desk.

'Dr Defoe will see you now. If you'd like to go through?'

Unpeeling himself from his seat with an embarrassing squelching sound, Williams lumbered through into Haddon Defoe's office.

'Mr Williams, hello! How can I help?'

Defoe's unexpected warmth put the PI even more on the back foot. Stepping out from behind his desk in rolled-up shirtsleeves, smiling broadly, Haddon offered Williams his outstretched hand. 'You wanted to talk to me about Doug Roberts?'

'That's right.' Williams pressed his clammy palm against Haddon's dry one. 'His wife – his widow, I should say – has received some pretty unpleasant threats. She's my client,' he added, by way of explanation. 'I'm wondering whether the person making them might have had some connection to her late husband.'

'Someone's been threatening Nikki?' Haddon's expression darkened. 'She never mentioned that to me.'

'Would she be likely to?' Williams asked casually. 'Are the two of you close?'

'Well, I . . .' The question seemed to catch Haddon off guard. 'Do the police know about these threats?' he asked, dodging it.

Williams gave a snort. 'The police? Oh yes. They know. But let's just say keeping Dr Roberts safe doesn't seem to be at the top of their priority list. That's why she hired me.' He handed Haddon his card. 'That and other reasons.'

Haddon examined the card curiously. Taking a seat, he gestured to Williams to do the same.

'What other reasons?' He looked at Williams quizzically.

Williams cleared his throat. 'When Doug Roberts died, I understand he had his mistress with him in the car?'

'Ah. That.' Haddon frowned.

'So it's true?'

'Yes. It's true. So that's what Nikki's hired you to investigate? Doug's affair?'

'That's part of it, yes. She told me she knew nothing about this mistress's existence until the day of the accident. Does that surprise you?'

Haddon groaned and rubbed his temples. 'No. Not really.'

'But *you* knew about her?' Williams surmised. 'I mean, you must have, right? You and Doug being such close friends, working together and everything.'

'We were very close, yes,' said Haddon, again not directly answering Williams' question. He sounded irritated now, his earlier warmth rapidly evaporating. 'I wish Nikki would let this go,' he said, shaking his head. 'For her sake and everybody else's. Doug's dead. Lenka's dead.'

'You told Nikki you'd never met Lenka.' Williams dropped in the information as if it were a trifling detail.

'That's right,' said Haddon. 'I never did.'

'Hmmm.' Williams looked puzzled. 'That's odd.' Pulling out his phone, he passed it across the desk to Defoe. 'Because this *looks* like a picture of the three of you at a fundraiser together two years ago. Action on Addiction's summer gala, I believe it was. You don't remember that evening?'

Haddon looked at the image calmly, before handing the phone back. It was a grainy group shot – everybody's features were blurred – but it plainly showed Doug Roberts with his arm around a woman who was considerably too tall and full-figured to be his wife.

'I'm afraid not, no. I go to a lot of fundraisers. She's the brunette, I assume?'

'She is, yes,' said Williams. 'But then I'm guessing you probably knew that already, seeing as you were the one who invited her that night, and introduced her to Doug Roberts in the first place.'

Haddon Defoe smiled thinly. 'You've done your homework. I see Nikki chose well when she hired you, Mr Williams.'

*He's a cool customer,* thought Williams, although he noticed the small muscle twitching involuntarily at the top of the doctor's jaw.

'But maybe not so well choosing her husband. Or her friends.' Williams smiled back.

'Oh, I wouldn't say that,' said Haddon, refusing to take the bait. 'Doug and Nikki had a solid marriage. And while I consider myself a friend of Nikki's, I was a closer friend to Doug. I wouldn't feel right betraying his secrets, especially now that he's gone. We all make mistakes, Mr Williams. Whatever wrongs Doug Roberts may have done, to his wife or anyone else, hasn't he more than paid for them? He's dead after all. Cut off in his prime.'

'*He's* paid for them, yes,' Williams agreed. 'But have you, Dr Defoe?'

Haddon's eyes narrowed. 'What do you mean by that?'

Williams leaned back in his chair. 'Here's what I'm thinking: You were jealous of Doug Roberts. Your so-called "friend" beat you at everything. He scored higher on his medical exams. Got a more prestigious internship. He founded your addiction clinics and got all the glory for them, all the PR, while *you* played second fiddle.'

Haddon laughed loudly. 'Don't be ridiculous, man! It's a charity, not a competition.'

'He married a beautiful girl,' Williams went on, ignoring him. 'A girl you'd always lusted after yourself. And, like you said, it was a strong marriage – unlike your own, that collapsed after what? A year?'

'Eighteen months,' Haddon muttered, through gritted teeth. Not even he could smile through the mention of his ex-wife, Christie, and the humiliation of being so publicly abandoned.

'But most of all you hated Doug for landing the top position at the Addiction Recovery Clinic at Cedars. You both applied for it, and you'd been led to believe that the job was yours, hadn't you? But then your *dear friend*, Mr Charisma himself, snatches that out from under you . . .'

'Oh, don't stop there, Mr Williams,' Haddon drawled, regaining his composure as Williams paused for breath. 'I'm a fan of good fiction. I want to know how this story ends.'

'It ends with you introducing Doug Roberts to a woman named Lenka Gordievski. Setting up a honeytrap to destroy his happy marriage.'

Haddon shook his head. 'Look,' he said, putting his palms up on the table. 'You might be right about some of this, OK? Maybe I *was* jealous of Doug. It was hard not to be, Mr Williams. He was an amazing, amazing man. One of a kind. But I was also his friend. And yes, I introduced him to Lenka. Nikki doesn't know that, and I'd rather it stays that way.'

'I'll bet you would,' said Williams, but Haddon cut him off impatiently.

'It wasn't what you think,' he insisted. 'I'd met her in New York, at another charity thing. She was a sweet girl, she had money, she cared about the issues Doug and I cared about. But it wasn't a *honeytrap*. It was a casual introduction. I never intended him to have an affair with her! Why would I?'

For a moment Derek Williams hesitated. He didn't like Haddon Defoe, didn't trust his goody-two-shoes image as far as he could throw it. Yet something about this last speech was oddly convincing.

'What do you know about Lenka's background? Her life back in Russia?' Williams asked him.

'Nothing,' said Haddon. 'Like I say, she was an acquaintance.'

Williams shook his head. 'I'm not buying that, Dr Defoe. You see, I've been doing my own research on Ms Gordievski this week. And the funny thing is, there's nothing to find.'

'I don't understand,' said Haddon.

'Nor do I!' Williams agreed. 'It's the darnedest thing. But there's no record of her having left Russia, or entered the US, although she obviously did both. No addresses on file before she arrived in LA, no credit report. You say she had money, but I can't find any record of bank accounts. Only a landlord here in LA, who gave me her surname incidentally, but said she always paid in cash. It's almost as if she was a spy or something!' Williams laughed coldly. 'Or someone living under an assumed identity. Witness protection, perhaps?'

'I told you, I barely knew her,' Haddon insisted.

'She was your best friend's lover for a year!' Williams scoffed. 'You must have met her multiple times. But you lied to Nikki about that, like you're lying to me now. Who *was* she, Dr Defoe?'

'I don't know!' Haddon yelled in frustration. 'Good God, man, what's wrong with you? You're right that I lied to Nikki about never having met Lenka. But wouldn't you, in my shoes? Doug loved Nikki,' he went on. 'The affair was a mistake, an infatuation. It would have ended eventually.'

'It did end eventually,' said Williams. 'In a ball of flames on the freeway, that conveniently left *you* running the entire charity operation, as well as creating the very opening you'd hoped for at Cedars. You've applied for Doug Roberts' old job, haven't you, Dr Defoe?'

Haddon scowled, no longer trying to rein in his anger.

'Yes, I applied for it. Because I'm a highly qualified candidate, and why wouldn't I? Doug would have wanted me to apply. He would have encouraged me – something you'd know if you knew anything at all about the man who Doug was. How dare you come into my office making accusations and insinuations?'

'I'm not making accusations.'

'Oh, I think you are.' Haddon's voice was rising again. 'You're accusing me of wanting Doug dead! That's what you think. Well, you're wrong. He was my *best friend*. So I'm sorry if that didn't show up in your research, Mr Williams. But that is the truth. That is a FACT.'

Williams opened his mouth to speak, but Haddon cut him off.

'Enough!' he barked, shaking with rage. 'Get the hell out of my office.'

*   *   *

Outside, standing in the sunshine on Bedford Drive, Derek Williams wondered whether he'd gone too far, and how the aftermath of his interview with Defoe would play out. Would Haddon call Nikki and complain about him? Tell her that her attack dog was on the wrong track about Lenka? Convince her to dump Williams and let the police handle everything?

On the whole, Williams doubted it. Haddon Defoe had lied to Nikki about Doug's mistress. That was a can of worms he had no wish to re-open. Nor would Haddon want to get into the murky details of his and Doug's professional rivalry, something else Williams would lay good money that Nikki knew nothing about. It was amazing how often people were willing to act against their own best interests through a desire not to the rock the boat. Derek Williams saw it happen every day.

Thankfully, Derek's own boat was empty and full of holes. He had nothing left to lose, no matter how hard people rocked it.

\* \* \*

Standing at his office window. Haddon Defoe watched Nikki's squat toad of a PI loitering on the sidewalk, lost in thought, before finally disappearing into the parking structure across the street.

Haddon's face betrayed no emotion. But in the pit of his stomach, a painful knot tightened.

He picked up the phone and dialed the number of a private calling service. Moments later, his call no longer traceable, he was put through.

'The PI was just here,' Haddon said. 'The guy Nikki hired. Williams.'

'And?'

'He's a problem,' Haddon said simply. 'Something needs to be done.'

\* \* \*

'So I have a dilemma.'

Anne Bateman looked over at Nikki, biting down anxiously on her lower lip. It was the first therapy session Anne had come to since their row at the concert, and both women wanted it to go well.

'It's about my husband. My ex-husband,' she blurted. 'But I need you to hear me out. Don't jump to conclusions.'

'OK,' Nikki said soothingly, as much to calm her own fears as to combat Anne's. She was encouraged by Anne's use of the term 'ex-husband.' That was new, and Nikki hoped it might mean that divorce proceedings were actually underway. But after everything Derek Williams had told her about Anne's ex, she still wasn't sure how best to handle things with Anne. Should she tell Anne what she knew? Warn her that her ex might not be who she thought he was at all? It would risk whatever shreds were left of their friendship, the intimacy between them that had come to mean so much to Nikki. On the other hand, if she didn't say anything, and Williams was right about Luis Rodriguez's secret life as a drug lord, and – God forbid – something were to happen to Anne . . . The whole thing was a mess.

'What about your ex?'

Anne took a deep breath. 'He's here,' she told Nikki. 'In Los Angeles. I've seen him.'

'I see,' said Nikki, with a calmness she was far from feeling. Luis Rodriguez was here? What did that mean for the case, and for her own safety? Did Williams know? Did the police?

*Don't say anything,* she told herself. *Let Anne talk. Let her come to you.*

'He told me he's here on business, but I don't know if I believe him,' said Anne. 'I think he came for me. To convince me to go back to him.'

'I see.' Nikki struggled to hide her shock. 'So how did you end up meeting with him?'

'It wasn't by choice!' Anne gabbled defensively. 'He ambushed me on the street. Right here actually, outside your office. The other day when I came for therapy.'

Nikki felt the hairs on her forearms stand on end. Rodriguez had been *here*? At her office? That was too close for comfort.

'I didn't tell you because I didn't want . . .' Anne wrung her fingers together miserably. 'I knew how you felt about him already. And I didn't want to make it worse. With us.'

Nikki reached across to the couch and took her hand. 'I'm so sorry I made you feel that way. I'll always be here for you, Anne. I hope you know that.'

'I do, now.' Anne sniffed.

'I'd like to know more about him,' said Nikki, seeing her chance to get Anne to open up.

Anne looked surprised. 'Really? Like what?'

'Anything, really,' Nikki smiled. 'I don't know if you realize but you've never even told me his name.'

'His name is Luis,' said Anne. 'Luis Rodriguez.'

'You never took his surname?' Nikki asked.

'I wouldn't go psychoanalyzing that,' Anne laughed, delighted that the conversation seemed to be going smoothly for once. 'I've always performed as Bateman so it made no sense to change.'

'Fair enough,' said Nikki. 'And you mentioned his business is in real estate?'

Anne nodded. 'That's right.'

'Is that his only business?'

The question was thrown out so casually, Anne barely seemed to notice it.

'As far as I know,' she replied. 'That's partly why I don't believe he's here on business. All his real estate deals are in Mexico City, so why would he come here, if not to see me?'

Her bafflement seemed genuine to Nikki. If Williams was right about Rodriguez's criminal empire, then his wife knew nothing about it. She'd stake her professional reputation on that. What was left of it.

'The truth is, he scared me that day outside your office. He was so forceful, so insistent that I agree to see him again. Not violent,' she added hastily. 'It's more that he, sort of, *overwhelms* me. Luis is a very strong-willed man, very determined. When he wants something, he simply doesn't stop until he gets it.'

'And he wants you,' Nikki said quietly.

Anne's voice was almost a whisper. 'Yes. He does. He wants me.'

Nikki allowed the silence to hold for a good twenty seconds before she spoke again.

'And what about you, Anne? What do you want?'

'I want to be free,' Anne said firmly, and with much more certainty than Nikki had expected. 'Part of me will always love him. That's the simple truth. But I want to live my life, Nikki. I want to stop looking over my shoulder day and night.'

'You're ready to let go.' Nikki smiled approvingly, sweet relief flooding her own body. She too wanted Anne to be free. One day, she hoped, she might be free herself. Once all this nightmare with the murders was over, and Derek Williams had found out the truth about Lenka and Doug's affair and everything that happened last year. Once the killing could stop.

'Yes,' said Anne. 'I am ready. But that's the dilemma I told you about before. I need Luis to let go as well. I need him to go home, not because I tell him to, but because *he* realizes it's over between us. I need his men to stop following me. But I don't think that can happen unless we, Luis and I, have some sort of closure. We need to agree to be friends, somehow. To reset our relationship.'

'I see,' said Nikki, still trying to adjust to this new, stronger Anne.

'That's what I wanted to ask you about,' said Anne, emboldened by Nikki's supportive responses. 'He's asked me to join his table at the End Addiction Ball at the Four Seasons tomorrow night. I think I should do it.'

A pained look swept over Nikki's features. She and Doug used to go to the End Addiction gala every year. The ball was one of their favorite nights, a rare chance for Nikki to dress up and for the two of them to go on a real 'date' together. Bittersweet memories from those times mingled with a genuine concern for Anne's welfare.

'You think you should go on a date with your ex-husband?' Nikki asked.

'It wouldn't be a date.'

'So why go?'

'To reset things between us, like I said,' explained Anne. 'To show him we can be friends, that he hasn't "lost me", but that our lives have to move on.'

It sounded so sensible, so rational the way Anne said it. And yet the alarm bells ringing in Nikki's head wouldn't stop. This was dangerous. This was wrong. Something bad was going to happen.

'Philanthropy is one of the few things Luis and I have in common,' Anne went on earnestly. 'He cares deeply about the drug problems in Mexico, and all around the world. Remember, I told you about his sister?'

Nikki nodded. She remembered. She was still having trouble squaring this image of Luis Rodriguez as the addiction-fighting hero with Williams' alternate characterization of him as a cocaine and Krok magnate, whose life of luxury was built entirely on the misery and despair of others.

'That's why I thought this event might be a good place for us to start. His sister's overdose changed his life for the better once. Maybe this could be the time for him to change it again? To begin a new chapter. What do you think?'

*This is my chance,* thought Nikki. *This is where I tell her what Williams told me.* If she were ever going to warn Anne, surely this was the moment.

'I'm not sure,' Nikki played for time.

Meanwhile, Anne continued to wax lyrical. 'Luis has donated millions of dollars to addiction charities and rehab programs over the years, like the one your husband ran,' Anne smiled, the connection apparently only just occurring to her. 'I know you don't want to believe it, but he isn't all bad, you know.'

'I'm sure he's not,' Nikki heard herself saying, cursing herself for her cowardice.

'So should I go with him to the gala? Or not?' Anne's big, doe eyes looked at her for guidance.

'I can't answer that,' said Nikki. She felt bad ducking the responsibility, but really what choice did she have? She herself had never met Luis Rodriguez. She had no way of knowing whether Williams' version of him, or Anne's, was the accurate one. Or if, as Derek had implied, both sides coexisted. After all, even Robin Hood used to rob the rich before he could help the poor. 'You must make up your own mind,' she told Anne. 'Hold on to your own conviction that you want your freedom. And then do whatever *you* believe is going to help you get it.'

After the session, Nikki tried to process her own conflicting feelings. While the thought of Anne attending a function with her ex was terrifying, on another Nikki felt profound relief. Because the big takeaways from today's therapy were surely that a) Anne's marriage was finally over; in her heart. And b) She knew nothing whatsoever about Luis's supposed 'secret life' as a drug baron. If indeed he even had one.

Again, Nikki found herself beginning to doubt Derek Williams' account of Luis Rodriguez's past. Goodman had warned her not to trust Williams. And while the PI's certainty in his own conclusions was definitely seductive, so far he'd provided no actual evidence of a link between Rodriguez and the missing au pair, Charlotte Clancy, or anything to indicate that Luis's fortune was based on something other than real estate. Nikki wanted to believe Williams. She wanted to think that Anne's controlling ex-husband was a criminal and a bad, bad man. But wanting to believe somebody was always a dangerous place to start.

Turning on her phone, she scrolled through her old messages till she found the one she wanted. It was more than a month old, and it was from Haddon.

*'Dr Haddon Defoe cordially invites you to be a guest at his table for this year's End Addiction Gala.'*

Nikki had already replied weeks ago, clicking the 'No' box. Since Doug's death, she'd taken to automatically declining all social invitations. The only thing worse than having your life disintegrate from grief, and shame, was having it happen in front of an audience. The five words Nikki now hated most in the entire English language were: 'I'm sorry for your loss.'

*How could you be sorry?* She wanted to scream whenever she heard it. *You don't even know me.*

But things were different now. Now she had a reason to go, a reason to put on her glad rags and smile and shake hands and tolerate the nauseating waves of sympathy. This would be her chance, perhaps her only chance, to see Luis Rodriguez for herself, in person. To form her own conclusions about him, not just blindly rely on Derek Williams' information, or Anne's. If there was even a remote possibility that he was involved in these Zombie Killings then she owed it to Trey and Lisa to learn whatever she could. Plus, she'd be in a better position to protect herself, and perhaps Anne too, if Luis really was the bad actor Williams claimed.

*Haddon will be pleased I've changed my mind,* Nikki thought, as she tapped out a new email.

What a rock Haddon had been since Doug's death.

'Hey,' she wrote. '*Is it too late for me to join your table tomorrow night?*'

The reply came back in seconds.

'*Of course not! Delighted. See you there. H xx*'

Nikki turned off her phone with a smile. She felt excited, and nervous at the same time. One way or another, things were starting to happen.

It was about time.

# 30

The Ballroom at the Four Seasons Hotel on Beverly Hills' iconic Rodeo Drive, is a grand, split-level room, dominated by a large, formal stage at one end. In the center of the ceiling a vast, spiral chandelier lamp hangs above a permanent dance floor surrounded by tables, illuminating a bright blue and gold carpet that wouldn't look out of place in a sultan's desert palace.

Tonight's charity, the luxuriously funded End Addiction, had spared no expense transforming the already lavish space into an enchanted vision of fairytale proportions. The flowers alone – vast arrangements of hydrangeas and white roses, each as tall as a grown man – must have cost hundreds of thousands of dollars. Polished silver charges gleamed and glinted in the candlelight atop tables dressed with crisp white linens, crystal-cut glasses and priceless Spode china flatware. An eighteen-piece string orchestra played in white tie from the stage, while waiting staff who all looked like movie stars glided between the milling guests, offering caviar blinis and flutes of vintage champagne, as well as exotic 'soft' cocktails for the AA and NA crowd.

The whole thing was so far over the top, it was like walking into a collapsing soufflé of decadence. Distasteful, in Nikki's opinion, especially when one considered the lives of the poor, lost souls, their lives wrecked by drugs, that tonight's event was supposed to help. But Nikki was an old enough hand at fundraising to know that, in LA at least, you had to spend money to make money. Yes, the indulgence was obscene, from the room to the Michelinstarred food to the couture dresses, some of which cost more than most of tonight's waiting staff made in a year. But with tickets going for a thousand dollars a head, and tables for twenty times that, plus an after-dinner auction that was tipped to raise well into seven figures, from the charity's point of view the evening was already a roaring success.

'Nikki! Darling. I'm so glad you could make it.'

Haddon Defoe, looking as dapper as ever in a beautifully cut Armani tux and pale blue silk tie, was all smiles as he glided over, kissing her on both cheeks. 'I could use the support, to be honest,' he confided. 'They've asked me to give a speech tonight, and I'm panicking. That was always more Doug's thing than mine.'

Nikki hugged him warmly, inhaling his smell of expensive aftershave mingled with mouthwash. Haddon had always been one of those people who ought to have been attractive but somehow just wasn't. 'You'll do fine,' she assured him. 'It's an honor they asked you to speak.'

'Yeah, an honor I couldn't refuse. End Addiction was one of our biggest donors this year.'

Nikki raised an eyebrow. In the past Haddon and Doug had struggled to find backing from the big, umbrella slush-funds that so many other small drug charities relied on. Largely because their own clinics were fiercely autonomous, and any donations they accepted had to be strictly no strings attached.

'That's good, isn't it?' she looked at Haddon questioningly.

'I think so,' he replied, intermittently looking over her shoulder to scan the arriving guests. 'I don't know. Maybe Doug wouldn't have approved. But these guys had so much money to give away this year. They got a couple of big new donors themselves. And they eased up on the whole needle-sharing thing, plus you know, with opening Venice we needed the cash really badly.'

'You don't have to justify yourself to me,' said Nikki, touching his arm. She looked beautiful tonight, Haddon thought admiringly, in a floor-length, off-the-shoulder red dress, with her dark hair pinned up and drop diamond earrings casting brilliant flashes of light over the smooth skin of her neck and shoulders. These were no widow's weeds, that was for sure. Was the dress some sort of statement? Was her official mourning period now over?

'Doug's gone,' she said, reading Haddon's mind. 'These are your decisions to make now. Besides,' she smiled, 'Doug wasn't perfect. Not all of his decisions were the right ones.'

'That's true,' said Haddon. *And nor are all of yours, Nikki,* he wanted to add, doing a double take as the rotund figure of Derek Williams, her obnoxious PI, suddenly appeared at the entrance to the ballroom. *What the hell is he doing here?*

Haddon had considered telling Nikki about his visit from Derek Williams, and the wild, offensive accusations the PI had decided to lob at him. But in the end he decided against it. If Williams ended up sharing his version of their interview with Nikki, then Haddon would be prepared to push back and defend himself. But if he didn't, then it would be better all round to let bygones be bygones. The last thing Haddon wanted was to re-open the Doug/Lenka conversation with Nikki. The dead should be allowed to rest in peace.

Following his gaze, Nikki frowned too. Williams hadn't mentioned anything to her about attending tonight. Then again, perhaps he didn't know that *she* was coming? She'd only added herself to the guest list at the last minute, after all, to have a chance to check out Luis Rodriguez. Was Derek doing the same thing? She hoped he hadn't forgotten that his priority was supposed to be finding out more about Lenka.

'I'll see you at our table later,' said Haddon, making his excuses and slipping off to glad-hand some of the other VIPs. Nikki was about to go over to Williams when she suddenly spotted Anne at the back of the room, deep in conversation with one of End Addiction's founders.

Walking over, Nikki waited patiently for the two of them to finish talking before approaching her.

'Surprise!'

'Nikki?'

For a moment Anne looked almost angry. In a short black flapper-style dress with a silk tasseled hemline, she looked even younger than usual, although her pale face seemed strained. 'What are you doing here?'

'I had a last-minute invitation,' Nikki blushed. Somewhat taken aback by Anne's reaction, she bent the truth a little. 'Doug's partner, Haddon Defoe, asked me to join his table.'

'Oh,' said Anne, softening a little. 'That's nice.'

'Is everything all right?' Nikki asked. 'You look a little tense.'

Anne exhaled. 'Luis isn't coming,' she said, disappointment etched on her face. 'Something came up, apparently, and he had to pull out.'

Nikki did her best to conceal her own disappointment. She wasn't sure exactly what she'd hoped to achieve by seeing Anne's husband face to face, but his absence left her feeling cheated.

'I'm sorry,' she told Anne. 'I know tonight meant a lot to you.'

Anne ran a hand through her hair in frustration. 'Eugh, I don't know. When I heard he wouldn't be here, I couldn't decide whether I was relieved or disappointed. I mean, I want to see him, but at the same time I don't. I hate that he still has this much power over me. Do you know what I mean?'

'Sure I do,' said Nikki truthfully. Doug still exerted enormous power over her emotions and actions, and he was dead. She could only imagine how hard it must be to break free from a complicated, controlling man like Luis Rodriguez, when he'd decided he didn't want you to.

A bell rang, indicating it was time for guests to take their seats for dinner. Nikki glanced around again for Derek Williams, but couldn't seem to see him anywhere. Meanwhile, Haddon was waving, beckoning her over to his table.

'What's wrong?' said Anne, noticing Nikki doing a double take.

Behind Haddon, standing by the entrance like sentries, were Detectives Goodman and Johnson. Looking up, Goodman raised a hand in greeting to Nikki across the room. He looked preposterously handsome in his tuxedo jacket and bow tie, a taller version of a young Frank Sinatra. Flustered, Nikki nodded briefly in reply.

'Oh, nothing,' she said casually to Anne. 'I just saw an old friend. Try to enjoy your evening, even without Luis. Maybe we can talk again later, after dinner?'

Something was up tonight. *First Williams and now the cops?*

The thought suddenly occurred to Nikki that perhaps *she* was that something. Were Goodman, Johnson and Williams all here because of her? Watching her? Protecting her? And if so, from what? Or from whom?

Or perhaps there was another reason, some other link between one of tonight's guests and Lisa and Trey's murders that she hadn't yet grasped. Another strand in the web.

And could it really be a coincidence that the police were here but – at the very last minute – Luis Rodriguez, the man of the hour, was not?

*       *       *

Dinner was delicious.

After a first course of tuna tartare and smoked sweet potato chips, Nikki was presented with a mouthwatering platter of thinly sliced

Kobe beef and freshly made spaghetti with shaved white truffles, all washed down with crisp, vintage Chablis. The combination of the food, the wine and the stimulating company helped Nikki start to relax. The man next to her was quite fascinating, a neuroscientist from Berkeley specializing in neuron pathway regeneration after drug-induced brain damage. By the time Haddon got up to speak, Nikki realized to her own surprise that she was actually enjoying herself. She'd forgotten all about Luis Rodriguez, and even about Anne, although she still had half an eye on Detective Goodman, not least because she was aware of his eyes on her.

'I wouldn't be standing here today if it weren't for an amazing man that many of you knew: the late, great Dr Douglas Roberts.'

Haddon's voice washed over Nikki like warm water. Even as he told stories about Doug and the old days, something that a few weeks ago would have reduced her to tears, she found she felt oddly fine, cocooned in a sort of fuzzy numbness. *Maybe I'm drunk?* As Haddon's speech drew to a close and the auction began, her attention wandered and her vision began to blur. Faces merged one into another, all bathed in a lovely, mellow light from the candles. She was supposed to be looking for someone. Who was that again? *Someone . . .*

\* \* \*

Lou Goodman watched as Nikki Roberts leaned back in her chair and closed her eyes. She looked stunning tonight, sexier than ever in that clinging red dress. It was a struggle to take his eyes off her even for a second. But he knew he must.

Two tables across from Nikki, right up against the stage where the auctioneer was whipping the crowd into a money-spending frenzy, Nathan Grolsch sat holding court beside his hollow wreck of a wife. Merely looking at Old Man Grolsch's wrinkled, spiteful, hypocritical face, yukking it up with his 'friends' was enough to turn Goodman's stomach. Surrounded by some of LA's best known superrich – the Grolsches' table included a Bel Air real estate mogul, a legendary Vegas casino boss and his wife, and the new Russian owner of LA Galaxy, among others – the old man was obviously enjoying playing the part of the generous philanthropist.

Goodman thought back to his brief interview with Brandon's parents at their home. He would never forget Nathan Grolsch's brutal lack of compassion for addicts, and how it even extended to his own son.

*'Brandon was an addict. A useless, lying, no-good scumbag who threw his life away for drugs.'*

Fran, Brandon's mother, had had more empathy, perhaps because she evidently had some sort of tranquilizer problem herself. But her husband's bullying had broken her down over the years, and she'd been no more use to poor Brandon when he was alive than his cold, self-righteous father. Yet now that he was dead, here they both were, at an End Addiction event, of all things, with Nathan throwing his money around as if he actually gave a shit.

'Psst, Goodman,' Johnson, back from the bar, whispered in his partner's ear. 'You wanna hear a good joke?'

'I'll tell you what's a joke. *That's* a joke,' said Goodman, gesturing with distaste towards the very public bidding war between Nathan Grolsch and one of the men on Nikki Roberts' table over a weekend on a super-yacht in Sardinia. The price had already passed the two hundred thousand dollar mark, and neither bidder seemed inclined to stop anytime soon. 'Grolsch is such a showboat. He turned his back on his own son. If he really cared, he'd write an anonymous check and be done with it.'

'Hmmm,' grunted Johnson. He wasn't inclined to shed too many crocodile tears for a rich, spoiled addict like Brandon Grolsch. So his dad was an asshole. Big deal. Whose wasn't?

'Look who's back,' he remarked, dragging a reluctant Goodman's attention away from the bidding towards the less expensive tables to their right, farthest from the stage. Derek Williams, looking not unlike Tweedle-Dee, squeezed into a cheap dinner suit at least two sizes too small for him and with the buttons on his white shirt gaping in the middle, was mingling with diners, taking notes and handing people his business card like a pesky used-car salesman.

'I'll get rid of him,' said Johnson, putting his beer down with a clatter.

'No,' said Goodman, putting a hand on his arm. 'Let me do it. You keep an eye on the tables.'

Johnson opened his mouth to protest but Goodman had already gone.

\* \* \*

Derek Williams was tired.

He'd shown up tonight because of a tip-off about Luis Rodriguez. The last time he'd been about to meet Rodriguez he'd been kidnapped, beaten and summarily deported. More than a decade had passed, but Williams had not forgotten about Charlotte Clancy and the mysterious American he was convinced Rodriguez had been protecting. He remembered his questions as if it were yesterday and he'd hoped tonight, he might finally have a chance to ask them, for Charlie's sake.

But it wasn't to be. Once again the bastard had slipped through his fingers, pulling a last-minute no-show. Thankfully, there were plenty of other guests here to occupy Williams' attention. Exhausted as he was, it wasn't long before the connections started firing in his brain, the synapses going off like fireworks, one after another.

Nikki was here, and as Haddon Defoe's guest, no less. Williams hadn't expected that. He still wasn't sure what to make of his interview with Dr Defoe, or whether he believed his protestations of innocence about Doug Roberts' mistress and her mysterious past. Or rather, her lack of a past. Increasingly, Williams was coming to the conclusion that 'Lenka Gordievski' was some sort of alias or alter ego. That the woman who had died in a ball of fire next to her lover, Nikki's husband, had begun her life as somebody else. Witness protection was certainly a possibility. But until he knew more, Williams decided he would keep silent. Nikki needed answers, not more questions, and right now that was all Williams had.

Williams' gaze shifted from Haddon and Nikki across to Rodriguez's estranged wife, Anne, the violinist with whom his client was obviously besotted. And less than twenty feet from where *she* stood were Brandon Grolsch's parents.

Williams now knew that Brandon was the eponymous 'zombie' so beloved of internet conspiracy theorists – the police had found his DNA on the bodies, or rather they'd found rotting cells from his body on Lisa Flannagan's, which was certainly creepy and bizarre if it was true. Maybe the serial killer was one of those trophy-keeping types who held on to fingernails and locks of hair and jewelry? Maybe he had Brandon's corpse floating somewhere in a vat of formaldehyde?

Surely it was odd that his folks were here tonight, sitting two tables away from Lisa Flannagan's former lover Willie Baden and his wife Valentina, a frozen-faced fossil of a woman, dripping in more diamonds than a gangster's whore. Earlier Williams had watched Valentina Baden and Fran Grolsch briefly acknowledge one another, exchanging the frosty nod of former friends. It was as if some mystery host had invited the entire cast of characters from the Zombie Killings files, right down to the moronic duo Johnson and Goodman, surely the Laurel and Hardy of the LAPD Homicide Division.

Right on cue, Detective Goodman popped up behind Williams like the ghost of Christmas past.

'Hello, Derek.'

Williams jumped.

'I would ask what you're doing here. But you wouldn't tell me the truth, would you?'

Suave, polite and very obviously educated, not to mention in perfect shape, Goodman wore the innately smug expression of a man who can't help but be aware of his own superiority over another. Williams, being that other, bristled.

'That's right, I wouldn't. Any more than you and Chubby Checker over there would tell me what brings *you* to a fancy party like this one. I'm pretty sure they're not serving donuts, you know.'

'Right.' Goodman's smile didn't waver. 'The only difference being that we're investigating officers on a double murder case, doing our jobs. Jobs that you tried and failed to get for yourself – how many times was it now? I forget. But the point is, we're working while you're . . . what's the word I'm looking for? That's it.' Goodman clicked his fingers patronizingly. '*Trespassing*. I'm assuming you don't have an actual invitation you can show me?'

Williams bit his lip. Boy, would he love to smash his fist into Detective Goodman's perfect features, to watch his straight white teeth fly out of his self-satisfied mouth like gleaming white bullets in a shower of blood.

'Oh, I've got something I can show you, pretty boy,' he replied menacingly. 'You wanna take this outside?'

Goodman raised a mocking eyebrow. 'You're not serious?'

'Aren't I?' snapped Williams. 'How's it going with Nikki, by the way? A little bird told me she still won't sleep with you. That's gotta hurt.'

'And when was the last time a woman slept with you, Derek?' Goodman shot back. 'Without you having to pay her, I mean.'

'Unlike you, I don't have sex on the brain,' Williams replied coolly. 'Especially not with Nikki. I'm actually trying to help the lady. Maybe that's why she trusts me, tells me things she wouldn't *dream* of sharing with you and shit-for-brains over there.' He nodded towards

Johnson, who had unhelpfully chosen that moment to start picking his nose.

For the briefest of moments, Williams was rewarded with the sight of Lou Goodman losing his legendary cool. His olive skin flushed an ugly red and his nostrils flared. 'Get out of here, Williams,' he snapped. 'Before I have you arrested.'

A mocking 'Arrested for what?' hung on Derek Williams' lips but he thought better of saying it. It was important to pick one's battles, and something told him there would be plenty of those ahead with Goodman and Johnson.

'I'll see you around, Detective.'

'Not if I see you first.'

Picking up his jacket, Williams made his shambolic way towards the exit. As he left, the first strains of Anne Bateman's haunting violin solo began echoing around the ballroom.

Sitting at her table, Nikki's befuddled senses jolted back to life as the first notes of Vaughan Williams' *The Lark Ascending* filled the air, stunning the room into an awestruck hush. There was Anne up on the stage, her eyes closed, a tiny, transfixed figure in black, her bow moving back and forth as if independent from her body. But for once it wasn't Anne who was mesmerizing Nikki, but the music itself and the overwhelming nostalgia it provoked. Doug had loved this piece. He and Nikki had listened to it countless times, making Sunday morning pancakes, in the car on one of their long drives up the coast. In bed. On their honeymoon . . .

All of a sudden, emotion overwhelmed her. With an awful, embarrassing noise, like a sort of deep, desperate gasp, she leaned forward over the table, putting her head in her hands.

'Are you all right, my dear?' The charming neuroscientist put a concerned hand on Nikki's shaking shoulder. 'Would you like to get some air?'

Nikki shook her head, blinded by tears. In recent months she'd somehow managed to keep her grief for Doug in check, to file it under 'pending' while she tried to make sense of the terrible, terrifying events spiraling around her. But now, thanks to Anne's exquisite playing, Pandora's box had been unlocked. There was no way back now, no way to stop the tears and the shaking and the awful, visceral pain ripping her in two, twisting in her gut like a dagger.

'It's OK, Professor Jameson.' Haddon Defoe's voice, deep and resonant and strong, rang in Nikki's ears. 'I've got this.'

Nikki didn't want Haddon's help either, but unlike the professor he wasn't taking no for an answer, lifting her to her feet and practically dragging her, sobbing, out of the ballroom and through some fire doors into a small courtyard garden.

'Sit here,' he said, lowering her gently onto a stone bench beside a softly trickling waterfall. Nikki was still crying, tears streaming down her cheeks and turning her eye make-up into muddy rivulets. But the wracking sobs had slowed to weak, intermittent shudders. The storm appeared to be subsiding.

'What happened in there?' Haddon asked, taking a seat beside her. Reaching over, he pulled her hair back from her face and offered her his handkerchief.

'I don't know,' Nikki sniffed, taking it. 'The music, I think. It made me think about Doug and I . . . I just felt so *sad*, Haddon! He's gone, and it's . . . it's incredibly sad. All of a sudden I couldn't hold it.'

Haddon pulled her into his arms. 'You poor, sweet thing.'

Exhausted, Nikki leaned into him trustingly. Haddon was like the big brother she'd never had. Solid. Steady. Not a superstar, like Doug had been, but a rock nonetheless, an anchor through all life's storms.

He was whispering in her ear. 'He didn't deserve you. You know that now, Nikki. He never deserved you.'

His tone was low and reassuring, and Nikki's head was still foggy enough that his actual words didn't sink in fully at first. It was only when she felt his hand pushing up underneath her dress, his hot and eager fingers digging into the flesh of her thigh, that alarm bells belatedly went off.

'Haddon!' She tried to push him away but his grip was like a vise. 'What the hell are you *doing*?!'

'What I should have done years ago,' he murmured, his voice thick and guttural with desire. 'Don't fight me, Nikki. You know you want this. We both do. I've loved you for so—'

'Haddon, no!' She was so shocked, she felt momentarily frozen. Haddon was leaning over her now, his full lips pressing down on hers, kissing her, pawing at her. 'I said NO.'

'Is everything OK out here?'

Detective Goodman's voice cut through the night air like razor wire. Haddon Defoe jumped back like a surprised cat.

Nikki stared up at Goodman with profound relief. She couldn't remember the last time she'd been so pleased to see someone. Actually, come to think of it, she could. It was the night the boy in the red car had scared off the lunatic trying to kill her. That whole incident felt like a dream now, or like something that happened multiple life-times ago.

*Had* she dreamt it? Tonight, more than ever, Nikki felt as if reality was slipping away from her.

'Everything's fine,' she told Goodman, straightening her hair and dress and getting to her feet, still in shock from Haddon's clumsy come-on. She glanced at Haddon, who looked back at her, mortified.

Did he really believe she wanted him? Wasn't that what he said? '*You know you want this. We both do.*' The idea was painful. Haddon had been Doug's friend, his best friend. How could he?

On the other hand, Doug *had* lied, to her, and perhaps to both of them. Perhaps Haddon had as much right to feel angry as Nikki did, to feel cheated by Doug's affair? Especially if he really had 'loved her for so long'.

But had he? Surely not. That was crazy! She'd have noticed. Wouldn't she? She was a psychologist, for heaven's sake. She'd have seen the signs. There would have been signs.

'Are you sure you're all right, Nikki?' Goodman pressed her.

'She told you,' Haddon snarled at him. 'She's fine.'

'I'm a little dizzy, that's all,' Nikki told Goodman. 'I probably had too much to drink. I think I should go home.'

'I'll get you a car,' Goodman and Haddon announced simultaneously.

Nikki looked from one to the other. 'Thank you both, but I'm perfectly capable of calling myself an Uber. I appreciate the concern but I'd like to be alone now. Please.'

*   *   *

Outside, on Rodeo Drive, two separate lines had formed, one for valet parking and the other for Uber pick-ups. Nikki waited in the second line, her thin cashmere shawl pulled tightly around her shoulders against a suddenly chill evening wind. She'd come here tonight to check out Luis Rodriguez for herself and to try to provide support or protection for Anne. But it turned out that she was the one who'd needed support, As for Luis Rodriguez, Nikki could barely remember now why she'd thought him so important. Something about drugs, and Trey and the girl who'd gone missing in Mexico City all those years ago . . . It was all a bit of a blur.

'Roberts! Car for Dr Roberts!'

Nikki stepped into a spotless sedan that smelled of peppermint and leather mixed with its owner's lemony aftershave. As she fastened her seatbelt, it took her a moment of intense concentration to be able to remember her own address.

*What's wrong with me?*

'Brentwood, please,' she told the driver. 'Tigertail Drive.'

As they pulled away from the hotel, there was a hard slam on the brakes and the car squealed to a halt. Nikki's seatbelt cut painfully into her skin and her neck snapped back against the headrest. A man, wild-eyed and obviously terrified, had jumped into the road in front of them. Nikki caught a glimpse of him tearing off in the direction of Santa Monica Boulevard, oblivious to the beeping horns and yelled insults behind him.

*Am I seeing things?* she thought. *Or was that Carter Berkeley?*

'Are you crazy?' the driver yelled through the window at the man's retreating back, in a heavy Jamaican accent. 'You could 'ave been killed, man!'

Turning back to Nikki, the driver made his apologies and they once again got on their way.

*That was Carter. I'm sure of it,* Nikki thought, as they passed the serried rows of palm trees swaying like drunken sentries along the Wilshire Corridor. *What was he doing here? And what was he so afraid of?*

The wind was back with a vengeance now. It wasn't the Santa Ana – it felt too cold for that, chill and menacing. Nikki tried to marshall her racing thoughts in the back of the cab, but nothing seemed to make sense. Then all of a sudden, she started to laugh.

*It doesn't matter! None of it matters!*

Who cared what Carter Berkeley had been running from, or that Haddon Defoe had declared his love for her, or that Luis Rodriguez had failed to turn up? Only one thing mattered in the entire world, and that was Doug.

Doug, her Doug, was dead.

He was never coming back.

Pulling out her phone, Nikki tapped out a text to Williams, her fingers misspelling the words wildly as the screen swam before her eyes. *'Any wrd n Lenka?'*

Williams' response was immediate and succinct. *'No.'*

Seconds later, a second reply arrived.

*'Let me know when you're home safe.'*

Nikki was touched. The gruff, abrasive PI actually cared about her. And she cared about him. Unlike everybody else in her life, from her patients to Haddon Defoe to Lou Goodman, Derek Williams had no ulterior motive for his kindness. Yes, Nikki paid him. But she'd have paid him anyway, and he knew it. His concern for her was genuine.

'He's a good man,' she said to her phone, blinking back tears.

Doug had been a good man too. Just a bad husband, as it turned out.

Defeated by grief, Nikki closed her eyes and sank instantly into very deep sleep. The last thing she remembered was thinking what a relief it would be if, this time, she never woke up.

# 31

Kevin Voss sat in the cafeteria at Cedars-Sinai Hospital in West Hollywood, tapping his fingers nervously on the plastic tabletop and glancing for the umpteenth time at his phone.

The PI, Williams, had asked to meet here at six a.m. It was six ten now . . . six eleven . . . and Kevin was starting to wonder whether he'd been punked. After all, it wasn't every day that someone called out of the blue offering 'hundreds of dollars' for 'anything you can tell me about Dr Doug Roberts and his girlfriend'. The truth was, Kevin didn't really have much to tell. Most of it was hearsay, gossip among the nurses, both male and female, many of whom had fancied Dr Roberts. What Kevin Voss did have, unfortunately, was debts. Credit card, personal, tax-related, you name it. Kevin's last boyfriend, Enzo, had bled him dry before he left, milking poor Kevin's modest chargenurse's salary for a lot more than it was worth.

'Kevin?'

A large, panting man who looked like a walking coronary, burst loudly into the cafeteria and marched over to Kevin's table, extending his clammy hand by way of introduction. Thankfully, the place was almost empty, because this fella was anything but discreet.

Looking around them anxiously, the nurse nodded, shook Williams' hand as briefly as he could and gestured for him to sit.

'What's good to eat around here?' Williams boomed. 'I had a late night, and I could use a decent breakfast.'

*Like a hole in the head,* thought Kevin, eyeing the sweat patches under the PI's arms with distaste. 'You said you wanted to talk privately,' he whispered, sotto voce.

'I do. And we are,' Williams grinned, striding up to the counter and ordering two blueberry muffins and a large latte before returning to his seat and telling Kevin, 'No one's interested in us, believe me.

Besides, you're not doing anything illegal, you know. All we're doing is talking about an old friend. No law against that, is there?'

'I guess not.' The nurse forced a smile. He couldn't help but wonder how much of a 'friend' of Dr Roberts this Williams guy really was. But he needed the money too badly to dwell on the issue.

'I can't say we were close,' he admitted, picking at his own oatmeal while Williams cheerfully devoured the first of his treats. 'But we worked together sometimes, Dr Roberts and I, and I liked him. Most people liked him. He was one of the good guys, but I'm guessing you know that already.'

'Who didn't like him?' Williams asked, taking a loud slurp of coffee.

'I'm sorry?'

'You just said most people liked him,' Williams clarified. 'Most implies "not all". Who didn't like Doug Roberts?'

Kevin Voss looked pained. 'He changed,' he said, staring down at his oatmeal. 'He met a woman. Supposedly she was Russian. Everything was different after that.'

'Supposedly?' Williams asked.

'She had a Russian name,' said Kevin. 'I forget it now. And she used to live in Moscow. But she seemed really American, you know, to talk to? Her English was perfect. Anyway, it was like Dr Roberts was under her spell or something. No one could understand it. She wasn't even that attractive. I always thought she looked kind of *haunted,* you know? Like, she might have been a looker when she was younger, but now she had the weight of the world on her shoulders? She was super tall,' he added idly. 'But apart from that, there was nothing special about her. Especially not compared to his wife.'

Williams nodded his agreement. The few grainy pictures he'd seen of Lenka Gordievski showed a lanky brunette, probably a bit younger than Nikki but nowhere near as striking, physically. She wore expensive clothes, but nothing overtly revealing or sexy, and was hardly the leggy, blonde 'Russian mistress' of popular imagination.

Despite his best efforts, Williams had failed to unearth any more information about her life or history since his interview with her landlord in LA. He could find nothing on her family, her employment history, her education. Haddon Defoe claimed she worked for a drug charity in New York, but no one Williams had spoken to in that community seemed to have heard of her. The woman was a ghost.

'You did meet her then?' he asked Kevin.

The nurse nodded. 'A few times. She came to the hospital quite a lot. They'd have lunch together right here.' He waved an arm around the still empty cafeteria. 'That was the weird part. They never made a secret of it. I think that was what bugged Dr Defoe the most. He and Doc Roberts were fighting a lot before the accident, and I'm pretty sure it was about *her*. Lenka, that was her name,' he added, pleased with himself for dredging it up.

'How did Doug Roberts and Lenka meet?' Williams asked.

Kevin thought for a moment. 'In New York, I think? I'm not sure. Some charity thing. Dr Roberts had a rehab clinic . . .'

'I know,' Williams cut him off. 'Do you know what she did for a living?'

'No.' Kevin looked worried, sensing that his 'hundreds of dollars' might be slipping away. 'But I know she was rich. Maybe that was one of the attractions, I don't know. But she always wore this watch, one of those platinum ones with diamonds round the face. *Chopard!*' he said, happy again to have come up with a name, although it was clear from Williams' expression it meant nothing to him. 'Those things are like fifteen, twenty thousand dollars a pop,' Kevin explained. 'And she carried a Hermès pocketbook, and one time she came in wearing an incredible sable jacket, I think it was like a Fendi or something? I remember that because Dr Roberts had a fight with her about it. I actually remember that really well, because he said something strange.'

'What was that?' asked Williams.

'He said, "Either you want to escape or you don't. Never wear that around me again!" He was really mad.'

'How did she react?' Williams asked, curious.

'She cried,' said Kevin, matter-of-factly. 'And then he backed down, like he always did. He could never resist a damsel in distress.'

'He had other girlfriends?' Williams suggested.

Kevin shook his head. 'I don't think so. No. Before Lenka came along he was totally into his wife. But you know, she was a doctor too, super capable. I don't think she needed him the way the Russian girl did. You know?'

Williams nodded, writing something in his notebook.

'I also heard she was friends with some bad people,' said Kevin, lowering his voice to a whisper. 'Powerful people.'

'What people?' Williams frowned.

'Don't know,' said Kevin. 'And I don't know if Doug Roberts was mixed up in that either. I'm not saying he was. But supposedly her friends had influence at City Hall. Awarding contracts, stuff like that. I heard some of the other surgeons talking about it.'

Williams looked skeptical.

'OK, Kevin,' he said, getting to his feet. Reaching into his wallet he put two hundred-dollar bills down on the table. 'Thank you for your time.'

'Two hundred? That's it?' The nurse failed to hide his disappointment or his desperation as he grabbed the cash and stuffed it into the pocket of his scrubs.

Williams shrugged. 'You haven't given me much, son. The name of her watchmaker and some vague rumors about City Hall?'

'They're not vague rumors!' Kevin protested, standing up himself. 'I have a contact there, someone who can tell you more. A lot more.'

Williams hesitated. 'Who?'

Kevin sat back down. 'I'll need another three hundred for the name.'

Williams turned to leave.

'Two hundred!' Kevin called after him. 'She can help you, Mr Williams. I know she can help you.'

Extracting another two notes, Williams sat back down and placed them on the table. Kevin reached forward eagerly, but Williams covered the money with his hand.

'I want the name. The address. And the cell phone number,' he said slowly. 'And this had better be worth my time, son.'

*   *   *

It turned out Kevin Voss hadn't been entirely straight with him.

Adrienne Washington did not work at City Hall. She was fired six months ago from her junior secretarial job in the Mayor's Office, and now worked as a part-time PA to a tech entrepreneur downtown.

'Best thing that ever happened to me, losing that job,' she told Williams, over lunch at an overpriced sushi place off of Figueroa. 'I mean it was awful at the time. *Awful.* So humiliating. But if I hadn't left the Mayor, I would never have found Michael, and he is like *the* nicest boss ever. *Of all time.* Plus the salary is like, double.'

A number of things struck Williams as he listened to Adrienne ramble enthusiastically on. The first was that she was blessed with beauty – long legs, a narrow waist and a mane of thick, red hair that gave her a look of Disney's Little Mermaid – but not brains. It was pretty clear to Williams on what basis both the Mayor and the tech entrepreneur had hired her. The second was, encouragingly, she was also wildly indiscreet.

'At first I thought Mayor Fuentes fired me because I wouldn't sleep with him,' she told Williams cheerfully, slurping down her sugary cocktail noisily through a straw. 'I mean, the man was *all hands*, if you know what I'm saying, and he's also, like, fifty years old, not to mention, like, *married*.'

Every third word was delivered with painful overemphasis, and 'likes' peppered her conversation like bullets. Williams would have fired her for that alone. It was like listening to a doll where you pull a string and she says something inane, only one day the string broke and the loop got stuck on repeat, endlessly.

'But then *later* I realized that, like, *maybe* it was because of what I *knew*.'

'And what was that, Adrienne?'

'That the Mayor was taking money from the Russians,' she said, in the same tone she might use to make a comment about the weather. 'Bribes and whatnot. Like, I heard my *boss*, Mrs *Drayton*, talking on the phone about it? I think it was, like, to a *reporter*?'

'Are you sure about this, sweetheart?' Williams asked kindly. 'That's a big accusation to make. And I've never read anything about the Mayor being involved in corruption.'

'Oh, I'm not *accusing* anyone!' Adrienne said, apparently genuinely surprised. 'I'm simply telling *you* what I *heard*. Just like I told Mayor Fuentes what I heard. And next thing I know, *boom*, I get fired. So that's why I'm thinking it was, like, *probably* that? And *not* the sex thing? Also, they fired Mrs D, and I don't mean to be catty or anything, but I'd be willing to make you a bet Mayor Fuentes wasn't trying to get *her* into bed. Now, my *new* boss, Michael, when I told him, he was like . . .'

It took Williams twenty minutes to get out of there, once he'd established to his satisfaction that Adrienne Washington knew nothing more about these mysterious Russians supposedly in cahoots with the Mayor, and nothing at all about Lenka Gordievski.

It took him another four hours to track down Tina Drayton, Adrienne's old boss at a run-down apartment in West Hollywood.

'Yes?'

She opened the door to him less than an inch. Three strong steel chains locked into place across the opening, and Williams could only see a section of her face on the other side. It was enough to reveal an exhausted and frightened middle-aged woman, barricaded inside a home where she clearly no longer felt safe.

'My name is Derek Williams, Mrs Drayton. I'm a private investigator. May I come in?'

After the briefest hesitation, Tina shook her head. 'I'm sorry. It's not a good time.'

She was about to shut the door when Williams interrupted her. 'I got your name from Adrienne Washington. She was worried about you.'

'Adrienne?' Tina's eyes widened. 'That stupid girl! Will she never learn to keep her mouth shut? I'm actually very fond of her, but she doesn't know what she's saying half the time, Mr . . . I'm sorry, I forgot your name.'

'Williams.' Pulling out a card, he passed it to her between the chains. 'But please call me Derek. I understand your hesitation, ma'am. And I agree with you about Adrienne. I think, unwittingly, she may be putting herself in danger. I'd really like to talk to you, Mrs Drayton. Only for a few minutes.'

Tina hesitated again. But this time she relented. 'Hang on.'

The door closed, and Williams heard each of the chains being removed one by one, before it reopened.

'You'd better come in,' the Mayor's ex-secretary sighed heavily. 'And please call me Tina. I don't have long to talk though I'm afraid. I'm moving again today. You say you're a private investigator, Derek?'

'That's right.'

Williams followed her into the dingy sitting room. Taking a seat in an armchair still covered in plastic wrapping, it was immediately obvious that this was temporary accommodation, and not Tina's's home. There were no photographs or personal items anywhere, not even a cushion or a throw rug to warm the place up.

'May I ask who you're working for?' said Tina, sitting opposite him.

'I never reveal my client's names,' Williams explained. 'Confidentiality is kind of a prerequisite in my business. But I will say that I'm working for a woman, a person of integrity, who may be a victim of some of the same people you fell foul of at City Hall. My client wants answers, Tina, that's all. Just like you.'

Tina rolled her eyes. 'I don't want answers, Derek. I want my life back.'

Although Adrienne was right to imply the older woman was no sex object, by Williams' lights Tina Drayton was an attractive woman for her age. Not 'pretty' perhaps, especially not in her current, washed-out, nervous state and dressed in an unflattering skirt and sweater. But there was an intelligence and spiritedness about her that Williams admired, a sort of confidence that, in other circumstances, might have been fun to be around.

'Do you move a lot?' Williams asked, already knowing the answer.

'I do now,' Tina sounded resigned. 'It's not safe to stay in one place too long.'

'That must be exhausting. And expensive,' he said, treading carefully. 'My client would be happy to pay you for any information you might have that could help us.'

Tina waved a hand dismissively. 'Thank you, Derek, but I wouldn't feel comfortable accepting payment simply for telling the truth. You seem like a nice man, and I daresay your client is trustworthy.'

'She is.'

'But I doubt either of you know what you're getting into,' Tina added. 'If we *are* dealing with the same people—'

'The Russians,' Williams interrupted her.

That simple word alone was enough to make the blood drain from Tina's face.

'Yes,' she whispered, 'then you should tell your client to walk away.'

Williams thought about Nikki and smiled. 'I don't think she'd take that advice. Not from me, anyway. She's tenacious.'

'This isn't a game,' Tina said, becoming agitated. 'People have died. The reporter I spoke to, at the LA Times? Robin Sanford? He's dead now.'

Williams started taking notes.

'They said it was a heart attack, but there was nothing wrong with Robin's heart. He was thirty-three years old and fit as a fiddle.'

'People are still dying, Tina,' said Williams. 'That's why I'm here.'

He talked to her about the slayings of Lisa Flannagan and Trey Raymond, and their links to Nikki Roberts and her husband Doug.

About the Roberts' involvement in drug addiction charities, and the wars between Mexican and Russian dealers for supremacy on the streets of LA.

'Doug Roberts died last year, in an "accident", alongside a Russian woman who may have been involved with the people you say were bribing Mayor Fuentes.'

Tina raised a hand. 'Bribing? Is that what Adrienne told you?'

Williams nodded.

'My God.' Tina shook her head. 'That child is going to get herself killed one of these days. And the irony is, she knows nothing. She's too stupid to understand any of this.'

'Yeah,' agreed Williams. 'I kind of got that impression.'

'All right, so firstly, I don't know if Fuentes personally was being bribed. I never said that. All I know is that he was being paid, or at least *someone* was being paid, via his accounts at City Hall. I'm talking large sums of money, and it was coming from the Russians.'

Williams was still writing. 'How large, and which Russians?'

'The amounts varied each time,' said Tina. 'Five hundred thousand, a hundred and fifty thousand. One was for over a million dollars. Every four to six weeks a new check would arrive. Perhaps it was three million in total. Or more, I don't know.'

'And the Russians making the payments. Do you have names?'

'No.' She looked down. Williams could smell the fear on her skin.

'A description, then. Did you ever see any of them in person?'

She shook her head, biting her lower lip. 'I'm sorry. I can't.'

'You must have taken phone calls at least,' Williams pressed her. 'Are we talking men or women? Two or twenty?'

'You don't understand—'

'Does the name Lenka Gordievski mean anything to you? This lady?' Getting up, Williams waved his iPhone in front of her frightened face. Despite herself, Tina looked at the image, the same one Williams had shown Haddon Defoe of Lenka, Haddon and Doug Roberts at the New York fundraiser, the night Lenka and Doug first met. The recognition in Tina's eyes was obvious and instant.

'I cannot talk about this, Derek. I'm sorry. I've already said too much.'

'Give me a company name, at least. Something I don't already know, one piece of this puzzle. Please, Tina. Tell me what you told Robin Sanford.'

Jerking her head up, she looked him square in the eye. 'They'll kill me!'

Williams held her gaze in silence for a few moments. Then he said quietly:

'Maybe they will. Maybe they'll kill both of us. But what if they're out there, killing other, innocent people *right now*, just to keep whatever this is a secret? Isn't the only way to be rid of them to uncover that secret? To bring it out in the open? You must have believed that when you called Sanford in the first place.'

'I did,' Tina acknowledged. In her lap, her hands trembled.

'I know you're scared, Tina. I'm scared too. But if we don't speak up, who will?'

Derek Williams watched the inner battle raging inside the poor woman opposite him. Tina Drayton was a brave person. She'd already proved that. But everybody had their limits.

'All right,' she said eventually. 'I'll do it. I'll tell you. But after I do you must never contact me again. Never. Not for any reason.'

Williams sat down and pulled out his pen again. 'You have my word.'

# 32

Gretchen Adler eased herself down into the warm water and felt the tensions of her day and the long drive downtown melt away.

Gretchen and Nikki had discovered Lucky Hot Springs in their senior year of High School and had been coming to the women-only, strictly naked Korean spa for girls' bonding sessions ever since. As teenagers, back when both their bodies were perfect, the whole 'naked' thing had felt weird and embarrassing. Now, in middle age and with pretty much everything sagging more than she would have liked, Gretchen couldn't care less about taking her clothes off, or about the other women and girls, from aged two to ninety-two, lazily wandering past her in the buff.

In fact, stepping into the naturally heated water as naked as God intended felt incredibly freeing, and one of the many reasons Gretchen Adler loved this place. It didn't matter to Gretchen that Nikki's body seemed to have stood the test of time far better than her own. Nikki with her cellulite-free thighs and small, pert breasts that bobbed like two apples on the surface of the water above a stomach so flat and taut you could have used it as a trampoline. Gretchen's own breasts were more like two sandbags, instantly submerging like a ship's ballast, and her belly was more stretchmark than skin at this point, courtesy of her three kids. But really, who cared? She was thirty-eight, and happily married to a very successful producer. Unlike lonely, widowed Nikki, who in recent years had seen her life lurch from one tragedy to the next, poor thing.

Sliding into the hot pool beside Gretchen, Nikki kicked off the girls' gossip session with a bombshell.

'Haddon Defoe tried to sleep with me the other day.'

Gretchen's jaw dropped open, cartoon style. '*Whaaat??* He did not!'

'He did,' said Nikki. 'It was at the End Addiction Ball. We were outside, and he was comforting me about Doug and then, I don't know,' she shrugged, 'suddenly he was kissing me and declaring his love, telling me how Doug never deserved me. He was kind of forceful.'

'Do we like "kind of forceful"?' Gretchen asked, astonished. She'd known Haddon Defoe for almost a decade, through Nikki and Doug, and was having immense difficulty picturing the scene Nikki described.

'Not from Haddon we don't!' Nikki blushed. 'I mean . . . *Haddon*. I had no idea.'

'Why would you?' said Gretchen.

'And obviously I could never. I'm not remotely attracted to him for one thing, but even if I was, he was like a brother to Doug. That would be too weird.'

'Biblical,' Gretchen agreed. 'Like in the Old Testament, when people die and the widows marry the brother? It's a thing!' she added defensively, seeing Nikki's baffled face.

'The truth is, I'm nowhere near ready to be with someone new,' said Nikki, dipping her whole head under the water and then rising up again, her hair sleek like an otter's. 'I'm not sure I ever will be.'

'Oh, baloney.' Gretchen said robustly. 'You're still young, you're gorgeous. Look at you! You'll meet someone. Someone you *are* remotely attracted to. Although I have to say, from where I'm sitting, Haddon's not bad. I mean, compared to Adam.'

'Give me a break,' said Nikki. 'You worship Adam.'

Adam Adler, Gretchen's husband, was a highly successful television producer, amazing father and husband and all round good guy. It was true he wasn't exactly Johnny Depp. But he was funny and generous and he and Gretchen adored each other. Gretchen would no more have traded Adam in for a new model than flown to the moon. Back before the accident, before she knew about Lenka, Nikki had thought of herself and Doug in the same light. The two couples used to go on vacations together. Christ, it all seemed so long ago now.

'I have been attracted to other people,' Nikki confided in Gretchen. 'It's not that. It's more that . . .'

'Whoa, whoa whoa. Back up,' said Gretchen. 'Attracted to other people? Like who?'

Nikki waved a hand dismissively. 'No one important. Nothing's happened.'

'Who?!' Gretchen repeated.

An embarrassed smile spread over Nikki's face. 'There's a guy. His name's Lou Goodman. He's actually one of the detectives investigating these murders.'

Gretchen clapped a hand over her mouth to stop herself laughing. 'You're hot for the detective?! Oh my God. Nikki!'

Nikki laughed herself. It was such a relief to talk to Gretchen about this stuff. Somehow her old friend's presence made everything seem more normal. More OK.

'Hold on, didn't you tell me he thought you were a possible suspect? In Lisa Flannagan's murder?' Gretchen remembered.

'That's the other one. His partner. Johnson,' said Nikki. 'No one in their right mind would be attracted to him, believe me.'

'So this Lou guy. You really like him?'

'Not really. I mean, yes, sometimes. He's smart. He's good-looking. But nothing's going to happen. We got drunk one night, talking about the case, and I almost . . . I thought about it.'

'Is he married?'

'Of course not,' said Nikki, suddenly serious. 'I wouldn't do that. Not after what Doug did to me.'

Instantly, the atmosphere changed. Nikki's mood darkened and her face fell, as it always did when she thought about Doug's affair. Gretchen had learned not to say anything at these moments, to lay low and let the storm pass. It always did, in the end. She and Adam were two of the very few people who Nikki had confided in about Doug's secret girlfriend, and the horrendous trauma of learning about it the way she did, the day that he died. They had both seen a profound change in Nikki since then, not just grief but a barely suppressed rage that hadn't existed in her before. Or at least, Gretchen didn't remember it.

As if sensing Gretchen's worry, Nikki suddenly said, 'I think there might be something wrong with me.'

'Why? Because you found someone attractive?'

'No. Not that.'

'There isn't anything wrong with you, Nik,' Gretchen said kindly.

'My emotions are all over the place.'

'That's called grief.'

'I know, but it's been a year,' said Nikki.

'A year? That's nothing,' insisted Gretchen. 'And then these terrible murders on top of everything? My God. Anyone else would be in an asylum by now.'

'Yeah, well. Maybe I should be in an asylum,' said Nikki glumly. 'I've been having feelings for one of my patients as well. A woman.'

She looked across at Gretchen, apparently determined to win her disapproval for something. Instead, her old friend simply looked intrigued.

'Really? Tell me more.'

'She's young. Very young,' said Nikki. 'And separated from her husband. And if that weren't complicated enough, Derek Williams, the private investigator I've hired, thinks her husband may have some connection to these murders, or at least to Trey . . .'

'Have you ever . . . you know . . . before? With a woman?' asked Gretchen, cutting her off. Evidently she was a lot more interested in Nikki's love life than any new developments in the case.

'No,' said Nikki.

'Not even in college?'

'You'd know if I had.'

'I guess that's true,' Gretchen shrugged. 'So these "feelings" you're having for this woman. I take it you haven't acted on them?'

'No. And I never will. I'm not that stupid.' Nikki ran a dripping hand through her wet hair. 'I honestly think I'm having a mid-life crisis, Gretch. Or I'm depressed or . . . something. Forget I said anything.'

The dark cloud was back, so Gretchen let it drop, changing the conversation to her kids and their latest dramas, before dragging Nikki into another room for a body scrub. The old Korean women who attacked them with hoses and loofas were so rough, turning them over and pummeling them like two slabs of meat on an abattoir table, that Nikki and Gretchen always ended up in fits of laughter.

Afterwards, feeling red-raw but energized and changed back into their clothes, the two women went to their usual sushi bar across the street for a late lunch. Only then, tentatively, did Gretchen return to the subject of Nikki's personal life.

'So you mentioned before about hiring a private detective?'

'Derek Williams,' Nikki nodded, deftly spearing some stray tendrils of seaweed salad with her chopsticks. 'He's good.'

'How did you find him?' asked Gretchen.

'I looked at reviews,' Nikki said casually. 'I don't really have any experience of this stuff. Although randomly,' she pointed a chopstick at Gretchen, 'guess what case he worked on ten years ago.'

Gretchen laughed. 'How am I supposed to guess that?'

'Charlotte Clancy's disappearance,' Nikki told her, grinning. 'Remember you were the one who brought that up, the last time I saw you? How Willie Baden's wife Valentina took up that case when Charlotte first went missing, got a whole load of media attention?'

'For the firefighter dad. Right.' Gretchen leaned in, fascinated.

'Tucker Clancy. He was the one who hired Williams to search for his missing daughter. I mean, how much of a coincidence is that?'

'Crazy,' Gretchen agreed. 'So what happened?'

'What do you mean?' asked Nikki.

'What happened with that case?'

'Oh, nothing, really. Williams got fired.'

'Because he couldn't find her?'

'He says it was because he found out she had a married lover and the dad didn't want to know about it. But maybe, I guess. Derek has some theory about an American banker and Anne's ex-husband and drug wars here in LA . . .'

She trailed off vaguely, and Gretchen watched her eat her California roll with growing concern. This all sounded like gobbledygook to her. Like people making connections where there couldn't possibly be any, trying to find meaning in a string of unrelated, awful, random events. In short, Derek Williams' wild theories sounded like the very last thing Nikki needed.

'Anyway, I wouldn't shed too many tears for Charlotte Clancy,' Nikki rambled on, oblivious to Gretchen's worried look, and to her silence. 'According to Williams, she wasn't the sweet, innocent everyone believed her to be. She was running around Mexico City, wrecking lives, breaking up families. I'd say she deserved what was coming to her.'

Gretchen sat up, shocked. 'You don't mean that, Nik. You don't really believe people deserve to *die* for having an affair.'

'Don't I?' Nikki sat up too, her eyes blazing in a blood-chilling flash of anger. 'Can you imagine turning on your iPad one night and seeing naked pictures of some slut Adam was seeing pop up on your screen?'

'That would be terrible,' admitted Gretchen. 'But I wouldn't—'

'And what if the slut was pregnant?!' Nikki demanded, her voice getting faster and louder by the second to the point where other customers were turning to stare. 'What if you'd been having fertility treatment, painful, exhausting, hopeless treatment for five YEARS,' Nikki's eyes welled with tears. 'And then you discover your husband's gone behind your back and got some other woman pregnant. And she sends the picture to his email, and you come home one night and BOOM, there it is. BOOM! Your entire life. GONE!' she was shouting now and shaking, like a woman possessed, her entire face contorted in absolute hatred.

Gretchen felt her stomach flip over and the bile rise up in her throat. When she spoke again, there was genuine fear in her voice.

'Lenka was pregnant?'

Nikki stared at her wild-eyed but silent. It was almost as if she were having some sort of fit.

'You told me – you told everyone – you knew nothing about her until the day Doug died!'

Nikki blinked and shook her head, like someone emerging from a trance.

'But you *knew*? You saw *pictures*? Jesus Christ, Nikki.'

Now it was Gretchen's turn to shake.

*Did Nikki have something to do with that accident?*

Gretchen hesitated, her hand on her purse, unsure whether to stay or go.

'I loved Doug,' said Nikki, sensing her unease and answering the unspoken question. 'I still love him. I would never have done anything to hurt him, Gretch. *He* was the one who did all the hurting, believe me,' she added, with more sadness than bitterness this time.

Gretchen put down her purse. 'OK. But you did know about the girl?'

Nikki nodded, staring guiltily down at her lap.

'Before?'

'Yes.' Nikki's voice had dropped from a roar to a whisper. 'About a month before. She sent him pictures.'

'And she was pregnant?'

Nikki nodded again. Then she started to cry. Instinctively, Gretchen leaned across the table and hugged her.

'Why didn't you tell me?' she asked.

'I was embarrassed,' said Nikki. 'I didn't know what to do!'

'Did you confront Doug?'

Nikki bit down hard on her lower lip. 'No. I know, I know. Pathetic, right? I should have thrown him out of the house then and there. But I didn't. I pretended I'd never seen the pictures. I thought – hoped – he'd come to his senses.' She looked at Gretchen, willing her friend to believe her. 'He was my whole life, Gretch!'

'And the baby?'

'I don't know,' Nikki admitted miserably. 'I hadn't thought that through. I don't know what I hoped for, it was all so new and so devastating and then,' she swallowed hard, 'then he died. He died and it was too late.'

The two women sat and talked for another hour after that. Despite her shock at the revelation, Gretchen was glad Nikki had told her. Obviously, the truth had been eating away at her for the last year, poisoning her from the inside out, corroding whatever chance she had for recovery or moving on.

'You have to go to therapy, Nik,' Gretchen told her. 'I mean it. You have to promise me.'

'I promise,' Nikki said meekly.

'All this anger, and talk about people deserving to die. It's not you, and I don't mind telling you, it's terrifying. You need help.'

Nikki nodded.

Later, before Gretchen left, they spoke about the future.

'Have you ever thought about moving?' Gretchen asked.

'Moving? Moving where?' replied Nikki, running an exhausted hand through her hair. Gretchen knew the truth now. She was the only person on earth who did. Nikki was still trying to figure out whether that was good or bad.

'Anywhere,' said Gretchen. 'New York? You could make a completely fresh start, away from all of this. Sell the house. I mean, you have no money worries, no dependants, nothing to tie you to LA. You could leave all the painful memories behind and begin again.'

Nikki had to admit it was a tempting idea, at least the way Gretchen put it. But life was never that simple. Memories were no respecters of geography, in Nikki's experience. And then there was her practice.

'I'd have to rebuild the business from scratch in New York,' she told Gretchen, signaling to their waitress for the check. 'Build a whole new client list.'

'That's true. But aren't your clients here part of the problem?' Gretchen countered. 'This "young girl" you say you've been infatuated with? And then there's what happened to Lisa Flannagan and Trey, not to mention the threats against you. I have no idea how you walk back into that office every day, Nikki. I know I couldn't do it.'

\* \* \*

Later, driving back to Brentwood, Nikki thought about what Gretchen had said. It hadn't ever occurred to her to leave Los Angeles, but perhaps that fact in itself should worry her. The psychologist in her began analyzing her own motives. *Why do I stay? What am I holding on to?*

The answer came more swiftly than Nikki expected, blindingly obvious all of a sudden after today's outpouring to Gretchen.

*It's my anger.*

*My anger with Doug.*

*I'm afraid to let my anger go.*

Just then, Derek Williams' number popped up on her Bluetooth. Nikki pulled over to take the call, parking under a jacaranda tree exploding with gorgeous violet blossoms. She felt a brief but acute moment of happiness – maybe she would go to New York? Let her anger go and be free! – that resonated in her voice as she picked up Williams' call.

'Derek! Hello. Thank you for your message after the gala the other night. I meant to call before and say that I—'

'Nikki, I need to see you urgently. Tonight.'

For the first time since she'd met him, Nikki heard fear in Derek Williams' voice. She wondered whether it was for her or for himself.

'Has something happened? Are you all right?'

'I'm fine. This drug-wars thing Luis Rodriguez has with the Russians is even bigger than we thought,' Williams gabbled, his words rushing out nineteen to the dozen. 'There's a ring, Nikki, at City Hall. The cartels are competing for influence across LA. The entire city's implicated – and I mean the entire city. The police department are part of it, but also banks and even charities.'

'What?' Nikki couldn't keep up.

'Charities. NGOs,' Williams explained. 'They're being used to launder drug money. Everybody's getting a cut. This is huge. *Huge!*'

'OK, OK. Slow down,' said Nikki cautiously. She was more concerned with Williams' tone than anything else, the naked, breathless panic in his voice. It wasn't like him.

'Have you found a direct link to the murders? Or to me?'

'Maybe.'

That wasn't reassuring.

'Maybe? Well, do you have any names?'

'Not over the phone,' Williams hissed. 'Tonight. Somewhere neutral.'

They agreed on a hotel.

'What about Lenka?' Nikki couldn't help but ask. 'Were you able to find out anything more about her?'

'Unfortunately, yes, I was,' said Williams. 'I'll tell you that too, when I see you. It's all connected.'

'Can't you tell me now?' Nikki begged. She'd waited so long for closure on Doug's mistress. Even another minute was torture.

'Not now,' Williams was firm. 'Seven o'clock, at the hotel.'

'But why . . . ?'

'Because I'm going home to pack a bag right now, and so should you. You're not safe here, Nikki. After we meet, you should get away. Far away. Lay low for a while. I'm serious.'

A litany of questions formed in Nikki's mind, but Williams hung up before she could ask any of them, clearly desperate to get off the phone. His paranoia was jarring, not least because it was so out of character. But Nikki's nerves were eclipsed by her excitement.

In a few hours, she would know who Doug's mistress really was.

*Then I can let go of my anger. I can and I will.*

*Once I know the truth, all this will be over.*

She was surprised when her phone rang again, this time from a blocked/unknown number. Williams must have switched phones.

'Derek?' Nikki picked up again. But it wasn't Derek Williams.

At first she didn't recognize the voice on the other end of the line. It was hard to make out anything through the sobbing, deafening, gut-wrenching howls of pain that echoed through Nikki's car speakers like the soundtrack from a horror film. But after a few seconds, she knew.

*No. That's impossible. It can't be!*

But it was.

'Dr Roberts?' Brandon Grolsch gasped. 'It is you, isn't it?'

'Yes, Brandon, it's me.' Nikki's heart pounded. 'Where are you?'

'I need help.' He began sobbing again. 'I think they're going to kill me!'

'I can help you, Brandon,' said Nikki. 'But you need to tell me where you are.'

'OK.' He inhaled deeply. 'I . . . I'm. I'm at the corner of . . .'

There was a loud *thud*.

Then the line went dead.

# 33

Nikki sat at the bar at the SLS Hotel in Beverly Hills sipping a 'mocktail', in this case a Moscow mule minus the vodka, and trying not to look nervous.

Her overnight bag was at her feet. She'd only packed a small weekender. She had no intention of being hounded out of her home for good, by Luis Rodriguez or anybody else. But after the unnerving call from Brandon Grolsch, she'd decided to take Derek Williams' warnings seriously.

*What will Derek say when I tell him Brandon's still alive?* she wondered. At some point she knew she would have to tell the police about Brandon as well. But Williams deserved to be the first to know. Besides, she wanted his take on it before she took another step.

Williams was late, which wasn't unusual, although Nikki's frayed nerves could have done without it tonight. She wanted to hear whatever he had to tell her about Lenka first, before she broached the subject of her call from Brandon. The terror and misery in Brandon's voice still haunted her, as did the abrupt end to his call, and she still had no idea what to make of any of it.

Had Brandon *really* been involved in Lisa and Trey's murders? Nikki didn't want to believe it. It didn't square in any way with the boy she remembered Brandon Grolsch to be, the lonely, troubled but intrinsically gentle individual who had turned to her for help when nobody else would help him, and who was still turning to her for help, although at this point God only knew what Nikki or anyone could do for him. And yet his DNA was there, on the bodies. That's what the police said, anyway. It was so hard to know whom to trust.

Nikki looked up at the clock on the wall: *7.22 p.m.* Williams was officially late now. Where the hell could he be?

She'd made an effort with her clothes tonight, and looked understatedly sexy in a pair of charcoal gray cigarette pants and a jade green silk blouse, low enough to reveal a hint of cleavage in her lace La Perla bra. Obviously not for Derek Williams' benefit. As ridiculous as it sounded, as ridiculous as it *was*, Nikki wanted to look her best when she heard the full story about Lenka. It was as if Doug's mistress were still alive, and in the room, and the two women were in some sort of stand-off or competition.

This ghost of a woman had robbed her not just of her happiness in the present, but of all her precious memories from a happy past. The opportunity to lay her to rest at last was a momentous occasion, one worth getting dressed up for.

Since her unexpected confession to Gretchen about Lenka's pregnancy, and the real circumstances under which she'd learned of Doug's affair, Nikki had had precious little time to question herself on *why* she'd chosen to conceal this information from Derek Williams. Was she embarrassed? Even now, after all this time and in the wake of so much tragedy? Embarrassed that another woman had so effortlessly provided Doug with the one thing Nikki couldn't give him – a child – and that she'd been so terrified by that prospect, she'd done nothing whatsoever about it. Until the fates intervened . . .

Would Williams have uncovered the truth himself by now? Was that his big 'news'? Or did he have other information, new information, something that might finally help Nikki make sense of Doug's infidelity and all the terrible things that had happened since?

Impatient, she texted Williams' number.

'*Where r u? Getting worried.*'

\* \* \*

Williams' phone buzzed on the desk as he pulled on his pants, the fabric sticking to his legs still wet from the shower.

'*Coming,*' he typed back hastily to Nikki. '*Sorry.*'

He'd explain the rest later, at the hotel. For once he had an excuse to be late. What he'd learned from Tina Drayton, Mayor Fuentes' former secretary, was so explosive he knew he needed to protect it, right now, before anything happened to Tina, or to himself. Even typing up a simple, bare-bones memo on the bald facts had taken longer than he imagined. And then he had to choose someone to mail it to as a backup, someone he could trust but who he would also be willing to be put at risk. Because there could be no doubt this information was potentially deadly. Knowledge was power, but it could also be lethal.

Pulling on his shirt and socks, Williams dashed over to his desk and, with a final, deep breath, hit 'send'. 'Don't hate me, Alan,' he whispered under his breath, imagining this bombshell email flying through the ether towards its unwitting recipient. Slipping his laptop into its case, he stuffed it into his suitcase and was just reaching for his shoes when his door buzzer rang.

*Really? Now?*

No one called on him at home any more. It was probably another summons from Lorraine's lawyers. Those leeches never quit.

He finished tying his shoes and zippered up the case before wheeling it down the hallway. Opening the door he was surprised to see a familiar face smiling at him.

'Oh! It's you. What are you doing here? Look I'm sorry but I'm really in a rush right now. I'm late to meet . . .'

The first bullet pierced him in the heart.

The second and third, to the head and neck, weren't necessary.

Williams fell where he stood, his eyes open, a look of profound surprise fixed eternally on his dead face.

\* \* \*

Derek Williams wasn't coming.

That left Nikki with three choices.

Take her bag, check into some anonymous hotel out of town as Williams had suggested, and lie low until he contacted her.

Go home and forget this crazy day ever happened.

Or stay here and order herself a real drink. Or two. Or three.

In the end it was an easy choice. After so much hope, so much expectation, the disappointment felt like a medicine ball to the stomach. She didn't care about Luis Rodriguez, or drug cartels, or corruption at City Hall. She didn't care that Brandon Grolsch was alive and that she needed to let Williams know it. All that mattered was that she would *not* learn the truth about Lenka tonight. She would *not* get closure, not now, maybe not ever. That small shred of comfort was to be denied her, after everything she'd been through, and was still going through. Why *not* drink?

It was ten o'clock by the time the barman touched her arm to rouse her. Nikki was so out of it, she must have nodded off at the bar.

'Do you want to settle up now, miss?' the barman asked kindly.

'It's OK. I've got this.'

Sliding onto the stool next to Nikki, Detective Goodman handed over his credit card. 'Could you put a couple of double espressos on there too? And a large glass of water, no ice.'

'Sure thing.'

The barman left them alone. Slowly, Nikki turned her head towards Goodman and tried to process what it meant that he was here.

'You're not Derek,' she slurred, trying to force his two, oscillating faces to merge into one.

'No,' Goodman agreed. 'I'm not.'

He tried not to focus on Nikki's half-open green silk shirt, disheveled hair, flushed cheeks and smudged make-up after what must have been a long night's drinking. She was usually so controlled, so together. There was something incredibly compelling about this unraveled version of the professional Dr Roberts. But this wasn't the time.

He cleared his throat. 'Nikki.'

'Where's Williams?' she interrupted him. 'He d'in show up.' Jabbing drunkenly at Goodman's chest with her finger she leaned in towards him like a falling tree. '*You* shun't be here, Lou. 'S after hours. You're following me again, aren't you?'

Their coffees arrived, not a moment too soon. Goodman waited until Nikki downed hers, wincing with distaste as the hot, strong liquid burned her throat and cut through the alcohol fog in her brain.

'Nikki, I need you to focus.' His voice was deadly serious. He pushed the glass of water towards her but she shook her head.

'I'm OK,' she told him, sounding less out of it than before. 'What is it? Wha's wrong?'

'I'm afraid I have bad news. Derek Williams is dead.'

Nikki frowned, shook her head. 'No. That's not right. He just texted me.'

'When?' Goodman asked.

Nikki looked at her watch. 'Tonight. About three hours ago.'

Goodman reached for her phone and she handed it over. He noted the times on their brief text exchange before passing it back to her.

'He was shot in the head and chest, probably right after he sent this message. Outside his apartment, point-blank range. It's only been a couple of hours but it looks like a professional hit. The killer's gun had a silencer.'

A low ringing sound in Nikki's ears grew louder. Soon it was deaf-ening. She could see Goodman's lips moving, but his words were lost to her, like he was shouting from the other side of a wall of sound-proofed glass. Her vision changed too. She no longer felt the drunken bleariness of a few moments ago. Instead she saw some things with crystal clarity. The slice of lemon floating on the top of her untouched water, glowed an almost fluorescent yellow. The freckles on the back of her own hand also seemed strangely vivid suddenly. Hyper-real. And yet her wider surroundings – the bar, the hotel lobby beyond, every-thing outside of the small circle encompassing her and Goodman and this awful new truth about Williams – that was all gone. Not blurred or faint. Actually *gone*. Disappeared.

'NIKKI.'

Goodman was shouting, shaking her roughly by the shoulders. She startled, and the mute button on his speech switched off.

'Nikki, you have to tell me what Derek Williams knew. What has he told you? What was he meeting you about tonight?'

She shook her head, still reeling with shock.

'It's vital that you tell me everything you know. I can't protect you unless you help me.'

*Poor Derek! He was a good man. A kind man. He was trying his best, to do his job, to help me, to get his own life back on track. And now he's dead. He's dead because he met me.*

'It's me,' she muttered dazedly to Goodman. 'It's because of me.'

'What was tonight's meeting about, Nikki?' Goodman forced her to focus.

'Lenka,' she replied blankly.

'Your husband's mistress,' said Goodman.

Nikki's eyes widened. 'You knew about that?'

'Johnson found out,' said Goodman. 'He also found out she was pregnant the night she died. Why'd you lie to us, Nikki?'

'I didn't lie,' she looked away. 'I didn't tell you, that's all.'

'Because?'

'Because it had nothing to do with the case, and because I don't have to tell you everything, OK? I don't!' Nikki's voice was becoming more hysterical.

'What if it did have something to do with the case?' Goodman asked. 'What if your husband's accident and these murders are connected?'

Nikki shrugged listlessly. She couldn't think about this now. Derek Williams was dead. *Dead.* That single, awful reality took up every inch of emotional space in her brain.

Goodman struggled to hide his impatience. 'Nikki, please focus. I need your help. Williams had a bag packed when we found him. You do too.' He looked down at Nikki's feet accusingly. 'Where were the two of you going?'

'Away,' she mumbled, adding hastily 'Not together. We were going to meet here and then take off. Separately. Williams said we weren't safe in LA. I guess he was right.'

'Did he say why you weren't safe?'

'Something about a ring . . . the drug cartels bribing city officials and a bunch of other people. I don't know,' Nikki mumbled.

'I know you're in shock,' said Goodman, taking Nikki's hands in his and forcing her to look him in the eye. 'But that's not good enough. I need names. I need details. I need something I can use.' Goodman's voice was rising. Other drinkers at the bar were looking increasingly uncomfortable. 'Derek Williams was *executed* tonight,' he whispered, lowering his volume but not the urgency of his tone. 'You could be next, if you don't help me.'

'I guess I could,' she replied, without a hint of emotion.

He was losing her. Somehow he had to reach her, to make a connection. Get her to talk to him, to open up. In desperation, he leaned in and kissed her, passionately, on the lips.

Nikki didn't resist. But neither did she respond, not really. It was as if someone had hit her 'off'' switch. As if her entire emotional, inner world had shut down, short-circuited. As if Derek Williams' death had been one trauma too many.

At last, Goodman pulled away. 'A name?' he asked again, softly.

'Luis Rodriguez.' Nikki sighed. 'Anne Bateman's exhusband. Derek Williams believed he might be involved, in the murders and in this "ring". He thought the Badens might be connected too, but Rodriguez was his big obsession. Those are the only names I have.'

Goodman frowned. 'Luis Rodriguez is a developer and a philanthropist. He probably gives more money to anti-drug charities than anyone else in Mexico.'

'I know,' said Nikki.

'Gives to the police too,' said Goodman. 'Why on earth would Williams think *he's* involved?'

Nikki sighed again. 'Derek was convinced he ran a massive illegal drug operation. He said the LAPD and FBI knew all about it but turned a blind eye.'

'That's baloney,' Goodman retorted angrily. Then he reminded himself that Derek Williams was dead, and it no longer made sense to pick a fight with him. 'And the Badens?'

'I don't know.' Nikki rubbed her eyes. 'I know he thought Valentina's charity was some sort of front for illegal activity. And that maybe Willie was helping Rodriguez in other ways here in LA. But, like I said, it was Rodriguez he really cared about.

'He said he had new information and he was going to tell me more tonight,' said Nikki. 'Something to do with Rodriguez and the Russians and this new drug Krokodil and corruption. According to Williams, City Hall was involved, and some investment banks. Even charities, like the Badens' Missing. Oh, and the cops,' she added. 'Corrupt cops. From the drug squad.'

'But he never told you any names?'

'He never got the chance, did he?' Nikki observed bitterly. 'I can think of some corrupt guys in your drug squad, if you're interested. Or ex-drug squad. One person in particular springs to mind.'

Mick Johnson's name hung unspoken in the air between them.

'OK.' Goodman leaned back on his chair. Apparently satisfied for now, he signaled to the barman and signed the tab for both of them. 'Was there anything else? Anything at all you can remember that might help us figure out who killed Derek Williams and why?'

Nikki contemplated telling him about the phone call she'd received earlier from Brandon Grolsch. She'd been going to tell Williams, but now Williams was gone. Somebody should know, surely? Somebody should be investigating it, trying to find Brandon, to help him. Why not Goodman? Goodman who flirted with her and rescued her and shouted at her and kissed her. Goodman who she could have loved, in another life.

But something held her back.

Derek Williams had never trusted Goodman. And Nikki had trusted Derek Williams. He'd been the only one left she did trust completely. And now he was gone too.

'No. There's nothing,' she told Goodman.

Reaching down, he picked up her overnight bag.

'I'm taking you home,' he said firmly.

'I can't go home,' she protested. 'It's not safe.'

'Not your home,' said Goodman. 'Mine.'

Their eyes met, and for a brief moment Nikki allowed herself to imagine what her life might be like if she let this happen. If she let Lou Goodman step in and take care of her, take over. Let him make the decisions, keep her safe, slay the dragons and banish the demons.

It was a lovely idea. Like most fairy tales.

But it wasn't to be.

It was far too late for all that.

'You're very sweet,' she said, kissing him on the lips, with feeling this time. 'But I can't.' Gently but firmly she prized her bag from his grip.

'Why not?' he asked, his fingers still touching hers.

'Because a long time ago, I gave my heart to my husband,' said Nikki. 'And he broke it. I'm sorry, Lou. There's nothing left to give.'

*   *   *

Anne Bateman drove carefully, blinded by her own tears as well as by the rain that was lashing down across her windshield.

It never rained in Los Angeles in May. But tonight the heavens had made an exception, as if the gods were watching the tragedy unfold below. Not Anne's personal tragedy. She wasn't arrogant or delusional enough to think that her own, small life counted for much. Her dashed hopes, her broken dreams, her loneliness. But the bigger tragedy, the one that seemed to emanate out from her in ripples, as if she were a stone dropped into a calm, clear lake. That, surely, was worthy of celestial attention. All she'd ever wanted to do was make music. And yet somehow pain and suffering seemed to cling to her, an unwanted smell she could never quite wash away.

And now here she was, again, turning to Nikki Roberts for help, for advice that she already knew in her heart she wouldn't have the strength to take. And yet Anne Bateman still needed Nikki. She needed the adulation, the adoration. The way that she, Anne, looked through the lens of Nikki's admiring, understanding, forgiving eyes. On some level, what Nikki gave her had replaced what Luis used to give her. Because he'd adored her too. If she could hold on to that fact somehow – choose good over evil, the future over the past, Nikki over Luis – then maybe, just maybe, the ripples would stop?

It was late, almost eleven o'clock, and the hour combined with the heavy rain meant the roads were practically empty. A full moon flickered in and out of the moving clouds. It bathed Brentwood's slick streets in a silvery glow, giving the grand homes and lush gardens an air of magic. Heading up Tigertail towards Nikki's house, Anne felt as if she were driving through an enchanted kingdom, a land where everything was clean and shiny and beautiful, where happy children slept soundly in their beds and bad things didn't happen.

*What if I'm the bad thing? What if I'm the monster, sneaking through the night, ready to pounce, to destroy, to devour?*

In her calmer, more rational moments, Anne knew that she wasn't intrinsically a bad person. It was Luis who'd brought the chaos into her life, Luis who'd made everything so very hard. But at other times, like tonight, she was gripped with a terrible self-loathing.

Why couldn't she break free, cut the ties for good? When Luis had failed to show up for the End Addiction Ball, why had she felt so desolate, so abandoned, so hurt? She'd complained to Nikki countless times about Luis refusing to let her go. But tonight it struck her for the first time that perhaps she was the one clinging on? That when she ran, there had always been a part of her that had expected – hoped – Luis would come running after.

And now he had, and with him, it seemed, the hounds of hell.

Anne needed Nikki. Not for advice this time but for something much more profound. For absolution.

Pulling up outside the house, she stepped out of her car into the rain. The downpour was less dramatic than it had been a few minutes ago, but still heavy enough to make a loud *rat-tat-tat* rhythm on the roof of Anne's car and the newly tarred street. The double gates were locked, but a wooden side door next to them opened easily, despite its slippery handle. Soaked to the skin, Anne stood in Nikki's forecourt looking up at the house. It was a gorgeous property, romantic and charming with its shutters and balconies and climbing roses, giving it an old world, European feel. All the lights were off – unsurprisingly, given the lateness of the hour – but Nikki was home. Her car was parked out front, raindrops bouncing off it in the moonlight like tiny silver bullets.

Anne was about to ring the bell – she felt foolish, rousing Nikki from sleep, but she'd driven all this way and her need to see her 'friend' had long since spilled over into a compulsion – but an unexpected noise made her hesitate. It was a cry. Not of fear but of sorrow. Anguish, even. Short at first but then followed by another, longer sound, keening and awful like an animal's howl. It was coming from the backyard.

A narrow passage led along the side of the house to the rear of the property. Anne followed it, being careful not to slip on the slick stone tiles. Rounding the corner at the end she saw Nikki, kneeling underneath a beautiful, spreading magnolia tree. The tree was in bloom, but the night's heavy rains had dashed many of its oversized white blossoms to the ground, creating a carpet of silken petals on the wet grass. It was on this carpet that Nikki knelt, wetter even than Anne was, her blouse clinging to her shivering body like damp seaweed on a rock. Her head was tilted up towards the moon, but her eyes were closed, and she was crying out piteously, like a dying she-wolf. Her kicked off shoes lay on the ground beside her and she was holding something in her right hand. Only as Anne drew nearer did she see what it was: a tiny, elegant pistol, glinting silver in the shadows.

'Nikki!' Anne called out to her loudly, shouting to make herself heard above both the howling and the rain. Running over, she sank down on the grass beside her friend. 'Nikki, it's me. It's Anne! Are you all right? What's happened?'

With a start, Nikki opened her eyes and turned to look at her. For what felt like a long time, both women stared at one another in shocked silence. Soaking wet, freezing cold, side by side beneath the magnolia tree Nikki had planted with Doug on their first wedding anniversary, there was so much to say. Too much. So instead they said nothing. Eventually Nikki stood up, as if in a trance. Still holding the Glock in her right hand, she offered Anne her left.

'You'd better come inside and get dry.'

Anne nodded. 'Thank you.'

Like two bedraggled ghosts, the two women went into the house.

*   *   *

Half an hour later, wearing a pair of Nikki's pajamas and swaddled in a faux fur blanket in front of the fire on Nikki's couch, Anne allowed herself to be coaxed into a deep, satisfying sleep. Nikki stroked her hair with an absent, repeating rhythm, her voice hypnotic and heavy as she told Anne to rest, to close her eyes, to let the warmth surround her and take her.

Nikki watched as the younger woman slipped effortlessly into sleep. *Like a baby,* she thought. That was the one part of the dream that she and Doug had missed out on: a child of their own. Long before she learned about Lenka, Nikki remembered how despairing her infertility had made her at the time. How not having children had felt like the biggest tragedy in the world. Before she knew what tragedy meant.

Would she have gone through with it tonight, if Anne hadn't shown up? Would she really have pulled the trigger and blown her own brains out? Her instinct told her that she would. But she would never know for sure now. All she did know was that the moment had passed. Anne had appeared, like an angel of mercy, and Nikki had taken the gun inside and put it back in the drawer and locked it, and she no longer wanted to die. Not today, anyway. There was too much left to do. Too much she still needed to understand.

Had God sent Anne to save her?

Or perhaps it was Doug who'd intervened, in some mysterious, spiritual way, from the afterlife? That was a nice thought.

Standing at the window, Nikki gazed out into the night. The rain had stopped, and all was peace and calm and stillness. She thought about Derek Williams, how he'd given his life for the truth. *Her* truth. She owed it to Williams to see this through.

*    *    *

From the safety of a warm, dry car, a figure watched in the darkness, their night vision goggles trained onto Nikki Roberts' living room window.

Sliding lower in their seat, they settled in for the night.

It wouldn't be long now.

# 34

Goodman sat alone in the booth at Joe's Diner, staring morosely at his phone. Johnson was in the men's room, where he'd been locked away ever since his ill-advised third cup of coffee twenty minutes ago. They were due back at Derek Williams' apartment for a meeting with forensics. But Nikki's email, sent at five this morning, had already thrown Goodman for a loop.

'Been thinking all last night,' she wrote. 'Not sure what to tell you, but I guess now Williams is dead I have to tell someone. Brandon Grolsch is alive. He called me yesterday, very distressed. I don't know where he is, or how he's connected to any of this, but I lied to you about not knowing him. I'm sorry.'

As if that weren't enough of a bombshell, she carried on.

'If Williams was right about a corrupt cop helping the cartels, then it has to be Johnson. I know you don't want to believe it. But it fits. He asked for this case, he's senior, he's ex-drug squad, and he's deliberately mishandled the investigation into these murders, trying to make me the scapegoat. He's deflecting and he's succeeding.'

There was a lot of paranoia in Nikki's note, shot through with micro-threads of truth, but perhaps that was to be expected, given her frazzled state of mind, especially since Williams' murder. But it was the last part of the email that troubled him much more.

'Watch Johnson, Lou. I don't think you're safe around him, and I don't want to see you hurt. I don't think I'm safe either, so I'll be gone for a while, off grid.

Try not to worry.

Take care. NR.'

Goodman felt his pulse quicken.

How long was 'a while'? And what the hell was 'off-grid' supposed to mean?

He'd already rung her twice since the note landed in his inbox, in addition to sending a brief email reply, but all her devices were switched off. *Off grid.*

*Not good.*

As for the rest of Nikki's suspicions about Johnson, without evidence there was little Goodman could do to pursue them. And in the meantime the two men were supposed to be a team.

'Jesus,' Johnson grumbled, shuffling back to the table clutching his distended belly. 'What the hell do they put in their coffee in this joint? I feel like I just gave birth.'

Goodman put away his phone, wrinkling his nose in distaste. 'Too much information, dude. Shall we go?'

'Ready when you are,' said Johnson. 'I hope forensics have got something concrete. Because that son of a bitch had so many enemies, half of Los Angeles might have taken him out. Hell, I had half a mind to do it myself!'

Goodman followed his partner to the car, trying to shake the feeling that Derek Williams' ghost had just walked over his grave.

*       *       *

Setting her bag down on the bed at the San Miguel Hacienda in Palm Springs, Nikki felt a surreal sense of déjà vu.

The last time she'd stayed here had been with Doug, five years ago, for their wedding anniversary. The small, intimate guesthouse had been built as a family home in the Moorish style, with warm tiled floors and ornate stone fountains and rooms that opened onto secret, sun-drenched courtyards, overgrown with bougainvillea. There was no air conditioning, astonishingly for a hotel out in the desert, and yet somehow the whitewashed walls and ceiling fans and the shade from the desert palm trees that surrounded the property ensured that guests were always comfortably cool inside. And outside, an old-fashioned, kidney-shaped pool, sparkling sapphire blue, provided frequent cooling relief from the punishing afternoon sun.

The Hacienda was intrinsically romantic. Even now, Nikki could still remember her delight walking in here, and Doug's pride and satisfaction that his surprise discovery had worked out so well. That he'd pleased her.

'One of Haddon's rich patients came back raving about this place,' Doug said, slipping his hands around Nikki's waist and pulling her towards him greedily. 'And I know how you hate those big corporate joints. So you like it?'

'I love it,' Nikki said, tossing her bag on to the white linen bed and floating into the simple bathroom, barefoot and happy and carefree in a way that seemed so alien to her now, she could hardly believe she was the same person.

*Perhaps I'm not the same person,* she thought, turning her phone back on and sitting soberly on the end of the bed beside her overnight case, the same one she'd brought to the SLS for her meeting with Derek Williams, the one that never happened.

Williams had told her to disappear to somewhere neutral and anonymous, 'somewhere nobody knows you'. The Hacienda was hardly that. But something had drawn her here. A half-remembered feeling of safety, perhaps, or of happiness? As if her soul were reaching subconsciously for the last vestiges of the life she'd lost.

Or maybe it was Doug again, pulling her strings from beyond the grave? She'd felt that last night, when Anne showed up. When she'd been ready to end it all, to screw up her courage and turn off the noise and the pain forever.

Was that really only last night? Less than twenty-four hours ago?

Nikki's phone began pinging with messages. *Goodman. Goodman. Gretchen. Goodman.* Ignoring them all, she pushed it to one side. With a faint knock, Señora Marchesa, the proprietress, stuck her smiling, heavily wrinkled face round the door of Nikki's room.

'How long you staying with us this time, Dr Roberts?' she asked. 'You know the room is free right through the end of June if you want it. Summer's pretty quiet up here.'

'I'm not sure yet, señora,' Nikki told her, returning the smile. 'Can we say a few days, and then I'll let you know?'

'Of course,' the older woman said, touching Nikki gently on the shoulder. 'You look tired. Try to rest.'

Nikki waited till she'd gone to drop the smile, suddenly and totally, like a too heavy weight. The pretense of happiness was too hard now, even for a few seconds. Inside her chest was a burned-out shell where her heart should have been, a scorched wasteland still smoldering with anger, white-hot to the touch.

*Damn you, Doug, for the happy memories! Damn you for lying, and cheating on me! Damn you for being dead! I hope you burn in hell, with your Russian witch and her child beside you!*

Nikki had told Anne Bateman last night that she loved her but she could no longer be her therapist.

'It's not personal,' she insisted. 'I'm in no fit state to practice, and you need a therapist who is and who can help you move forward.' She still hadn't broached the subject of Luis Rodriguez and Derek Williams' wild accusations about his secret life as a drug lord. And she knew now that she never would. Without evidence, Williams' theories would have to die with him. If Luis really intended to hurt Anne, Nikki reasoned, he would have done it by now. Either way, there was nothing that Nikki could save her from. And if Williams was right about Luis Rodriguez, she needed to save herself.

Numb with her own pain, Anne had agreed to part ways, and the two women had said warm goodbyes to one another when dawn broke this morning, both of them knowing that they wouldn't see one another again.

Anne had seen the gun in Nikki's hand last night. She'd said nothing, but that shared moment of what should have been private anguish had changed everything. Nikki couldn't be Anne's rock. She couldn't be anybody's rock, not until she'd laid her own demons to rest.

Once Anne had gone, Nikki composed an email to Goodman. She then sent four others. Two to her remaining patients, Carter Berkeley and Lana Grey, terminating her role as their therapist and asking their forgiveness. One to her new secretary and ill-fated office manager, Kim Choy, to whom she also transferred three months' wages in lieu of notice. And a fourth and final note to Gretchen. That had been the hardest to write. Because Nikki wanted to believe so badly that this wasn't goodbye. That one day, when all this was over, maybe she really *could* move to New York and start again. And Gretchen could come and stay with her, and they'd have Thanksgiving together and go to shows and exhibitions and restaurants and Nikki would build a new practice and life would have meaning again.

She knew it was a pipe dream. But writing that note to her oldest friend, it was a pipe dream she didn't have the strength to let go, not completely.

Once the email was sent, she ate a quick breakfast and got on the road, putting fifty miles between herself and the city before LA's morning rush hour began in earnest. In the past, Nikki had always found the drive out to the desert liberating. Palm Springs itself might be a bizarre throwback to the long-gone glamour days of its Rat Pack past, but the vast open spaces that surrounded it, the mile upon mile of nothing, of rock and sky, that led one there – that landscape had a magic to it, for anyone willing to appreciate it.

This morning, however, Nikki felt no freedom, no elation on the long, empty roads. Next to her on the passenger seat was her cell phone, which she'd been forced to switch off after the third call from Goodman, and a letter, handwritten, from Derek Williams. She hadn't opened the letter yet. She would do that at the Hacienda, where she felt safe, and alone. But its mere presence was enough to suck any joy out of the car and replace it with fear, the sort of brooding dread that came with knowing a sleeping rattlesnake was coiled up beside you.

The letter had arrived at Nikki's offices, roughly four hours before Williams' murder. Kim had had the forethought to drive it up to the house and deliver it to Nikki personally, rather than wait for the police to seize it in their regular trawls of Nikki's business mail.

Now the letter sat propped up against the pillow on Nikki's bed. She'd been about to open it when Señora Marchesa walked in. Once the señora was gone, she had to screw up her courage all over again.

*Tequila,* Nikki thought. *Tequila will help.*

Slipping on her bikini, she grabbed two miniatures of Jose Cuervo from the fridge in her room, along with Williams' letter, and marched defiantly out to the pool, stretching out her slender limbs on a sun lounger. *I'll open it when I'm ready,* she decided, letting the hot dry air warm her skin and the cold tequila warm her throat and calm her jangled nerves. Whatever Williams had chosen to put in his final letter to her had been his decision. But Nikki got to decide when she opened Pandora's Box, and she clung to that tiny shred of control like a life raft in a stormy ocean.

She fell asleep quickly and without even realizing it. When she woke her skin was burning, her mouth dry and her head throbbing with an awful, insistent ringing noise that went on and on and on . . .

'Are you gonna get that?' An angry woman in an ugly printed one-piece and a large straw hat loomed over Nikki's lounger. 'Because if you aren't, maybe you could turn your cell phone off? Some of us are trying to relax here.'

Groggily realizing what was happening, Nikki reached for her phone.

'Hello?' Her voice sounded hideously raspy, as if she'd been gargling with sand.

'Nikki? Oh my God, thank God. Thank *God!* Where were you? I've been calling and calling . . .' Anne was hysterical, speaking so fast and so loudly that Nikki had to hold her cell away from her ear.

'Anne. I told you this morning. I can't help you any more,' she said patiently. 'Whatever's happened, you need—'

'NO!' Anne cut her off, screaming wildly. 'Please! You don't understand. I found out something terrible . . . about Luis.'

A shiver ran down Nikki's spine. *She knows.* So Williams was right all along?

'I can't talk on the phone,' Anne babbled. 'It's not safe. You *have* to meet me!'

'I don't have to do anything,' said Nikki bluntly.

Anne burst into tears.

'I am begging you, Nikki. Please!' she sobbed. 'If I ever meant anything to you. It's for your sake as much as mine.'

'How is it for my sake?' asked Nikki.

'It just is, OK? I have evidence, something I need to show you in person. I swear to God, after this I will never contact you again.'

'Can't you go to the police?' Nikki asked wearily.

'No!' It was almost a shriek. 'I need you.'

Nikki put a hand to her burning cheek. She felt torn. She'd never heard Anne this desperate before, and that was saying something. If she really had found proof that Luis *was* what Williams insisted he was, that would account for it. But what did she expect Nikki to do about it? On the other hand, this was Anne. Her Anne. Anne who had saved her life last night, whether she intended to or not.

*I could meet her,* Nikki thought. *One last time.*

But where, and how? The idea of turning around and driving all the way back to LA tomorrow filled her with dread. She'd only just escaped the city. Plus if Goodman found out she was back, or worse, Johnson, she'd be screwed.

Perhaps she should ask Anne to come to her instead? To drive out to the desert. But that presented its own problems. She didn't want anyone to know where she was. And if Luis was still having Anne followed . . . No. It was too dangerous.

'Be at my office at six o'clock tomorrow night,' she said at last. 'I'll have Kim let you in through the back door.'

'Not your office,' Anne replied. 'Luis has people watching. Your home too. And mine, and the concert hall.'

The fear in her voice made the hairs on Nikki's arms stand on end.

Anne blurted out an address downtown. 'It's a warehouse in the old clothing district but it's been empty for months. I pass it on my way to rehearsal.' She gave Nikki instructions on how to get in. 'Six o'clock, yes?'

'OK,' Nikki said reluctantly. 'Tomorrow at six.'

With a click, the line went dead.

# 35

Strangely, Nikki woke the next morning feeling enormously better. Perhaps it was the temporary euphoria of an unbroken night's sleep, her first in many days. The Hacienda's cloud-soft bed had welcomed her like a lover, stinging sunburned skin and all. And though she awoke looking like a half-boiled lobster, with flakes of skin peeling painfully from her nose, cheekbones and the tops of her red-raw shoulders, her raging anxiety seemed to have gone and with it all the anger and sadness that had felt so overwhelming the night before.

*How strange human emotions are,* Nikki mused, as she wolfed down an enormous late breakfast of bacon frittata, fresh fruit, toast and cottage cheese, all washed down with gallons of strong Italian coffee. Her appetite was back too, apparently. *And how resilient.*

She no longer felt afraid of tonight's meeting with Anne. And although the drive back to the city was an inconvenience, it would be worth it to end that fraught relationship on a solid, kind note. Plus, although no longer obsessed with the case, she had to admit she was curious about this 'evidence' Anne wanted to show her. If it was significant, she would find a way to pass the lead on to Lou Goodman. Then, her conscience clear, she would head back to Palm Springs and after that, who knew? Maybe Arizona. Or Utah? If she were going to lose herself, to lay low until this case was resolved, she might as well do it somewhere beautiful and wild, exploring places she'd never been before like Zion and Moab, or maybe Monument Valley.

After a morning spent reading inside, her sore face covered in soothing aloe gel, she showered, changed and headed to the reception desk.

'I'll be back tonight but very late,' she told Señora Marchesa. 'Do I need a key to the front gate?'

'No, Dr Roberts,' the hostess smiled. 'Your room key works for both. Would you like me to leave a supper tray in your room?'

'Maybe some fruit,' said Nikki, heading out to her car. 'Thank you.'

'You're welcome,' the older woman muttered under her breath, watching Nikki go. As soon as her car had pulled out of the gates, Señora Marchesa picked up the phone.

'She just left,' she whispered.

Hanging up as another guest came in, she fixed her welcoming smile back in place. 'Buenos días, señor. Welcome to the San Miguel Hacienda. How may I assist you?'

\* \* \*

Stopping for gas at the Exxon station right before the freeway on-ramp, Nikki reached into her purse to retrieve her wallet and ended up pulling out Williams' letter. Suddenly all her fear and over-thinking seemed ridiculous. Right there at the pump she tore open the envelope and pulled out the single sheet of paper inside.

A few minutes later, a worried attendant came over. Nikki was bent double, clutching the paper, tears streaming down her face.

'Miss? Are you OK? Do you need some help?' He touched her shaking shoulders nervously.

Nikki jerked upright and turned around, wiping away her tears.

Embarrassed and relieved, the attendant saw that she'd actually been crying with laughter.

'I'm fine. I'm sorry!' she said, screwing the petrol cap back on and getting back into the car, the paper still in her hand. 'It's . . . it's an invoice.'

'I'm sorry?'

'A bill! For services rendered!' Nikki waved the paper delightedly in front of the man's face. 'The last thing he sent me, his oh-so-important message from beyond the grave? It was a bill!' She laughed again, shaking her head.

'OK, miss. Well as long as you're all right,' the baffled attendant said. In his experience, bills really weren't all that funny. Then again, this was Palm Springs. If he had a dollar for all the crazies he ran into around here, he'd be able to pay all his bills and then some.

\* \* \*

Goodman sat at his desk at the precinct, idly re-reading the meager forensics report on Derek Williams' killing. No fingerprints. No hairs. No DNA or clothing fibers, other than the deceased's.

Ballistics had had marginally more success. They'd retrieved two bullets, 9 mm Elite V-Crown hollow-points, and had a good idea of the gun the killer used, a Sig Sauer P938. Unfortunately those were a dime a dozen on the streets of LA. The only real lead was the suppressor the assassin had used, something called a Dead Air Ghost M, a much rarer, top-of-the-range, specialist piece of kit only stocked by a handful of gun stores. If it had been bought legally, the purchaser would have had to file an application for it with BAFTE.

Mick Johnson was out interviewing Dead Air suppliers right now and Goodman was supposed to be trawling the BAFTE records. But he already knew in his heart that Derek Williams' killer would never be caught. What worried him were the live threats still out there, specifically Dr Nikki Roberts, who was somewhere on the run and who clearly had zero intention of returning any of Goodman's calls. So far, Johnson didn't even know Nikki had left town, in direct contravention of police instructions to remain 'available' while the Flannagan and Raymond murder investigation was ongoing. Even Goodman had to admit that Nikki taking off the day after her PI got whacked didn't look good. Innocent or not, it was what Washington politicians referred to as 'bad optics'.

'This came for you.'

The bored new desk officer, a young mother named Latisha Hall who'd joined the force to escape the dull routine of domesticity, only to find herself wasting her days filing and delivering mail to a bunch of ungrateful detectives, tossed an envelope lazily in Goodman's general direction.

'You opened it?' Goodman frowned accusingly, seeing the rip across the top.

'Course not, Detective,' Latisha defended herself. 'It came like that.'

Flipping the envelope over, Goodman went white. It was addressed to 'Dr Nicola Roberts'. Inside were two pieces of paper. The first was a neatly typed bill for 'services rendered in April/May' from 'the offices of Derek. B. Williams, PI.' It was dated May 12th, the day Williams died. On the back of the invoice, someone had written by hand the word *'Grayling'* and the number *777*.

The second piece of paper had been roughly torn off a pad and was in Nikki's own hand, hastily scrawled.

'*Thought you should have this,*' it read. '*Hopefully, it means more to you than it does to me. Don't come after me. But please watch your back, Lou. Johnson's in this up to his neck. NR.*'

Goodman's heart began pounding, speeding up like an overloaded freight train heading downhill.

'Where did you get this?' he demanded, glaring at Latisha as if she'd delivered some personal affront. 'Who gave it to you?'

'No one "gave it" to me. I—'

'Did it come in the regular mail?' Goodman interrupted impatiently. 'Why didn't you give it to me earlier?'

'Because I only saw it now, on my desk, when I got back from the bathroom. *Sir,*' the girl shot back sassily. Goodman might be a senior officer, but Latisha Brown didn't take shit from no one. 'Someone musta dropped it off in person. I already gave out the regular afternoon mail, two hours ago.'

Pushing past her, Goodman scrambled to the window and looked out at the parking lot below and the street beyond. Nikki must have been here! Maybe even in the last few minutes. He scanned the lot, staring down at the handful of milling people, willing her to be there. But of course she wasn't. He'd lost her. So close, and he'd lost her!

Turning the paper over, he stared at it and the envelope again intently. There was nothing untoward about Derek Williams' invoice, nothing unusual or noteworthy about it at all as far as Goodman could see, other than the date. And yet Nikki had felt it important enough to leave it for him. To risk coming here to the station in person. *Why?*

Only the writing on the back, 'Grayling 777', was in any way unusual, although even that looked harmless enough, like it could have been anything or nothing. Surely she wouldn't have come back to LA and taken such a risk just for that?

'Call Detective Johnson,' he barked at Latisha.

'OK,' she replied sullenly. 'Call him and say what?'

'Tell him to get his ass back here,' Goodman snapped. 'Right away.'

# 36

The address Anne had given Nikki was for a small, deserted warehouse, situated right on the edge of Downtown's fashion district, off San Julian Street. Wedged between two much larger buildings, one a printing shop and the other a factory full of seamstresses, it nestled in almost total shadow, hidden from the surrounding streets by its neighbors, as well as by a double-height brick wall to the rear.

It was an area Nikki used to know well. Doug and Haddon's first drop-in clinic had been only a few blocks away, although a lot had changed since those days. The junkies were still here of course. But rising real estate values and the insane amounts of money pouring into downtown had seen them driven further and further east, past Olympic Boulevard. The new mayor's clampdown on homelessness had also had an impact. Five years ago, unused spaces like the one Anne had chosen for their meeting would have been full of rough sleepers. Now they sat, still empty but untouched, while landlords waited for a tenant rich enough to pay their outrageous rent hikes, or for a development offer they couldn't refuse.

Parking at a meter a few blocks up the street, Nikki worried about Anne. Meeting somewhere neutral and private, especially if she had sensitive information to impart, was one thing. But to pick such an eerie, desolate spot seemed at best eccentric and at worst a sign that Anne must be genuinely afraid of being seen with Nikki. This wasn't a meeting place so much as a hiding place. But hiding from whom?

Nikki's first assumption was Luis, and Anne had pretty much implied as much over the phone. But why would her ex suddenly want to hurt her now, after all this time? Nikki's view of Anne's husband had always been that he was both jealous and controlling, but that, by his own lights, he did love his wife. He might threaten and cajole and intimidate, to try to win her back. But he had never raised a hand to Anne, whatever else he may have done.

And yet the fear, the panic in Anne's voice when they spoke yesterday had been unmistakable. She sounded petrified. It was a feeling Nikki had come to know intimately herself over the course of the last few weeks. She hoped she would be able to help Anne this one last time, before she returned to her own hiding place, running from her own demons.

She checked her watch. It was five to six when she approached the warehouse, tapping the five-digit code Anne had given her into the keypad beside the front gates. With a satisfying 'click' the heavy steel door unlocked, allowing Nikki through to a thin strip of open space, and concrete stairs up to the building itself. Here the sliding doors were already part open, as Anne had said they would be. *You can let yourself in. If I'm late, please wait for me. I promise I'll be there.*

Instinctively, Nikki drew her thin cashmere cardigan more tightly around her as she stepped into a cold, dark room. A trickle of early evening light streamed through two dirty upper windows, but the overall feeling was one of institutional gloom. The gray concrete floor was scratched and pitted, and other than a few desultory plastic chairs and tables stacked against one wall, the space was devoid of furniture. A few scraps of discarded fabric lay scattered here and there, presumably remnants of the last business to occupy the space. Straight ahead, at one end of the room was a double-wide elevator, designed for moving stock rather than people. To both the left and right of it, ugly metal fire stairs led up to a mezzanine level, and then up again, presumably to a second and third floor.

'Anne?'

Nikki's voice bounced off the walls, the echo seeming to drift upwards until it died away. There was no response. Somewhere above Nikki's head a bird shrieked and she could hear the sound of frenzied flapping before silence fell again.

*Poor thing. It must be trapped.*

Striding towards the fire stairs, determined not to give in to the uneasiness that gripped her, Nikki climbed to the mezzanine level and continued straight on up to the next floor. Here the space was divided into a series of smaller rooms, presumably once offices, along a long, narrow corridor. It was a lot darker than downstairs, with the only available natural light coming from only one side of the building. And there was an awful smell, the unmistakable stench of human feces. Reaching up, Nikki touched a switch on the wall. With a flicker, then a glare, and a loud buzz from the revived electrical current, all the strip lighting along the windowless walls burst into life.

Nikki screamed, a shrill, strangled sound that half-caught in her throat.

There, nailed to a wooden beam against the wall with outstretched arms, like a grotesque parody of Jesus, hung a naked, bloated male corpse. Beaten and bloodied almost beyond recognition, it took Nikki a moment to register who it was:

*Willie Baden!*

Someone had stuffed a wad of money into his mouth, presumably a final insult in what looked like a gruesome ritual killing. Nikki felt the bile rise up in her throat, partly in disgust and partly in terror. She was no expert, but from the blood still dripping from the wounds on his groin, Baden didn't look like he'd been dead for long. If whoever did this was still here . . .

'Nikki! Over here.' Anne's voice sounded reedy and thin.

'Anne!' Turning away from Baden's corpse Nikki blinked, her eyes stinging under the bright lights. 'Where are you? I can't see you.'

Like a faun stepping out from the protective cover of the forest, Anne emerged from one of the box-like 'offices' into the long corridor where Nikki was standing. Barely glancing at the crucified body hanging only a few feet away, she stumbled towards Nikki. Only as she came close did Nikki see the bruises, from Anne's eye, all the way down the right side of her face and neck, where the skin was blue gray and swollen.

Nikki rushed towards her. 'He hit you?'

Anne looked down, ashamed, biting her lower lip.

'Did he kill Willie Baden, Anne?' Nikki put a protective arm around her as she turned back to the grisly apparition nailed to the beam. 'Did you see what happened? Were you here? The poor man was obviously tortured.'

'I'm sorry,' Anne mumbled. She was obviously still in shock.

'What for?' said Nikki. 'It isn't your fault. None of this is your fault.'

'You're wrong,' Anne sobbed, shaking.

'Listen, we need to get you out of here.' Nikki's practical side kicked in. 'Whatever's happened, neither of us are safe—'

'It is my fault,' Anne interrupted her. 'I wish . . . I wish things could have been different. But he made me do it. He made me watch.'

She looked at Baden's corpse then, for the first time. 'He made me film it.' She held up her phone to Nikki with a shaking hand. 'And he made me bring you. He wanted you to see. I'm so sorry.'

From the rooms behind her, two heavyset men in dark suits suddenly appeared. 'This way please, Mrs Rodriguez,' one of them said politely, while the other one firmly grabbed Anne by the upper arm. With a lurching stomach, Nikki noticed that his hand was covered in dried blood. Presumably poor Willie Baden's. Although what on earth Baden had to do with any of this she couldn't imagine. 'We'll escort you to your car.'

Nikki watched helplessly as a sobbing Anne was bundled into a different, smaller elevator and disappeared from view.

'Wait!' she called after them. 'Don't hurt her! Don't you touch her!' But the doors had already closed.

Frantically, Nikki tried to gather her thoughts. Anne had been upset to see the two men, but not surprised. She knew they were coming, knew she'd be taken away. What was it she'd just said? '*He made me bring you. He wanted you to see.*'

Nikki had seen enough. She had to get out of here. Had to save herself, even if she couldn't save Anne. Turning around, she started back the same way she came in, averting her eyes from the hunk of flesh that had once been Lisa Flannagan's lover and running along the corridor. But before she'd gone more than a few yards, a tall, distinguished-looking man in a dark suit stepped casually in front of her, blocking her path.

He was relaxed and smiling, and she recognized him instantly from the picture on Google that Derek Williams had shown her.

'Mr Rodriguez.'

Luis nodded, still smiling all the way to his brown eyes.

'Dr Roberts. We meet at last. So glad you could make it.'

Pulling a pistol out of his inside jacket pocket, he pointed it right between Nikki's eyes.

*    *    *

Mick Johnson looked at Officer Latisha Hall as if she were something unpleasant he'd found stuck to the bottom of his shoe.

'You said Goodman needed me back here. You *said* it was urgent.'

'That's what Detective Goodman told me, sir.' Latisha knew better than to risk the same levels of sass with Johnson that she had with his partner. You did *not* want to get on the wrong side of Mick Johnson. Everyone in the department knew that. And if you weren't Irish, Catholic, White and Male, you already had four strikes against you.

'So where is he?' Johnson asked through gritted teeth.

'I don't know, sir.'

'You don't know,' Johnson repeated, in a whisper that could only be described as menacing. Sinking down into his chair in the room he shared with Goodman, he closed his eyes and literally willed himself not to lose his temper. Not because the lazy, stupid desk officer didn't deserve it. But because he didn't have the time or the energy to waste on her. Things were getting serious now. Deadly serious. He needed to know where Goodman was.

It didn't help that the two of them had been lying to each other for a long time. Johnson hadn't spent this afternoon trailing around muffler dealers, any more than Goodman had spent it checking up on BAFTE license applications. He'd been at Carter Berkeley's Investment Bank, Berkeley Hammond Rudd, strong-arming the accounts department into handing over the files he needed. Files that made *very* interesting reading and that he'd only gotten halfway through copying when he received Goodman's summons.

Johnson knew why *he'd* been lying. He'd stopped trusting his partner in this cursed case a long time ago. But he hadn't been sure of Goodman's motives for concealing so much from him. Not till today.

Today, sitting in Carter Berkeley's offices, it had suddenly come to him. A reason for Goodman to lie, to operate in the same murky world of half-truths that had blinded both of them.

'Detective Goodman did receive a phone call, sir,' Latisha said nervously. 'Shortly after I spoke with you. I can't say who that call was from, but he took off after that, sir. Like a bat out of hell, if you'll pardon the expression.'

Johnson's mind raced, his stomach sour with fear.

Waving Latisha away, he closed the door to the glass box of an office, and sat down not at his own desk, but at Goodman's.

The net was tightening, but he mustn't panic.

*Think.*

Unlike Johnson's own desk, Goodman's was clean and organized, as neat as a pin. The envelope addressed to Dr Roberts was still lying there, as was Goodman's cell phone, a sure sign that he must have left not just in a hurry but in a flat-spin panic. Johnson looked at the envelope first, carefully reading both Williams' invoice and the writing on the back, and Nikki's note to Goodman. His chest tightened when he saw his own name. *'Johnson's in this up to his neck.'* Stupid woman! She was about to find out what being in something up to your neck really meant.

Slipping the envelope into his pocket, Johnson picked up Goodman's cell phone. Typing in the access code he'd memorized long ago, he began scrolling through his partner's messages and calls, as well as his search history.

It didn't take him long to find what he needed.

Forwarding the information to his own phone, he quickly deleted the record from Goodman's sent items. The feeling of fear in his chest intensified as he looked at his watch. Six twenty already! How had that happened? What if he was too late?

Reloading his gun, he ran out of the door.

It was time to finish this thing once and for all.

*   *   *

Nikki closed her eyes and braced herself for the bullet that would end her life. At least, in her case, it looked as if the end would be swift, and not the protracted agony inflicted on poor Willie Baden. Strangely, now that it had come to this, she felt very little fear. More resignation, and a sort of dull ache of disappointment that she was going to die before she understood anything at all.

But the shot didn't come. Opening her eyes, she was surprised to find Luis Rodriguez staring at her, his expression a combination of cruelty and amusement.

'Why the rush, Dr Roberts? Don't you want to talk before you meet your maker?'

'You murdered Willie Baden.' Nikki looked at him coolly. He was going to kill her at some point. But as long as she was alive she wanted answers.

'Indeed.' Rodriguez gave a little bow, as if accepting a compliment.

'Why?'

'Why not?' he laughed. Then, seeing Nikki's appalled face, added, 'Oh, come along now, Dr Roberts. Don't tell me you disapprove? He was a cheating pig, you must have despised the man.'

'Why?' Nikki asked again.

'He got greedy,' Rodriguez said simply. 'He'd been taking more than his agreed cut on a little business deal we had together. For a long time, as it turned out. In Mexico he was careful, but here in LA he believed he was untouchable.' He turned to look appraisingly at Baden's mutilated, naked body. 'I disabused him of that notion. No one's untouchable. Make an enemy of me and I will find you.'

His eyes blazed murderously into Nikki's and she half expected him to shoot her on the spot. Instead he waited for the wave of anger to subside and said quietly, 'Next question.'

'What did you do to Anne?'

Rodriguez seemed surprised that this was what Nikki wanted to ask.

'To Anne? Nothing that she didn't want me to do,' he replied, smiling smugly. 'My wife likes to be dominated, you see, Dr Roberts. I'm surprised you haven't figured that out by now. But then again, you never really knew Anne. Not like I do.'

'I knew she was afraid of you,' said Nikki. 'I knew she ran because she couldn't stand one more day in the cage of a life you'd condemned her to.'

His smile died on his lips.

'You know it amuses me to listen to you try to defend her. Even now, after she brought you here to die.'

'Because you forced her to. The same way you forced her to watch what you did to Willie Baden. You terrorized her. You beat her!' Nikki insisted.

Luis shook his head. 'No, Dr Roberts. You still don't get it, do you? She does these things because she *loves* me. In the end, whatever she feels for you, Anne will do anything to please me, and to protect me. Because, despite your best efforts to destroy us, her heart is still mine.'

'That's not true,' said Nikki. But she could hear her own conviction wavering. Anne had brought her here, after all, led her into Rodriguez's trap. And who knew what role she'd really played in Baden's killing?

'I should have stepped in a long time ago,' Luis went on, his gun still pointed firmly at Nikki's head. 'The irony is that I was going to get rid of you before you even met my wife. As soon as I discovered that that buffoon Berkeley had been reckless enough to put himself in *therapy*. Of all the moronic things to do.'

'You mean Carter?' Nikki's eyes widened. 'What does Carter Berkeley have to do with any of this?'

Luis's smile broadened. 'You really don't know, do you?'

'No,' Nikki said truthfully. 'I don't.'

'All right, Dr Roberts. In that case, I'm going to tell you a little story. Just for fun. And you see if you can fit some of the pieces together. Once upon a time, there was a man. Not a young man, but a man in his prime.'

His voice was deep and mellifluous, like an actor's, and there was a hypnotic quality about the way he spoke that compelled one to listen. Nikki could quite see how a younger, more vulnerable Anne could have fallen under his spell.

'Try and picture this man in a forest, a few miles outside Mexico City. A beautiful, secluded spot. It's a hot, dark night. The moon is full. He's waiting for a girl. A special girl. A girl whose soft, young body he's been pleasuring himself with for months now, but not like this. Not like tonight. Tonight will be different. Even *more* special.'

Nikki felt a cold, prickling sensation creep over her. She shivered. Rodriguez was becoming excited, telling the story. Carter Berkeley's words came rushing back to her, from their last session together, when Carter had slipped almost into a trance. '*I see a clearing in the trees. It's nighttime. It's dark but there's moonlight. It's hot.*'

'He sees her coming,' Rodriguez went on. 'She's stumbling through the fields, taking glances at the little map he's made for her. Her reddish blond hair, newly washed, swings from side to side as she walks. She's tall, very tall, and her long, slim legs picking their way over fallen branches and rocks remind him of a young deer. *Perfection.* She's so beautiful it's almost painful to watch her. So young. So innocent! Are you with me, Dr Roberts?'

Nikki nodded, appalled but mesmerized. The pieces were starting to fall into place. Some of them, anyway.

'Charlotte Clancy. You're talking about Charlotte Clancy, aren't you?'

'Very good,' Rodriguez grinned. 'More than anything, it was her innocence that had drawn the man in. It was intoxicating, something he wanted because he had never had it. He'd been young once himself, of course, a long time before. But he'd never been truly innocent. Not like Charlotte. The two of them came from different worlds, different planets. Their stars had never been intended to collide. But collided they had, and here he was, watching her, drinking in the wonder of her as she rushed to meet him.'

'What happened then?' Nikki asked, as if this were a therapy session and she was drawing her client out. Which, in a way, she was.

'Well then, the man got silently out of his car and tiptoed the few hundred feet to the clearing, so he would be there to greet her when she arrived,' said Rodriguez, playing along. 'He felt aroused. Excited. He'd been hesitant before but not now. He wanted this. He called out through the darkness:

'"Cara!"

'"I'm here! I'm here my love," she called back.'

He mimicked Charlotte Clancy's voice in a squeaky falsetto that made Nikki's stomach churn.

'Then she stepped into the clearing and stood shyly in front of him, maybe ten feet away. She tried to come closer but he held up a hand to stop her. Told her he wanted to remember her there, just as she was. Can you picture her?'

'I can,' said Nikki, repulsed. 'She was eighteen years old. A child. What did you do to her, Luis?'

He made another little ingratiating bow and chuckled. 'Right again, Dr Roberts. So the young lady is Charlotte and the man is me. You're almost there. I was married at the time, to my second wife – this is a few years before Anne – and I'd had a fabulous summer fling with Charlotte. But then, very unfortunately, she decided to overstep the boundaries. And she really left me with no choice but to finish things.

'What did I do to her? I asked her to take off her dress. Like Anne, you see, Charlotte liked to be dominated. She was happy to comply. *Eager*, even.' He salivated at the memory. 'I can picture her now, raising her arms, pulling the thin cotton over her head. She had these lovely, high, round, apple breasts and a flat, taut stomach above a *tiny* pair of lace underwear. Oh, she was perfect, Dr Roberts! She really was. I asked her to dance for me, but she was shy, and she didn't want to, not at all. So I had to give her a little helping hand. Have you ever seen the human body under machine-gun fire?'

He let out a sadistic high-pitched giggle. 'I don't suppose you have. They're dead long before they fall to the ground, but before that they all do this amusing sort of jerky, jumpy little dance to the rhythm of the bullets, legs and arms flying everywhere. It's a bit of a mess by the end, but it's well worth watching, if you've never seen it before.

'Carter Berkeley was one of my bankers. I liked him, but my God he was uptight! Anyway, I'd hoped he would enjoy the little show I put on for him with Charlotte. He'd introduced us in the first place, so he deserved a little thank you, and I'd promised him a surprise, you see. He came along and watched from the car. But he was boringly squeamish about the whole thing, shaking and crying like a little girl. I *think* he thought I was going to let him sleep with her.'

He laughed again, looking back up at Nikki.

'I mean, can you imagine? Why would I allow that? What's mine is mine, Dr Roberts. And always will be.'

It took Nikki a few seconds fully to process everything he was saying, and to square it with what Williams had told her before he died. When she spoke it was as much to herself as to Rodriguez.

'So Carter was the American banker. The man with the green Jaguar. But he was never Charlotte's boyfriend. *You* were.'

'I'm not sure I was her *boyfriend*,' Luis clarified amiably, as if they weren't talking about a cold-blooded murder.

'Does Carter still work for you?'

Luis's expression darkened. 'My organization isn't like a bank. People don't come and go. Once you're in, you're in. We're like a family.'

The word sounded horribly chilling on Luis's lips.

'Unfortunately, over the years Carter Berkeley became one of our more dysfunctional members. Hence his visits to you.'

'And by "organization" you mean your drug cartel?' asked Nikki.

'I wouldn't call it that. Narcotics is a part of our business. So is real estate. We have broad-based interests.'

'Bullshit,' Nikki said boldly. If she was going to die, she wasn't going to do it on this man's terms. 'Your property empire's nothing but a giant *laundromat* for your drug-trade profits. Same as your so-called philanthropy. You push Krok for a living, Mr Rodriguez. You're just another low-life drug dealer, no more, no less.'

Luis cocked his head curiously to one side, but didn't seem angry. If anything, he appeared to enjoy being challenged.

'Firstly, I don't have to "push" Krokodil, Dr Roberts, any more than I had to "push" cocaine. Demand is high. I don't create it. I simply meet it.'

Nikki's eyes narrowed in disgust. 'You know what that stuff does to people.'

'Yes, I do. And so do they. I'm not responsible for my customers' choices,' Luis shot back, unapologetic. 'Nor was Carter Berkeley. He's been my finance guy on the West Coast for years. He was a damn good one too, until he started getting cold feet. There's truly nothing more irksome than a late-developing conscience, don't you agree? Like Lisa Flannagan's.'

Nikki's ears pricked up at the mention of Lisa. What did Rodriguez know about her, or her conscience?

'Anyway, all of a sudden Berkeley's heart started to bleed for these poor, pathetic junkies,' Rodriguez went on, bringing the conversation back to Carter. 'Needless to say, that was *after* he'd taken his cut. He felt bad enough to spill his guts to a therapist, but never to give back any of the millions of dollars he made from me. He became greedy and weak. Just like Mr Baden over there. Never a good combination.'

*Carter was part of this 'ring' Williams was trying to warn me about,* thought Nikki. He must have been the 'crooked banker'. And Baden had obviously been part of it too, although where he would have fit in, Nikki still wasn't sure. Not that it mattered now. Her mind raced. Who else had Derek said was involved? A politician, possibly the Mayor himself. A cop. And someone in the charity world, all taking their slices of Rodriguez's Krokodil pie.

'I've made many mistakes here in LA, Dr Roberts,' said Rodriguez, glancing down at the gun in his hand. 'I admit it. My first was relying on Berkeley. Carter's a smart guy but he had no balls, as it turned out, and you need those in our business. My second was letting Valentina Baden talk me into working with her husband. Valentina's a professional. She comes from the same world that I do and she understands the way things work. But her old man was a liability. And then there was my biggest mistake of all, hiring that wrecked boy Grolsch to get rid of you. What a goddamned mess he made of everything.'

Nikki winced. She still found it hard to believe that Brandon would hurt anybody, never mind murder and torture. But the idea that he would agree to kill *her*, the one person who'd helped him, or tried to help him, more than anyone? That was mind-boggling. What had Rodriguez's drugs done to him?

'I should have known the kid was too far gone, too deep in his addiction to do a decent job. But Valentina was obsessed with him and she lobbied for him so *persuasively.* She and Brandon had been lovers, you see. Back when he still had his looks, before the drugs ravaged him.'

'That's ridiculous,' said Nikki. 'Brandon's nineteen. Valentina Baden's old enough to be his grandmother.'

Rodriguez shrugged. 'In addiction, as in love, there are no barriers, Dr Roberts, no boundaries. Your husband understood that. I'm surprised you don't. In any event, I think it excited the old bitch, the idea of lover-boy killing somebody for her. '*Brandon knows Dr Roberts*,' she told me. '*He knows her habits, her movements. He can do this, Luis. Give him a chance.*' Stupidly, I let her have her way. It was in the early days of my association with Willie, and I thought it made sense to keep both the Badens sweet.' Luis shook his head bitterly. 'My God, what a fiasco. All Grolsch had to do was wait for you outside your office and stick a knife in your heart. I mean, how hard is that? But the whole thing became a comedy of errors. Lisa Flannagan comes out wearing your raincoat, and *oops!* The moron goes and kills her instead. I mean, he literally cut that poor girl to ribbons.'

Nikki thought about this. It was Goodman's 'mistaken identity' theory. That the killer had mistaken Lisa for Nikki, because it was dark and she was wearing Nikki's coat. On the one hand, she supposed it was technically possible that Brandon could have been high enough and so amped-up to kill that he would make that sort of 'mistake'. But surely it was more likely that Valentina Baden had instructed him to kill Lisa, her husband's mistress, instead of Nikki?

She assumed this possibility must have occurred to Rodriguez too. Although he seemed to have a bizarre trust in Valentina Baden's word and judgment that ran counter to everything else Nikki knew about him. It struck her that Luis Rodriguez would make a fascinating psychological case study, if only he weren't about to blow her brains out.

'So,' he continued, 'Brandon killed the girl. I had some of my guys here try and clean up the body, but that was a mess too. They were rushed and they panicked and some of that idiot's rotten, Krok-infested skin gave the cops a DNA match. So now I have a murder investigation on my hands and a three-ring media circus and the Badens and Brandon panicking – and all the time, *you're* still alive, Dr Roberts. Which was a very unsatisfactory situation, given the fact you were seeing Anne. My Anne.'

As he said his wife's name, his entire face changed. Suddenly his chatty, convivial tone was gone. He looked at Nikki with raw hatred.

'Of all the thousands of shrinks in LA, *my wife* picks *you*. The same woman who's been listening to my banker spill his guts for the past year, who I've been trying and failing to get rid of like a damned cockroach. *You* were the one Anne turned to. What are the odds, eh?'

*Slim,* thought Nikki. The odds were slim. Someone must have recommended her to Anne. Someone who knew about the Carter Berkeley connection and who actively wanted to put her life in danger. She tried to think who that might be, and why – someone connected to this 'ring' perhaps? – but her mind was a blank.

She was still grappling with the idea that Brandon Grolsch had taken money to kill her, and that he had killed poor Lisa. All this time she'd protected Brandon from Goodman and defended him to Williams. And then, only days ago Brandon had called her, begging for help and forgiveness. *Forgiveness!*

'Don't get me wrong,' Luis continued, interrupting Nikki's muddled thoughts. 'I would have killed you anyway. Carter Berkeley signed your death warrant the day he walked into your consulting room. But it wasn't personal at that point. When I found out you were seeing Anne, that's when things changed.' His eyes narrowed. 'That was when I began to despise you, Dr Roberts.'

Nikki listened to Rodriguez rant about Anne, and how Nikki had tried to 'turn her against him'. He was growing more agitated, veering wildly from boastful revelations about having planted listening devices in Anne's pocketbook and car in order to spy on their sessions, to increasingly bitter name-calling: Nikki was a predator, a pervert. She wanted Anne for herself and had badmouthed him out of sexual jealousy.

As he rambled on, for the first time it crossed Nikki's mind to try and look for a means of escape. Luis Rodriguez was plainly deranged. But perhaps Nikki could use his disturbed mental state to her advantage? She was a psychologist, after all. At a minimum she could keep him talking for a while, play on his ego to buy herself some time. In the end, though, if she was going to live she would need to distract him sufficiently to try to knock the weapon out of his hands.

But even if she succeeded, then what? Run, presumably, but where? There was the elevator behind her, just past Willie Baden's hanging corpse, the one Anne had taken with Luis's two goons. But unless she actually managed to knock Luis out cold, Nikki could hardly afford to press the call button and wait. If she could grab Luis's gun, get hold of it herself, that would change things. But glancing around she could see nothing she could use to overpower him, neither in the corridor nor the offices that lined it. She didn't even have a purse with her; all she had was the set of car keys still clenched in her hand.

The more she began to think rationally, and practically, the more her earlier feeling of calm left her and fear began to creep in. She wasn't ready to die after all, not today, and not at the hands of this sadistic madman.

There must be a way out. There just must be.

\* \* \*

By the time Goodman turned into San Julian Street, his shirt was drenched with sweat and his clammy palms could barely grip the steering wheel. Fear had churned his stomach and drained the blood from his face. It had dried out his mouth and elevated his heart rate to a relentless gallop that made it hard to breathe normally.

The only upside to the fear was the adrenaline coursing through his veins, overriding everything else and compelling him to act: Drive. Park. Run. Draw his weapon. Yes, he was afraid. But he wasn't frozen. Some deep-seated survival instinct reminded him that he couldn't afford to be.

This was it. Do or die.

Life or death.

The street was deserted, except for the occasional straggling seamstress, late leaving work, making their weary way to the tram stop on 8th Avenue. No one seemed to notice Goodman pull over, jump out of his car, and make his way at a jog towards the empty warehouse. About thirty yards from the front of the building, he slowed his place. Two burly men in dark suits, their biceps rippling preposterously beneath the formal fabric, emerged from the warehouse escorting a slight, young woman. It only took Goodman a moment to recognize her as Anne Bateman, Luis's wife.

The two goons led her to a town car with blacked-out windows. One of them displayed bloodied hands as he opened the door to usher her inside. They exchanged a few words with the driver, then the car sped away to the other end of San Julian Street. The suited men watched it go before drawing their guns and making their way into the shadows, one crouched on either side of the front of the building.

Goodman tried not to think about the blood and whose it might be. What mattered was that he now knew for sure what he'd suspected back at the station: Luis Rodriguez was inside the warehouse. Anne's 'summons' to Nikki to come and meet her urgently had been a ploy to lure Nikki here. Luis Rodriguez couldn't afford to let Dr Roberts 'disappear' and reinvent herself. Not in this world at any rate. And Goodman knew why.

Fingering his service weapon, he swiftly ran through his options. He was alone, and Rodriguez had at least two armed men in support, maybe more. He could call for backup – that would be proper procedure. But it would take too long. Alternatively, he could try to take out the two thugs on the door. But that was a gamble too. What if he failed, or if he got inside to find the place swarming with more of Rodriguez's men? He'd be dead within seconds.

Glancing around, he noticed a narrow passageway to his right. It wasn't even a true alley, because no vehicle other than a motorbike could have fit down it. Instead it looked like it had been designed for maintenance access of some kind. Darting into it unseen, Goodman discovered two locked power boxes bolted to one of the walls, next to a very rickety-looking fire ladder. The only other thing of interest was a grate, almost like a cattle grid but with narrower bars, set into the ground. Reaching down, he gripped it tightly and pulled hard. Harder than he needed to, as it happened, because the thing came loose easily, sending him flying backwards with a clatter and leaving him staring into the entrance to some sort of tunnel. It might have been the mouth of a ventilation shaft, or an air-conditioning duct. Whatever it was, it appeared to lead into the bowels of the warehouse.

Goodman hated small spaces. They made him feel like a trapped rat. But he knew the two men out front would have heard the clatter of the grate. Any second now, one of them could come tearing around the corner to investigate the sudden loud noise. When they did, Lou Goodman knew from experience they'd be unlikely to ask questions.

There was nothing else for it. Easing himself down into the shaft, feet first, he grabbed the grate and slid it back loosely into place on top of him.

Inching his way deeper into the darkness, his mind turned angrily to Nikki Roberts.

*Stupid, reckless woman*! Why the hell had she come here on her own? Jumping to Anne Bateman's command like a trusting lamb. Wasn't Derek Williams' death warning enough for her?

Nikki might be beautiful and smart. But she'd got herself into deep water this time. Only Lou Goodman knew exactly how deep.

*　*　*

'Tell me about Trey. Were you the one who had him abducted?'

Nikki looked defiantly into Luis Rodriguez's eyes as he once again raised his gun and pointed it at her, arm locked, ready to shoot. His long rant about Anne, and what he perceived as Nikki's jealous meddling in their marriage, had reignited his anger to murderous levels. Nikki's only hope was to keep him talking, and pray that his desire to boast would outweigh his desire to kill her, for a few more minutes at least.

It worked. Lowering his arm, Luis rolled his eyes dramatically.

'Stupid boy. He could have lived if he chose to. We gave him every chance.'

'What do you mean, "every chance"? Every chance to what? Did he owe you money?' Nikki asked, remembering Derek Williams' theory about Trey still working for one of the Westmont gangs, and thinking grimly about the bills crudely crammed into Willie Baden's gaping mouth.

'He owed a little money, but it wasn't about that,' Luis said dismissively.

'What then? You resented him starting a new life? Getting clean, breaking away from the gangs?'

Luis smiled chillingly. 'You confuse me with someone who had the slightest interest in Trey Raymond's life, Dr Roberts. I've told you before, I'm a businessman. Trey wasn't part of the family. He was a user. A customer. Customers come, customers go.'

Nikki frowned. 'Trey was tortured, brutally tortured before he died. What could he possibly have done to deserve that?'

Rodriguez yawned, and Nikki felt a surge of rage and hatred rush through her body as if she'd been electrocuted. How could Anne have married this monster? This vile sadist? Even if she didn't know the truth about his illegal businesses, the fortune he'd made peddling despair and death, Anne couldn't have lived with this man and not seen the casual cruelty that drove him. No one could be that blind. Could they?

'Trey Raymond had something I wanted,' said Luis. 'I offered him a fair price, but he refused to give it to me. That was a grave mistake.'

'What could Trey possibly have had that you wanted?' asked Nikki, her eyes filling with tears suddenly. So many terrible things had happened, she'd allowed herself to push the horror of Trey's death and her grief for him to one side. But now, facing her own death, they came flooding back like water through a breaking dam. 'You're worth hundreds of millions of dollars. Trey had nothing! The most valuable thing he owned was a stupid skateboard that Doug bought him.'

'He had information,' Luis said simply. 'About your sessions with my wife, the ones I was unable to surveil myself. I asked him, very nicely, to deliver me that information. He refused. So he died.'

'But . . . he didn't know anything!' Nikki gasped. 'All our sessions were private.'

'Liar!' Luis snapped, irritated. 'You keep notes. The police have copies.'

'Not of my sessions with Anne, they don't,' said Nikki truthfully. 'I never recorded those.'

Luis looked skeptical. 'Never recorded them? Why not?'

Nikki shrugged helplessly. 'She wouldn't allow it. I should have insisted . . .' She looked away, guilt and regret overwhelming her. 'You were asking Trey to give you information he never had. No one had it, because it didn't exist – other than in here.' She tapped the side of her head. 'You killed him for nothing!'

Luis paused for a moment to take this in. Then he started to laugh, quietly at first, but then the laughs got louder and fuller and more menacing.

'And so the comedy of errors goes on!' he said, wiping tears of mirth from his eyes. 'I'm glad you shared that with me, Dr Roberts. Truly I am. Quite the irony. But at least you can rest assured *your* death won't be for nothing.' Lifting his gun a third time, the look in his eyes left Nikki in no doubt: her time had run out.

'Like all good plays, my dear, I'm afraid there must be a final act. And this is yours. Goodbye, Dr Roberts.'

'Burn in hell!' Nikki snarled back at him.

And with a single, deafening bang, everything went black.

# 37

First came the darkness.

Then the quiet.

No breath. No movement. Only stillness.

Peace.

So this was death.

It was nice while it lasted. Unfortunately for Nikki, it didn't last long. The darkness remained, but at some point she realized she could hear her own heartbeat, her pulse *thud, thudding* inside her aching skull. Time began to speed back up, but gradually, like an animal emerging hesitantly from a long hibernation. And when it did, the pain began, waves of it, sharp and burning.

*My leg.* Reaching down her fingers found the warm, sticky wound. She'd been shot just below the knee. She realized then that the darkness surrounding wasn't a product of her own lost consciousness, but a real, external thing. *There must have been a power cut!* Like an act of God. Only Nikki didn't believe in God. In the confusion, Rodriguez must have misfired and hit her leg. Christ, it hurt. She wondered how much blood she'd lost. Touching the wound again she made a sound, involuntary, a sort of high-pitched, keening whine, like an animal caught in a trap.

It was a mistake.

She heard him instantly, turning and shuffling in the pitch-darkness, moving towards the sound, lunging blindly. Then a clatter as he slipped and lost his footing. He was cursing in Spanish, wheezing – was he hurt too? – but no. When he spoke his voice was strong. The quiver Nikki heard in it wasn't pain but anger.

'I hear you, you bitch!'

She froze. He was close, only feet away.

'I'm coming for you!'

\*   \*   \*

The darkness was total and instant.

Flipping the main fuse had been an instinct, a spur of the moment impulse to confuse Luis Rodriguez and whatever men he had upstairs to buy himself some time. But now that it was done, Goodman regretted it at once. Trapped and disorientated in the cramped basement, he struggled to contain his panic. He felt as if he were in a coffin. No light! No escape! His heart raced, pounding wildly to the beat of his own terror. It took every ounce of his self-control to try to calm his breathing. *In. Out. In. Out.*

*Now think.*

He fumbled in his pocket for his cell phone. It wasn't there. With trembling fingers he checked every pocket, realizing as he did so that the phone must be back at the office. Fortunately he had a Maglite on his keychain. As soon as he twisted the head, the light came on and reality reasserted itself. The lid of the coffin was merely the basement's low ceiling, its fat, aluminum-clad pipes draped with cobwebs. Behind him was the opening to the ventilation shaft he'd used to get in, that led up to street level in the alley. In front of him, about twenty feet from the fuse box, was a set of rickety metal stairs.

Goodman moved slowly towards them on his hands and knees, feeling warily for any live wires or nails or other hazards on the filthy floor. Everything was quiet. There'd been a loud 'bang' when the lights went off, but since then, nothing. *Was Rodriguez even still in the building?* He might have killed Nikki and left while Goodman was worming his way inside. *Maybe I'm the only one crawling around in the dark in here?*

As he had the thought, he heard a scream from above. A single, piercing scream. *Nikki?* Drawing his gun, he scrambled to the staircase and began to climb.

\* \* \*

Luis Rodriguez froze and listened, eagerly, like a wolf. She was close, very close. He could hear her breaths, short and rapid from the pain of his bullet.

His hand tightened on his gun as he lunged furiously towards the sound. Once he reached her, even in the pitch-dark he would find her neck and hold her down and fire a second shot deep into her skull.

*Bitch.* Nikki Roberts had tried to brainwash Anne, to take her from him. Luis wouldn't stop until Dr Roberts' 'brilliant' mind was splattered all over the walls like vomit. 'Where are you?' he grunted, shuffling forwards. There was nowhere for her to go, no escape other than to go past him in the narrow corridor. And yet as he reached out he felt nothing but air. *Where the hell could she have gone?*

The pain hit him then, like a gunshot. A fist, hard and determined, slamming at full force into the soft flesh between his legs. He doubled over, his roar of pain morphing into a dry retch as he sank to his knees. Behind him he heard scrambling, like the scuttle of a mouse racing for its hole.

*She got past me! The bitch scrambled straight through my legs! She's going for the stairs.*

Still doubled over in agony, he twisted his upper body around and fired wildly into the darkness. 'I'll kill you!' he rasped. 'I will kill you!'

*       *       *

*I made it! I'm out.*

Nikki heard the shots ring out as she reached the top of the fire stairs, but elation trumped fear. Faint glimmers of evening light were visible here, rising up from the ground floor below. All she had to do was make it down these stairs and out onto the street. Someone would be there, surely? Someone would help her. Save her. But she must hurry. Rodriguez would be on his feet soon.

Clinging on to the handrail she took one step, then two before sliding uncontrollably to the ground, writhing in agony. *My leg!* Adrenaline had seen her this far, but now the deep bullet wound reasserted itself. She couldn't move. The pain was overwhelming. Hard metal tore into her back as she fell onto the stairs, blacking out for a moment as she rolled down to the first landing. Willing herself back into consciousness, she used her last ounce of strength to drag herself over to the corner of the landing, curling up into a tiny alcove cut into the concrete wall.

For a moment she felt overwhelming sadness. Her eyes filled with tears. She could *see* the way out. Peering through the shadows, there was the fire door, no more than twenty feet below her. *I'm so close!* But she couldn't get there. Couldn't move another muscle. Nikki knew with certainty that this spot, this alcove was the end of the line.

Closing her eyes, a strange sensation of heat crept over her. It was really quite pleasant. As swiftly as it had arrived, the sadness left her and with it the pain and fear, all three replaced by a thick, warm blanket of exhaustion.

*Sleep. I need to sleep now.*

\*   \*   \*

At the top of the stairs, Goodman finally stood up tall, pressing his back hard against a brick pillar for cover as he squinted into the gloom. The high, dirty windows afforded only the faintest rays of natural light this late in the evening, but after the darkness of the basement, his eyes adjusted quickly and he was able to switch off his flashlight. Satisfying himself that he was alone – the entire floor was one, vast empty room – he began to move stealthily towards the service elevator on the far wall when a familiar voice stopped him in his tracks.

'Goodman! You in here?'

Mick Johnson's gruff, Boston-Irish twang echoed off the walls.

*No. How was it possible? How the hell had that fat slob made it here?*

'Where are you, Lou?'

Goodman's blood ran cold. Now he had *two* of them to worry about, Rodriguez *and* Johnson. He had to find Nikki before his partner did. It was either that or kill Mick before he made his move. He hoped it didn't come to that. Despite everything, Lou Goodman still felt some kinship with Mick Johnson, some residual affection for his comrade of the last year. But this was a life-or-death situation. There could be no room for sentiment or hesitation.

He started to run.

\*   \*   \*

Whacking his head on the low ceiling of the basement, Mick Johnson cursed under his breath as his flashlight clattered to the floor. *Damn Goodman.* Johnson had found his partner's car abandoned a few blocks up and followed what he assumed had been his path towards the warehouse. Pausing at the narrow passageway as Goodman had done, he'd noticed the dislodged grate and put two and two together. With some effort, he managed to squeeze his own, more considerable girth inside, emerging as his partner had done into the basement electrical room.

Goodman had come this way, all right. His shoe and hand prints were everywhere in the dust. Reaching down for his dropped flashlight, Johnson picked up one of his partner's white monogrammed cotton handkerchiefs from the filthy floor, where he must have dropped it in the confusion of the blackout. *Who the hell carried handkerchiefs in this day and age?* Not so long ago, Johnson would have been irritated by Goodman's vanity and dandyish ways. But not now. Now Goodman had shifted from 'irritating' to 'dangerous', a threat that must be stopped at all costs.

Dr Nikki Roberts should never have gotten herself involved with him. But the good doctor made her own bed. Mick Johnson knew what he had to do – if Luis Rodriguez, *the boss*, hadn't already done it for him.

Turning on his flashlight, Johnson swiftly found the fuse box and flipped up the main switch. Light flooded the cramped space, momentarily blinding him. He heard footsteps, running, on the floor above.

'Luis!' he called out, his deep voice echoing up the empty stairwell.

He started to climb.

*     *     *

Luis Rodriguez shielded his eyes against the dazzling light, instinctively pressing his back against the wall and raising his gun blindly. He could hear someone calling to him from below, but he didn't give him much thought. He would deal with them later. Right now he was on the hunt, his nostrils flaring for the scent of blood. Dr Roberts' blood.

The thought of the kill excited him. He could almost taste her. 'I'm coming!' he called out in a sing-song voice, taunting, like a child playing hide and go seek. As his eyes began to adjust to the light, he saw dark splashes of blood, leading towards the staircase. His groin still throbbed but the pain was nothing compared to the thrill of the chase. Killing Willie Baden had been the hors d'oeuvre, an amuse-bouche before the main event. After all this time, he was finally going to do it. He was going to execute that bitch. Then he and Anne would live happily ever after.

'Come out, come out wherever you are!'

He pushed open the door to the stairs.

*     *     *

Nikki had been asleep when the lights came back on, dazzlingly bright, dragging her reluctantly back into consciousness. *The land of the living.* But not for long. Rodriguez would find her and kill her, like he had killed Baden. She knew that now. She couldn't move and no one was coming to save her. But she didn't care.

Soon she would be with Doug. Then she would know the truth at last. Either that, or she would be in a place where truth no longer mattered.

*I'm so tired.*

Her eyelids fluttered. She gazed blankly at the bloody wound below her knee. Her whole leg had stiffened and no longer felt part of her. There was pain, but it wasn't the sharp, stinging pain of before. More of a numbing ache, like the kind you get swimming in the cold ocean.

With a click, the door above her opened. She heard Rodriguez's voice, taunting her, thick with cruelty and excitement. 'Where are you, Doctor? I'm coming.'

Fear returned to her then, unexpected. Some primal instinct to survive, its roots deeper than exhaustion, deeper than pain, took hold. She shrank back into her alcove, her terror building with each slow, deliberate step he took towards her. She saw his boots first, black and polished, then the legs of his suit trousers. She heard a whimper of fear and submission, before realizing with shame that the noise came from her own lips.

'There you are, my dear.' He loomed above her like a malevolent giant, his legs slightly apart, his gun held casually at his side as she cowered beneath him. 'Look at me, please.'

Nikki shook her head, pleading.

'I SAID LOOK AT ME, BITCH!' Luis roared, his voice ricocheting off the stairwell walls like the boom of a canon.

Shaking uncontrollably with fright, Nikki did as he said. She found herself looking up into a face that might have been handsome were it not so contorted with hatred. Luis's eyes were two hard brown stones of polished cruelty, glinting down at his victim, compassionless and cold. He raised his gun slowly, savoring the moment, a wolfish smile spreading over his thin, sadist's lips.

'Rodriguez! Put your hands in the air! Police!'

Goodman's voice sounded distant to Nikki. Unreal, like a voice in a dream.

Apparently, Luis Rodriguez felt the same as he continued raising his gun and smiling, unconcerned.

'I'm right behind you, Luis. Do not shoot her.'

Nikki saw Goodman then, standing on the top landing, his service weapon pointed directly at Rodriguez's back. He wasn't in uniform, but everything about him radiated confidence and authority. The firm set of his jaw, the steady command in his voice.

*He's come to save me! Everything's going to be all right after all.*

The relief was overwhelming. Nikki looked from Goodman to Rodriguez and back again as for a long, tense moment, neither man lowered their weapon. Then, his smile still fixed, Rodriguez slowly lowered his arm and let his pistol clatter to the ground.

Turning around, he seemed oddly relaxed, greeting Goodman almost like an old friend. 'See, Detective? I didn't shoot her. I'm sure she appreciates your romantic gesture.' He chuckled, as if all this were some sort of elaborate practical joke. 'So what happens now? Are you going to arrest me?'

He held out his arms as if for handcuffs, still grinning.

*He's insane,* thought Nikki, wondering how she hadn't realized this before. *He's not just bad, he's mad. Crazy. Deranged.*

She looked gratefully up at Goodman, waiting for him to read Rodriguez his rights, and wondering if any backup were on its way. She wouldn't feel completely safe until Rodriguez was cuffed and taken away. Even without his gun he was a strong man and . . .

*Bang!*

A single shot rang out. At such close range, Rodriguez's skull exploded. Shards of bone and brain tissue spewed onto the walls of the stairwell. Nikki's blouse, face and hands were all liberally splattered with blood.

Coolly stepping over Rodriguez's corpse, Goodman walked down to where Nikki lay, curled up in the cramped alcove. He crouched next to her.

'You killed him,' she whispered. She was in shock, her breath coming in short, erratic gasps.

'Yes.' Reaching out, Goodman laid a hand softly against her blood-splattered cheek.

'You didn't try to arrest him.'

'No,' he said soothingly. 'I didn't.'

Nikki started to tremble violently. Then she started to cry, her body dissolving into long, shuddering sobs of relief.

'Thank you!' Reaching up, she put her hands around his neck and hugged him.

After a few moments clinging to him, breathing in his familiar scent, the scent of safety and normalcy and hope, she finally let go, sinking back weakly against the wall. Her leg was completely numb now, like a stone. She needed to get to hospital, fast.

'You saved my life,' she said gratefully, her eyes seeking out his own.

He looked back at her, and for a second Nikki was filled with confusion. His expression was exactly like Rodriguez's had been. Evil.

'You really are an incredibly stupid woman,' he sneered, pressing his gun to Nikki's temple.

\* \* \*

Outside in the street, a seamstress heard another loud bang from the empty warehouse. Then nothing.

Quickening her pace, she hurried to her bus stop and hopped aboard.

She didn't look back.

# 38

Fiona McManus loved her job at Good Samaritan Hospital. Not that Fiona saw nursing as a 'job' per se. In her view it was more of a vocation. A calling, to help others, to serve. 'Just as long as it's a calling that pays the bills,' Fiona's mother Jenny liked to remind her, wryly.

Luckily, it was. The wages were good, the doctors and nurses she worked with every day inspirational, and the patients . . . well, the patients were mixed. Some were incredibly brave. Many were also kind and respectful, grateful for the treatment and care they received from Fiona and her colleagues. But of course there were others too. Drunks and addicts who could be abusive. People who had a hard time with pain, or even discomfort. And then there were those made angry by suffering and grief, those who couldn't be helped or whose injuries or illnesses were beyond treatment.

Pulling open the curtains to allow the sunlight into the room, Fiona glanced across at the bed where this morning's patient was sleeping peacefully. Gunshot wounds could be notoriously difficult. Even following successful surgery, patients could collapse or suffer heart failure from shock hours, days, or even weeks after the event. The sleeping figure in the bed looked better to Fiona than they had yesterday, with more color in the cheeks and good oxygen levels in the blood. Although that might be the morphine.

Rearranging a vase of flowers on the windowsill, Fiona looked down at the milling crowd of reporters and television crews still gathered in the parking lot, like vultures waiting for a fresh carcass. Like the policemen stationed outside, in the corridor of the private wing, they reminded Fiona that this morning's patient was an important person. Not because of who they were, necessarily, but because of the circumstances that had brought them here, circumstances that were still all over the news, forty-eight hours later.

'Hello?'

A voice from the bed, surprisingly strong, made Fiona spin around.

'Oh my goodness! You're awake. Let me get Dr Riley.'

She started to move towards the door but a wail of distress from the patient stopped her in her tracks.

'Why am I here? I shouldn't be here.'

'It's all right. Try to stay calm now,' Fiona said soothingly. 'You're at Good Samaritan Hospital. You were brought here after—'

'NO!' It was a shout. 'I'M DEAD!'

The patient slumped back against the pillow, seemingly unconscious. A cacophony of beeping began as, one by one, the vitals started to drop.

Fiona pulled open the door and yelled down the corridor. 'We need Dr Riley in here. Right now!'

\* \* \*

Sam Riley burst into the room at a run. Normally Good Samaritan's most eligible surgeon would have stopped to exchange flirtatious pleasantries with the pretty, red-headed Nurse McManus. But there was no time for that today. This patient had to live. Sam had fought too hard to have it go any other way, not now.

'What happened?' he asked accusingly as he lifted each unresponsive eyelid in turn. The beeping had stopped now and the heart rate stabilized, but these sorts of abrupt losses of consciousness were not a good sign.

'Nothing happened.' Fiona defended herself. 'I opened the curtains and she opened her eyes. She said "Hello" – she was calm at first, but then she quickly became agitated. She said she was dead, that she shouldn't be here. And then she just, sort of, stopped.'

Dr Sam Riley looked down at the sleeping face of Dr Nikki Roberts. Sam had seen Dr Roberts before, on the news, as the famous Beverly Hills psychologist at the center of the Zombie Killings mystery. She'd looked beautiful then, on screen. No doubt that was one of the reasons the story had run for so long, despite there being no more victims or arrests. But she was even more beautiful in the flesh, regardless of the bruises, with her soft skin, dark eyes and fragile, feminine features. He hadn't fully appreciated it before. He'd been too busy trying to save Nikki's leg and repair the damage caused by Luis Rodriguez's bullet as it tore through the flesh and ligaments.

The operation had gone as well as Sam could have hoped, but the risk of infection was ever present, as was postoperative heart failure.

'Stop the morphine,' he instructed Nurse McManus.

'Reduce the dose, you mean?' Fiona asked innocently.

Sam fixed her with a gimlet eye. 'Is that what I said?'

'Well, no,' Fiona stammered. It wasn't like Dr Riley to be so tetchy. Thanks to the media attention they were all feeling the pressure with this particular patient. 'But the pain, Dr Riley. She's going to need something.'

'She needs to be awake,' Sam said firmly, walking over and disconnecting Nikki's morphine drip himself, replacing the bag with plain saline solution. 'Besides,' he added, looking down at Nikki's bruised and scratched complexion, 'I suspect this lady has a high tolerance for pain. She's certainly used to it.'

He was right. When Nikki woke an hour later she was lucid, but her right leg felt as if someone were slowly pouring acid into an open wound. Gritting her teeth, she asked the nurse to give her something for the pain.

'I can give you a strong ibuprofen with codeine,' Fiona explained apologetically. It was late afternoon now, and the sun was throwing long shadows into the room, stretching all the way from the window to the head of Nikki's bed. 'I'm afraid Dr Riley's said no more morphine or opiates.'

Nikki turned her head away, resigned. The pain had its upside. It reminded her she was still alive, although she still didn't know how that was possible. The last thing she remembered was Lou Goodman, her friend, her savior, at one time almost her lover, pressing his gun to her head and preparing to shoot her.

'*You really are an incredibly stupid woman.*' Those had been his last words to her. And Nikki could only assume he was right, because she had no idea *why* Lou Goodman would want her dead, or why he'd killed Luis Rodriguez, if not to protect her? It made no sense. None of it made any sense.

What had happened after that was a total blank.

Crunching the pain pills the nurse gave her, she fought down a wave of nausea and began to ask some questions. The nurse seemed to know nothing about what had happened at the warehouse or how Nikki had survived. 'You were shot in the leg and the ambulance brought you here,' was all she said. She was more informative about what had happened since. Nikki had gone straight into surgery on arrival. Dr Riley had operated on her leg for nine hours. The operation had gone well and Dr Riley was 'hopeful', whatever that meant, that Nikki's leg would now heal.

'He can tell you more about that when you see him,' the nurse said, smiling. 'I've paged him to let him know you're awake. And your other visitor's still here. I don't think he's left the hospital since they took you in for surgery, bless him.' She smiled, and Nikki noticed for the first time what a pretty girl she was, with her red hair and freckles. *Wholesome* was the word that sprang to mind.

'What visitor?' Nikki asked.

'The cop,' said the nurse. 'The one who brought you in? He came with you in the ambulance. He's been beside himself with worry, poor man.'

Nikki's mind raced, full of confused images. Goodman had brought her in? But hadn't he just tried to kill her? Or was that whole scene a figment of her imagination, some sort of delirium brought on by blood loss or . . . something?

'Can I see him? The cop.'

'Sure you can!' the nurse brightened. 'As long as you feel up to it. I'll pop out and let him know.'

'You will come back though?' Nikki blurted, suddenly fearful. 'I mean, you will stay with me, while he's here? In the room? Just in case I . . . need anything?'

Fiona looked at her patient curiously. Dr Roberts had shown incredible physical bravery up till now. Most people would have hit the ceiling after a wound like that once they switched the morphine off. But this brave woman was visibly afraid at this moment.

Perhaps, after everything she'd been through, it was to be expected?

'Certainly I'll stay,' Fiona said kindly. 'And if you start to feel tired or need to rest, I'll kick him out pronto, don't you worry.'

She left, and Nikki lay there for what felt like an age.

What would she say to Goodman? What should she ask? She tried to think of possible, rational explanations for his words and actions at the warehouse, but there were none. And yet, he'd saved her – twice. He'd brought her here. Her palms started to sweat from fear and pain and she dug her nails into her flesh to try to distract herself. At last she heard footsteps and the nurse's voice – 'She's right in here. She's still very tired from the operation so try to be patient . . .'

The door opened. Nikki held her breath.

'Hello, Dr Roberts.' Detective Johnson's fat red face lit up. 'Welcome back!'

# 39

'**Y**ou . . . ?'
     Nikki's eyes narrowed as she took in the familiar, hated figure of the bigoted detective who had made her life so intolerable these last few weeks. 'What are *you* doing here?'

'Waiting for you to wake up,' Johnson said cheerfully, either missing her hostility or choosing to ignore it as he took a seat beside her bed. 'I hear you're gonna keep your leg? That's good news, Doc. You always did have great legs.'

Nikki scowled. Was there literally no circumstance in which this awful man could refrain from being sexist, or racist, or otherwise insulting?

'You know, you're a great-looking woman, but you'd look even better if you smiled once in a while,' Johnson went on, adding insult to injury. 'I mean, not to blow my own trumpet or anything, but I did save your life.'

'What do you mean?' Nikki sat up in bed, wincing at the pain in her leg as she moved. She loathed Detective Jonson, but her need to understand what had happened trumped her instinct to throw him out of the room. 'How did *you* save my life? What happened back there?'

Now it was Johnson's turn to sit up. Cocking his head to one side like a curious dog, he looked at her and said, 'Seriously? You don't remember?'

Nikki shook her head.

'I remember some.' She frowned in confusion. 'I went there to meet Anne. She called me out in the desert. I remember seeing Willie Baden, dead, nailed to the wall like a piece of meat.' Her face crumpled as the grotesque image came back to her.

'What else?' asked Johnson.

'Two men came and took Anne away. Her husband was there. Luis Rodriguez. He'd beaten her. He made her call me.'

'I wouldn't waste too many tears on Anne Bateman, if I were you,' Johnson said brusquely 'Beaten or not, she must have known her old man planned to whack you when she lured you there.'

'Luis tried to shoot me. Twice!' Nikki became agitated as the memories rushed back to her. 'He told me everything. How he'd murdered Charlotte Clancy and made Carter Berkeley watch. How Willie Baden had tried to cheat him, so he'd tortured and killed him too, and made Anne watch. How he hired Brandon to kill me. Then the lights went out, just as he fired his gun. That must have been when he shot me in the leg. I hit him – in the groin I think? – and I got away.'

Johnson nodded again.

Fiona stepped forward. 'Try to keep yourself calm now, Dr Roberts. Your body's been through enough shock. It's important not to—'

'I'm fine. I'm calm,' said Nikki, waving away her objections like a horse dispatching a fly with an impatient flick of the tail. She needed to talk about this, needed to remember. It helped. 'The first time the lights went out, and the second time . . . I was on the stairs?'

She looked to Johnson for confirmation. 'Yup.'

'Rodriguez was about to finish me off when Goodman showed up. *He* saved me.' She looked at Johnson again. '*He* killed Rodriguez. Blew the top of his head right off.'

Fiona winced at this gruesome detail, but Johnson was unfazed. If anything, he seemed pleased Nikki remembered so vividly.

'Good,' he said. 'That's right. And after that?'

Nikki looked pale. Then she started to shake. It was coming back to her: Goodman's face, his mocking, vicious expression swam before her eyes.

'After that I . . . I don't remember.'

'I think you do,' Johnson persisted. 'Goodman was going to shoot you next.'

'No,' Nikki shook her head. 'He wouldn't have done that. I know he wouldn't. He . . . we were friends.'

'Friends like you and Brandon Grolsch, you mean?' Detective Johnson laughed, but there was anger there too. Anger at Nikki's willful blindness. 'Lou Goodman was a liar and a fraud, and if I hadn't killed him right then and there he would have sent your brains flying around that stairwell just like Rodriguez's.'

'NO!' Nikki sat bolt upright. 'That's not right! That can't be right!'

'Sure it's right,' Johnson snapped. 'Goodman had been in Rodriguez's pay for at least two years, maybe longer. He grew up poor – he told you about that, didn't he? He knew what it was like to lose everything. The only thing driving him since his dad's suicide was the pursuit of money. Wealth. Security. Rodriguez offered him a fast track to millions of dollars and he grabbed it with both, greedy hands. But even that wasn't enough. He wanted to run the show.'

'You're lying!' Nikki wheezed, feeling suddenly dizzy.

Nurse McManus could take no more. 'Right. Out!' she commanded Detective Johnson. 'We discussed this outside. She's supposed to be *resting*. If I'd known you were going to upset her like this, I would never have brought you in.'

Johnson lumbered angrily to his feet. 'And if I'd known she was going to insist on keeping her blinkers on even *now* – even after I saved her goddamned *life* – I'd have let my partner shoot her!'

Nurse McManus opened her mouth to interject, but Johnson waved her angrily away. 'Save your breath. I'm leaving,' he said. Turning back to Nikki he snapped, 'And *you* . . . if you don't believe me, try turning on the news. Good luck to you, Dr Roberts.'

Like a cloud of storm and fury, he was gone.

'I'm so sorry.' Fiona fussed nervously around her patient's pillows. If Dr Riley found out she'd allowed a visitor and then the patient's condition deteriorated . . . 'I had no idea he was going to upset you like that. He seemed so nice out in the waiting room and he's been ever so concerned, keeping vigil all through your operation and afterwards.'

'It's OK,' Nikki said blankly, her mind struggling to process everything that Johnson had said. The worst part was that it tallied with her own, fractured memories. Goodman *had* been about to shoot her. Someone, presumably Johnson, must have stopped him. Or she wouldn't be lying here, alive and wondering. Would she? And now Goodman was dead too, and so was Luis Rodriguez. Two more bodies to add to the roll call of the dead: Doug, Lenka, Lisa, Trey, Williams. One by one they'd fallen around her.

*But I'm still here.*

*Do I really have that bigot Johnson to thank for it?*

'What did he mean, about turning on the news?' she asked the nurse.

'Oh, nothing, I expect,' the girl replied dismissively. 'There's been some coverage about the shoot-out at the warehouse. He probably meant that. But you should rest. I'll page Dr Riley and be back in a tick.'

Nikki waited till she was alone to pick up the TV remote, attached by a wire to the side of her bed. Flipping the channel to ABC news, she was shocked to see a picture of her own face immediately filling the screen. It was an old professional headshot, taken a few months before Doug's accident, and if her name hadn't been printed underneath, Nikki would have had trouble recognizing that pretty, carefree young woman as herself.

'Beverly Hills Psychologist Dr Nicola Roberts, the woman believed to be at the center of the infamous Zombie Killings case, is said to be in a stable and comfortable condition at Good Samaritan Hospital, after Wednesday night's shooting incident on San Julian Street downtown, following the reported murder of Rams owner Willie Baden at that same location.'

*I wouldn't say 'comfortable'*, thought Nikki, flinching at the pain in her leg as she listened eagerly to the reporter's voice.

'One police officer, Detective Lou Goodman, was also confirmed dead at the scene, along with Mexican businessman and philanthropist, Luis Rodriguez. Both men died from gunshot wounds. Mr Baden's cause of death has not yet been confirmed by police, although we understand that it was not gun-related. And again at this point we are unclear about the connection between the three victims. Although, as we know, Willie Baden had admitted to an extra-marital relationship with Lisa Flannagan, the first victim of the so-called Zombie Killer. So it would seem there are lots of threads to follow as this story develops.'

The screenshot of Nikki's face disappeared, replaced by live images of the warehouse, the streets around it now criss-crossed with yellow police tape.

'Dr Roberts was carried bleeding from this building' – the reporter gestured over her shoulder – 'by Detective Michael Johnson, one of the senior officers assigned to the Zombie Killings along with the deceased Detective Goodman.

'The LAPD have yet to make any official statement regarding Wednesday's events. However, we can confirm that in the forty-eight hours since the shootings took place, multiple arrests have been made, possibly pertaining to a drug ring that Mr Rodriguez *may* have been involved with . . . As I say, Chase, details are still scarce at this stage.'

'That's right, Karina.' They cut back to the TV studio where a blandly handsome anchor in a jacket and tie – presumably 'Chase' – took over the narrative from behind the news desk.

'Things are still pretty confusing on this story but it does appear that drugs were involved, and that Wednesday's slayings, possibly including that of Willie Baden, may have been a part of a long-running battle for control of LA's illegal narcotics trade between Mexican and Russian gangs. Last night saw the arrest of prominent LA Philharmonic violinist Anne Bateman, the estranged wife of one of the deceased, Luis Rodriguez. Ms Bateman was actually detained on the tarmac at John Wayne Airport, where we understand she was attempting to board a private plane to Mexico City. Then this morning, as you know, Karina, investment banker Carter Berkeley was arrested at his multimillion-dollar home in the small hours, as was eminent surgeon Haddon Defoe. Also Frankie Jay, a senior official at City Hall, all three men reportedly woken from their beds by armed police as part of the same operation.

'Police also want to speak to Mrs Valentina Baden, but she is reported to have suffered a collapse following her husband's death and is not fit to answer questions at this time.'

Stills of Haddon and Carter and the Badens in happier times flashed in front of Nikki's eyes like part of a dream. *So Haddon's a part of this too?*

'Now we can't confirm this ourselves,' the anchor went on, 'but the *LA Times* are saying that unnamed sources at the FBI have told them these arrests and the recent shootings are all part of the same operation, and that both the deceased, Rodriguez, *and* the individuals taken into custody were all involved in the supply of a street drug known as "Krokodil".'

'Exactly, Chase.' Karina reclaimed the baton at that point, cutting away from the studio to the warehouse shot and explaining to viewers what Krok was and its gruesome effects on users. But Nikki was no longer listening. Instead she was glued to the images on her screen of Haddon Defoe, still in his pajamas, being led out to a squad car, stony-faced but unresisting.

'It does look at this point as if the police are closing in on a high-level ring of corruption and possibly money-laundering relating to the supply and sale of Krokodil. Interestingly, we're also getting reports of some connection between these arrests and the Charlotte Clancy case of maybe ten years ago. D'you remember that case, Karina?' Chase asked.

Charlotte's name brought Nikki's focus back to the report.

'I sure do,' his colleague nodded sagely, no doubt having just been fed the information on autocue. 'Charlotte was an au pair from San Diego who went missing in Mexico City. Now exactly how Monday's victims might fit into this complex picture remains unclear, Chase,' Karina added helpfully. 'But we'll keep you updated as soon as we know more.'

Nikki hit the 'off' button and stared at the ceiling.

It was all about the ring.

Williams' ring.

Goodman had been part of it. And Haddon. And Carter. And the Badens.

And the one man Nikki had hated all along; the one person she'd been *certain* was a liar and a bigot and corrupt – Detective Johnson – *he'd* been the one good apple in the whole, rotten barrel.

*He saved my life.*

She was still staring at the ceiling when her surgeon came back in.

'How are you doing?' he asked. Mistaking Nikki's tears for physical pain, he started to apologize about withdrawing the morphine. 'I know it hurts like hell, and I'm truly sorry. But right now it's important, vital, that you really *feel* it. That you stay connected to reality, no matter how hard that is.'

'I understand,' said Nikki, tears streaming down her face.

And for the first time in many months, she did.

# 40

Two months later . . .

'**A**unt Nikki! Aunt Nikki! Look at me!'
Lucas Adler, Nikki's godson and the oldest child of her BFF Gretchen, balanced precariously on the handlebars of his (moving) bike on only his hands. Arms outstretched, ten-year-old legs thrust ramrod straight in the air, he looked like a broken neck waiting to happen.

*Thank God he's riding on grass,* thought Nikki, watching nervously from the back porch as her budding acrobat godson hurtled across the Adlers' enormous lawn. She'd been staying with Gretchen and Adam for two months now, in one of the countless guest rooms at their Beverly Hills estate. It was as nice a place to recuperate as she could have wished for: a beautiful, luxurious home but also a happy one, full of kids and laughter and noise and company. Plenty to distract her from her own, brooding thoughts, on the days when she cared to be distracted. And on the days when she didn't, Gretchen was there, refusing to take no for an answer, dragging Nikki up and out of her depression with a no-nonsense firmness that had quite probably saved Nikki's life.

'You're alive, Nik,' Gretchen never stopped reminding her. 'You survived. There's a reason for that.'

'I didn't survive,' Nikki would answer. 'I was saved. There's a difference. Saved by a man who stands for everything I don't. A racist, sexist, deceitful . . .' She never seemed to run out of adjectives when it came to describing the loathsome Mick Johnson. And yet part of her knew that the anger pouring out of her towards the cop who saved her life was really anger at herself. For having misjudged him, at least in part. Just as she'd misjudged so many others.

'Well, I don't care if he lives under a bridge and eats billy goats,' Gretchen replied robustly. 'Anyone who saved your life is a good guy in my books. And besides, Nik, this isn't about him, it's about you. What are *you* going to do with the rest of your life? Because as much as we love having you, you can't sit around on our porch reading the newspaper for the rest of your life.'

That much was true. At Gretchen's prompting, Nikki had closed down her practice and given up her lease on the Century City office. She'd also put her and Doug's Brentwood house – 'that mausoleum' as Gretchen called it – on the market.

'You're rich, you're beautiful, you're healthy, you're educated,' Gretchen insisted, thrusting listings for yet more swish New York condos under Nikki's nose while she packed the kids' lunchboxes one morning. Nikki moving to New York for a 'fresh start' had become a minor obsession with Gretchen, who Nikki was starting to suspect might be living out some sort of escape fantasy of her own. 'You're still young, Nik.'

'I'm not young!' Nikki laughed. 'And neither are you.'

'Well, we're not old,' Gretchen countered, slathering yet more peanut butter and jelly onto slices of crustless bread. 'You don't want to be alone for the rest of your life.'

*Don't I?* Nikki wondered.

Watching Lucas deftly lower himself from his handstand and successfully plant his butt back on the saddle with a punch of triumph, she smiled and gave a thumbs up sign before returning to her newspaper.

Today was the first day of Haddon Defoe's trial. The charges were money-laundering and corruption. Apparently, ever since Doug's death, and perhaps even earlier, Haddon had been using his and their charity to channel Luis Rodriguez's drug money, 90 per cent of it profits from the Krokodil trade. If prosecutors were to be believed, he'd earned millions of dollars in kickbacks, as had the other members of the LA 'ring', including the Badens. Willie had made a fortune laundering Rodriguez's cash before he was murdered, funneling funds into everything from shopping center developments across Southern California to his beloved football team. As for Valentina, her connection to the cartel stretched back decades, with her charity, Missing, profiting from abductions and sex-trafficking, and acting as a front for illicit, even murderous, activity, just as Derek Williams had suspected.

It went deeper than that, though. According to prosecutors, Mrs Baden was a deeply troubled individual, and may even have had a hand in her own sister's disappearance all those years ago. Old family friends had come out of the woodwork to speak openly about Valentina's obsessive jealousy of her sister, María, who had evidently always been the more beautiful of the two sisters. Like so many other Americans, Gretchen couldn't get enough of the story. Valentina's trial wouldn't begin for months at the earliest, if it happened at all. Since Willie's murder, she'd been 'resting' at a secure psychiatric facility near Oxnard. But her trial-by-tabloid was already well underway, and utterly gripping.

*Williams was right about so much*, Nikki thought sadly.

He totally called it on Missing. More importantly, he'd been the first person to blow the whistle on Rodriguez's secret life and the waves of corruption and conspiracy that rippled out from it. But it was the FBI who were taking all the credit for that, the same way they were claiming to have 'solved' the mystery of Charlotte Clancy's disappearance – now officially classified as murder.

*In death as in life*, thought Nikki, *Williams was robbed of recognition. Poor Derek.*

Nikki had attempted a complete detox from all media coverage of the trials. But with the *LA Times* devoting multiple pages to the story every day, and every cable news show leading with it, it wasn't that easy simply to switch off. Not often did LA reporters get their teeth into a case involving quite so many of the city's elite, from politicians to bankers, surgeons to cops, philanthropists to lawyers and even judges; not to mention the sensational 'foreign meddling' angle, with Russians and Mexicans fighting a deadly turf war on US soil. It certainly made a change from the usual inane showbiz gossip. It wasn't only Gretchen who was addicted to the latest twists in the story. The entire city of LA was gripped.

'Hey!'

Nikki jumped as Gretchen snuck up behind her, reaching over her wicker recliner and snatching the newspaper out of her hands.

'You promised not to look, remember?'

'I know,' said Nikki. 'But it's Haddon's trial. His picture's all over the front page.'

'All the more reason not to read,' said Gretchen, folding the paper under her arm.

'He looks so gaunt,' said Nikki. 'He must have aged ten years.'

Gretchen frowned. 'I hope you're not feeling *sorry* for him? My God, Nik. After everything Haddon Defoe did to you? All the lies? Not to mention those poor people whose lives got ruined by that terrible drug.'

'I know,' Nikki said sadly. 'You're right.'

'You bet I'm right!' Gretchen said indignantly. 'First he profits from their addiction, then he swoops in and acts like their savior. Think how much value all that good PR added to his surgical practice, on top of the millions he got paid by Rodriguez!' She shook her head bitterly. 'He betrayed Doug as well as you, you know. I hope they throw away the key.'

Nikki nodded, too depressed to respond in words. Everything Gretchen said was true, and sometimes she felt the same. But at other times it was hard, changing your opinion and feelings about a person 180 degrees overnight. It wasn't like Lucas, flipping upside down then right side up on his bicycle, as deftly and easily as a fish gliding through the water. Nikki had known Haddon for years, decades, not just as a friend but as a *good man*. And while it was true that his recent clumsy come-ons towards her had dented that image somewhat, now she was being asked to accept that he was a *bad man,* that he had been all along. How did one do that? How did one begin? Facts were facts and could change on a dime, but feelings? Feelings were another story.

It had been hard enough with Lou Goodman, who she'd only known for a few months and never gotten truly close to. Goodman had put a gun to her head and would have killed her like a stray dog if Johnson hadn't come along. Killed her for money.

That was a fact.

He'd also murdered Derek Williams in cold blood.

That, tragically, was another fact, one that the police victims' liaison officer had had to explain to Nikki days after she left the hospital: 'There's no doubt, I'm afraid. We found the silencer in Detective Goodman's belongings, and blood splatters belonging to Mr Williams in fibers of his clothing.'

But Nikki's feelings still hadn't caught up to the new reality. As irrational as it was, part of her still grieved Goodman's death, still pitied him for his painful childhood and the demons that drove him so powerfully. She couldn't seem to let go of the man she'd imagined him to be, any more than she could re-cast Johnson in the role of hero, simply because the 'facts' demanded it.

'Come on,' said Gretchen, sensing Nikki's thoughts spiraling back into a dark place. 'Adam's on set all day today so I'm taking the kids to

Pasadena. I thought we'd do the Huntingdon Gardens and get a late lunch at the pagoda in the Chinese Garden. You can help me wrangle the three of them.'

'I'm OK,' said Nikki. 'I think I'll stay here and rest.'

'Oh, it's not a request,' Gretchen said firmly, dropping a bottle of suntan lotion and a map of the botanical gardens into Nikki's lap. 'You're coming.'

Without breaking stride, she turned towards the lawn and yelled, *'Lucas! Get off that bike before you break something – and help me find your brothers! I need you in the car in five minutes!'*

\* \* \*

The botanical gardens at the Huntingdon were stunning, but punishingly hot. Less than twenty miles from Beverly Hills, the temperature had somehow soared almost fifteen degrees, pushing the thermometer to almost a hundred as Nikki, Gretchen and the boys weaved their way through the acres of roses, desert blooms and oriental gardens complete with carp ponds, bridges, and miniature temples alive with countless species of butterflies.

Nikki, who still walked slowly and with the help of a cane thanks to the bullet Luis Rodriguez had fired into her lower left leg, struggled to keep up with Gretchen and the kids. Sweat poured down her face and between her breasts, leaving her sticky and uncomfortable. Worse than the heat were the stares and whispers of strangers, many of whom Nikki was sure recognized her from the newspapers or the TV news.

*In New York, I'll be anonymous again,* she thought, trying to focus on the positive. *It'll be cooler too. With seasons.*

She'd missed seasons.

Spotting a stone bench in the shade of an acid-green willow, she sat to catch her breath and take a sip of water. The *ding ding* of a text on her phone surprised her. *Who could that be?* No one called her these days. Nikki had long since grown distant from family and friends, apart from Gretchen. The police investigation was over, and her practice shut down. Her phone had pretty much become a camera with which to record the exploits of the Adler children.

Looking down at the screen in her palm she felt her stomach lurch. She recognized the number immediately, even though she'd long since deleted its owner's contact from her phone.

Detective Johnson's text was typically brief, self-important and rude.

'*Meet me tomorrow. Denny's Pico/34th.*'

That was it. No 'please'. No 'How are you?' No explanation as to why Nikki should meet him or what the meeting was about, still less any thought as to whether the time and place were convenient for her.

She contemplated texting back '*Forget it,*' before deciding on balance that complete silence would send the same message more effectively. Glancing up she saw Gretchen walking towards her and swiftly deleted the text.

'Everything OK?' Gretchen looked suspiciously at the phone. 'You're not watching coverage of Haddon's trial are you?'

'Nope,' said Nikki. 'Scouts honor.'

She imagined Mick Johnson sitting at Denny's alone, confidently waiting for her to arrive, only slowly realizing that she wasn't coming. Not now. Not ever.

He no longer had any power over her at all. She smiled.

And it struck her then, for the first time.

*I hate him even more than I used to.*

*I hate him for saving my life.*

\* \* \*

In the visitors' room at Valley State Prison, Jerry Kovak scratched his red neck anxiously. It was well over a hundred in Chowchilla and Jerry had gotten sunburnt simply walking from the prison yard back to his cell.

'Did she reply?'

Mick Johnson stared down at his phone. 'Not yet.'

The scratching intensified.

'But you think she will? I mean, you will see her?'

It pained Mick to see Jerry like this. So scared. So desperate.

'Oh, I'll see her all right,' he told his friend. 'You can count on that. I'm not done with Dr Roberts yet.'

\* \* \*

'He looks mad,' whispered the waitress, refilling the coffee pot.

'Real mad,' her friend whispered back. 'How much longer d'you think he'll wait?'

The girls at Denny's knew Detective Mick Johnson well. He'd been a regular for years, and although he didn't say much, he was a generous tipper. Occasionally he came in with other cops, but usually he ate alone, giant stacks of pancakes and bacon, no matter what time of day he came in. Today, however, he'd specifically mentioned he was expecting 'a friend' and asked for a booth at the back, 'somewhere private'.

It was obviously a woman he was expecting, and the waitress felt bad for him, getting stood up in front of everybody. She was about to go over and refill his coffee cup for the third time when a petite brunette walked in and headed straight for Johnson's table.

'Wow,' whispered her friend. 'She's so pretty. She can't be his date, can she?'

The first girl shrugged. 'Who knows? Maybe he has money stashed away somewhere.'

Her friend laughed. 'Yeah, right. That's why he eats here four times a week. Maybe he's hung like a donkey,' she winked.

'Carla! Don't be gross. I'm going to take their order.'

Grabbing two laminated menus she slid over to Johnson's booth.

'Hi there!' She smiled at the brunette, who looked awfully familiar. 'What can I get you?'

'We're fine,' Johnson snapped. 'We need some privacy, OK?'

The waitress retreated, stung. *Jerk.* There was no pleasing some people. And here she'd been, feeling sorry for him . . .

* * *

Johnson looked across the table at Nikki with narrowed, angry eyes.

'You took your time,' he grumbled.

'You're lucky I came at all,' Nikki shot back frostily. 'I wasn't going to.'

Johnson's face turned so red he looked as if he were being boiled from the inside. 'You're a piece of work, Dr Roberts, you know that?'

'Oh, *I'm* a piece of work?'

'I saved your life!' Johnson raised his voice.

'I never asked you to,' Nikki hissed back at him. 'I didn't want you to!'

'Oh really? You're telling me you wanted to die in that warehouse? You wanted lover-boy Goodman to put a bullet in your head? Because it sure didn't look that way when you were lying there whimpering like a stuck piglet, begging for your life.'

'We were never lovers.' Nikki quivered with rage. 'And yes, I wanted to live. Who doesn't? I just didn't want *you* to be the one . . . I hate you!' she blurted. 'You've made my life hell, ever since this nightmare started.'

'Me?' Johnson sounded genuinely taken aback. 'How do you work that out?'

Nikki looked at him, incredulous.

'Are you serious? You tried to pin Lisa and Trey's murders on me. You even accused me of having a hand in my own husband's death.'

'I didn't try to "pin" anything on anyone,' Johnson grumbled defensively. 'I thought you were guilty. At the beginning anyway.'

'Based on what?' Nikki threw her arms wide in exasperation. 'A *hunch*? Your *cop's instinct*?'

'Oh, that's right,' Johnson sneered. 'You go ahead and dismiss those things. Because you understand what it means to be a police officer *so well*, don't you, Doc? You being such an insightful psychologist and all.'

The dig hit home, but Nikki tried not to show it. She was glad she'd come, glad to be having it out with Johnson at last, telling him to his fat, ignorant face what she really thought of him.

'Oh, I've made mistakes,' she said. 'I'll be the first to admit it. I've made big mistakes, and I've paid for them, Detective. But that doesn't make your Neanderthal, racist, sexist, homophobic worldview any less loathsome. You falsely accused me of murdering people I loved – my husband, my friend, my patient – for no better reason than that you disliked me. Why don't *you* explain to *me* how that's OK?'

Johnson opened his mouth to yell at her – his blood was up, as it always seemed to be around this infuriating woman – but for once he held back. Sure, he was angry. But he also wanted her, needed her, to understand him. One of them had to bridge the chasm between them.

Holding up his hands in a *Let's slow down* gesture, he made a concerted effort to speak calmly and slowly.

'OK, look. It's true I thought you were involved at the beginning. And I was wrong about that. Even though God knows you gave me enough reason to suspect you. But you ought to know, *I* wasn't lying and I wasn't trying to frame you. I genuinely thought you had orchestrated those killings.'

'Why? Because I held back information?' asked Nikki, mirroring his more measured tone. 'That's a bit flimsy, isn't it?'

'It was more than that,' said Johnson. 'You had a motive.'

Nikki raised an eyebrow. 'I did?'

'Sure. Your husband cheated on you,' Johnson explained. 'Plus you stood to inherit everything in his will. That's a motive for his murder. Lisa Flannagan was a mistress, and you hated that. That's a motive for hers.'

'And Trey?' Nikki asked.

'I don't know about Trey,' Johnson shrugged. 'I thought, maybe he knew things about you and your husband that you didn't want getting out there. Or maybe he covered for your husband's affair? The fact is that all the deceased were linked to you, Doc. You had motive, you had opportunity, and you had the financial means to do it. You had the smarts, the cunning.'

'And you didn't like me, right, Detective?' Nikki said bitterly. 'An educated, successful woman, a woman who wasn't impressed by your badge and bravado.'

'How about a liar?' Johnson replied, struggling not to let his anger get the better of him. 'You lied to us about Brandon Grolsch. You said you'd never heard of him.'

Nikki flushed. 'That's true. I guess I . . . I didn't trust you to treat him fairly.'

'Oh, right. You didn't trust us. And what was that – a hunch? A *psychologist's instinct?*'

*Touché*, thought Nikki.

'I was wrong to lie to you about Brandon,' she admitted. 'But that didn't excuse you hounding me . . .'

'I didn't hound you, lady,' Johnson shook his head. 'I was doing my job, investigating those murders. I had reason to suspect you, but once I started looking into it, other leads came up that made me see things differently. I'd already started on the drugs angle and I was looking into Rodriguez, thanks to some of my old friends on the drug squad. It didn't help having your man Williams trampling all over my turf,' he couldn't help adding, 'interfering with potential witnesses. But I don't like to speak ill of the dead.'

He crossed himself and Nikki decided to let it go. She had no right to get angry on Derek Williams' behalf. If it hadn't been for her, Williams would still be alive.

'How did you know I'd be at the warehouse?' Nikki asked.

'That was lucky,' said Johnson. 'Goodman got sloppy. He left deleted emails on the server, and I'd already hacked into his texts.

Once I interviewed the dealers on the streets in Trey's old neighborhood and I got a sense of the turf war over the Krokodil market between Rodriguez and the Russian gangs, I knew someone in our department had to be helping Rodriguez. I suspected Goodman right off the bat, but I didn't know for sure until the day before you showed up at the station. That was when I put the tracker on his car.'

Nikki shuddered. Without that tracker, and Johnson's foresight, she would certainly not be alive right now.

'Look. I am grateful,' she told him.

'Really?' he frowned. 'You've got an odd way of showing it.'

'It was very brave, what you did,' said Nikki. 'But it doesn't erase everything that went before. You're bigoted. You're self-righteous.' She counted his character flaws off on her fingers, like a disappointed schoolteacher. 'You blatantly lie in court to protect fellow officers.'

'I'm loyal to my friends!' Johnson defended himself. 'So are you, Doc. Look at the way you protected Brandon. Only difference is, my friends are decent guys who've devoted their lives to public service, whereas yours are good-for-nothing junkies who cut innocent people to ribbons with butcher's knives just so they can afford their next hit.'

Nikki winced. She wished with all her heart that this weren't an accurate description of Brandon Grolsch. But it was. Even if Luis Rodriguez and Valentina Baden had been pulling the strings, Brandon must still be held accountable for the terrible things he'd done.

'Does the name Jerry Kovak mean anything to you?' Johnson asked, out of the blue.

*Kovak.* Something stirred in Nikki's memory, but she couldn't quite place it.

'Detective Jerry Kovak, drug squad. Great officer. Lost his wife. He was involved in an incident with a lowlife drug dealer back in the early 2000s. The judge gave him twenty years.'

'Kovak . . .' Nikki murmured the name out loud. 'Not the guy who beat the young black boy nearly to death?'

'That "young black boy" was a ruthless dealer and killer by the name of Kelsey James.' Johnson spat out his name as if it were poison. 'Jerry, on the other hand, was a decorated detective, not to mention a great husband and father. He was out of his mind with grief at the time. But you testified against him. You told the judge he was OK mentally, and that bitch put him away for two decades. Totally destroyed the man.'

Nikki could see the anger and resentment etched on Johnson's face. *He genuinely thinks an injustice was done,* she thought. Choosing her words carefully, she said, 'I remember. It was a tragic case.'

'It didn't need to be,' said Johnson. 'You stuck the knife in, Doc.'

Nikki looked him in the eye. 'I meant tragic for everyone. For your friend, but also for the murdered man and his family.'

''Course you did,' said Johnson bitterly.

'Grief is a terrible thing,' said Nikki. 'I know that as well as anyone. But you can't go round beating people half to death.'

'Kelsey James wasn't "people". He was scum. Him and his family and the whole community of bastards who closed ranks around him. You think I'm a racist, Doc? You ever ask yourself why?'

'No, I don't ask myself that,' said Nikki, still defiant but less angry than before. She saw now that Mick Johnson wasn't an intrinsically bad man. Only a deeply misguided one. 'Because it doesn't matter why. Wrong is wrong. What your friend did was wrong. And that's that.'

'That's that,' Mick repeated, shaking his head in a mixture of amusement and despair. 'What a cozy, black-and-white world you live in, Dr Roberts. For us cops out on the street – you know, the guys risking our lives to save yours – it ain't like that. Nothing's ever black-and-white. Everything's gray.'

*We're never going to agree,* thought Nikki. *I'll never get him to see the world my way, and he'll never get me to see it his way. But we're both trying to live by our own conscience.*

She felt the last of her own anger melt away and a deep sense of relief sweep in to take its place.

'Why did you ask me here today, Detective Johnson?'

Johnson eyed her thoughtfully, as if considering how best to solve a complex problem. Which, in a way, he was.

'To call in a favor,' he said, clearing his throat. 'Or perhaps you could say to make a trade? I saved your life. So maybe you might do something for me in return.'

'If I can,' said Nikki. 'What's the favor?'

'Jerry Kovak's got a parole hearing next month.' Johnson looked her square on. 'I'd like you to speak in his defense.'

Nikki's face fell. 'Come on, Detective. Be reasonable. You know I can't do that.'

'Sure you can.'

'He was guilty of that crime,' said Nikki. 'He was no more insane than you or I. My opinion hasn't changed. I'm sorry.'

'This isn't about guilt or innocence,' said Johnson, waving away her objections with an impatient hand. 'It's about mercy. About showing compassion for a decent man.'

Nikki hesitated. As they'd been talking, details of the Kovak case came back to her. The terrible injuries that Kelsey James had sustained, leaving his face unrecognizable, even to his own family. What Johnson's friend had done was the act of an animal, a savage beast. No 'decent man' could have done that, not under any circumstances. And Kovak's record had shown a history of racially motivated incidents, with a string of alleged assaults on black victims dating back years, well before his wife's death.

'I'm sorry,' she looked down at her hands. 'I can't do what you're asking.'

'Hmmm. I thought you might say that.' To her surprise, Johnson sounded disappointed rather than furious. 'Well, in that case, I guess I can't share the FBI file on your husband's mistress I just got me a copy of. *Pregnant* mistress, I should say. Something else you decided in your wisdom not to share with us. Ah well. That's too bad.'

Dropping a twenty on the table, he stood up to leave.

'Wait!' Nikki called after him.

He kept walking.

'Detective Johnson! Hold on, please.'

He stopped and turned, smiling.

'What happened, Doc?' he asked mockingly. 'Things suddenly get a little grayer, did they?'

He'd got her over a barrel and they both knew it. Nikki didn't know whether to be angry or to laugh. In the end, for reasons she couldn't explain, she chose the latter.

'All right,' she said. 'You win. I'll come to the parole hearing.'

'And put in a good word for him? An unequivocal good word?'

It was wrong. But everybody had their price. The truth was Nikki would have sold her soul to know who Lenka Gordievski really was, and how she'd gotten her claws into Doug.

'Yes,' she said. 'Now, please, show me what you have.'

*　*　*

Ten minutes later, a desolate Nikki looked up at Mick Johnson.

'This doesn't tell me anything.'

While she'd been reading the file on Lenka, he'd ordered himself a second stack of pancakes from the still-peeved waitress, and was two thirds of the way through them when Nikki spoke.

'I'd say it tells you plenty,' he said, dabbing syrup from the sides of his mouth with a napkin and swallowing his current mouthful. 'Lenka was the go-between who helped Luis Rodriguez import his initial batches of Krokodil from Moscow. She'd changed her name to Gordievski five years earlier, after she turned state's witness on one of the St Petersburg cartels. That's why your friend Williams couldn't find any history. Before that she went by Natalia Driskov.'

'I don't care about her name!' Nikki said, exasperated. 'I care about her relationship with my husband.'

'It's all connected, honey,' said Johnson, not unkindly. 'Lenka introduced Rodriguez to her network of suppliers and drug runners back in Russia. She was already living in LA and familiar with the networks on the ground here. I'm guessing she was well compensated, but that was always a dangerous game to play. The Russian gangs wouldn't have appreciated anyone bringing one of the Mexican cartels onto their turf.'

'So you think the Russians murdered her?' asked Nikki. 'By tampering with the computer on Doug's car? He was collateral damage, is that what you're saying?'

Johnson shrugged. 'You've read the report, same as I have. Yes, I think your husband was definitely collateral damage. But I don't believe the Russians were behind that crash. I'd say it was Rodriguez.'

Nikki frowned, confused.

'But . . . if Lenka worked for Rodriguez . . . ?'

'She'd outlived her usefulness,' said Johnson. 'Like Willie Baden. And you saw with your own eyes what happened to him.'

Nikki shivered.

'By the beginning of last year, Rodriguez's crew already owned the Krok market on the West Coast,' said Johnson. 'With Goodman's help, he'd effectively driven the Russians out and he was producing his own shit, down in Mexico City. He already had huge facilities down there for processing coke. Charlotte Clancy found out about those years ago, which was why she got whacked. All Luis had to do was re-fit that operation, turn it into giant Krok labs. After that he didn't need Lenka any more. You wanna know what my theory is, about her and your husband?'

'Sure,' Nikki said wearily.

'I think this woman knew she was on borrowed time with Rodriguez. So she tried to make herself useful to him in other ways. That was where your old man came in. She offered to get close to him, in hopes of pumping him for information about you and your patients. She had Haddon Defoe introduce the two of them, and the thing went from there. After all, by that point you were treating Carter Berkeley, one of his key money men in LA and witness to Charlotte Clancy's murder. I reckon the affair with your husband was Lenka's last-ditch attempt to keep herself relevant to Rodriguez. Relevant and alive. Not such a great plan, as it turned out.'

Nikki gazed blankly out of the window. *So it was my fault? Lenka targeted Doug to get at me?* After what felt like an age, she turned back to look at Johnson.

'The thing is,' she said sadly, 'what this doesn't tell me is why *Doug* did it. Let's say you're right about Lenka's motivations, and Rodriguez's. And maybe you are, because it all fits. It still doesn't answer the biggest question of all, at least for me. Which is, why would *my* husband cheat on *me* with this person? This stranger. One minute we were happy – really happy – and the next, it was all gone. Why did that happen?'

Mick Johnson looked at her with genuine pity.

'I don't know, sweetheart. Maybe she fed him a sob story. Maybe she confessed she'd gotten mixed up with the cartels and Rodriguez and she was trying to break free? From what I heard, your husband was big on helping people in trouble. Second chances and all that?'

'He got her *pregnant!*' Nikki's eyes welled with tears.

'So maybe that was part of it too?' offered Johnson. 'He was trying to help her, they got close, he made a mistake and slept with her – and remember, all this time she's fighting for her life, doing everything she can to seduce him and get close to him, because her own life depends on it. And maybe he regrets it, but then boom, she's pregnant, and what's he gonna do? Maybe that's his one and only chance to have a child, because you guys couldn't. That's a tough thing to walk away from. Isn't it?'

Nikki nodded mutely. *Maybe.* There were too many maybes. Johnson's file had given her facts about Lenka, and he'd offered her theories. But facts and theories couldn't explain emotions. Nor could they heal a broken heart.

Sighing, Nikki passed the folder of papers back to him across the table.

'Oh, that's OK,' said Johnson. 'Those are for you. You can keep 'em.'

'No thanks,' said Nikki. 'It's time to start letting go of the past. I might as well start here.'

An awkward silence fell. Pushing the cold remnants of his pancakes to one side, Johnson signaled to the waitress for the check.

'So, er, what are your plans now?' he asked, feeling someone ought to say something. 'Will you go back to work?'

'No.' Nikki spoke with a firmness that surprised herself. 'I shut down my office here and put my house on the market. I was toying with the idea of starting a new psychology practice in New York, but I've changed my mind. I'm sure I'll do something out there, I just haven't figured out what yet. Luckily I can afford to wait. Take some time out.'

'You're moving to New York?' Johnson looked surprised. 'When?'

'Now, I guess,' Nikki shrugged. 'I mean, soon. There's nothing keeping me here. I think today was the first time I understood that fully.'

'OK. But our deal still stands, right?' Johnson asked distrustfully. 'You'll speak up for Jerry at the parole hearing? Because that's in a month.'

'Sure,' said Nikki, adding with a weak smile, 'A deal's a deal, Detective. I'll fly back for it. What about you?'

'What about me?' Johnson raised an eyebrow.

'What are your plans?' Nikki clarified.

'My *plans*?' He seemed to find the question amusing. 'I'm a cop. That's the only plan I got. I'll move on to the next case, and then the next one, till I croak. I'm not complaining,' he added quickly. 'I love the job.'

*How could anyone love that job?* Nikki thought, watching Johnson pay his check. Police work meant low pay, constant danger, and you didn't even get public respect any more, not after all the corruption scandals. She still didn't approve of the way Mick Johnson led his professional life, of the entitled way he behaved, a walking behemoth of white male privilege. And yet, after everything she'd been through, she found she could understand it. It must be exhausting to have to live in a permanent state of battle-readiness. She knew she couldn't do it.

'So, I don't know if you heard,' Johnson mumbled awkwardly, 'but they're giving me a service medal, kind of like a valor thing. For that night at the warehouse.'

'They are?' Nikki's face broke into a genuine smile. 'Congratulations! That's amazing.'

'I mean, you're probably gonna be busy.' Johnson was blushing like a schoolboy. 'But I just thought, you know, if you wanted to come . . . what I mean is, you'd be welcome.'

'I'd be honored,' said Nikki. She was touched, knowing how much it must have cost him to extend the invitation. They'd been through a lot, the two of them, and she recognized this was Detective Johnson's way of offering an olive branch.

'Let me know the date and I'll be there.' Standing up, she shook his hand. 'Take care, Detective.'

'You too, Doc.'

Mick Johnson shook Nikki's hand and watched her leave the restaurant and disappear down the street.

She was a piece of work, all right. But she was also a survivor.

Mick Johnson respected that.

He hoped she found the happiness she was searching for in New York, but somehow, he doubted that she would. Sadness seemed to cling to her like mist to the ocean.

Oh well. He'd done what he could.

Like she'd said, it was time to let go of the past.

# 41

It was another scorching day in downtown LA, up in the high nineties, but inside the Grand Ballroom at the Hollywood and Highland Entertainment Complex, all was cool. Sitting towards the back of the packed auditorium, directly below an air conditioning vent, Nikki wished she'd brought a cardigan. Today was Detective Johnson's medal of valor ceremony, and she'd flown in specially, more to honor a promise than from any desire to be there. It was painful coming back to LA so soon, but at least she would manage to kill three birds with one stone on this trip: Johnson's ceremony, the Kovak parole hearing, and the final trip to her attorney's office to sign the sale papers on her Brentwood house. After this, she could fly away and never look back. In theory anyway.

'We're here today to celebrate an act of extraordinary courage,' the Chief of Police, Brian Finnigan announced proudly from the podium. 'Members of our police force are called upon to perform acts of courage every single day in the line of duty. And all of those acts are worthy of recognition. But occasionally, an officer steps outside the bounds of his, or her, normal service . . .'

He droned on in this vein for a number of minutes to a rapt audience, almost all of them either cops themselves or their families. Beside him on the podium, Mick Johnson sat looking awkward and heavier than ever in his tight-fitting formal uniform, with his stomach spilling over the belt and his broad chest looking as if it might burst, Superman style, through his starched shirt at any moment, sending the buttons flying around the room like bullets. *Poor man*, thought Nikki. He deserved the medal and was proud of his honor, but would clearly far rather have received the thing anonymously in the mail. Aware of the media presence – anything connected to the Zombie Killings and the Rodriguez Krok Ring, however tangential, brought them out of the woodwork like maggots – Nikki had signaled to Johnson earlier, making him aware of her presence, but after that slunk back into the shadows. Dressed to disappear in a shapeless, gray-black shift dress and dark glasses, with no make-up on and her longer, grayer hair tied back in a messy bun, she was unrecognizable as the glamorous Dr Nikki Roberts people remembered from the TV news reports.

While the commissioner rambled on, her mind wandered.

It was only three weeks since she'd moved out of Gretchen's place, but already it felt like years. The day she left, all the LA channels ran the breaking news story that the prime suspect in the Zombie Killings, Brandon Grolsch, had finally been tracked down to an apartment in Fresno. Sordid details of his affair with Valentina Baden had already begun to emerge, and the live-action cameras were all trained with an expectant hush on the Fresno apartment as the police broke in.

In the days prior to that, Charlotte Clancy's remains had been found at long last, in a shallow grave on the outskirts of Mexico City, their whereabouts divulged by Carter Berkeley as part of his plea deal for turning state's witness. The news had been full of tearful, angry images of the Clancy family, furious that Carter had received only a four-year sentence for his role in laundering Rodriguez's drug money and covering up their daughter's death, while Dr Haddon Defoe, a far more minor figure in the Los Angeles 'Krok' ring, received a ten-year term. Even worse was the media's fawning adoration for Anne Bateman, the beautiful young violinist who had been married to Rodriguez and claimed to have had no prior knowledge of any of his crimes. Anne's trial would not begin for some months, the list of charges against her being longer and more complex than some of the other players involved.

But for Nikki, the day they found Brandon Grolsch was the hardest, and the most personal. Nikki and Gretchen watched together from Nikki's bedroom, standing over her half-packed suitcase, as armed police broke down the door of Brandon's apartment and entered. Nikki held her breath and waited. She was still watching when, an hour and a half later, the same men emerged bearing a body bag on a stretcher. Brandon was dead from an apparent overdose. Over the course of the afternoon it emerged that his corpse was already partially rotted when the cops found it. That he'd likely been dead and undisturbed for several days, if not weeks.

Nikki sank down on the edge of the bed, feeling suddenly faint.

'You shouldn't let it get to you,' Gretchen told her. 'He tried to kill you.'

'I know.'

'You can't save everyone, Nik.'

'I know that too.'

The problem was that, apparently, Nikki couldn't save anyone. If she'd succeeded with Brandon, if she'd only been able to help *him*, Lisa Flannagan would still be alive. So would Trey – maybe.

That last day at Gretchen's place got even worse at dinner, after Adam got home.

'Guess what?' Adam asked innocently, kissing both his wife and Nikki on the cheek as they all sat down at the table with the kids.

'I heard today they're gonna make a movie about the Zombie Killings.'

'Cool!' Nikki's godson Lucas piped up excitedly. 'Is Aunt Nik gonna be in it? Who's playing her?'

'You're not serious,' Nikki looked aghast at Adam.

'Totally serious,' he said, helping himself to a large bowlful of Gretchen's Thai beef salad and a cold beer. 'There's already a three-parter script in the works at Warner. Part One's the Charlotte Clancy case, set in Mexico City in the early 2000s. Part Two flashes forward to the Flannagan and Raymond murders, with some of the Krok wars thrown in. I'm guessing your character would have to be central in there.'

'Awesome!' the Adler children exclaimed in unison.

'And Part Three covers Rodriguez's LA drugs ring and how it got smashed, ending with Willie Baden's murder and a big shoot-out scene at the warehouse. That's more of a Michael Bey, *Fast & Furious* type vibe, I think, while the first two scripts are a little more slow burn. Like *Traffic*. Did you ever see that movie? With Michael Douglas?'

Nikki sat frozen with shock. Gretchen's husband was a sweetheart. Adam would never knowingly try to upset her. Yet he seemed strangely oblivious to how awful it was to talk about these murders as if they were entertainment. As if Lisa and Trey and Brandon and even Nikki herself were fictional characters, to be polished and airbrushed and regurgitated onto the screen for general public amusement.

'I know you don't even want to think about this right now,' Adam plowed on. 'But this could actually be great news for you, Nikki. If these pictures get off the ground, or even if they don't and they never get past the development stage, people are gonna be beating down your door to act as a consultant, maybe even to exec produce. Those gigs can be really lucrative.'

That dinner was the moment Nikki's last ounce of hesitation or regret at leaving LA left her. This city was insane and rotten to the core. Even really good people like the Adlers became tainted by it after a while. As for Nikki, she wasn't so much 'tainted' as immersed, covered in a stench of corruption and violence and death and lies and filth so strong that she didn't know if she would ever fully get rid of it.

A ripple of applause broke her reverie. Suddenly she was back in the auditorium. Detective Johnson. The medal ceremony.

'And now, without further ado,' the commissioner was saying, 'it is my duty, my honor and my pleasure to present the LAPD Medal of Valor to Detective Michael Johnson of the Homicide Division. Detective Johnson, please stand.'

Nikki watched as Johnson got awkwardly to his feet and lumbered over to the center of the podium to receive his award. To the left and right of her, the audience clapped and cheered and within a few seconds most got to their feet. Nikki stood and joined them, cheering the man who had saved her life and who she'd belatedly come to see as more than just a redneck – although that side to him was still alive and well. She was glad they'd buried the hatchet, but at the same time she wouldn't be sorry to see the back of Detective Johnson and the rest of the LAPD, and all the other small, daily reminders of this terrible case.

Slipping out early, Nikki walked along Grand Avenue in the direction of Union Station. She would take an Uber back to her hotel, rather than a train, but it was a beautiful old building and it gave her somewhere to walk to on this hot, dazzling day.

Passing a flower stall, she bought an overpriced bunch of peonies to take back to her hotel room. Recently she'd been taking Gretchen's advice and trying to appreciate the little things, like fresh flowers or a warm, blue-skied day. It might be corny, but Nikki knew from her own practice it was as good a way as any to fight depression. Tiny step by tiny step.

To the left and right of her, gleaming tower blocks in glass and concrete and steel rose like the behemoths of wealth and status that they were. Some were banks or insurance companies. Others were law firms. In and out of them, like tiny termites, scurried well-dressed workers, the women coiffed and uncomfortable-looking in their pencil skirts and high heels, the men simply overheated in their formal suits and ties.

Out on the sidewalks, directly in the shadow of these buildings, homeless people sat or stood or lay, some pushing shopping carts laden with blankets and clothes and their other meager possessions, others ragged and dirty and even barefoot. It felt to Nikki as if America was at war, a war between the haves and have-nots, and that these people were members of the losing army. If such a war really existed then Los Angeles was surely its front line. So much wealth and fame and glamour here, so much luxury, and yet at the same time so much despair.

Veering off down a narrower street about half a mile from the station, one young woman caught Nikki's eye. She was skinny, with lank, thinning blond hair and striking high cheekbones beneath her sallow skin. She wore the prostitute's uniform of frayed denim hot-pants, tank top and cheap plastic wedge sandals, but she didn't seem to be looking for work. Slumped against a garage wall, she stared vacantly ahead of her, there but not there. In other circumstances, this girl would probably have been pretty. As it was, Nikki saw the tell-tale green, swollen forearms of the Krokodil addict. Her legs had not yet turned gangrenous, but the skin peeled from them like dried paper, or the bark from a eucalyptus tree.

There was a time, not so long ago, when Nikki would have tried to help this young woman. When she would have walked over and asked her name and tried to get her into some sort of rehab program. But not now. Now she knew better. Her compassion was still there. It was the hope that had gone. That, and her faith in her own judgment.

*Who am I to try to help anyone?* a voice in her head reminded her relentlessly. *Most days I can't even help myself.*

She hurried on to the station, but she no longer felt any pleasure in the walk, not even in the sunshine on her back. Climbing into an Uber, still clutching her peonies like a talisman, she gave the driver the address of her hotel in Malibu – if she had to be back in LA, Nikki decided, she wanted to be by the ocean and as far away from all her old stomping grounds as possible – and gazed mindlessly out of the window.

Her depression came in waves, ebbing and flowing, and she'd learned to live with it, welcoming the sadness that was now a part of her like an old friend. She imagined her mental state as being something akin to the pains of childbirth – a powerful, all-consuming pain that you could feel coming, and peaking and then fading away. Like a contraction you could either try to resist it, which made the pain worse, or accept it. *Breathe through it,* as all the childbirth books said. Of course, Nikki would only ever know about the experience of childbirth from books, and from her imagination. It was too late for motherhood now, as it was too late for so many things.

Some days she felt a thousand years old.

'Actually, could we make a quick stop first? Would you wait for me?' She gave the driver a different address.

'We're not really supposed to make stops,' the man said. 'I'll take you there and then you can call for a new ride when you're done.'

'I'll only be a few moments,' Nikki assured him. 'In and out, I swear.'

* * *

The graveyard was small and perfectly manicured, with neatly trimmed box hedges lining winding gravel paths, enabling mourners to meander through the headstones. Doug's stone was simple and understated, as he would have wanted it, a plain gray slab inscribed with his name and the dates of his birth and death.

Nikki laid her bunch of peonies down in front of it and brushed away a couple of stray dead leaves. Then she stared for a moment at all that was left of her old, happy life and the love that had once been her everything.

*I'll always love you, Doug.*

*But I don't think I'll ever forgive.*

Turning around, Nikki Roberts walked to her waiting car without looking back.

She knew she would never return.

# Acknowledgements

With sincere thanks to Alexandra Sheldon, and the whole Sheldon family, for their continued support and encouragement. Also to my marvelous editors, Kimberley Young and Charlotte Brabbin, and the whole team at HarperCollins in London, who have worked so tirelessly on this book. It's been a joy to collaborate with all of you. Thanks also to my agents, Hellie Ogden in London and Luke Janklow in New York, for all that you do and for putting up with my nagging. And last but not least, to my family, especially my husband Robin and our four fantastic children, Sef, Zac, Theo and Summer. I love you all incredibly.

*The Silent Widow* is dedicated to my beautiful sister Alice. So much love to you Big Al, and I hope you enjoy the book. Tills xx

TB 2018.